The Watcher's Guide

Christopher Golden *and* **Nancy Holder**

with **Keith R.A. DeCandido**

POCKET BOOKS
New York   London   Toronto   Sydney   Singapore

Special thanks to the people at Pocket Books, Twentieth Century Fox, and Buffy the Vampire Slayer *who made this book possible:*

Gina Centrello, Donna O'Neill, Lisa Feuer, Julie Blattberg, Gina DiMarco, Nancy Pines, Patricia MacDonald, Twisne Fan, Jennifer Sebree, Debbie Olshan, Caroline Kallas, Todd McIntosh, and Lili Schwartz.

An *Original* Publication of POCKET BOOKS

Edited by: Lisa A. Clancy
Design by: Lili Schwartz

POCKET BOOKS, a division of Simon & Schuster Inc.
1230 Avenue of the Americas, New York, NY 10020-1586

ISBN: 0-671-02433-7

First Pocket Books trade paperback printing November 1998

20 19 18 17 16 15 14

Printed in the U.S.A.

In memory of my father, J. Laurence Golden Jr., who used to wake me up in the middle of the night to watch Kolchak: The Night Stalker. *this one's for you, Dad. You would've loved it.*
—CG

In memory of my grandmother, Lucile M. Jones, and my father, Kenneth Paul Jones, who both hoped I would write someday. And for the mensch and the friend and the writer he is, thank you, Chris Golden. You made it happen.
—NH

For Laura Anne Gilman. She knows why.
—KRAD

A book of this magnitude requires the infinite patience and the invaluable assistance—not to mention the simple moral support—of a great many people. For all of that, the authors would like to thank the following:

Joss Whedon and the entire cast and crew of *Buffy*, with a very special thanks to Caroline Kallas (your name should be on the cover, Coywoman!), Todd McIntosh and Jeff Pruitt; our editor, Lisa Clancy, and her tireless assistant, Elizabeth Shiflett; and our agents, Howard Morhaim and Lori Perkins.

Christopher would like to thank: Lucy Russo, Colleen Viscarra, Stefan & Carole Nathanson, Jeff & Gail Galin (for their forbearance), Ruth and Rachel Satrape, and Tom Sniegoski, for his help in juggling. And thanks to Nicholas and Daniel, for their love and laughter, with hope that they grow to be as brave and noble as Xander and as clever and gentle as Oz.

Nancy would like to thank: Lindsay Sagnette, Leslie Jones, all the Simpsons and the Holders, the Baby-sitter Battalion (Ida Khabazian, April Koljonen, Andi Craft, and Bekah "Bah" Simpson), Maryelizabeth Hart, Stinne Lighthart, Karen Hackett, Linda Wilcox, Susan Klug, Barbara Nierman, Brenda Van De Ven, Susie Johnson, Margie Morel, and all my other friends who so politely ignored me.

Keith would like to thank: Helga Borck, Peg Carr, Cathy (a.k.a. BuffyChic4), Amiee Collier, GraceAnne Andreassi DeCandido, Livia DeCandido, Robert L. DeCandido, Edward DeVere, John S. Drew, Laura Anne Gilman (a.k.a. Meerkat), Orenthal V. Hawkins, Alan "Anime Nut" Hufana, the Inner Circle of *Buffy* Geeks (you know who you are), Kate (a.k.a. hrprobe), Andrea K. Lipinski, Peter Liverakos, Dave Logsdon, Sonja Marie, Pam McLaughlin, John Nestoriak, Carolyn Oldham, John Edward Peters, RayneFire, Leslie Remencus, Scott Robinson, Rainier Robles, Lisa Rose, Wendy Tillis, Jack Welsh, Jennifer Whildin, Sarah Winsor, and generally everyone on Buffy-L@planetx.com.

And most of all, we'd like to thank our respective, long-suffering spouses: Connie Golden (you were right, sweetie, but it looks phenomenal! —CG); Wayne Holder (*Dai suki*—NH); and Marina Frants (hey, look, dear, it's finally a *book!*—KRAD)

CONTENTS

FOREWORD

Buffy the Vampire Slayer wasn't always the hip success it now is. Before the show aired, there was often a certain amount of derision involved in conversations about it. A cheerleader named *Buffy*, who slew vampires. It sounded a little goofy, truth be told.

But the first time you saw it, you just knew.

Joss Whedon has proven to Hollywood that it isn't impossible to mix action, comedy, drama, and horror and still have a compelling hour-long show...in fact, one of the most compelling hours on television. Critics fall all over themselves naming it one of the best shows on the air.

Here is a series unlike anything else on TV. Things *change*. Characters feel pain. Yes, this is a world of horror and fantasy, but the ongoing subplots don't feel like storylines. They feel like people's lives. It's a world of angst and the terror of simply being a teenager that anyone can relate to. Joss Whedon is often, mostly in fits of hyperbole, called a genius. And while it might not have taken genius to come up with the basic plot of *Buffy*—high school girl chosen to save the world from vampires—it certainly took genius, or something like it, to make of that idea a series that speaks to viewers of all ages on a universal level. Nobody knows what it's like to be a Slayer, because there's no such thing. (No such thing as vampires, either.)

But we all can relate to what Buffy and her friends are going through.

As the series progresses and the characters move through high school, graduate, and go out into the world, we can be certain of one thing. There will be a great deal of change. And, as always, change will bring some joy, and a great deal of pain.

We wouldn't miss it for the world, and we know you'll be right there with us.

You hold in your hands a very special book: the official companion and guide to the hit television series *Buffy the Vampire Slayer*. It contains nearly forty exclusive interviews with principal cast members and major guest stars, the executive producers, the production crew, and the creator of *Buffy* himself—Joss Whedon.

Illustrated with photographs from the set, as well as from the personal archives of *Buffy* professionals such as makeup artist Todd McIntosh and stunt coordinator Jeff Pruitt, the *Watcher's Guide* offers a behind-the-scenes look at what it takes to transform Joss Whedon's unique vision into a series that continues to intrigue and delight devoted fans...and capture new ones each week.

Everything you need to know about the series and its mythology, as well as everything you'd like to know about how the show is put together and the people who bring it to you week after week—it's all in here.

On the following pages, you'll find out things about this series you can't get anywhere else!

It was a true pleasure putting this book together for all of you. We hope that you enjoy it as much as we did.

Christopher Golden & Nancy Holder
with Keith R.A. DeCandido

THE MYTHOLOGY
OF BUFFY

Who and What is a Slayer?

Don't you get the feeling that the Watcher Rupert Giles knows an awful lot more than he's telling "The Harvest," part two of the two-hour premiere of *Buffy the Vampire Slayer,* opens with Giles beginning to explain to Willow Rosenberg and Xander Harris just what it is they have gotten themselves involved in by discovering Buffy Summers's secret identity as the Slayer.

"This world is older than any of you know, and contrary to popular mythology, it did not begin as a paradise. For untold eons, demons walked the Earth, made it their home, their Hell. In time, they lost their purchase on this reality, and the way was made for mortal animals. For Man. What remains of the Old Ones are vestiges: certain magicks, certain creatures. . . .

"The books tell that the last demon to leave this reality fed off a human, mixed their blood. He was a human form possessed—infected—by the demon's soul. He bit another and another . . . and so they walk the Earth, feeding. Killing some, mixing their blood with others to make more of their kind. Waiting for the animals to die out and the Old Ones to return."

Not a pretty picture, is it? Fortunately, the forces of good reacted almost instantly. As Giles says later in that very same episode, "As long as there have been vampires, there has been the Slayer." More precisely, "a" Slayer, for each time a Slayer dies, a new one is ready and waiting to take her place, with a Watcher prepared to instruct and guide the new Slayer in her role as the scourge of Darkness.

How all this happens is still quite a mystery. Since the Slayer herself is slightly more than human—stronger, faster, more resilient—it is probably safe to assume that, even as the forces of Darkness created the vampires, there are forces of good that have created the Slayer legacy as counterpoint to the evils of the world.

Giles: "Into each generation, a Slayer is born. One girl, in all the world, a Chosen One. One born with the . . ."

Buffy: ". . . the strength and skill to hunt the vampires, to stop the spread of evil, blah blah. I've heard it, okay?"
— *"Welcome to the Hellmouth"*

Indeed, there are many questions unanswered. Who was the first Watcher? How does a Watcher know that it is his time and the time for his Slayer? Is there some ruling council among Watchers? This is fertile territory, fascinating questions whose fascinating answers still exist only in the mind of Joss Whedon. For the moment, let's take a look at what we do know.

Slayer

The current Slayer is Buffy Summers, a seventeen-year-old junior at Sunnydale High

School. After her parents' divorce, Buffy believed that her and her mother's move to Sunnydale was their own choice, but obviously larger forces were at work. After all, upon her arrival, Buffy discovered that Sunnydale was once also called "Boca del Infierno" or "the Hellmouth."

Giles: "Dig a bit into the history of this place and you'll find there's been a steady stream of fairly odd occurrences. I believe this area is a center of mystical energy. Things gravitate toward it that you might not find elsewhere."
Buffy: "Like death."
Giles: "Like werewolves. Zombies. Succubi. Incubi. Everything you ever dreaded was under your bed and told yourself couldn't be by the light of day. They're all *real.*"
Buffy: "What, did you send away for the *Time-Life* series?"
Giles: "Uh, yes."
Buffy: "Did you get the free phone?"
Giles: "The calendar."
—*"Welcome to the Hellmouth"*

1927: Forty-one bodies were found near Union Station. Shortly after the arrival of this young woman, the mysterious murders stopped. Now, in 1997, it's starting all over again."
Voice-over narration at the beginning of "Welcome to the Hellmouth"

> Later, Giles did indeed get "the calendar." The erstwhile Watcher's only love interest on the series thus far has been technopagan Gypsy computer teacher Jenny Calendar.

"A Slayer hunts vampires; Buffy is the Slayer; don't tell anyone. I think that's all the vampire information you need."
Giles, in "The Harvest"

Information about other Watchers and Slayers has been revealed sparingly over the course of the first two seasons. The very first episode began with a short trailer that discussed some of them, including Lucy Hanover, in Virginia, 1866. But other references have been even more vague. We do know, interestingly enough, that the vampire Spike has killed two Slayers in his time, and his lover, Drusilla, has also killed at least one—namely, Kendra.

"Virginia, 1866: The disappearance of local Civil War widows shocked an already devastated community. These events ended when Lucy Hanover arrived in town. Chicago, May

"I knew a Slayer in the '30s. Korean chick. Very hot. We're talking muscle tone. Man, we had some times."
Sid, the demon-hunting dummy, in "The Puppet Show"

"So this is the Slayer. You're prettier than the last one."
The Master, to Buffy, in "Nightmares"

"You know what I find works real good with Slayers? Killing them. . . . Oh, yeah, I did a couple Slayers in my time. I don't like to brag. Oh, who am I kidding; I *love* to brag. There was this one Slayer, during the Boxer Rebellion . . ."
Spike, in "School Hard"

Yes, time is unkind to Slayers. They don't tend to live very long. Take Kendra, for example.

When Buffy drowned, only to be revived by Xander, she was, technically, albeit temporarily, dead. Thus, Kendra was "activated" as the Slayer, and her Watcher, Mr. Zabuto—whom Giles notes is "very well respected" among Watchers—sent her to Sunnydale because of the great evil rising there.

Willow: "Is that even possible? I mean, two Slayers at the same time?"

Giles: "Not to my knowledge. The new Slayer is only called after the previous Slayer has died. . . . Good Lord, you *were* dead, Buffy."

Buffy: "I was only gone for a minute."

Giles: "Clearly it doesn't matter how long you were gone. You were physically dead, thus causing the activation of the next Slayer."

Kendra: "She . . . died?"

Buffy: Just a *little*."

—*"What's My Line? Part 2"*

In the end, Kendra didn't live very long. But why? What is it that keeps Buffy going? That keeps her alive? Her training, certainly. Her determination. But even in the face of prophecies about her death, what seems to keep Buffy alive more than anything else is this: she's unpredictable. The very thing about her that frustrates Giles to no end—her lack of attention to tradition—may be what makes her so very hard to kill.

For starters, Buffy uses her street smarts as much as she does the profound perception of a Slayer.

Giles: "Can you tell me if there's a vampire in this building?"

Buffy: "Maybe?"

Giles: "You should know! Even through this mass and this din you should be able to sense them. Try. Reach out with your mind. You have to hone your senses, focus until the energy washes over you, till you can feel every particle of—"

Buffy: "There's one."

Giles: "What? Where?"

Buffy: "Down there. Talking to that girl."

Giles: "But you don't know . . ."

Buffy: "Oh, please. Look at his jacket. He's got the sleeves rolled up. And the shirt . . . deal with that outfit for a moment."

Giles: "It's dated?"

Buffy: "It's carbon-dated! Trust me: only someone who's been living underground for ten years would think that was the look."

—*"Welcome to the Hellmouth"*

Kendra: "My parents—they sent me to my Watcher when I was very young."

Buffy: "How young?"

Kendra: "I don't remember them actually. . . . I've seen pictures. But that's how seriously the calling is taken by my people. My mother and father gave me to my Watcher because they believed they were doing the right thing for me—and for the world. [Then, off Buffy's look] Please. I don't feel sorry for myself. Why should you?"

Buffy: "It just sounds very lonely."

Kendra: "Emotions are weakness, Buffy. You shouldn't entertain them."

Buffy: "Kendra, my emotions give me power. They're total assets."

—*"What's My Line? Part 2"*

Yes, even in the nastiest of situations, Buffy's ability to improvise has saved her time and again.

"There was this time I was pinned down by this guy that played left tackle for varsity. . . . Well, at least he used to before he was a vampire. Anyway, he's got one of those really thick necks and all I've got is a little Exacto knife. . . ."

Buffy, *in "The Harvest"*

Buffy (looking at some crossbow bolts): "Huh, check out these babies; good-bye, stakes, hello, flying fatality. What can I shoot?"

Giles: "Nothing. The crossbow comes later. You must become proficient with the basic tools of combat. And let's begin with the quarter-staff. Which, incidentally, requires countless hours of rigorous training. I speak from experience."

Buffy: "Giles, twentieth century. I'm not gonna be fighting Friar Tuck."

Giles: "You never know with whom—or what—you may be fighting. And these traditions have been handed down through the ages. Now you show me good, steady progress with the quarterstaff and in due time we'll discuss the crossbow."

Buffy demolishes him with the quarterstaff.

Giles (on the floor, breathing hard): "Good. Let's move on to the crossbow." —*"Angel"*

Of course, given Buffy's penchant for doing things her way, she has clashed time and again with both Giles, as her Watcher, and particularly with Kendra, whose training was far more traditional . . . and restrictive in a way that Buffy would never stand for.

Buffy: "Then why the hell did you attack me?"
Kendra: "I thought you were a vampire."
Buffy: "Ooh, a swing and a miss for the rookie."
—*"What's My Line? Part 2"*

Kendra: "Here. In case the curse does not succeed . . . This is my lucky stake. I have killed many vampires with it. I call it Mr. Pointy."
Buffy: "You named your stake."
Kendra (embarrassed): "Yes."
Buffy: "Remind me to get you a stuffed animal." —*"Becoming, Part 1"*

Giles: "Kendra. There are a few people—civilians if you like—who know Buffy's identity. Willow is one of them. And they also spend time together. Socially."
Kendra: "And you allow this, sir?"
Giles: "Well . . ."
Kendra: "But the Slayer must work in secret. For security . . ."
Giles: "Of course. With Buffy, however, it's . . . some flexibility is required."
—*"What's My Line? Part 2"*

Kendra: "We can return to your Watcher for orders."
Buffy: "I don't take orders. I do things my way."
Kendra: "No wonder you died."
—*"What's My Line? Part 2"*

Giles: "You see, Spike has also called out the Order of Taraka to keep Buffy out of the way."
Kendra: "The assassins? I read of them in the writings of Dramius."
Giles: "Really? Which volume?"
Kendra: "I believe it was six, sir."
Buffy (to Kendra): "How do you know all this?"
Kendra: "From my studies."
Buffy: "So, obviously you have a lot of free time."
Kendra: "I study because it is required. The Slayer handbook insists on it."
Willow: "There's a Slayer handbook?"
Buffy: "Handbook? What handbook? How come I don't have a handbook?"
Willow: "Is there a T-shirt, too? 'Cause that would be cool."
Giles: "After meeting you, Buffy, I was quite sure the handbook would be of no use in your case." —*"What's My Line? Part 2"*

Kendra: "Buffy's a student here?"
Giles: "Yes."
Kendra: "Right. Of course. And I imagine she's a cheerleader as well."
Giles: "Actually, she had to give up cheerleading. It's quite an amusing story, really . . .
—*"What's My Line? Part 2"*

Buffy's most persistent crisis, however, has little to do with vampires or Demons. Instead, it is the struggle to create some kind of life for herself, some sort of "normal" teenage existence, and still do her duty as the Slayer. Surely she cannot be the first Slayer to have struggled with these issues, but before she was approached by the late Watcher Merrick, at Hemery High, where she spent her freshman year in Los Angeles, she was living the life of a typical, popular, fifteen-year-old girl: boys, clothes, cheerleading, and dreaming about the future, those were her primary topics of conversation. All of that has changed.

Kendra: "Did anyone explain to you what 'secret identity' means?"
Buffy: "Nope. Must be in the handbook. Right after the chapter on personality removal."
— *"What's My Line? Part 2"*

Buffy: "I'm guessing dating isn't big with your Watcher, either."
Kendra: "I am not permitted to speak with boys."
Buffy: "Unless you're pummeling them."
— *"What's My Line? Part 2"*

Buffy: "Have I ever let you down?"
Giles: "Do you want me to answer that, or shall I just glare?"
— *"The Dark Age"*

Buffy: "I told one lie, I had one drink."
Giles: "Yes. And you nearly got devoured by a giant demon-snake. I think the words 'let that be a lesson' are a tad redundant at this juncture."
— *"Reptile Boy"*

FROM THE ORIGINAL TELEPLAY
"WHAT'S MY LINE? PART 2"
Kendra: "I'm not allowed to watch television. My Watcher says it promotes intellectual laziness."
Buffy: "And he says it like it's a bad thing?"
— *"What's My Line? Part 2"*

"Do you think any of the other Slayers ever had to go to high school?"
Buffy, in "School Hard"

In "The Harvest," we see that Buffy keeps Slayer supplies in a false bottom of a trunk in her closet. Later, in "School Hard," we see that she also keeps such supplies in a drawer in her dresser, including stakes, a cross, a bottle with "Holy Water" inscribed on it, and spiked brass knuckles.

Angel: "I thought we had...you know."
Buffy: "A date? So did I. But who am I kidding? Dates are things normal girls have. Girls who have time to think about nail polish and facials. You know what I think about? Ambush tactics. Beheading. Not exactly the stuff dreams are made of."
— *"Halloween"*

Giles: "Buffy, maintaining a normal social life when you're a Slayer is problematic at best."
Buffy: "This is the '90s! The *1990s*, in point of fact, and I can do both. Clark Kent has a job. I just wanna go on a date."
— *"Never Kill a Boy on the First Date"*

Giles: "Buffy, you think I don't know what it's like to be sixteen?"
Buffy: "No. I think you don't know what it's like to be sixteen, *and* a girl, *and* a Slayer."
Giles: "Fair enough. Well, I don't. . . ."
Buffy: "Or what it's like to stake vampires while you're having fuzzy feelings toward one."

Giles: "Ohh . . . ahh . . ."

Buffy: "Digging on the undead doesn't exactly do wonders for your social life."

— *"Reptile Boy"*

Given the life she leads, Buffy is often cynical about being the Slayer. She frequently talks about what life might be like if she didn't have that burden.

Willow: "You're not even a teensy-weensy bit curious about what kind of career you could have had? I mean, if you weren't already the Slayer and all."

Buffy: "Do the words 'sealed' and 'fate' ring any bells for you, Will? Why go there?"

— *"What's My Line? Part 1"*

Buffy: "I wonder if it would be so bad, being replaced."

Willow: "You mean, like, letting Kendra take over?"

Buffy: "Maybe. Maybe after this thing with Spike and the assassins is over, I could say, 'Kendra, you slay, I'm going to Disneyland.'"

Willow: "But not forever, right?"

Buffy: "No, Disneyland would get boring after a few months. But I could do . . . other stuff. Career-day stuff. Maybe I could even have, like, a normal life."

— *"What's My Line? Part 2"*

Giles: "I'll research all the possibilities, ghosts included. Xander, if you're not doing anything, would you like to help me?"

Xander: "What, there's homework now? When did that happen?"

Buffy: "It's all part of the glamorous world of vampire slaying."

— *"Out of Mind, Out of Sight"*

Joyce: "A little responsibility, Buffy, that's all I ask. Honestly, don't you ever think about anything besides boys and clothes?"

Buffy: "Saving the world from vampires."

Joyce: "I swear, sometimes I don't know what goes on in your head."

— *"Bad Eggs"*

FROM THE ORIGINAL TELEPLAY "WHAT'S MY LINE? PART 1"

Buffy: "This career business has me contemplating the el weirdo that I am. Let's face it—instead of a job I have a calling. Okay? No chess club or football games for me. I spend my free time in graveyards and dark alleys."

Angel: "Is that what you want? Football games?"

Buffy: "Maybe. Maybe not. But you know what? I'm never going to get the chance to find out. I'm stuck in this deal."

— *"What's My Line? Part 1"*

Despite her many complaints, however, Buffy is dedicated to her sacred duty. Never was there a Slayer who had to bear so much horror. That may well be because she refuses to turn her heart off, to her friends and family, and to Angel, the vampire she loves. Still, in the end, Buffy is a Slayer, through and through.

"If the apocalypse comes—beep me."
Buffy, in *"Never Kill a Boy on the First Date"*

" . . . and you never let her do anything, except work and patrol and—I know she's the Chosen One, but you're killing her with the pressure. I mean she's sixteen going on forty!"
Willow, to *Giles,* in *"Reptile Boy"*

"Who needs a social life when they've got their very own Hellmouth?"
Buffy, in *"Reptile Boy"*

Kendra: "You talk about slaying like it's a job. It's not. It's who you are."

Buffy: "You get that from the handbook?"

Kendra: "From you."

Buffy: "I guess it's something I really can't fight. I'm a freak."

Kendra: "But not the only freak."

Buffy: "Not anymore."

— *"What's My Line? Part 2"*

Buffy: "You know, I'm the Chosen One. It's my job to fight guys like that. What's your excuse?"

Angel: "Somebody has to." — *"Angel"*

"Grown-ups don't believe you, right? Well, I do. We both know there are real monsters. But there are also real heroes, that fight monsters. And that's me."

Buffy, in "Killed by Death"

Angel: "That's everything, huh? No weapons, no friends. No hope. Take all that away and what's left?"
Buffy: "Me." —*"Becoming, Part 2"*

Giles: "He seems like a nice lad."
Buffy: "Yeah, but he wants to be Dangerman. You, Xander, Willow, you guys know the score. You're careful. Two days in my world and Owen really would get himself killed. Or I'd get him killed."
—*"Never Kill a Boy on the First Date"*

Willow: "Come on, Buffy. One night of rest isn't going to kill you."
Buffy: "No. But it might kill somebody else."
—*"Killed by Death"*

Buffy: "Open your eyes, Mom. What do you think has been going on for the last two years? The fights, the weird occurrences—how many times have you washed blood out of my clothes? You still haven't figured it out?"
Joyce: "Well, it stops now."
Buffy: "It doesn't stop! Do you think I chose to be like this? Do you know how lonely it is? How dangerous? I would love to be upstairs watching TV or gossiping about boys, or God, even studying. But I have to save the world. Again." —*"Becoming, Part 2"*

"Mom, I'm a Slayer, not a postal worker. The cops just can't handle demons. I have to do it."
Buffy, in "Becoming, Part 2"

No matter how she might fight it, in the end, Buffy will accept her destiny. Even if that destiny is her death. That is a kind of courage that is rare in the human race, and it is even rarer for one so young to be mature enough to understand the nature of sacrifice.

Merrick: "There isn't much time. You must come with me. Your destiny awaits."
Buffy: "I don't have a destiny. I'm destiny-free. Really."
Merrick: "Yes, you have. You are the Chosen One. You alone can stop them."
Buffy: "Who?"
Merrick: "The vampires." —*"Becoming, Part 1"*

> Some of Giles's books include *The Black Chronicles, The Tiberius Manifesto,* the *Writings of Dramius, Legends of Vishnu,* and *The Pergamum Codex.*

Giles: "Some prophecies are a bit dodgy. They're mutable. Buffy herself has thwarted them time and again. But this is *The Pergamum Codex.* There is nothing in it that does not come to pass."
Angel: "Then you're reading it wrong."
Giles: "I wish to God I were. But it's very plain. Tomorrow night, Buffy will face the Master. And she will die."
Buffy: "So that's it, huh? My time is up. I remember the drill. 'One Slayer dies, the next is called.' I wonder who she is. [Then, to Giles] Will you train her? Or will they send someone else?"
Giles: "Buffy, I . . ."
Buffy: "Does it say how he's gonna kill me? [small voice] Do you think it'll hurt? [Angel reaches out to comfort her.] Don't touch me! [beat] Were you guys even gonna tell me?"
Giles: "I was hoping I wouldn't have to. That there was some way around it."
Buffy: "Oh, I've got a way around it. I quit."
Angel: "It's not that simple."
Buffy: "I'm making it that simple! I quit! I resign! I'm fired! You can find someone else to stop the Master from taking over."
Giles: "I'm not sure that anyone else can. The signs all indicate—"
Buffy: "The signs? Read me the signs! Tell me my fortune! You're *so* useful, sitting here with all your books. You're really a lot of help!"
Giles: "I don't suppose I am."
Angel: "I know this is hard . . ."
Buffy: "What do *you* know about this? You're never gonna die."

Angel: "You think I want anything to happen to you? Do you think I could stand it? We just have to figure out a way—"

Buffy: "I already did. I quit, remember? Pay attention."

Giles: "Buffy, if the Master rises . . ."

Buffy: "I don't care! I don't care. Giles, I'm sixteen years old. I don't want to die."

—"Prophecy Girl"

"Bottom line is, even if you see 'em coming, you're not ready for the big moments. No one asks for their life to change, not really. But it does. So, what, are we helpless? Puppets? No. The big moments are gonna come, can't help that. It's what you do afterward that counts. That's when you find out who you are."

Whistler, in voice-over, as Buffy discovers Kendra's corpse, in "Becoming, Part 1"

"She's gonna have it tough, that Slayer. She's just a kid. And the world is full of big bad things."

Whistler, in "Becoming, Part 1"

Watcher

As we have previously noted, one of Buffy's strengths is that she does not work alone. All Slayers have had a Watcher, but it is certain that few are as dedicated, as loyal, and as passionate as Rupert Giles. His perseverance in the face of Buffy's inner struggle, and his position at her side in many of her physical battles, mark him as a tremendously courageous man.

Giles: "I was ten years old when my father told me I was destined to be a Watcher. He was one, and his mother before him, and I was to be next."

Buffy: "Were you thrilled beyond all measure?"

Giles: "No. I had very definite plans about my future. I was going to be a fighter pilot. Or possibly a grocer. My father gave me a very tiresome speech about responsibility and sacrifice."

—"Never Kill a Boy on the First Date"

"Buffy, I have volumes of lore, of prophecies and of predictions. But I *don't* have an instruction manual. We feel our way as we go along. And I must say, as a Slayer you're doing pretty well."

Giles, in "Never Kill a Boy on the First Date"

"It's who you are? The Watcher? Sniveling tweed-clad guardian of the Slayer and her kin?"

Ethan Rayne, to Giles, in "Halloween"

Buffy: "Maybe you should consider a career as a Watcher."

Willow: "Oh, no. I don't think I could take the stress."

Xander: "And the dental plan is *crap*."

Willow: "I don't know how Giles does it."

Buffy: "I don't think he has a choice."

—"The Dark Age"

Willow: "How is it you *always* know this stuff? You always know what's going on. I *never* know what's going on."

Giles: "Well, you weren't here from midnight to six researching it." *—"Angel"*

Buffy: "There's something supernatural at work. Get your books. Look stuff up!"
Willow: "What are you going to do?"
Giles: "Get my books. Look stuff up."
— *"The Pack"*

Giles: "I've studied all the extant volumes, of course. But the most salient books of Slayer prophecy have been lost. *The Tiberius Manifesto, The Pergamum Codex—*"
Angel: "*The Codex . . .*"
Giles: "It is reputed to contain the most complete prophecies about the Slayer's role in the end years. Unfortunately, the book was lost in the fifteenth century."
Angel: "Not lost. Misplaced. I can get it."
Giles: "That would be most helpful. My own volumes seem to be rather useless of late. . . . There's an invisible girl terrorizing the school."
Angel: "That's not really my area of expertise."
— *"Out of Mind, Out of Sight"*

Now, for those of you who believe you have the courage and the fortitude—and particularly the lack of any real social life—which will make you perfectly suited for the position of Slayer, we have provided here a step-by-step program to train you for the job in the event you are the Chosen One.

Rules of the Game
or The Slayer Handbook According to Buffy Summers

Rule One:

Walk tough. Talk tough. Be tough.

"I don't think we've been properly introduced.
I'm Buffy and you're...history."
Buffy, in "Never Kill a Boy on the First Date"

"I've lost friends tonight, and I may lose more.
If you have information worth hearing
then I am grateful for it. If you want
to make jokes then I will pull out your
rib cage and wear it as a hat."
Buffy, to Spike, in "Becoming, Part 2"

Rule Two:

**Provide whatever assistance you can, but
know your strengths and weaknesses.**

Buffy: "You have to admit, I kinda lack in the
book area. You guys are the brains. I'd only be
here for moral support."
Xander: "That's not true, Buffy. You totally con-
tribute. You go for snacks."
—*"What's My Line? Part 1"*

Xander: "So. Okay. Get started, Buffy. Dissect it
or something."
Buffy: "Dissect it? Why me?"
Xander: "Because you're the Slayer."
Buffy: "And I slayed! My work here is done."
—*"Bad Eggs"*

Rule Three:

**Be properly respectful about your
calling and its traditions.**

"Sacred duty, yadda yadda yadda."
Buffy, in "Surprise"

Rule Four:

**Keep your cool. Don't let little things like
homicidal boyfriends distract you.**

"I know how hard this is for you. But as the
Slayer, you do *not* have the luxury of being a
slave to your passions. You mustn't let
Angel get to you, regardless of how provocative
his behavior may become."
Giles, in "Passion"

"It should simply be *plunge* and
move on, *plunge* and . . . "
Giles, in "Never Kill a Boy on the First Date"

Rule Five:

**Don't be fooled by a lull in Slayage.
Stake all you want, they'll make more.**

"When you live atop a mystical convergence,
it's only a matter of time before a fresh hell
breaks loose. Now is the time that you should
train more strictly, you should hunt and
patrol more keenly, you should hone
your skills day and night."
Giles, in "Reptile Boy"

"Just because the paranormal has been more
normal and less . . . para lately, is no excuse for
tardiness or letting your guard down."
Giles, to Buffy, in "Reptile Boy"

Rule Six:

Seek a proper balance in your life.

"Buffy, when I said you could slay vampires and
have a social life, I didn't mean at the same time!"
Giles, in "Never Kill a Boy on the First Date"

Rule Seven:

Be vigilant in regard to personal morale.

"A cranky Slayer is a careless Slayer."
Buffy, in "Never Kill a Boy on the First Date"

Rule Eight:

**Personal appearance is important in making a
good first impression.**

Xander: "Is she gonna be okay?" [re: an elec-
trocuted Buffy]
Giles: "She was only grounded for a moment.
[then, to Buffy] Still, if you'd been anyone but
the Slayer. . . ."
Buffy: "Tell me the truth. How's my hair?"
Xander: "It's great. It's your best hair ever."
Giles: "Oh, yes."   *—"I, Robot, You Jane"*

Rule Nine:

**When faced with the unknown,
go with your instincts.**

Xander: "You don't know how to kill this thing."
Buffy: "I thought I might try violence."
Xander: "Solid call."   *—"Killed by Death"*

Rule Ten:

**Wherever you can, inspire faith in your allies
and loathing in your enemies.**

"Not to state the obvious, but this looks
like a job for Buffy."
*Xander, in "Never Kill a Boy
on the First Date"*

"He was young, and he was careful. And still
the Slayer takes him, as she's taken
so many of my family. It wears thin."
The Master, in "Angel"

Rule Eleven:

Be patient.

"Ninety percent of the vampire-slaying
game is waiting."
Giles, in "Never Kill a Boy on the First Date"

Rule Twelve:

**Safeguard your identity as the
Slayer at all times.**

"If your identity as the Slayer is revealed,
it could put you and those around you
in grave danger."
Giles, in "Never Kill a Boy on the First Date"

Spike: "What, your mum doesn't know?"
Joyce: "Know what?"
Buffy: "That, uh, that I'm in a rock band. . . .
Yes, a rock band with Spike here."
Spike: "Right, she plays the . . . triangle."
Buffy: "Drums."
Spike: "Drums, yeah, she's hell on the old
skins, you know."
Joyce: "And what do you do?"
Spike: "Well, I sing."   *—"Becoming, Part 2"*

"Buffy, you aren't by any chance giving
away your secret identity just to impress
cute boys, are you?"
Giles, in "Lie to Me"

**Follow these words of wisdom, and one
day perhaps your Watcher will arrive,
and you, too, may be called to save the
world from Darkness.**

WELCOME *to* SUNNYDALE
Enjoy Your Stay!

POPULATION 36,500   ESTABLISHED 1909

SUNNYDALE
GUIDEBOOK

Buffy the vampire slayer

EXCERPT FROM
*Sunnydale
Official Board
of Tourism
and Commerce*
BROCHURE

Welcome to beautiful Sunnydale!

"It's two hours on the freeway past Neiman Marcus."
RE: SUNNYDALE, **BUFFY** IN "WELCOME TO THE HELLMOUTH"

The Sunnydale Chamber of Commerce welcomes you to lovely Sunnydale, home to many scenic attractions, including a pristine strip of Southern California beach, a world-class museum, and the fully accredited Crestwood College, a magnet for liberal-arts majors from all corners of the globe. Browse for curios at our art gallery, have a cappuccino at our young people's "hangout," the Bronze...and get to know the friendly locals, who are always glad to show you around their town. Colonized by the Spanish centuries ago and given the quaint and colorful name Boca del Infierno, Sunnydale is a community steeped in history. Nowadays, all kinds of interesting folks make their homes in Sunnydale...and once you've been here for a little while, you'll see why!

Sunnydale...come for an hour...stay for a lifetime!

The Historical Society has prepared this Tour of Sunnydale. Many of the attractions are clustered in our central downtown section, while the beach, docks, skating rink, and other places of interest make diverting excursions by car or bus (a map to our **bus depot** and **airport** is located on the back of this brochure).

Sunnydale is a town on the grow . . . and our young people are our lifeblood. The lovely Spanish-style campus of the **Sunnydale High School** features an attractive **Quad**, where the annual May Queen is announced, and an Olympic-sized **swimming pool**, complete with an exquisite **underground grotto**. Sunnydale High is home to the fierce Razorbacks. In 1977, our cheerleading squad won the tri-county championship, and this year we took state semifinals in boys' swimming. Everyone turns out to view the exhibits at our annual science fair, and it's standing room only at the spectacular talent show in our large, professionally equipped **auditorium**. Come have a snack and "hang out" with the class of '99 in our student-decorated **lounge**! Our **cafeteria** recently won "Best Burritos" for the third year in a row. We have a fully computerized **library**, and we're also members of the "Let's Get Together" foreign-exchange-student program.

There are 43 churches in Sunnydale...but some claim there are 44! Ghost stories about a **sunken church** across from the school persist,

THE LIBRARY
According to Willow, in the pilot, it's "where the books live."

"**Ew**, libraries. All those books. What's up with that?"
MITCH, IN "OUT OF MIND, OUT OF SIGHT"

"Ooh, Sunnydale bus depot. Classy. What better way to introduce someone to our country than with the stench of urine."
XANDER, IN "INCA MUMMY GIRL"

XANDER: "Buffy, this is not about looking at a bunch of animals. This is about not being in class."

BUFFY: "You know, you're right! Suddenly the animals look shiny and new."
—ON A FIELD TRIP TO THE ZOO, IN "THE PACK"

WILLOW: "Everything seems normal. Not a snake, not a wasp."

CORDELIA: "Yep. School can open again tomorrow."

XANDER: "Explain to me again how that's a good thing."

CORDELIA: "I'm drawing a blank—"
—"I ONLY HAVE EYES FOR YOU"

despite the fact that no such structure has ever been located. Museum archeologists have explored the vast warren of tunnels beneath the town itself, but to no avail. Still, the legend of the Master's Lair never dies . . . will you be the one to unlock its secrets?

Continue on a few blocks directly from the campus, and you'll come across another very nice example of Spanish architecture. These multi-storied buildings have been turned into condos. **Rupert Giles,** the school librarian, lives here.

Doubling-back to the campus, take a short walk toward the edge of town. **The Bronze** is the local hangout for high school students and older young adults. The place has an appealingly dive-y earthiness; no waiting in line for the bouncer to decide if you're cool or not! Just pay the cover and get your hand stamped if you're old enough to drink.

The Bronze is dark, crowded, noisy...and fun! Live bands play almost every night of the week, and the club also hosts the annual May Queen dance, a spooky celebration of Halloween, the World Culture fiesta, and other exciting community get-togethers. The coffee bar serves a delicious array of croissants and pastries.

"An affluent Southern California school."
JOSS WHEDON'S DESCRIPTION OF SUNNYDALE HIGH IN THE SCRIPT FOR "WELCOME TO THE HELLMOUTH"

Approximately ten blocks to the northeast of the Bronze are a number of abandoned warehouses, where, until recently, an attractive brick **factory** occupied most of a city block. Discussions with the city fathers were under way to transform the factory into a spaghetti restaurant or possibly a wax museum, when, unfortunately, a fire burned the factory to the ground.

Also located in this part of town are two very "colorful" establishments, the rough-and-tumble **Fish Tank** and **Willi's Alibi Room.** (No one under twenty-one admitted.)

In addition, you'll need to know "the password" to enter the private **Sunset Club**. And the word is . . . "Lestat"! This Goth club, it is said, once played host to some "real vampires" . . . but you be the judge as you walk among its denizens clad in black lace and blood-red velvet! (Hours vary.) Admission by invitation only.

A ten-block walk east will lead you to the main gate of the **Sunnydale Armory**. Currently under the command of Colonel Newsome, the Armory is home to the 33rd (the legendary "Skull & Crossbones" unit). The Armory offers a tour of its Weapons Museum on Saturdays from 1–3 P.M. A number of interesting armaments have been recovered during excavations in and around Sunnydale (including our new and exciting high-rise towers!). These fascinating objects of battles gone by are showcased alongside examples of the military's most up-to-date weapons systems. (Civilians, please check in at the Visitors' Gate.)

OZ: "Hey, did everybody just see that guy turn into dust?"
WILLOW: "Uh, sort of."
XANDER: "Yep. Vampires are real; lot of 'em live in Sunnydale. Willow'll fill you in."
WILLOW: "I know it's hard to accept at first...."
OZ: "No, actually, it explains a lot...."
—"SURPRISE"

BUFFY: "There's this amazing place you can go and sit down in the dark—and there are these moving pictures. And the pictures tell a story."
GILES: "Ha ha. Very droll. I'll have you know I have many relaxing hobbies."
BUFFY: "Such as?"
GILES: "Well, I enjoy cross-referencing."
BUFFY: "Do you stuff your own shirts or do you send them out?"
—"HALLOWEEN"

Rounding the perimeter of the Armory and heading back west, you'll come to the **Sunnydale Hospital**. Our E.R. is a busy, bustling trauma center, and our on-site physicians are ready to service your every need, be it a gang-related incident, a run-in with a backed-up sewer line, or an inconvenient tumble down the stairs. Our viral-containment unit is world-class. All our blood products are irradiated, and we have a twenty-four-hour pharmacy.

Continue past the **police station** and the city administration building, and you will come to our lovely **Sunnydale Mall**. Recently refurbished, it boasts a multiplex cinema offering first-run movies, as well as many shops and a lavish food court. Be sure to check out the cool video-game parlor on the upper level!

Leaving the mall and continuing past the community parking lot, our business district offers more fascinating shopping. Not for the faint-hearted, the **Dragon's Cove Magic Shop** carries voodoo dolls, love potions, and Ouija boards. It also sells an attractive line of crystal globe paperweights called "Orbs of Thesulah." Pick up a few for your New Age friends! Nearby, a number of shops specialize in theatrical-costume rentals and Halloween gear. Flash those vampire teeth and say, "Blood!" The oldest costume shop is **Party Town**, and last year, **Ethan's** was a big hit. (Currently closed.)

> XANDER: "Hel-lo! Excuse me, but have you ever heard of knocking?"
> STUDENT: "We're supposed to get some books on Stalin. For a report."
> XANDER: "Does this look like a Barnes & Noble?"
> GILES: "Xander! This is the school library."
> —"PASSION"

After an hour or so of browsing, continue down the lane that leads into one of our loveliest residential areas. Wide boulevards and Deodora pines grace the yards of several Arts and Crafts homes on **Revello Drive**, as well as typical Southern California ranch and Mediterranean styles on the attractive cross streets.

If you continue on, you'll come to **Weatherly Park**, a meeting place for young people and senior citizens alike. This large park is suitable for biking, hiking, and picnicking. Skateboarding is prohibited. (A note of caution: it's probably best to stick to the trails and paved walkways. The occasional unlicensed dog may run loose.) The gates are locked at 10 P.M.

A few blocks farther north, you'll come to the local **playground**, where children can let off steam on the jungle gym and the swings. There are picnic tables, too.

Continue on for approximately another mile, and you'll come upon one of the largest and most beautiful buildings in Sunnydale: the **Sunnydale Natural History Museum**.

> **"Uuhhggh. Parts."**
> **BUFFY** AT THE SUNNYDALE FUNERAL HOME, "NEVER KILL A BOY ON THE FIRST DATE"
>
> WILLOW: "Oh, I'm good with medical stuff. Xander and I used to play doctor all the time."
> XANDER: "*No*, she's being literal. She used to have these medical volumes and diagnose me with stuff. I didn't have the heart to tell her she was playing it wrong."
> —"KILLED BY DEATH"
>
> GILES: "A transport vehicle is delivering a supply of blood to the hospital."
> BUFFY: "Aha. Vampire meals-on-wheels."
> GILES: "Well, hopefully not. We should meet in front of the hospital at 8:30 sharp. I'll bring the weapons."
> XANDER: "I'll bring the party mix."
> —"THE DARK AGE"

Boasting several impressive collections of anthropological artifacts as well as scientific specimens, the museum also plays host to several touring exhibitions each year. Recently, the Inca Princess exhibit drew record crowds. Be sure to visit the Douglas Perren Memorial Room, where a large collection of curios from in and around Sunnydale is on display.

> "Typical museum trick. Promise human sacrifice, deliver old pots and pans."
> **XANDER,** IN "INCA MUMMY GIRL"

Beyond the museum are a number of lovely homes. Rumor has it that members of the popular local band Dingoes Ate My Baby live in this area. Watch out for groupies!

The next stop on any tour of Sunnydale would have to be the **Sunnydale Zoo**. Home to many rare and exotic species, the zoo is a favorite field-trip destination for all ages and grades. Open year-round. (Sorry, the Hyena House is under repair and will be closed until further notice.)

Our youth like to stop to admire the view at "the point," which actually affords a nice view of our town. Make sure that emergency brake is on! Another well-known congregating spot is the humorously named "Makeout Park," near the zoo. Teen Angel, where are you?

Next stop...surf city! Hang ten at the **Sunnydale Beach**. Take I-17 west (municipal bus #13, "Beach" stop.) There's plenty of free parking in the lot. Bonfires are permitted; however, alcoholic beverages and glass containers are not permitted. (*Note:* There have been several unverified shark sightings, but the Sunnydale Water Safety Commission advises that there is, at present, no cause for alarm.) **Our waters are safe**.

And speaking of sharks, if it's fishing you're after, be sure to visit the **Sunnydale Docks**! Home to a healthy shipping industry, the docks house deep-sea fishing boats that are available for charter, from half-day excursions to long, lost weekends lazing in the sun, waiting for that good, strong tug....Call 555-FISH for details.

Take I-17 in the opposite direction, go past the Sunnydale exit, and take the Kallas off-ramp, for a cool spin at the **Sunnydale Ice Rink**. (Bus #66, "Ice Rink" stop.) Go for the gold—and be sure to warm up with some nice hot chocolate and a sugary *churros* at the concession stand. Closed Tuesdays.

Head back into town to spend a few quiet moments in the "Graveyard in the Woods," **Sunnydale Cemetery**. The Mausoleum is also on the grounds. In this hallowed ground, the town's deceased are buried. Prominent Sunnydalians laid to rest here are: Sunnydale principal Robert Flutie, all-state football star Daryl Epps, and many, many others. The historic **Sunnydale Funeral Home** is located nearby. A full-service funeral home providing burial services and with a fully licensed, on-site crematorium, its motto for over four generations has been: "We'll take care of the rest."

XANDER: "We saw the zebras mating! Thank you, very exciting..."
WILLOW: "It looked like the Heimlich. With stripes." —"THE PACK"

CORDELIA: "The Bronze. It's the only club worth going to around here. They let anybody in, but it's still the scene. It's in the bad part of town."
BUFFY: "Where's that?"
CORDELIA: "About half a block from the good part of town. We don't have a whole lot of town."
—"WELCOME TO THE HELLMOUTH"

GILES: "We'll deal with that when we've ruled out evil curses."
BUFFY: "Someday I'm going to live in a town where evil curses are just generally ruled out without even saying."
—"INCA MUMMY GIRL"

Abutting the cemetery's south wall stand the Sunnydale woods, a bucolic wonderland of deciduous evergreens, and just beyond the woods, the abandoned but still splendid **Delta Zeta Kappa fraternity house**. Once chartered by **Crestwood College**, on whose campus the house stands, the fraternity chose to disband last year after a scandal involving questionable initiation rituals. The college itself remains in excellent academic standing. Last year, the drama department mounted an excellent production of *The Sound of Music*.

About two miles past the north wall of the college stands **Sunnydale Technology Park**, home to a small but prosperous cluster of high-tech companies, including Lorrin Software. The park was also home to CRD, now unfortunately in Chapter 11 bankruptcy proceedings. The structure recently sustained some damage due to an electrical problem and has been condemned.

> WILLOW: "Now there's a killer? We don't know there's a—"
> GILES: "No. But this being Sunnydale and all..." —"REPTILE BOY"

A quick turn down the street and you're at the **Mini-Golf**! Providing wholesome family entertainment, Sunnydale's miniature golf course is a great place to catch up with old friends...or get better acquainted with new ones!

On the outskirts of town stands a **mansion**, which is reputed to be the home of a retired silent-film star who deeded it to the town upon her death. The Historical Society recently leased it to a reclusive gentleman named "Mr. A." Movers report that the mansion is filled with beautiful Art Deco statuary and fixtures. Perhaps one day Mr. A will open his doors for a *grande soiree*, as has been suggested by some "in the know."

We hope that this brochure has added to your enjoyment of our beautiful town. Who knows? Maybe once you've spent some time in Sunnydale, you'll find you just can't leave!

> "Not a lot happens in a one-Starbuck's town like Sunnydale."
> XANDER, IN "WELCOME TO THE HELLMOUTH"

> BUFFY: "And on your right, once again—the beautiful campus. I think you've now seen everything there is to see in Sunnydale."
> FORD: "Well, it's really..."
> BUFFY: "Feel free to say 'dull.'"
> FORD: "Okay. Dull's good. Or maybe not so dull.... Is that more vampires?"
> —"LIE TO ME"

> GILES: "There are forty-three churches in Sunnydale? That seems a little excessive."
> WILLOW: "It's the extra evil vibe from the Hellmouth. Makes some people pray harder."
> —"WHAT'S MY LINE? PART 2"

> GAGE: "So that . . . was the thing that killed Cameron?"
> BUFFY: "No, that was something else."
> GAGE: "Something else?"
> BUFFY: "Unfortunately, there are a lot of 'something elses' in this town."
> —"GO FISH"

CHARACTER GUIDE

Buffy Summers

Buffy Anne Summers was born in 1981 ("Nightmares," "Surprise," "Innocence") to the now-divorced Hank and Joyce Summers. As a child, she would pretend to be the superhero Power Girl, which would turn out to be a prophetic choice of alter ego. She was very close to her cousin Celia until Celia died in a hospital, leading Buffy to hate hospitals ("Killed by Death").

Buffy started attending Hemery High School, in Los Angeles, in the fall of 1995. She was elected the equivalent of the May Queen in 1996 ("Out of Mind, Out of Sight"), and it was also then that she learned from a Watcher named Merrick that she was the Chosen One, the Slayer of vampires ("Welcome to the Hellmouth," "Becoming, Part 1"). During her initial foray into Slayerhood, Merrick was killed and she burned down the school gymnasium ("Welcome to the Hellmouth"). Her parents—who had been having marital difficulties for some time ("Becoming, Part 1")—finalized their divorce that same year ("Nightmares").

Her mother gained custody of Buffy in the divorce, and the pair moved to a house at 1630 Revello Drive ("Angel") in Sunnydale, California, and Buffy enrolled as a sophomore at Sunnydale High School ("Welcome to the Hellmouth"). Reluctantly at first, she again took up her duties as the Slayer, with Rupert Giles as her new Watcher ("The Harvest").

In addition to her increased strength, agility, and stamina thanks to being the Slayer, Buffy is also a skilled ice skater—she went through a "Dorothy Hamill phase" as a child, down to the haircut ("What's My Line? Part 1"). She also sometimes has prophetic dreams ("Welcome to the Hellmouth," "Prophecy Girl," "Surprise," "Innocence"). Giles seemed to think that she should be able to sense vampires ("Welcome to the Hellmouth"), an ability Buffy has been developing over the last two years.

> "I think I speak for everyone here when I say, 'Huh?'"
> —to Giles, in "Out of Mind, Out of Sight"

> "Everyone has them in L.A. Pepper spray is so passé."
> —about her stake, in "Welcome to the Hellmouth"

Buffy's success with relationships has been limited. Her fifth-grade crush on Billy "Ford" Fordham went unrequited, though the two had been very close friends through to high school ("Lie to Me"). She briefly dated a boy named Tyler, but dumped him in fairly short order ("Becoming, Part 1"). She became vaguely involved with two Sunnydale High boys, Owen Thurman ("Never Kill a Boy on the First Date") and Cameron Walker ("Go Fish"), but the former was more interested in Buffy's wild lifestyle than in Buffy

> "Giles, CARE. I'm putting my life on the line, battling the undead! Look, I broke a nail, okay? I'm wearing a press-on. The least you could do is exhibit some casual interest. You could go 'Hmmm.'"
> —"Prophecy Girl"

herself, and Cameron turned out to be as dull as dishwater (and a gill monster, to boot). A college boy named Tom Warner came on to her, but he was interested only in sacrificing her to the Demon his fraternity worshiped ("Reptile Boy"). She turned down two other propositions ("Halloween," "I Only Have Eyes for You"), as well as Xander's numerous advances ("The Witch," "Prophecy Girl"). Her only successful relationship—with Angel—ended very badly ("Angel," etc.). Buffy and Angel, a vampire with a soul, fell in love and actually managed to sustain a relationship.

Unfortunately, the curse that gave Angel his soul was predicated on his suffering forever for his past evil deeds; having sex with Buffy led to him to revert to his former vampiric self, Angelus ("Surprise," "Innocence"), which put something of a damper on the relationship.

Buffy's style of Slayerhood has proven to be unique. She has a support system beyond her Watcher (Xander, Willow, Cordelia, and Oz, plus Angel, until he reverted, and Jenny Calendar, until she was murdered), the peculiarity of which was commented on by Spike ("School Hard"), and her training has focused almost exclusively on the physical elements of Slayerdom, Giles having foregone the intellectual side ("What's My Line? Part 2"; until that episode, Buffy had no idea there even was a Slayer's handbook). However, she has done a superlative job, having killed the Master, one of the oldest and most powerful vampires ("Prophecy Girl"), and prevented Hell from spilling over onto Earth ("Becoming, Part 2").

Buffy is played by Sarah Michelle Gellar. Her eight-year-old self was played by Mimi Paley in "Killed by Death," and she was also played by an anonymous rat for parts of "Bewitched, Bothered, and Bewildered."

Quot-aBLe Buffy

QUOT- ABLE Buffy

"She's the gnat in my ear. The gristle in my teeth. She's the bloody thorn in my bloody side!"

Spike, on Buffy, in "What's My Line? Part 1"

Buffy: "I wasn't gonna use violence. I don't always use violence, do I?"
Xander: "The important thing is, *you* believe that."　　**—"Inca Mummy Girl"**

"Now, we can do this the hard way, or . . . well, actually, there's just the hard way."
—"Welcome to the Hellmouth"

"I've had it. Spike is going down. You can attack me, you can send assassins after me . . . that's fine. But nobody messes with my boyfriend."
—"What's My Line? Part 2"

"When this is over, I'm thinking pineapple pizza and teen-video movie fest—possibly something from the Ringwald oeuvre."
—"What's My Line? Part 2"

Buffy: "I kill vampires. That's my job."
Giles: "True, although you don't usually beat them into quite such a bloody pulp beforehand."　　**—"Ted"**

Xander: "Can you say 'overreaction'?"
Buffy: "Can you say 'sucking chest wound?'"
—"Ted'"

Willow: "Don't forget, you're supposed to be a meek little girlie-girl like the rest of us."
Buffy: "Spoil my fun."　　**—"Phases"**

Ted: "Buffy, your mother and I are taking one step at a time, and if things go the way I hope, someday soon I may just ask her to tie the knot. How would you feel about that? It's okay to have feelings, Buffy, and it's okay to express them."
Buffy: "I'd feel like killing myself."　**—"Ted"**

Willow: "I'm sure it wasn't your fault. He started it!"
Buffy: "Yeah, that defense only works in six-year-old court, Will."　　**—"Ted"**

Giles: "Let's not jump to any conclusions."
Buffy: "I didn't jump. I took a tiny step, and there conclusions were." **—"Phases"**

Cain: "You know, sis, if that thing out there harms anyone, it's going to be on your pretty little head. I hope you can live with that."
Buffy: "I live with that every day."
—"Phases"

"The Master. I went by his grave last night and they have a vacancy." **—"When She Was Bad"**

"Destructo-Girl, that's me." **—"Teacher's Pet"**

Buffy: "So what's the scuttlebutt? Anybody besides Larry fit our werewolf pro- file?"
Willow: "There is one name that keeps get- ting spit out. Aggressive behavior, run-ins with the 'authorities,' about a screenful of violent inci- dents."
Buffy: "Okay, most of those weren't my fault. Somebody else started this. I was just standing up for myself."
Willow: "They say it's a good idea to count to ten and say you're sorry."
—"Phases"

"I am trying to save you! You are playing in some serious traffic here, do you understand that? You're gonna *die*. And the only hope you have of surviving is to get out of this pit right now and, my God, could you *have* a dorkier outfit?

—to "Diego" and the True Believers, in "Lie to Me"

"I'd suggest a box of Oreos dunked in apple juice...but maybe she's over that phase."

Ford's first line, in "Lie to Me"

"We need to find the rest of the swim team and lock them up before they get in touch with their inner halibut." **—"Go Fish"**

Coach Marin: "You've got quite an imagination, missy."
Buffy: "Right now I'm imagining you in jail....You're wearing a big orange suit and—oh, look! The guards are beating you!" **—"Go Fish"**

"Can you vague that up for me?"

—"Welcome to the Hellmouth"

"People, listen to me. This is not the mother ship, okay? This is ugly death come to play."

—"Lie to Me"

Joyce: "Are you going out tonight, honey?"
Buffy: "Yeah, Mom, I'm going to a club."
Joyce: "Will there be boys there?"
Buffy: "No, Mom, it's a nun club."

—"Welcome to the Hellmouth"

FROM THE ORIGINAL TELEPLAY:
"I'm not a big secret-sharer. I like my secrets. They're secret." **—"Inca Mummy Girl"**

Angel

An Irish gentleman born in the early 1700s, Angelus was a ne'er-do-well who was more interested in drinking than in doing an honest day's work. On one such drunken binge, he encountered a vampire named Darla, who turned him into a vampire ("Angel," "Becoming, Part 1"). Although he had never left his home of Galway as a human, as a vampire he traveled extensively. In England in 1860, he murdered the family of a woman named Drusilla, driving her mad before finally turning her into a vampire ("Lie to Me," "Becoming, Part 1"). In Romania in 1898, he killed the favorite daughter of a Romany tribe and was thereafter cursed by the tribe's elders: they restored his soul to him, forcing him to live in anguish over the acts he had committed as a vampire ("Angel," "Becoming, Part 1").

From that point on, Angel suffered. He drifted, eventually winding up as a homeless person in a New York City alleyway in the 1990s. It was there that the demon Whistler found him and encouraged him to make something of himself ("Becoming, Part 1"). He traveled to California and

decided he would help the Slayer. Initially, his help came in the form of cryptic advice ("Welcome to the Hellmouth," "The Harvest," "Teacher's Pet," "Never Kill a Boy on the First Date"), but his and Buffy's growing feelings for each other led to him becoming closer both to her and to her circle of friends. He also revealed to her that he is a vampire and how he came to regain his soul ("Angel"). Angel became a valued ally to Buffy, Giles, and the Slayerettes, and his vampiric strength and abilities proved especially useful against the demon Eyghon ("The Dark Age"), the minions of the demon Machida ("Reptile Boy"), and against the various vampires that have infested Sunnydale ("Angel," "School Hard," "Lie to Me," etc.).

Despite the lunacy of it (though Giles called it "poetic" in "Out of Mind, Out of Sight"), Angel and Buffy fell hopelessly in love with each other, eventually consummating the relationship on Buffy's seventeenth birthday ("Surprise"). Unfortunately, the Romany curse was predicated on Angel remaining tortured. By experiencing joy, the curse was lifted and he reverted to his old self ("Innocence"). He remained un-souled until Willow recast the spell—but, right after that Buffy was forced to impale him and send him to Hell to prevent the world from being destroyed ("Becoming, Part 2").

Angel is played by David Boreanaz.

> "Angel's our friend. Except I don't like him."
> —Xander, in "What's My Line? Part 2"

> "Don't worry, I'm not here to eat."
> —"Out of Mind, Out of Sight"

> "Aren't you a 'throw himself to the lions' sort of chap these days?"
> —Spike, in "What's My Line? Part 2"

> "If I can go a little while without being shot or stabbed, I'll be okay."
> —"Angel"

QUOT-ABLE Angel

Willy: "I'm living right, Angel."
Angel: "Sure you are, Willy. And I'm taking up sunbathing."
—**"What's My Line? Part 1"**

Buffy: "It's Angel. He's Drusilla's sire."
Xander: "Man, that guy got some major neck in his day!"
—**"What's My Line? Part 2"**

Angel: "I want to learn from you."
Whistler: "Okay."
Angel: "But I don't want to dress like you."
—**"Becoming, Part 1"**

Angel: "The [Romany elders] conjured the perfect punishment for me."
Buffy: "What, they were all out of boils and blinding torment?"
Angel: "When you become a vampire, the demon takes your body. But it doesn't get your soul. That's gone. No conscience, no remorse...it's an easy way to live. You have no idea what it's like to have done the things I've done, and to care. I haven't fed on a living human being since that day."
—**"Angel"**

Spike: "No more of this 'I've got a soul' crap?"

Angel: "What can I say? I was going through a phase." **—"Innocence"**

"I can walk like a man, but I'm not one. I wanted to kill you tonight."

—to Buffy, in "Angel"

Buffy: "I invited you into my home. And then you attacked my family."

Angel: "Why not? I killed mine. I killed their friends and their friends' children. For a hundred years, I offered an ugly death to everyone I met. And I did it with a song in my heart."

—"Angel"

Buffy: "...I know what you are."

Angel: "I'm just an animal, right?"

Buffy: "You're not an animal. Animals I like." **—"Angel"**

Angel: "What?"

Xander: "You were checking out my neck! I saw that."

Angel: "No, I wasn't."

Xander: "Just keep your distance, pal."

Angel: "I wasn't looking at your neck."

Xander: "I told you to eat before we left." **—"Prophecy Girl"**

QuotABLe Angel

Xander Harris

Alexander LaVelle Harris has lived in Sunnydale, California, all his life. His best friend growing up was Willow Rosenberg—they used to play literal "doctor," with Willow using actual medical texts ("Killed by Death"), Willow was at Xander's sixth birthday party when he was menaced by a clown ("Nightmares"), and each used to regularly sleep over at the other's house ("Bewitched, Bothered, and Bewildered")—and they remain best friends to this day. He was also best friends with Jesse, until he was turned into a vampire and Xander inadvertently staked him ("The Harvest"). Xander learned of Buffy's secret by overhearing her and Giles speaking in the library about it ("Welcome to the Hellmouth"), and, along with Willow, he insisted on helping Buffy in her subsequent adventures ("The Witch").

Little is known about the Harris family. Xander's father supposedly once considered selling his son to some Armenians ("Inca Mummy Girl"), and apparently neither parent can cook—Xander once invited Willow over for dinner by saying, "Mom's making her famous phone call to the Chinese place," prompting Willow to ask if they even had a stove in their house ("Out of Mind, Out of Sight").

Although not unintelligent by any means, despite referring to himself as the "king of cretins" ("The Witch"), Xander has

never excelled academically ("Bewitched, Bothered, and Bewildered," "Go Fish," etc.), relying on Willow to tutor him in many subjects, especially math ("Welcome to the Hellmouth," "The Pack," "Becoming, Part 2").

Xander's love life has not been the most successful. Remaining cheerfully oblivious to how Willow feels about him (except for one moment in "When She Was Bad" and "Innocence"), he instead pursued a variety of women who were no good for him, ranging from a sexy substitute teacher who turned out to be a praying mantis out for his head ("Teacher's Pet"), to an exchange student who turned out to be a mummy that needed to drain the life out of people ("Inca Mummy Girl"), to Buffy, for whom he has carried a torch from the moment he saw her and crashed his skateboard ("Welcome to the Hellmouth") but who has not shown any interest (except for one moment in "Phases" and under a spell in "Bewitched, Bothered, and Bewildered"). Although he had often declared himself treasurer of the We Hate Cordelia Chase Fan Club ("Innocence"), Xander and Cordelia found themselves necking when they were trapped in Buffy's basement ("What's My Line? Part 2"), and the pair of them have become, against all odds, an item. After Cordelia broke up with him, Xander conscripted Amy Madison to cast a love spell on her, which backfired rather spectacularly, causing every woman in Sunnydale *except* Cordelia to fall for him and nearly starting a riot. The desperate gesture, however, was enough to make Cordelia give the relationship another chance ("Bewitched, Bothered, and Bewildered").

He continues to pine for Buffy, which irks both Cordelia and Willow and caused a great deal of friction between him and Angel before Angel's soul was taken ("Surprise")—and led to a not-entirely-unjustified "I told you so" ("Passion") and a lack of desire to see the vampire re-souled ("Becoming").

Xander's primary contribution to the Slayerettes is not really physical—Buffy, Giles, and Angel are all better suited to the hand-to-hand stuff—nor intellectual—Willow and Giles are more inclined in that direction—though he has done both (he's slain a vampire or two in his time, e.g., "Phases," and it was he who came up with a way to stop the Judge in "Innocence" and the maggot assassin in "What's My Line? Part 2"). His most important qualities are his loyalty to Buffy and the others and his willingness to do whatever is necessary to help out (overcoming his inner demons in "Nightmares," going undercover on the swim team in "Go Fish," challenging the vampires in their lair in "The Harvest," "Prophecy Girl," "When She Was Bad," "Innocence," and "Becoming, Part 2," rescuing Cordelia from a fire-filled room in "Some Assembly Required," etc.), though sometimes that gets in the way of his better judgment (e.g., shadowing Buffy and Cordelia to the frat party in "Reptile Boy").

Xander is played by Nicholas Brendon.

QUOT-ABLE Xander

"Okay, this is where I have a problem, see, because we're talking about vampires. We're having a talk with *vampires* in it."
—**"The Harvest"**

"Rodney Munson. God's gift to the Bell Curve. What he lacks in smarts, he makes up for in lack of smarts." —**"Inca Mummy Girl"**

"Can I just say one thing? *HEEELLLLLPPP!*"
—**"Teacher's Pet"**

Ampata: "You are strange."
Xander: "Girls always tell me that. Right before they run away."
—**"Inca Mummy Girl"**

Ford: "I'd love to go [to the Bronze], but if you guys had plans—would I be imposing?"
Xander: "Only in the literal sense."
—**"Lie to Me"**

"Cavalry's here; cavalry's a frightened guy with a rock, but it's here."
—**"Becoming, Part 2"**

Buffy: "Xander, how do you feel about rifling through Giles's personal files, see if you can shed some light?"
Xander: "I feel pretty good about it. Does that make me a sociopath?"
—**"The Dark Age"**

"Wow. Wow, I think I'm having a thought. I am. I'm having a thought. And now I'm having a plan. [The lights go out.] And now I'm having a wiggins." —**"Innocence"**

"I'm seventeen. Looking at *linoleum* makes me wanna have sex." —**"Innocence"**

Mr. Whitmore: "How many of us have lost countless productive hours plagued by unwanted sexual thoughts and feelings? [Xander's hand shoots up.] That was a rhetorical question, Mr. Harris. Not a poll." —**"Bad Eggs"**

"Man, Buffy. My whole life just flashed before my eyes. I've got to get me a life."
—**"Killed by Death"**

"Ready to get down, you funky party weasel?"
—**to Giles, in "Surprise"**

"Buffy! I feel a pre-birthday spanking coming on—" —**"Surprise"**

Giles: "I suppose there is a sort of Machiavellian ingenuity to your transgression."
Xander: "I resent that! Or possibly, thank you..."
Giles: "Bit of both would suit." —**"Bad Eggs"**

Giles: "The She-Mantis assumes the form of a beautiful woman and lures innocent virgins back to her nest."
Buffy: "Well, Xander's not a...I mean, he's probably . . ."
Willow: "Going to die!" —**"Teacher's Pet"**

"Principal Snyder! Great career fair, sir. Really. In fact, I'm so inspired by your leadership—I'm thinking principal school. I want to walk in your shoes. Not your actual shoes, of course. Because you're a tiny person. Not tiny in the small sense, of course . . . Okay. Done now." —**"What's My Line? Part 1"**

"Whatever comes out of your mouth is a meaningless waste of breath. An airborne toxic event."
—**Principal Snyder to Xander, in "What's My Line? Part 1"**

Jenny: "Cordelia is going to meet us."

Xander: "Ooh, gang, did you hear that? A bonus day of class, plus Cordelia! Mix in a little bit of rectal surgery and it's my *best day ever!*"

—**"The Dark Age"**

Buffy: "Winning equals trophies equals prestige for the school. You see how they're treated. It's been like that forever."

Xander: "Sure, discus throwers got the best seats at all the crucifixions."

—**"Go Fish"**

"That's it. This has gotta stop. It's time for me to act like a man. And hide."

—**"Bewitched, Bothered, and Bewildered"**

Giles: "I can't believe you'd be fool enough to do something like this."

Xander: "Oh, no. I'm twice the fool it takes to do something like this."

—**"Bewitched, Bothered, and Bewildered"**

"On behalf of my gender: Hey!"   —**"Phases"**

"I can translate American Salivating Boy-talk. He said 'you're beautiful.'"

Buffy, translating Xander's reaction to Ampata, in "Inca Mummy Girl"

"This is just too much. I mean, yesterday my life is like, 'uh-oh, pop quiz.' Today it's 'rain of toads.'"   —**"The Harvest"**

"That's creepy on a level I hardly knew existed."

—**"Ted"**

Buffy: "Willow, grow up. Not everything is about kissing."

Xander: "Yeah. Some stuff is about groping."

—**"When She Was Bad"**

Willow Rosenberg

Willow Rosenberg was born and raised in Sunnydale, the daugher of Ira Rosenberg and his wife in a very Jewish household ("Bad Eggs," "Passion"). A fairly reserved and shy person, she is best friends with Xander and had established a reputation as the person to go to for tutoring help ("Welcome to the Hellmouth"). Willow can be charmingly naive at times—when she was a child, her idea of playing "doctor" was to actually read medical texts and test them out on Xander ("Killed by Death").

Willow's computer skills are both prodigious and legendary. During Sunnydale High's Career Week, she was one of only two students (the other being Oz) selected to be interviewed by an unnamed but very prestigious computer-software company ("What's My Line?"), and she was chosen to substitute for computer-science teacher Jenny Calendar after she was murdered ("Passion"). When an adequate replacement couldn't be found, Principal Snyder asked her to fill in for the remainder of the term, an impressive request to make of a junior ("Go Fish"). Acquiring the latest software tends to make her incoherent ("Ted"), and she has continually upgraded her own equipment, having gone from a desktop

("I Robot, You Jane") to a laptop ("Lie to Me"). She was also involved in Jenny's project to scan several texts into the school computers ("I Robot, You Jane").

Willow and Buffy became friends soon after they met. Unfortunately, Buffy's encouragement for her to seize the moment led to her flirting with a boy at the Bronze who turned out to be a vampire ("Welcome to the Hellmouth"). Buffy rescued her; Willow later helped locate the Master's lair by hacking into the city records ("The Harvest"). Like Xander, Willow insisted on helping Buffy out on subsequent adventures ("The Witch"), and her computer skills in particular have come in handy, especially given Giles's technophobia. (at one point she comments, "I'm probably the only girl in school who has the coroner's office bookmarked as a favorite place" ("Some Assembly Required").

Willow has long carried a torch for Xander. They "dated" when they were five years old, but she broke it off when he stole her Barbie doll ("Welcome to the Hellmouth"). In adolescence, she has waited for Xander to notice her but, aside from a fleeting moment shortly before the start of junior year ("When She Was Bad"), he has remained only a friend to her and nothing else, preferring to lust after praying mantises ("Teacher's Pet"), mummies ("Inca Mummy Girl"), Buffy ("Welcome to the Hellmouth," etc.), and Cordelia ("What's My Line? Part 2," etc.). Throughout all this, Willow has remained a true friend even as her heart has broken, encouraging Xander to invite Ampata to a dance ("Inca Mummy Girl").

She carried on an on-line correspondence with a boy named Malcolm, who turned out to be the demon Moloch, which was a pity, as she seemed to have had more success with him than any other boy up to that point ("I Robot, You Jane"). She met up with Oz at the Career Fair, shortly after which he saved her life ("What's My Line? Part 2"), and they eventually started dating ("Surprise"). The later revelation that Oz is a werewolf did not deter their relationship ("Phases"), and when Willow awakened from a coma, Oz was whom she first asked for ("Becoming, Part 2").

After Jenny's death, Willow started going through the techno-pagan's programs, Web sites, and books on the occult, and when she and Buffy discovered the translated spell to restore Angel's soul to him, it was Willow who cast it, despite the risks ("Becoming"). It has yet to be determined whether or not she will continue to dabble in magic.

Willow is played by Alyson Hannigan.

> "Once again, I'm banished to the demon section of the card catalog."
> —"The Puppet Show"

> "So he is a good vampire. I mean, on a scale of one to ten, ten being someone who's killing and maiming every night and one being someone who's . . . not."
> —"Angel"

Quot-able Willow

Willow: "About the spiders. Did you talk to Giles about . . ."

Xander: "Oh. The spiders. Willow's been kinda . . . what's the word I'm looking for . . . insane about what happened yesterday."

Willow: "I don't like spiders, okay? Their furry bodies, their sticky webs—what do they need all those legs for anyway? I'll tell you: for crawling across your face in the middle of the night. *Ew*." —**"Nightmares"**

"I'm not okay. I knew those guys. I go to that room every day. And when I walked in there . . . it wasn't our world anymore. They made it theirs. And they had fun."

—to Buffy, about vampires slaughtering students right there in school, in "Prophecy Girl"

"Uh, Angel, if I say something you don't really wanna hear, do you promise not to bite me?"
—"Lie to Me"

Willow: "I know—we could go to the Bronze, sneak in our own tea bags, and ask for hot water."

Xander: "Hop off the outlaw train, Will, before you land us all in jail."
—"Reptile Boy"

Willow: "I don't get wild. Wild on me equals 'spaz.'" **—"Halloween"**

"I swear, men can be such jerks sometimes . . . dead or alive." **—"Passion"**

". . . and you, I mean, you're gonna live forever, you don't have time for a cup of coffee?"
—to Angel, in "Reptile Boy"

Xander: "Angel was in your bedroom?"
Willow: "Ours is a forbidden love."
—"Lie to Me "

Xander: "You gotta take care of the egg; it's a baby, gotta keep it safe and teach it Christian values."
Willow: "My egg is Jewish." **—"Bad Eggs"**

Willow: "Our friends are in trouble. Now we have to put our heads together and get them out of it. And if you two aren't with me a hundred and ten percent, *then get the hell out of my library!*"
Cordelia: "We're sorry."
Xander: "We'll be good." **—"The Dark Age"**

Buffy: "I'll fight [Angel]. If I have to, I'll kill him. But if I lose or I don't find him in time . . . Willow might be our only hope."
Willow: "I don't want to be our only hope. I crumble under pressure. Let's have another hope."
—"Becoming, Part 1"

Angel: "I guess I need help. And you're the first person I thought of."
Willow: "Help? You mean like on homework? No, 'cause you're old and you already know stuff."
Angel: "I want you to track someone down. On the Net."
Willow: "Oh! Great. I'm so the Net girl."
—"Lie to Me"

Xander: "Sheila's definitely intense. That guy with her? That's the guy she *can* bring home to mother."
Willow: "She was already smoking in fifth grade. Once I was lookout for her."
Xander: "You're bad to the bone."
Willow: "I'm a rebel." **—"School Hard"**

Willow: "I'll give Xander a call. What's his number? Oh, yeah: '1-800-I'm-Dating-A-Skanky-Ho.'"
Buffy: "Me-ow!"
Willow: "Really? Thanks! I've never gotten a 'me-ow' before." **—Phases**

"Oh, Will, you're supposed to use your powers for good!" **Buffy, in "Ted"**

"Don't warn the tadpoles!"
—upon awakening from a dream in **"What's My Line? Part 1"**

"Even I was bored. And I'm a science nerd."
—**about a particularly dull biology class, in "Prophecy Girl"**

QUOT-aBLe
Willow

Rupert Giles

Rupert Giles comes from a family of Watchers—both his father and grandmother also served in that capacity—and he was told at age ten that he too would become one, which disappointed him since he had plans to be either a fighter pilot or a grocer ("Never Kill a Boy on the First Date"). He attended Oxford University, where one of his friends, Carlyle Ferris, fought a She-Mantis and lost both the battle and his sanity ("Teacher's Pet"). Giles eventually rejected the family destiny and dropped out of Oxford, choosing instead to dabble in the occult—he and five friends summoned a demon called Eyghon to the Earth. Only two of that group—Giles and Ethan Rayne—still survive, the others having been killed by the demon ("The Dark Age"). Although he is no longer the practitioner he was in his youth, his skills in spellmaking have proven useful on more than one occasion ("The Witch," "I Robot, You Jane," "Bewitched, Bothered, and Bewildered").

He was the curator at a museum in England, possibly the British Museum, prior to being assigned by the Watchers to Buffy ("Welcome to the Hellmouth"). He also plays the guitar ("The Dark Age") though one suspects it's been a while since he picked the thing up, can read five languages "on a good day" ("Nightmares"), has some skill in fencing ("Reptile Boy") and in shooting a tranquilizer gun ("Phases," "Go Fish"), and lists cross-referencing among his favorite hobbies ("Halloween").

Giles is presently the school librarian for Sunnydale High ("Welcome to the Hellmouth"). It is presumed that he has either a master's degree in library science or the British equivalent in order to qualify for his current position. It is also presumed that Principal Flutie gave him broad discretion in choosing the contents of the library, since it includes several ancient texts that would be out of place in an ordinary school library ("I Robot, You Jane")—these are extremely useful when he needs information to help Buffy fight a particular demon or counter the latest plot from the Master, Spike, Drusilla, or Angel.

Aside from Jenny Calendar ("I Robot, You Jane," etc.) and Dr. Gregory ("Teacher's Pet"; after Gregory was murdered, Giles professed that he liked him), his relationship with his fellow faculty members has not been extensively chronicled. He did date Jenny for some time, though Jenny's possession by Eyghon put a hitch in things ("The Dark Age"), and the truth about her Romany background and that she was sent to Sunnydale to keep an eye on Angel put in an even bigger hitch ("Surprise," "Innocence"). They had made steps toward a reconciliation right before Angel murdered her ("Passion").

Although not a Slayer, Giles has proven quite physically resilient. He has suffered several attacks on his person ("Never Kill a Boy on the First Date," "The Pack," "Prophecy Girl," "The Dark Age," "Bad Eggs," "Passion," and "Becoming"), Jenny once shot him with a crossbow bolt at frighteningly short range ("Ted"), and he was able to resist giving Angel information under torture ("Becoming, Part 2"; he did eventually give in to Drusilla's hypnotic manipulations).

As a general rule, Giles is the picture of the stiff-upper-lip Brit: restrained, stuffy, always wears tweed, somewhat befuddled, what little humor that escapes is dry as toast. However, he also has a ferocity that tends to show through when his emotions are engaged, whether negative—as seen in his rather brutal treatment of Ethan ("Halloween," "The Dark Age") and his attack on Angel ("Passion")—or positive his tremendous protectiveness of and devotion to Buffy ("The Witch," "Nightmares," and "Bewitched, Bothered, and Bewildered," in particular). His time in the company of the Slayerettes, and dating the rather freewheeling Jenny, has loosened him up somewhat. His witticisms are coming more frequently, and he seems more relaxed around Buffy and the gang. He appears, however, to be suffering some residual mental trauma from Jenny's brutal murder ("I Only Have Eyes for You"), the full extent of which has yet to be explored.

Giles is played by Anthony Stewart Head.

Giles: "I've been indexing the Watcher Diaries covering the last couple of centuries. You'd be amazed at how numbingly pompous and long-winded some of these Watchers were."

Buffy: "Color me stunned."

        —"What's My Line?, Part 1"

Cordelia: "What?"

Giles: "I'm sorry . . . your hair."

Cordelia: "There's something wrong with my hair? Oh, my God." [She exits]

Giles: "Xander was right. It worked liked a charm."   **—"The Puppet Show"**

Willow: "...that they had...they had...you know . . . . Uh, you *do* know, right?"

Giles: "Oh, yes. Sorry."

Willow: "Oh, good. Because I just realized, you being a librarian and all, maybe you didn't know."

        —re: sex, in "Passion"

Giles: "Two more of the Brethren were here. They came after me, but I was more than a match for them."

Buffy: "Meaning?"

Giles: "I hid."

        —"Never Kill a Boy on the First Date"

Ethan: "How does Ripper inspire such goodness?"

Buffy: "Because he's Giles."

        —"The Dark Age"

Xander: "I knew this would happen. Nobody can be wound as straight and narrow as Giles without a dark side erupting. My uncle Rory was the stodgiest taxidermist you ever met—by day—by night, it was booze, whores, and fur flying . . . . Were there any whores?"

Buffy: "He was alone."

Xander: "Give it time."   **—"The Dark Age"**

Buffy: "It's not noise. It's music."

Giles: "I know music. Music has notes. This is noise."

Buffy: "I'm aerobicizing. I must have the beat."

Giles: "Wonderful. You work on your muscle tone while my brains dribble out my ears."   **—"The Dark Age"**

"One of these days, you have to get a grown-up car."

        Buffy, disparaging Giles' mode of transportation, in "Inca Mummy Girl"

Xander: "Giles lived for school. He's still bitter there were only twelve grades."

Buffy: "He probably sat in math class thinking, There should be more math! This could be mathier."

Willow: "Come on. You don't think he ever got restless as a kid?"

Buffy: "Are you kidding? His diapers were tweed."   **—"The Dark Age"**

Buffy: "I was a little sloppy on the roundhouse. You want me to try it again?"

Giles: "No, that's fine. You run along to class and I'll wait for the feeling to return to my arms."   **—"The Pack"**

"The Bay City Rollers, now *that's* music."

        Giles, "The Dark Age"

Quotable Giles

Giles HeRO LiBRARiaN

It should come as no surprise that *Buffy the Vampire Slayer* in general and the character of Rupert Giles in particular have been embraced by the library community. After all, one of the three male leads is the school librarian and the library is the Slayerettes' central meeting place.

The show is a hot topic of conversation on Stumpers Talk, an e-mail list created to discuss reference questions and other minutiae. The "listserv" was founded by and is primarily populated by librarians, many of whom have waxed enthusiastic about that rarest of rarities, a librarian hero on television. "I think this is the first time in years, if not decades, that a librarian is a major character in a television show," says Pam McLaughlin of the Warren-Newport Public Library. "Not only that, but what a librarian!" (The Fox series *Party Girl*—based on a feature film—also had a librarian as its lead character, but the show was canceled after only a few episodes.) Library consultant GraceAnne Andreassi DeCandido used Giles as a shining example of a pop-culture librarian icon in a speech that she gave to both Oxford University librarians (Giles's alma mater) and the California Library Association (to which Giles likely belongs).

> **Buffy:** "See, this is a school, and we have students and they check out books and then they learn things."
> **Giles:** "I was beginning to suspect that was just a myth."
> —**"Never Kill a Boy on the First Date"**

Recognizing this enthusiasm, the American Library Association has made *Buffy* the focus of its latest "READ" promotional poster. The poster includes the entire *Buffy* cast and the caption "Slay Ignorance at the Library." It can be ordered from ALA Graphics at 1-800-545-2433 (press 7 to order a poster) or at their Web site: http://www.ala.org/market/graphics/index.html.

In a world where the general public is mostly unaware that librarianship is a profession that requires a master's degree, a show such as *Buffy* that presents the librarian and the library as focal points of the Slayer's ongoing battle against evil is deeply heartening. So is the fact that the librarian isn't a middle-aged woman who says "Shhh!" a lot. Most episodes of *Buffy* hinge on hours of research by Giles (aided and abetted by Willow, Xander, and Cordelia), and the show rarely soft-pedals the difficulty of that research.

Not every librarian thinks Giles is the ideal, however. For one thing, he is rarely seen actually doing what school librarians do. As Priscilla E. Emrich, library director of the Murphy Memorial Library, points out, "The one time that I saw someone come in the library other than Buffy and her friends, Rupert ran them off."

> **Xander:** "Hel-lo! Excuse me, but have you ever heard of knocking?"
> **Student:** "We're supposed to get some books on Stalin. For a report."
> **Xander:** "Does this look like a Barnes & Noble?"
> **Giles:** "Xander! This is the school library."
> **Xander:** "Since when?"
> —**"Passion"**

More to the point, Giles is a technophobe, which makes him something of an oddity. As Carolyn Oldham, director of library resources at American InterContinental University, says, "Most librarians these days are expected to be technology literate." Will Caine of OCLC adds, "It's anachronistic that Giles—since he's not dumb and not working at an underfunded school in the slums—is not a computer user. Librarians today are big-time computer users; everything's on-line, on CD-ROM, on the Web, etc., and it has been that way for a decade or so. In many schools, the librarian would be the primary computer user." Libraries have been on the cutting edge of information technology, and librarians have been among the top professionals making use of the Internet in recent years.

> **Giles:** "Ms. Calendar, I'm sure that your computer-science class is fascinating, but I happen to believe that one can function in modern society without being a slave to the idiot box."
> **Jenny:** "That's TV. The idiot box is the TV. This is a good box."
> **Giles:** "Well, I still prefer a good book." —**"I Robot, You Jane"**

Still, the library and the librarian's critical role on the show is important to librarians. That importance is best summed up by library/pro-literacy advocate and cartoonist Edward DeVere (who was instrumental in getting the *Buffy* READ poster to happen): "The *Buffy the Vampire Slayer* series sets a precedent as far as presenting a first-time-ever hero who is a librarian. If ever there was a ready-made message just waiting for representation on a poster, it was this series being used to promote the idea that books, reading, libraries, and their many available avenues of research are a vitally important tool in combating the forces of Darkness—a metaphor for ignorance if ever I saw one."

Cordelia Chase

The prototype of the most popular girl on campus, Cordelia Chase is attractive, snobby, completely self-centered, fashion-conscious (and makes sure no one else is copying her outfits, "Angel," "Bewitched, Bothered, and Bewildered") head cheerleader (as of "Some Assembly Required," having gotten on the squad in "The Witch"), the object of desire of much of the school's male population, was elected May Queen in her sophomore year ("Out of Mind, Out of Sight"), and is often surrounded by a group of admirers who hang on her every word.

Cordelia was born and raised in Sunnydale. Her mother has Epstein-Barr syndrome ("The Harvest"). Her parents gave her a car ("Prophecy Girl") after she passed driver's ed (some time after "The Witch"). Her dating calendar tends to be full and varied. She used to be very fond of Daryl Epps before his tragic death ("Some Assembly Required"), she took Mitch Fargo to the May Queen dance ("Out of Mind, Out of Sight"), and she dated Devon, the lead singer of Dingoes Ate My Baby ("Inca Mummy Girl"), though she eventually dumped him because he wasn't paying sufficient attention to her ("Halloween"). She has also made plays for both Owen Thurman ("Never Kill a Boy on the First Date") and Angel ("Some Assembly Required," "Reptile Boy," "Halloween"), both of whom preferred Buffy to Cordelia, to the latter's disgust. She also attempted to get into a relationship with Richard Anderson, from the local college, but he was interested only in sacrificing her to the demon he worshiped ("Reptile Boy"). Cordelia and Xander found themselves wildly kissing after arguing while trapped in Buffy's basement by a Tarakan assassin ("What's My Line? Part 2") and, against all odds, have actually managed to build a relationship despite having gone through most of their lives despising each other (dating back to when they were small children, according to Willow in "Out of Mind, Out of Sight").

"People who think their problems are so huge craze me. Like the time I sort of ran over this girl with my bike, and it was the most traumatizing event of my life, and she's trying to make it all about *her* leg! Like my pain meant nothing!"
—in Out of Mind, Out of Sight"

Cordelia initially made friends with Buffy, thinking that, being from Los Angeles, she had to be cool, but when Buffy *a)* mistakenly attacked her with a stake while searching for a vampire in the back area of the Bronze and *b)* started hanging around with "losers" like Willow and Xander, Cordelia shunned the Slayerettes as the lamest of the lame ("Welcome to the Hellmouth," "The Harvest," etc.). This changed when Cordy was threatened by an invisible attacker, and she went to Buffy for help, figuring, based on all the violence that surrounds Buffy, that she was in a gang or something ("Out of Mind, Out of Sight"). Cordy had the truth about vampires in Sunnydale shoved in her face when the Master was freed from his imprisonment, and she was there when Buffy slew him ("Prophecy Girl"). She found herself hanging around with the Slayerettes more and more as time went on, becoming "official" when she was awakened early in the morning to drive Xander to Buffy's house after she'd gone missing ("What's My Line? Part 1").

When her relationship with Xander went public ("Innocence"), she became alienated from her roving band of followers, and she initially broke up with him to appease them. However, realizing that her "friends" were just sheep who hung around her because they wanted her cool to rub off on them, she decided she'd date anyone she wanted, "no matter how lame he is" ("Bewitched, Bothered, and Bewildered").

"Hello? Can we deal with my pain, please?"
—to the Scooby Gang, in "Some Assembly Required"

"This exchange-student thing has been a horrible nightmare. They don't even speak American!"
—in "Inca Mummy Girl"

Cordelia once summed up her own character perfectly: "Tact is just not saying true stuff. I'll pass" ("Killed by Death"; Giles later described her as "Homerically insensitive"). She expresses her opinion and isn't interested if she hurts anyone's feelings. This might be the reason she has found herself gravitating to the Slayerettes, who have also been completely open in their feelings for her (usually by insulting her, but still...).

Cordelia is played by Charisma Carpenter.

QUOTABLE Cordelia

"Being this popular is not just my right, but my responsibility, and I want you to know I take it very seriously."

> **—in her May Queen speech, from "Out of Mind, Out of Sight"**

"What an ordeal. And you know what the worst part is? It stays with you forever. No matter what they tell you, none of that rust and blood and grime comes out. You can dry-clean till judgment day; you're living with those stains."

> **—after Buffy has saved her from becoming a human sacrifice, in "When She Was Bad"**

Eric: "Cordelia is so fine. You know, she'd be just perfect for us."
Chris: "Don't be an idiot. She's alive."

> **—"Some Assembly Required"**

"I think you splashed on just a little too much 'Obsession for Dorks.'"

> **—to Xander, in "Phases"**

Xander: "Wendell, what is wrong with you? Don't you know that she [Cordelia] is the center of the universe...the rest of us merely revolve around her."
Cordelia: "Why don't you revolve yourselves out of my light?"
Xander (to Buffy and Willow): "Wendell was in Cordelia's light."
Wendell: "I'm so ashamed."
Willow: "Why is she so Evita-like?"
Buffy: "It's the hair."
Willow: "Weighs heavy on the cerebral cortex." **—"Nightmares"**

"Gym is canceled due to the extreme dead guy in the locker."

> **—"Welcome to the Hellmouth"**

Giles: "Do you know, I don't recall ever seeing you here (the library) before."
Cordelia: "Oh, no. I have a life."

> **—"Out of Mind, Out of Sight"**

Cordelia: "You're really campaigning for bitch of the year, aren't you?"
Buffy: "As defending champion, you nervous?"
Cordelia: "I can hold my own."

> **—"When She Was Bad"**

"I am, of course, having my dress specially made. Off-the-rack gives me hives."

> **—in "Out of Mind, Out of Sight"**

"God, what is your childhood trauma?"

> **—to Buffy, in "Welcome to the Hellmouth"**

"'I aspire to help my fellow man.' Check. I mean, as long as he's not, like, smelly or dirty or something gross."

> **—"What's My Line? Part 1"**

Cordelia: "She (Buffy) is like this Superman. Shouldn't there be different rules for her?"
Willow: "Sure, in a fascist society."
Cordelia: "Right! Why can't we have one of those?" **—"Ted"**

"Darn, I have cheerleader practice tonight. Boy, I wish I knew you were gonna be digging up dead people sooner; I would have canceled."

> **—"Some Assembly Required"**

Giles: "She (Buffy) has taken a human life. The guilt . . . is pretty hard to bear. It won't go away soon."

Cordelia: "I guess you should know since you helped raise that Demon that killed that guy that time."

Giles: "Yes, do let's bring that up as often as possible."
— **"Ted"**

"Feels like home. If it's the '50s and you're a psycho."
— **in "Ted"**

"Is murder *always* a crime?"
Xander, waxing homicidal about Cordelia, in "What's My Line? Part 1"

"She's a wonderland tour."
— **Oz, on Cordelia, in "Inca Mummy Girl"**

"Did I ever tell you about when Buffy attacked me? With a spear when I came out of the ladies' room at the Bronze. I still relive the trauma every time I see a pencil. I can only use felt-tip now."
— **in "Out of Mind, Out of Sight"**

"Boy, that Cordelia is a regular breath of vile air."
Xander, in "Angel"

"Cordelia, I don't want to hurt you...some of the time...."
Xander, stating the obvious, in "Bad Eggs"

"And almost sixty-five percent of that was actual compliment. [to Cordy] Is that a personal best?"
— **Xander, in "Becoming, Part 1"**

Cordelia: "I hope you guys weren't planning on going to this Sadie Hawkins dance tonight—because I'm totally organizing a boycott. Do you realize that the girls are supposed to ask the guys—and pay and everything? I mean, whose genius idea was that?"

Xander: "Obviously some hairy-legged feminist."

Cordelia: "Really. We have to nip this in the bud or things could get way scary."
— **"I Only Have Eyes for You"**

Cordelia: "And do what? Besides be afraid and die?"

Xander: "Nobody's asking you to go, Cordy. If the vampires need grooming tips, we'll give you a call."
— **"Innocence"**

Giles: "The more I study the Judge, the less I like him. His touch can literally burn the humanity out of you. A true creature of evil can survive the process. No human ever has."

Xander: "So what's the problem? We send Cordy to fight this guy and we go for pizza."
— **"Surprise"**

"I just don't see why everyone is always ragging on Marie Antoinette. I can so relate to her. She worked really hard to look that good. People don't appreciate that kind of effort."
— **participating in history class, in "Lie to Me"**

Cordelia (re: Giles): "No, he was perfectly normal yesterday when I saw him talking to the police."

Buffy: "And you waited until now to tell us because . . . ?"

Cordelia: "I didn't think it was important."

Xander: "We understand. It wasn't about you." —**"The Dark Age"**

Xander: "...Cordy, you should go with Giles."

Giles (petulant): "But why do I have— [stops himself] Good thinking. I could use a research assistant."

Cordelia: "Let's go, tact guy." —**"Killed by Death"**

Cordelia: "Nobody told me I was supposed to bring a gift. I was out of the loop on gifts."

Giles: "Well, it's common among . . . people." —**"Killed by Death"**

"Well, let me know when you want to move up to the big leagues."

—**to Owen re: Buffy, in "Never Kill a Boy on the First Date"**

"Doesn't Owen realize he's hitting a major backspace by hanging out with that loser?"

—**re: Buffy and Owen, "Never Kill a Boy on the First Date"**

"Buffy, love your hair. It just *screams* street urchin." —**in "Halloween"**

"Half the school is out with this flu. It's a serious deal, Buffy. We're all worried about how gross you look." —**in "Killed by Death"**

"Excuse me, I have to call everyone I ever met right now."

—**reveling in Buffy's bizarreness, in "Welcome to the Hellmouth"**

Oz

"I'm shot. Wow. It's . . . odd. And painful." —**"What's My Line? Part 2"**

"I was on the phone all night, listening to Willow cry about you. I don't know exactly what happened, but I was left with the very strong urge to hit you." —**to Xander, in "Bewitched, Bothered, and Bewildered"**

Many details about Oz are still unknown. He is a senior at Sunnydale High School ("Surprise"), and the guitarist for the rock band Dingoes Ate My Baby, which plays regular gigs in the area, including at least two special-occasion concerts at the Bronze, a costume dance in honor of the arrival of foreign-exchange students ("Inca Mummy Girl"), and the Valentine's Day dance ("Bewitched, Bothered, and Bewildered"), which indicates that the band is well regarded by the Bronze's management.

Oz is apparently quite brilliant—he was one of only two Sunnydale High students recruited by a large, unnamed computer-software company during Career Week ("What's My Line? Part 1")—but shows very little ambition, beyond mastering the E-flat, diminished ninth chord on the guitar which he refers to as "a man's chord—you could lose a finger," ("What's My Line? Part 2"). He tends to not pay attention in class ("Innocence"), though he does test very well.

Midway through his senior year, Oz was bitten by his cousin Jordy, who, it turns out, is a werewolf. The bite transmitted the lycanthropy to Oz, and he now changes into a were-wolf on the night of the full moon as well as the nights before and after. His initial foray into werewolfdom nearly caused a panic—not to mention almost getting him killed by a hunter after his pelt—but he now knows to lock himself up three nights a month ("Phases").

Oz tends to take things in stride. He was very nonchalant at the revelation that *a)* his cousin is a werewolf and *b)* so now is he ("Phases"), and he was equally blasé when he discovered that there are vampires in Sunnydale and Buffy is the Slayer ("Surprise"). He has joined the inner circle of Slayerettes, so far providing transportation in his van ("Innocence," "Becoming, Part 2") and tracking down Buffy when she was turned into a rat ("Bewitched, Bothered, and Bewildered").

Oz found himself attracted to Willow from the moment he saw her in an Eskimo outfit ("Inca Mummy Girl"), and more so when he saw her in her rather revealing Halloween out-fit ("Halloween"), though they didn't actually speak until they found themselves together in the recruitment area for the software company ("What's My Line? Part 1"). Oz saved Willow's life from one of the Tarakan assassins ("What's My Line? Part 2"), and they started dating a short while later ("Surprise"). His lycanthropy has not noticeably inter-fered with their relationship, though Oz was willing to break it off if she wanted (she did-n't, "Phases").

Oz is played by Seth Green.

QUOT-ABLE OZ

Willow: "Do you guys have a...gig tonight?"
Oz: "Practice. The band's kind of moving toward this new sound where we suck. So, practice."   —**"Surprise"**

Xander: "Vampires are real; lot of 'em live in Sunnydale. Willow'll fill you in."
Willow: "I know it's hard to accept at first...."
Oz: "No, actually, it explains a lot...."
                              —**"Surprise"**

Devon: "What does a girl have to do to impress you?"
Oz: "Well, it involves a feather boa and the theme from *A Summer Place*. I can't discuss it here."
Devon: "You're too picky, man. You know how many girls you could have? You're lead guitar, Oz, that's cur-rency!"
Oz: "I'm not picky. You're just impressed by any pretty girl that can walk and talk."
Devon: "She doesn't have to talk...."
                              —**"Inca Mummy Girl"**

Jenny Calendar

Born Janna, of a very old Romanian Gypsy tribe, she took on the name Jennifer Calendar when she was sent to Sunnydale, California, to keep an eye on the vampire Angelus, who had been cursed by her tribe eighty years before ("Angel," "Surprise," "Innocence"). Presumably, Janna was sent after the demon Whistler brought Angel from New York to Sunnydale ("Becoming, Part 1"). Jenny was hired as a computer-science teacher at Sunnydale High School. It was there that she met Rupert Giles and worked with him when she initiated a project to scan several of the school library's works into the computer system; when the demon Moloch was scanned into the Internet via this project, Jenny helped Giles exorcise the demon ("I Robot, You Jane"). Jenny also saw the signs of the Master's eventual freedom from imprisonment and offered to help Giles and Buffy stop him ("Prophecy Girl"). A very modern woman, Jenny dressed in similar fashions to her students, spoke in slang, and had an excellent rapport with her students.

Despite their differing philosophies—Giles is very much a technophobe—Jenny and Giles were attracted to each other, and, after months of flirting, started dating in the fall of 1997 ("Some Assembly Required"). Their relationship stalled when Jenny was possessed by Eyghon, a demon that Giles had helped conjure up twenty years before ("The Dark Age"), though Jenny eventually was able to forgive him ("Ted"). Less easy to forgive was the revelation that Jenny was, for all intents and purposes, a spy for the Romany elders ("Innocence").

She was the one who explained to Buffy and Giles the specifics of the curse on Angel—that if he achieved even a moment of happiness, the curse would end ("Surprise," "Innocence"). Wanting to make up for deceiving her friends, and having no desire to see Angel continue to be evil (among other things, he murdered Jenny's uncle Enyos, "Innocence"), Jenny tried to find a way to retrieve the spell that had cursed Angel the first time ("Becoming, Part 1"); using a computer program she wrote, she translated it, but was murdered by Angel before she had a chance to use it ("Passion"). Angel destroyed the hard copy and hard drive, but Jenny had backed the file up to a disk that was eventually found by Willow and Buffy ("Becoming, Part 1"). Willow was able to cast the spell, with the help of Oz and Cordelia ("Becoming, Part 2"), thus fulfilling what was, in essence, Jenny's dying wish.

Jenny was played by Robia LaMorte.

> "Wrong and wrong, snobby. You think the realm of the mystical is limited to ancient texts and relics? That bad old science made the magic go away? The divine exists in cyberspace same as out here."
>
> —to Giles, in "I Robot, You Jane"

Joyce Summers

Joyce Summers met Hank Summers, her future husband, at her high school prom. She didn't have a date and so went alone. She was miserable for the first hour, then met Hank. He *did* have a date, but they still met and clicked, and later married ("Prophecy Girl"). By the time their daughter, Buffy, reached high school, their fighting had escalated ("Becoming, Part 1"), and they were divorced in her first year ("Nightmares"). The pair seem to be getting along well since the divorce ("When She Was Bad").

Joyce works at an art gallery, where her duties include acquiring and selling pieces, a job which requires long hours and keeps her away from home sometimes ("What's My Line?"). She has tried to connect with her daughter, but—despite their occasional bonding over movies and ice cream ("Ted," "Bewitched, Bothered, and Bewildered")—finds understanding of her daughter elusive. She appreciates that her daughter can take care of herself ("School Hard"), but has grown frustrated with Buffy's inability to do what she is told for no obvious reason ("Bad Eggs") and for not confiding in her about anything, such as the fact that she was dating Angel ("Passion"). Despite having seen some evidence of the bizarre activity in Sunnydale ("Angel," "School Hard," "Bad Eggs"), she remained oblivious to her daughter's secrets right up until circumstances compelled Buffy to spell it out for her ("Becoming, Part 2"). The ultimate consequences of Joyce learning that her daughter is the Chosen One have yet to be established.

Joyce is played by Kristine Sutherland.

> "That much quality time with my mom would probably lead to some quality matricide."
> —**Buffy, to Amy, in "Witch"**
>
> "Seeing my mother frenching a guy is definitely a ticket to therapyland."
> —**Buffy, in "Ted"**

Buffy: "But . . . don't you understand? This is so important!"

Joyce: "It's an outfit. An outfit you may never buy."

Buffy: "But . . . I looked good in it!"

Joyce: "You looked like a streetwalker."

Buffy: "But a *thin* streetwalker! That's probably not gonna be the winning argument, is it?"

Joyce: "You're just too young to wear that."

Buffy: "I'm gonna be too young to wear that till I'm too old to wear that."

Joyce: "That's the plan."

—**"Bad Eggs"**

Willow: "I just hate to think of you solo on Valentine's Day."

Buffy: "I'll be fine. Mom and I are gonna have a pig-out and vidfest. It's a time-honored tradition among the loveless."

—**"Bewitched, Bothered, and Bewildered"**

Quot-aBLe Mrs. Summers

QUOTABLE
Mrs. Summers

Buffy: "Did I ask for backseat mommying?"

Joyce: "What's the matter, did your egg keep you up all night?"

Buffy: "You're killing me."

Joyce: "Wait till it starts dating."
— **"Bad Eggs"**

Buffy: "I made a mistake."

Joyce: "Don't just say that to shut me up, because I think you really did."

Buffy: "I know that. Mom, my life is so... I can't tell you everything."

Joyce: "How about *anything*? Buffy, you can shut me out of your life, I'm pretty much used to that, but don't expect me to stop caring about you, 'cause it's never gonna happen. I love you more than anything in the world."
— **"Passion"**

Joyce: "So, what did you do on your birthday? Did you have fun?"

Buffy: "I got older."
— **"Innocence"**

Joyce: "Was he the first?"

Buffy: "...Yes. He was the first. I mean, the only."

Joyce: "He's older than you."

Buffy: "I know."

Joyce: "*Too* old, Buffy. And he's obviously not very stable. I really wish ... I thought you would show more judgment."

Buffy: "Mom, I—he wasn't like this before."

Joyce: "Are you in love with him?"

Buffy: "I was."

Joyce: "Were you careful?"

Buffy: "Mom—"

Joyce: "Don't 'Mom' me, Buffy—you don't get out of this. You had sex with a boy you didn't even see fit to tell me you were dating."
— **"Passion"**

Joyce: "So does seventeen feel any different than sixteen?"

Buffy: "Funny you should ask that—You know, I actually woke up feeling more mature, responsible, and level-headed."

Joyce: "Really? That's uncanny."

Buffy: "I now possess the qualities one looks for in a licensed driver."
— **"Surprise"**

"Try not to get kicked out."
— **to Buffy, in "Welcome to the Hellmouth"**

Principal Bob Flutie
Principal Snyder

Sunnydale High School has gone through two principals in the past two years. The first was Bob Flutie. Flutie was a more "touchy-feely" type of principal, concerned with how the students felt and with relating to them as people, not just faceless students under his care. He assured Buffy that she would be starting at Sunnydale High School with a "clean slate" (though he did put the fact that she burned down the Hemery High gym on her permanent record) and that she would be given every opportunity to start over ("Welcome to the Hellmouth"). When the dead body of Dr. Gregory was found in the cafeteria, Flutie insisted that everyone who saw the body attend a session with a counselor ("Teacher's Pet"). In an attempt to foster school spirit, Flutie purchased a pig to serve as a mascot for the Sunnydale High Razorbacks (it is unclear which team the pig was meant to be a mascot for, since all the school sports teams are named "the Razorbacks"—perhaps it was an all-purpose pig); that pig, however, was devoured by five students possessed by the spirit of a hyena. Four of those five students—notorious troublemakers even before they were possessed—were summoned to Flutie's office, wherein they proceeded to eat *him* alive ("The Pack"). The official story was that wild dogs ate him.

Flutie was apparently married—he wore a wedding ring ("The Pack")—and tried to be friendly with his students—he wanted them to call him "Bob," though none of them did ("Welcome to the Hellmouth").

His replacement, Principal Snyder, is somewhat more authoritarian and less interested in the needs of his students. Indeed, he decried Flutie's attitude as the kind of "woolly-headed liberal thinking that leads to getting eaten" ("The Puppet Show"). He hates children—which led Giles to question his choice of vocation ("When She Was Bad")—but was apparently given this position by the Sunnydale City Council because he could "handle this job" ("I Only Have Eyes for You"). He is also fully aware that Sunnydale sits on the Hellmouth and has twice been seen coming up with cover stories for the strange events in the town ("School Hard," "I Only Have Eyes for You").

The one characteristic he shares with Flutie is a desire to foster school spirit. To that end, he has encouraged such events as a school talent show ("Puppet") and done what he could to boost the position of the swim team when it started winning ("Go Fish").

He seems to have it in for Buffy in particular, having singled her out for discipline on more than one occasion ("School Hard," "Halloween," "What's My Line? Part 1," "I Only Have Eyes for You"). Not until he expelled her when she was on the run after mistakenly being accused of Kendra's murder is it made clear that he knows who Buffy really is—and either doesn't care or wants to see her fail ("Becoming, Part 2"). The full consequences of Snyder's actions and the full story behind what he and the city council and the mayor of Sunnydale know have yet to be explored.

Flutie was played by Ken Lerner; Snyder is played by Armin Shimerman.

Amy Madison

The only daughter of Catherine Madison, Sunnydale High's most decorated cheerleader and Homecoming Queen, Amy was raised by Catherine alone after her father, the Homecoming King, ran off with a woman identified only as "Ms. Trailer Trash" when Amy was twelve. Catherine insisted that Amy follow in her mother's footsteps and trained Amy to become a cheerleader, though Amy herself had no interest in it. Frustrated with that disinterest and her daughter's increased weight, Catherine took to witchcraft. By the time cheerleading tryouts for the 1996–97 school year took place, Catherine had switched bodies with her daughter, then—when she proved unable to make her unfamiliar new body do what she wanted, leaving her only as third alternate on the squad—she cast spells on other cheerleaders to clear a space for herself. Amy was left to stay at home in her mother's body and do her homework for her. Catherine's actions were discovered by Buffy and Giles, and all the spells were reversed, putting Amy back in her own body. Catherine's attempt to banish Buffy to a nether realm was reversed in a mirror to a banishment of Catherine herself. Amy then went to live with her father and stepmother ("The Witch"), which she found "cool."

Although never interested in following in her mother's footsteps as far as cheerleading went, she was apparently intrigued by the occult. By the following school year, she had mastered several spells, including one to make a teacher believe she had handed in homework when she hadn't and another to transform a person into a rat. Her attempt at a love potion did not work as intended, however, and instead of making Cordelia love Xander, it made every woman in Sunnydale *except* Cordelia love Xander—including Amy herself. With Giles's help, that spell was reversed ("Bewitched, Bothered, and Bewildered"). It is unknown whether Amy will continue her pursuit of witchcraft.

Amy is played by Elizabeth Anne Allen.

Kendra

Very little is known about Kendra. Her accent suggests a background on a British, or formerly British, Caribbean island, but her homeland is never identified by name. However, her people are aware of vampires, as Kendra's parents knew that she was destined to become a Slayer and sent her to be trained with her Watcher, Sam Zabuto, at a very early age ("What's My Line? Part 2").

Kendra's training has been much more traditional than Buffy's—she was given the Slayer handbook to read, which Buffy had never even heard of ("What's My Line? Part 2")—and she works in less overt ways than Buffy, including hitching a ride from her home to Sunnydale in a cargo hold rather than traveling openly in an airline seat ("What's My Line? Part 1"). Her life has been very cloistered, with no friends or family (and she doesn't hug), and her manner of living is quite Spartan—she seems to own only one shirt ("What's My Line? Part 2"). Her one concession to whimsy was to name her favorite stake "Mr. Pointy" ("Becoming, Part 1").

"Get a load of the She-Giles."
—Buffy, to Willow, in "What's My Line?, Part 2"

"A Slayer? I knew this 'I'm the only one, I'm the only one' thing was just an attention-getter."
—Xander, in "What's My Line? Part 2"

"It's all right. Kendra killed the bad lamp."
—Buffy, in "What's My Line? Part 2"

Kendra became active as a Slayer after Buffy died fighting the Master ("Prophecy Girl"). When Spike found the du Lac manuscript and the key to deciphering it, signaling that he would be trying to revive Drusilla, Zabuto sent Kendra to Sunnydale ("What's My Line?"). She appears to have all the same abilities as Buffy—and a similar fighting style—though, like Buffy, she has not mastered the ability to sense vampires ("Welcome to the Hellmouth"), since she mistook Buffy for a vampire based on her kissing Angel ("What's My Line? Part 1"). After

helping Buffy stop Spike and Drusilla, Kendra returned home, coming back to Sunnydale, when Angel stole the sarcophagus of Acathla, to provide Buffy with a sword that would aid in defeating the Demon. She was killed by Drusilla while trying to protect the Slayerettes ("Becoming, Part 1").

Kendra was played by Bianca Lawson.

QUOT-ABLE Villains

Spike

"You have your way with him [Giles], you'll never get to destroy the world. And I don't fancy spending next month trying to get librarian out of the carpet."
—to Angel about Giles, in "Becoming, Part 2"

Willy: "What're you gonna do with him [Angel] anyway?"
Spike: "I'm thinking—maybe dinner and a movie. I don't want to rush into anything. I've been hurt, y'know."
—"What's My Line? Part 2"

"Do I have anyone on watch here? It's called security, people. Are you all asleep? Or did we finally find a restaurant that delivers?"
—on Ford's arrival at the Factory in "Lie to Me"

"It's paradise! Big windows and lovely gardens. They'll be perfect for when we want the sunlight to *kill us*."
—on their new mansion, in "I Only Have Eyes for You"

Spike: "A Slayer with family and friends. That sure as hell wasn't in the brochure."
Drusilla: "You'll kill her. And then we'll have a nice party." **—"School Hard"**

Buffy: "It's your lucky day, Spike."
Kendra: "Two Slayers."
Buffy: "No waiting."
—"What's My Line? Part 2"

"I'll only kill you this once."
—to Willy, in "What's My Line? Part 2"

"My mummy used to sing me to sleep at night. 'Run and catch, the lamb is caught in the blackberry patch. . . . What will your mummy sing when they find your body?" **Drusilla**
—to a small boy, in "Lie to Me"

Spike: "Are we feeling better then?"
Drusilla: "I'm naming all the stars."
Spike: "Can't see the stars, love. That's the ceiling. Also, it's day."
Drusilla: "I can see them. But I've named them all the same name, and there's terrible confusion. I fear there may be a duel."
—"Innocence"

"I met an old man. I didn't like him. He got stuck in my teeth." **—"Becoming, Part 1"**

The Master

"My ascension is at hand. Pray that when it comes, I'm in a better mood."

—in "The Harvest"

"You've got something in your eye."

—to a vampire henchman he's just blinded with a talon, in "The Harvest"

Quot-ABLe Knowledge

"I defined something? Accurately? Check me out. [He slams a book on the table shut.] Guess I'm done with the book learning!"

Xander, in "I Only Have Eyes for You"

Xander (to Giles): "After classes, I'll come back and help you research."
Cordelia: "Yeah, you might find something useful—if it's in an 'I Can Read' book." **—"Innocence"**

"You remember: you fail math, you flunk out of school, you end up being the guy at the pizza place that sweeps the floor and says 'Hey, kids, where's the cool parties this weekend?'"

Willow, to Xander, in "The Pack"

Cordelia: "This is not right. School on a Saturday? That throws off my internal clock."
Xander: "When are we going to use computers in real life, anyway?"
Jenny: "Let's see, there's home, schoolwork, games—"
Xander: "Computers are on the way out. I think paper is about to make a big comeback."
Willow: "And the abacus." **—"The Dark Age"**

"Well, evil just compounds evil, doesn't it? First I'm sentenced to a computer tutorial on Saturday, now I have to read some computer book. There are books about computers? Isn't that the point of computers, to *replace* books?"

Cordelia, in "The Dark Age"

Jenny: "I'm reviewing some computer basics for a couple of students who have fallen behind. Willow's helping for extra credit."
Xander: "Hah! Those poor schlubs. Having to give up their Saturday—"
Jenny: "Nine A.M. okay with you, Xander?"
—"The Dark Age"

"Buffy, this is not about looking at a bunch of animals. This is about *not being in class.*"

—Xander, on a field trip to the zoo, in "The Pack"

Joyce: "She talks about you all the time. . . . It's important to have teachers who make an impression."
Giles: "She makes quite an impression herself."
Joyce: "I know she's having trouble with history. Is it too difficult for her, or is she not applying herself?"
Giles: "She lives very much in the now, and history, of course, is very much about 'the then. . . .'" **—"Angel"**

quot- aBLe
Knowledge

Buffy: "Mom, this is Mr. Giles."
Joyce: "The librarian from your school? What's he doing here?"
Giles: "I just came to pay my respects, wish you a speedy recovery."
Joyce: "Boy, the teachers really *do* care in this town...."
—in Joyce's hospital room, in "Angel"

Willow: "This means I can't help you study for tomorrow's finals."
Buffy: "I'll wing it. Of course, if we go to Hell by then, I won't have to take them. [sudden fear] Or maybe I'll be taking them forever...."
—"Becoming, Part 1"

"I mean, in the real world, when am I ever gonna need to use chemistry, math, history, or the English language?"
—Buffy, in "Becoming, Part 1"

Willow: "I'm gonna get you through this semester if I have to sweat blood."
Xander: "Do you think you're likely to? 'Cause I'd like to be elsewhere."
Willow: "It was only metaphor blood."
Oz: "I think you'd sweat cute blood."
—"Becoming, Part 1"

Buffy: "We'd better get back. I haven't even *started* studying for finals."
Xander: "Oh, yeah, finals. Why didn't you let me die?" **—"Becoming, Part 1"**

"Sorry. I pretty much repress anything math related."
—Buffy, in "I Only Have Eyes for You"

"Oh. Yeah. . . .I remember now. Weren't there chalkboards and pencils and desks and stuff?"
Buffy, on her late, great Algebra II class, in "I Only Have Eyes for You"

Cordelia: "School can open again tomorrow."
Xander: "Explain to me again how that's a good thing."
—"I Only Have Eyes for You"

"Ha! This time I am ready for you. No F for Xander today. No, this baby's my ticket to a sweet D-minus."
Xander, on his homework, in "Bewitched, Bothered, and Bewildered"

Jenny: "You here again? You kids really dig on the library, don't you?"
Buffy: "We're literary."
Xander: "To read English is makes our speaking English good."
—"I Robot, You Jane"

Giles: "Does this look familiar to either of you?"
Buffy: "Yeah, sure. It looks like a book."
Xander: "I knew that one."
—"I Robot, You Jane"

Jenny: "Honestly, what is it about [computers] that bothers you so much?"
Giles: "The smell."
Jenny: "Computers don't smell, Rupert."
Giles. "I know. Smell is the most powerful memory trigger there is. A certain flower or a whiff of smoke can bring up experiences long forgotten. Books smell—musty and rich. The knowledge gained from a computer has no texture, no context. It's there and then it's gone. If it's to last, then the getting of knowledge should be tangible. It should be smelly."
—"I Robot, You Jane"

"You start a school, you get desks, some blackboards, and some mean kids."
—Xander, in "The Pack"

Giles: "So, apparently, Angel has decided to step up his harassment of you."

Cordelia: "By sneaking into her room at night and leaving stuff? Why not just slash her throat or strangle her in her sleep or cut out her heart? . . . What? I'm trying to help."

Giles: "It's a classic battle strategy to throw one's opponent off his game. He's trying to provoke you. To taunt you... goad you into a misstep of some sort."

Xander: "The 'nyah nyah nyah nyah' approach to battle."

Giles: "Yes, Xander, once again you've managed to boil a complex thought down to its simplest form."   **—"Passion"**

Willow: "Buffy. How come you weren't in class?"

Buffy: "Vampire issues. Did Mr. Whitmore notice that I was tardy?"

Xander: "I think the word you're searching for is 'absent.'"

Buffy: "Oh. Right."

Willow: "And, yes, he noticed. So he wanted me to give you this." [Hands her the egg.]

Buffy: "As punishments go, this is fairly abstract."   **—"Bad Eggs"**

Buffy: "Homework."

Willow: "It's my way of saying, 'Get well soon.'"

Buffy: "You know, chocolate says that even better."

Willow: "I did all of your assignments. All you have to do is sign your name."

Buffy (awestruck): "Chocolate means nothing to me."   **—"Killed by Death"**

"A couple more days and we'll get to do the two things every American teen should have the chance to do. Die young . . . and stay pretty."

**Ford, to the True Believers,
in "Lie to Me"**

Buffy: "'Cause I'm *not* well. I feel all oogy."

Xander: "Increased oogy-ness. That's a danger signal."   **—"Killed by Death"**

> **Angel:** "They're children, making up bedtime
> stories of friendly vampires to comfort themselves
> in the dark."
> **Willow:** "Is that so bad? I mean the dark can get pretty
> dark. Sometimes you need a story."
> —**"LIE TO ME"**

**Here it is, your handy-dandy guide to each and every
episode from the first two seasons of** *Buffy the Vampire Slayer,*
**including writer and director credits, complete cast list,
and a plot summary, plus pop-ups, sidebars,
and the following subsections:**

Quote of the week:

"Could you vague that up for me?"

Love, Slayer style:

The relationships on *Buffy* are complex and critical to the overall plots
(Angel/Buffy, Giles/Jenny, Xander/Cordelia). This section shows the major
relationship turning points for each episode.

BUFFY'S BAG OF TRICKS:

A catalog of Buffy's weapons in each episode.

POP-CULTURE IQ:

The characters in *Buffy* are almost preternaturally aware of pop culture—it's
part of their hip factor. We'll note some references from the show here, and
explain them to the uninitiated.

CONTINUITY:

A hallmark of *Buffy* is the show's sense of its own internal history and
chronology. This section will detail bits of continuity, character-establishing
moments, references to past episodes, and foreshadowing of future ones.

From the Original Teleplay:

Exclusive text from the original script that was cut solely to accommodate
the required length of an episode for broadcast.

EPISODE NUMBER	EPISODE NAME	ORIGINAL AIRDATE
1	Welcome to the Hellmouth	10-Mar
2	The Harvest	10-Mar
3	The Witch	17-Mar
4	Teacher's Pet	25-Mar
5	Never Kill a Boy on the First Date	31-Mar
6	The Pack	7-Apr
7	Angel	14-Apr
8	I Robot, You Jane	28-Apr
9	The Puppet Show	5-May
10	Nightmares	12-May
11	Out of Mind, Out of Sight	19-May
12	Prophecy Girl	2-Jun

★ STARRING ★

Sarah Michelle Gellar.................Buffy Summers

Nicholas Brendon ....Xander Harris

Alyson Hannigan ....Willow Rosenberg

Charisma Carpenter....................Cordelia Chase

Anthony Stewart Head ....Rupert Giles

Welcome to the Hellmouth/ The Harvest

WRITTEN BY Joss Whedon; **DIRECTED BY** Charles Martin Smith (Part 1) and John T. Kertchmer (Part 2). **GUEST STARS:** Mark Metcalf as the Master, Brian Thompson as Luke, David Boreanaz as Angel, Ken Lerner as Principal Flutie, Kristine Sutherland as Joyce Summers, Julie Benz as Darla; with Mercedes McNab as Harmony.

Buffy Summers and her mother, Joyce, have moved from Los Angeles to the suburb of Sunnydale, California, and Joyce drives Buffy to her first day at the prosaically named Sunnydale High School. Her first day at the new school, Buffy meets a new world of people who will have a profound effect on her life. Principal Bob Flutie says that he believes in clean slates and won't hold the fact that she burned down her previous school's gymnasium against her. Cordelia, popular girl on campus, gives Buffy a test for her "coolness factor" and extends the hand of friendship—until Buffy starts to hang out with Willow, a horribly shy computer nerd, and her friends Xander and Jesse. Giles, the school librarian, not only knows that Buffy is the Slayer but has been assigned to be her Watcher.

Later that night, Buffy meets the mysterious Angel, who informs her that Sunnydale is located on the Hellmouth, a focal point of demonic activity of all sorts that attracts vampires like moths to a flame, and that she needs to be ready for the Harvest. Buffy ignores both Giles and Angel, hoping to return to some semblance of a normal life after her experience with vampires in L.A.

In the catacombs underneath the town, the vampiric Luke awakens the Master so he will be ready for the Harvest. The Master, a very old, very powerful vampire, has been trapped underneath Sunnydale for sixty years, ever since his attempt to open the Hellmouth was foiled by an untimely earthquake. The time is right for the Harvest, which will give him the power to break free.

Luke sends vampires out for food, and Jesse is captured, although Buffy saves Willow and Xander—and also realizes that she must fulfill her duties as Slayer, or people will die. She goes to rescue Jesse, with some unwanted help from Xander, only to find that Jesse has been turned into a vampire. They escape and then must stop Luke, who serves as the Master's vessel and is attacking the Bronze. With assistance from Giles, Willow, and Xander, Buffy kills Luke and several other vampires (Xander winds up inadvertently staking his old friend Jesse), though Darla survives.

Quote of the week:

Cordelia: "It's in the bad side of town."
Buffy: "Where's that?"
Cordelia: "It's about half a block from the good side of town. We don't have a whole lot of town here."

Love, Slayer Style:

Xander's first sight of Buffy causes him to crash into a railing while skateboarding, and he gamely attempts to flirt with her. Angel and Buffy meet and are immediately at odds, thanks to his being overwhelmingly cryptic.

POP-CULTURE IQ:

"Don't go all *Wild Bunch* on me."

Buffy's warning to Giles, Willow, and Xander when they storm the Bronze, referring to the famous ending of that film

BUFFY'S BAG OF TRICKS:

Buffy carries a stake and uses several random items (tree branches, pool cues, and the like) as substitute stakes. She beheads one vampire with a drum cymbal. At the climax, she unpacks her supplies from a trunk with a false bottom, which include several stakes, vials of holy water, garlic, and crosses.

CONTINUITY:

Viewers of the movie *Buffy the Vampire Slayer* might be confused at the repeated references to Buffy burning the gym down, since that didn't happen in the movie. The solution is simple: Joss Whedon has spun this series off of his *original* movie script for *Buffy*, which did indeed have Buffy performing a touch of necessary arson on the gym. Two previous Slayers—Lucy Hanover in 1866 Virginia and an unidentified woman in 1927 Chicago—are mentioned in an opening montage, thereby extending the Slayer lore, although neither reference is to be found as such in Whedon's screenplay, nor in any other episode.

Buffy has the first of many prophetic dreams ("Prophecy Girl," "Surprise," "Innocence"). Joyce's parting words to Buffy as she drops her off are to extract a promise not to get kicked out of this school, a promise she will wind up breaking a year and a half later ("Becoming, Part 2"). Angel acts as if he's never seen Buffy before, which belies the flashback in "Becoming, Part 1." The Master's first attempt to open the Hellmouth was in 1937; his next will be in "Prophecy Girl."

Witch

WRITTEN BY Dana Reston; **DIRECTED BY** Stephen Cragg. **GUEST STARS:** Kristine Sutherland as Joyce Summers, Elizabeth Anne Allen as Amy Madison, and Robin Riker as Catherine Madison; with Amanda Wilmshurst, Nicole Prescott, Jim Doughan, and William Monaghan.

Cheerleading tryouts at Sunnydale High prove to be more exciting than expected, when Amber Grove, the most talented of the girls who try out, catches fire. Meanwhile, Amy Madison is under fierce pressure from her mother, Catherine, the former cheerleading champion of Sunnydale High, to live up to her own reputation from years before. Unfortunately, Amy is the third alternate, which means she only gets on the squad if something happens to three people on the team. Sure enough, something happens to three people on the team—Cordelia is struck blind, Lishanne's mouth is sealed over, and then Buffy is turned into a gibbering idiot, as the result of a Bloodstone Vengeance spell.

Giles and a weakened Buffy go to the Madison house to discover that it isn't Amy who's casting the spells at all—it's her mother, Catherine, who has switched bodies with Amy in order to relive her glory days. Fortunately, Giles is able to reverse all the spells, even as Buffy battles Catherine, whose final spell is repelled and ironically traps the witch herself inside the cheerleading trophy she won when she attended Sunnydale High.

Quote of the week:

"I laugh in the face of danger—then I hide until it goes away."

Xander, summing up his approach to life

Love, Slayer style:

Xander gives Buffy a charm bracelet that reads, "Yours, always," then queries Willow as to whether he should ask Buffy out, to Willow's obvious-to-anyone-but-Xander chagrin.

POP-CULTURE IQ:

"So Amber has this power to make herself be on fire.
Like the Human Torch, only it hurts."

Xander, speculating on Amber's combustion, referring to the
Marvel Comics superhero

"She's our Sabrina."

Buffy, describing Amy, referring to the Archie comics
and TV show character Sabrina the Teenage Witch

Buffy: "Mom, I accepted that you've had sex. I'm not ready to know that you had Farrah hair."
Joyce: "This is Gidget hair. Don't they teach you anything in history?"
—**Dishing about the hairstyles of sex symbols from the '60s and '70s.**

CONTINUITY:

Willow coins the term "Slayerettes," and Joyce's occupation as the owner of an art gallery is first discussed. Cordelia is taking driver's ed, having failed twice before—sometime between this episode and "Prophecy Girl," she passes her driver's test. Giles's affinity for the occult is first revealed ("The Dark Age," "I Robot, You Jane," "Bewitched, Bothered, and Bewildered"), though he claims that the spell he casts here is his first casting, a statement proven false in later episodes ("Halloween," "The Dark Age").

From the original teleplay:

There are a lot of lines in the original script that don't show up in the finished episode. Xander, at one point, says, "Hey, we've fought vampires. Anything else'll be a walk in the park." Giles observes, "If I had the power of the black mass, I'd set my sights a little higher than making the pep squad." And then there's this exchange:

Xander: "Wow, you've got a killer streak I've never seen before. Hope I never cross you."
Willow: "I do, too. Then I'd have to carve you up into little pieces."

Finally, when Giles is searching for a test to figure out if Amy is a witch, he comes upon something in a book . . . "Yes, the ducking stool! We throw her in the pond. If she floats, she's a witch; if she drowns, she's innocent...[then, off their looks]...some of my texts are a bit outdated."

> When Buffy wakes up in bed, early in "Witch," she's wearing a T-shirt with a black cat on the front, a symbol sometimes synonymous with witchcraft.

Teacher's Pet

WRITTEN BY David Greenwalt; **DIRECTED BY** Bruce Seth Green. **GUEST STARS:** David Boreanaz as Angel, Ken Lerner as Principal Flutie, Musetta Vander as Natalie French, Jackson Price as Blayne Mall, Jean Speegle Howard as Claw; with William Monaghan as Dr. Gregory, and Jack Knight, Michael Ross, and Karim Oliver.

Buffy receives an encouraging pep talk from her biology teacher, Dr. Gregory, who, sadly, turns up the next day without his head. His substitute is a sultry, sexy woman named Natalie French, who talks at length about praying mantises and has all the boys' hormones in overdrive. Buffy at first suspects Claw, a vampire whose hand has been replaced by sharp implements, as the culprit for the biology teacher's murder, but is surprised when she sees that very vampire whimper and flee at the sight of Ms. French.

Giles seeks advice from his friend Dr. Carlyle Ferris, who is an expert in entomology and mythology, and who is also quite mad since hunting a She-Mantis at Oxford. Meanwhile, Ms. French, apparently the same creature that Carlyle hunted, has taken both Xander and Blayne prisoner, with the intent of mating with them then killing them. Buffy manages to kill the creature before the boys are decapitated.

Quote of the week:

> **"You were right all along, about everything....Well, no, you weren't right about your mother coming back as a Pekingese."**
> Giles's half of the conversation with Carlyle

58

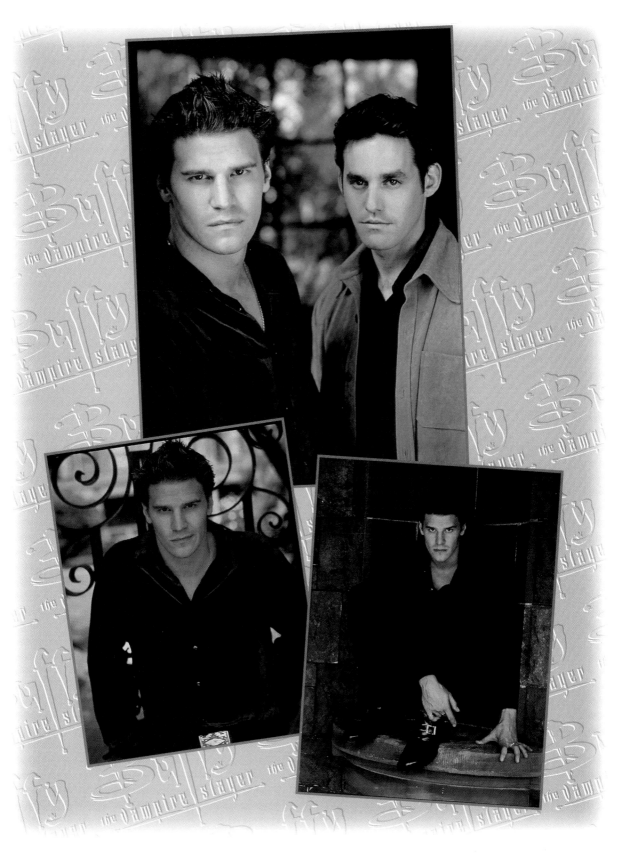

BUFFY'S BAG OF TRICKS:

She uses a machete on the She-Mantis, after driving it bonkers with an audiotape of bat sonar.

POP-CULTURE IQ:

"We're talking full-on *Exorcist* twist."

Buffy, describing Ms. French's head twisting all the way around,
referring to the most famous scene from *The Exorcist*

"Oh, this is fun. We're on Monster Island."

Xander, complaining about the Hellmouth, in reference to the Pacific
island where Godzilla and friends reside in Japanese monster movies

Love, Slayer style:

Xander continues to moon for Buffy and is not thrilled when Angel gives her his leather jacket. However, the minute Xander lays eyes on Ms. French, he only has eyes for her—as does every other male in the school. Xander refuses to believe Buffy's warning that Ms. French is a praying mantis, preferring to delude himself into thinking that she's jealous.

CONTINUITY:

Xander's falling for a She-Mantis becomes a running joke throughout the series ("Inca Mummy Girl," "What's My Line? Part 2," etc.).

From the Original teleplay:

The following scene was cut from the "Teacher's Pet" script because of length.

Buffy: "Dr. Gregory didn't chew me out or anything. He was really cool. But Flutie showed him my permanent record. Apparently, I fall somewhere between Charles Manson and a really bad person."

Willow: "And you can't tell Dr. Gregory what really happened at your old school?"

Buffy: "I was fighting vampires? I'm thinking he might not believe me."

Willow: "Yeah, he probably gets that excuse all the time."

Cordelia (just arriving): "Here lies a problem. What used to be my table occupied by pitiful losers. Of course, we'll have to burn it."

Buffy: "Sad, you have so many memories here. You and Lawrence, you and Mark, you and John. You spent the better part of your 'J' through 'M' here."

> Xander fantasizes about being a guitar god, impressing Buffy with his amazing musical talents. Of course, we later learn that Giles did actually play guitar in a rock band in his youth, and Oz is lead guitarist of Dingoes Ate My Baby. So, clearly, guitar is the hot instrument of the moment.

Xander Harris, Buffy's self-proclaimed knight in shining armor, is like all other great heroes in that he has one tragic flaw: snack food. A Hostess cake or a chocolate bar waved in front of his face during battle would be all an opponent would need to cause a fatal distraction. Check out these examples of the X-Man's obsession....

"Ho-Ho's are a vital part of my cognitive process."
—*What's My Line? Part 1"*

"Someone else's loss is my chocolaty goodness." — *"Nightmares"*

Giles: "A full moon tends to bring out our darkest qualities."
Xander: "Yet, ironically, also led to the invention of the moon pie." **—"PHASES"**

"It's a delicious, spongy, golden cake, stuffed with a delightful, white creamy substance of goodness. And here's how you eat it . . . . Good, huh? And the exciting part is, they have no ingredients that a human can pronounce. So it doesn't leave you with that heavy food feeling in your stomach."
—re: Twinkies, in "Inca Mummy Girl"

"Okay. On sleazing extra candy. Tears are key. Tears'll usually get you a double-bagger. You can also try the old 'you missed me' routine—but it's risky. Only go there for chocolate. Understood?"
—trick-or-treat advice, from "Halloween "

Yep. Keep an eye on that Harris boy. His sweet tooth is going to turn out to be his Achilles' heel for sure.

Never Kill a Boy on the First Date

WRITTEN BY Rob Des Hotel and Dean Batali; **DIRECTED BY** David Semel. **GUEST STARS:** Mark Metcalf as the Master, David Boreanaz as Angel, Christopher Wiehl as Owen Thurman, Andrew J. Ferchland as the Anointed One, Geoff Meed as Andrew Vorba; with Paul Felix Montez and Robert Mont.

The Master wishes to raise the Anointed One, who will be his primary weapon against the Slayer. Meanwhile, Buffy kills a member of the Order of Aurelius, the presence of which alerts Giles to the Master's plan. While Giles tries to decipher the prophecies relating to the rising of the Anointed One, Buffy attempts to have a social life with Owen Thurman, a

> Cemetery sequences in season one were shot at Rosedale cemetery in Los Angeles.

quiet student who likes Emily Dickinson. Their date, however, is cut short by the need to save Giles from a vampire attack at a funeral home—where he went in Buffy's place to see if the Anointed One would rise, so Buffy could have her date—made more complicated by Owen following Buffy. They believe that the vampire they find and kill is the Anointed One. Unfortunately, Owen turns out to be a danger junkie, and Buffy has to refuse to date him again in order to keep him safe.

Quote of the week:

Giles: "All right, I'll just drop in my time machine, go back to the twelfth century, and ask the vampires to postpone their ancient prophecy for a few days while you take in dinner and a show."

Buffy: "Okay, at this point, you're abusing sarcasm."

—**Discussing the inconvenience of the prophecy of the Anointed One coming to pass on the night Buffy has a date**

Love, Slayer style:

Buffy has a crush on Owen, which does not make Xander (or Cordelia, or Angel) happy. Xander does what he can to sabotage the relationship (and also continue his own fawning after Buffy, including sneaking a peek at her changing clothes), but Buffy eventually breaks it off herself.

POP-CULTURE IQ:

"Here endeth the lesson."

The Master, parroting dialogue from both Sean Connery and Kevin Costner in *The Untouchables*

"Clark Kent had a job."

Buffy, referring to her desire to have a life, citing the DC Comics character Superman's secret identity

CONTINUITY:

The Master creates the Anointed One, a small boy who remains a factor in the series until the second season events of "School Hard." Buffy and the gang think they've taken care of the Anointed One, and don't learn the truth until "Prophecy Girl." Giles says he has no instruction manual, which belies information learned in "What's My Line? Part 2" about the Slayer handbook.

CONSPIRACY THEORY

Throughout the second season, the creators of *Buffy* have been developing a sub-plot one tiny bit of dialogue at a time. It's a conspiracy fit for Oliver Stone, and it's happening right here in Sunnydale! The mayor. The chief of police. Principal Snyder. They know Buffy's the Slayer. They don't like her—particularly Snyder. Whatever their super-secret agenda is, it's probably sinister, and it is definitely something they'd like to keep Buffy from finding out!

Here are some of the moments that have led us to formulate this conspiracy theory.

Police Chief: "I'll need to say something to the media."
Snyder: "So?"
Police Chief: "So . . . usual story? Gang-related, PCP?"
Snyder: "What did you have in mind? The truth?"
Police Chief: "Right. Gang-related. PCP." **—"SCHOOL HARD"**

Police Chief: "Schoolboy prank?"
Snyder: "Never sell."
Police Chief: "Backed-up sewer lines?"
Snyder: "Better...I can probably make that one fly. But this is getting out of hand. People will talk."
Police Chief: "You'll take care of it."
Snyder: "I'm doing everything I can. But you people have to realize—[as people pass]—backed-up sewer line, this happened in San Diego just last week—[the people are gone]—that we are on a Hellmouth. Sooner or later, people are going to figure that out."
Police Chief: "The city council was told you could handle this job. If you feel you can't . . . perhaps you'd like to take that up . . . with the mayor."
Snyder: "I'll handle it. I will." **—"I ONLY HAVE EYES FOR YOU"**

"Just give me a reason to kick you out, Summers. Just give me a reason."
Principal Snyder, in *"Becoming, Part 1"*

Snyder: "In case you didn't notice, the police in Sunnydale are deeply stupid. It doesn't matter, anyway. Whatever they find, you've proved too much of a liability for this school....These are moments you want to savor. You wish time would stop so you can live them over and over again. You're expelled."
Buffy: "You never ever got a single date when you were in high school, did you?"
Snyder: "Your point being?" [Buffy leaves; he speed-dials on a cell phone.] "It's Snyder. Tell the mayor I have good news." **—"BECOMING, PART 2"**

WRITTEN BY Matt Kiene and Joe Reinkemeyer; **DIRECTED BY** Bruce Seth Green. **GUEST STARS:** Ken Lerner as Principal Flutie, Eion Bailey as Rhonda, Michael McRaine as Kyle, Brian Gross as Tor, Jennifer Sky as Heidi, Jeff Maynard as Lance, and James Stephens as the zookeeper; with Gregory White, Jeffrey Steven Smith, David Brisbin, Barbara Whinnery, Justin Jon Ross, and Patrese Borem.

> The zoo segments in this shot were filmed at the Santa Ana Zoo.

Among the attendees at a school field trip to the zoo are Buffy and the gang, as well as the four biggest troublemakers in the school—Kyle, Rhonda, Tor, and Heidi—and Lance, the nerdy object of their scorn. The quartet leads Lance into the closed hyena exhibit. Xander goes after them to keep them out of trouble—and all save Lance find themselves imbued with the predatory spirit of the hyena. Xander starts to hang around with the quartet, acting very un-Xander-like—including verbally abusing Willow. The five of them devour Herbert, the school's new pig mascot, and later, when Principal Flutie brings Kyle, Rhonda, Tor, and Heidi to his office to accuse them of attacking the pig, they eat the principal alive as well.

Giles digs up references to "Primals," animal worshipers who can draw the spirits of animals into themselves. The keeper of the Hyena House—to whom Giles and Buffy turn for help—is, in fact, one such Primal, and he attempts to draw the power into himself and out of the students. He succeeds, but then Buffy tosses him to the actual hyenas.

Quote of the week:

"It's devastating—he's turned into a sixteen-year-old boy. Of course, you'll have to kill him."

Giles, initially skeptical after Buffy describes Xander's odd behavior

Love, Slayer style:

> One line that was cut: Xander says, "Welcome to the jungle."

Buffy and Willow discuss their respective attraction for Angel and Xander in the Bronze. (Willow on Xander: "He makes my head go tingly.") This makes it all the more devastating for Willow when Xander publicly humiliates her in front of the rest of the Pack. The possessed Xander is also much more aggressive in his pursuit of Buffy. (Buffy hits him with a desk for his troubles.)

POP-CULTURE IQ:

"I cannot believe that you of all people are trying to Scully me."

Buffy, to Giles, when he refuses to accept that something's wrong with Xander, referring to Dana Scully's skepticism on *The X-Files*

"Oh, great, it's the winged monkeys."

Buffy, talking about the Pack, in a reference to *The Wizard of Oz*

Xander will find his experiences as a hyena useful when Buffy and her friends are trying to find a werewolf ("Phases"). Buffy is still wearing the leather jacket Angel gave her in "Teacher's Pet."

WRITTEN BY David Greenwalt;
DIRECTED BY Scott Brazil.
GUEST STARS: Mark Metcalf as the Master, David Boreanaz as Angel, Kristine Sutherland as Joyce Summers, Julie Benz as Darla; with Andrew J. Ferchland as the Anointed One; with Charles Wesley.

Angel

After hovering on the periphery for several episodes, Angel's secret is finally revealed: he's a vampire. This realization does not come until he and Buffy admit their feelings for each other and share their first kiss. At first this leads Buffy to think that Angel's past actions are part of a plot to set her up for a fall, especially after she finds her mother in Angel's arms with bite marks on her neck. (In light of Angel's actions in the latter half of the second season, this is an even more reasonable assumption.)

Soon enough, Buffy learns the whole truth. Angel was "sired" (vampire language for turning a human into a vampire) by Darla 240 years before. Eighty years ago, he tortured and killed a Romany woman, and her clan put a curse on him: they restored his soul. He became a vampire with a conscience, a unique creature among the undead. Darla's attempts to bring him back to the Master's fold fail, and she winds up on the wrong end of a stake wielded by Angel.

Quote of the week:

"Angel's a vampire. You're a Slayer.
I think it's obvious what you have to do."

Xander, laying it out for Buffy after
Angel's vampirism is revealed

Love, Slayer style:

The Angel/Buffy relationship goes into full bloom here, starting with his spending the night in her bedroom (though he is, as she says, a perfect gentleman), continuing to their first kiss, and ending with another kiss that, thanks to Buffy's crucifix necklace, leaves a burning impression on Angel's chest. Their continued insistence that "This can't ever be anything" rings hollow even as they say it, more so in light of where the relationship does actually go.

Meanwhile, a hint of the future with Cordelia and Xander comes in an early scene on the dance floor ("Boy, that Cordelia's a breath of vile air"), and Willow continues to moon for Xander to Buffy, though Buffy's continued urges for Willow to actually say something are met with vehement refusal ("No, no, no, no. No speaking up. That way leads to madness and sweaty palms").

BUFFY'S BAG OF TRICKS:

Giles trains Buffy in both quarterstaffs and crossbow. She uses the latter on Darla (piercing her in the stomach rather than the heart), and tries and fails to use it on Angel (the impression being that her shot went wild on purpose).

CONTINUITY:

The Master has begun training the Anointed One ("Never Kill a Boy on the First Date"). Buffy invites Angel into her home for the first time ("Passion"). Angel describes Darla making him and his cursing at the hands of the Romany, both later dramatized in "Becoming, Part 1."

WRITTEN BY Ashley Gable and Tom Swyden; **DIRECTED BY** Stephen Posey. **GUEST STARS:** Robia LaMorte as Jenny Calendar; with Chad Lindberg, and Jamison Ryan.

I Robot, You Jane

In fifteenth-century Italy, a monk is able to imprison the demon Moloch, the Corruptor, in a book as the actual text of the tome. Since the demon can be freed only if the words are read aloud, the monk seals the book in a box, where it remains for over 500 years—until it is opened in Sunnydale High School's library as one of Giles's new acquisitions. The book is scanned into the computer as part of a project developed by the school's computer-science teacher,

Jenny Calendar—a freewheeling, hip-dressing, slang-speaking young woman who seems to be the diametric opposite of Rupert Giles. Scanning the book, however, releases the demon into cyberspace, and Moloch soon begins his work. As "Malcolm," he begins an on-line relationship with Willow, subverts Fritz and Dave, the school's biggest computer geeks, and uses a now-defunct electronics company to build himself a robot body.

Alyson Hannigan is hooked into the Net, but says she's not the "Net girl" that Willow is.

With the unexpected assistance of Jenny—revealed to be a technopagan who is familiar with Moloch and other such creatures—Giles manages to bind the Corruptor into the robot body, giving Buffy the opportunity to kill the demon by blowing up the robot with a handy wiring box.

Quote of the week:

"I know our ways are strange to you, but soon you will join us in the twentieth century— with three whole years to spare!"

Jenny, in one of her many book vs. computer arguments with Giles.

Love, Slayer style:

Jenny and Giles go from open hostility to grudging respect over the course of the episode, and Jenny makes something of a pass at Giles at the very end, sowing the seeds of their future relationship (if not its tragic end). Xander also shows fierce jealousy when Willow starts cyberdating "Malcolm."

POP-CULTURE IQ:

"I can just tell something's wrong. My spider-sense is tingling."

Buffy, when she, Giles, and Xander are discussing the odd behavior of both Willow and Dave, referring to the Marvel Comics character Spider-Man's ability to sense danger

CONTINUITY:

Buffy and Xander attempt to cheer Willow by pointing out that, yes, Willow's boyfriend turned out to be a demon, but Buffy has the hots for a vampire ("Angel") and the teacher Xander had a crush on was a praying mantis ("Teacher's Pet"). Jenny's assisting Giles will lead to her being brought into the "inner circle" of Slayerettes ("Prophecy Girl").

The episode features the first appearance of Ms. Calendar. Though her first name is never used in this episode, it was originally to be "Nicki" and was later changed to avoid any confusion on set with actor Nicholas Brendon, whose friends call him Nicky.

THE REHABILITATION OF CORDY

At first, Cordelia Chase seemed like the stereotypical shallow, popular, vapid, bitchy...well, you get the idea. It was very easy to picture her in the role of Buffy's school-bound nemesis. And that would have been the easy way to go. But, interestingly, though Cordelia remains somewhat shallow, bitchy, and still very popular, over time, she's turned out to have a heart and soul after all.

Witness, then, the rehabilitation of Cordelia.

At first, Ms. Chase was best known for her cruel, humorless barbs. In one scene in the premiere episode, Cordelia gets off several nasty lines. Spotting Buffy hanging out with Willow and Xander, she says, "I don't want to interrupt your downward mobility...." and moments later, sneers at Xander, "Don't you have an elsewhere to be?" Not exactly the winner of the How to Make Friends and Influence People contest. Actually, Cordelia's enormous lack of charm is the subject of quite a bit of humor among our heroes for the first season.

But then, something begins to change. Slowly at first. In "Out of Mind, Out of Sight," Cordelia first approaches Buffy for her help, realizing that there's more to the Slayer than meets the eye. Then, discussing the hapless "invisible girl," we get our first glimpse at the human side of the wicked witch of Sunnydale High, with this exchange.

Cordelia: "It's awful to feel that lonely."
Buffy: "Oh, so you've read something about the feeling?"
Cordelia: "Hey, you think I'm never lonesome 'cause I'm so cute and popular? I can be surrounded by people and be completely alone. It's not like any of them really know me. I don't even know if they like me half the time. People just want to be in the popular zone. Sometimes when I talk, everyone's so busy agreeing with me, they don't hear a word I say."
Buffy: "If you feel so alone, why do you work so hard at being popular?"
Cordelia: "Well, it beats being alone all by yourself." —**"OUT OF MIND, OUT OF SIGHT"**

At the end of the first season, in the episode "Prophecy Girl," Cordelia takes her biggest step toward her rehabilitation, when she saves Willow and Ms. Calendar from an army of vampires. Then, in the first episode of season two, "When She Was Bad," the amazing Ms. Chase actually steps in when she sees how badly Buffy is screwing up her relationships with her friends. "Whatever's causing the Joan Collins 'tude, deal with it, embrace the pain, spank your inner moppet, whatever," Cordy tells Buffy. "But get over it, 'cause pretty soon you won't even have the loser friends you've got now."

Okay, so maybe she could have come up with a nicer approach, but this *is* Cordelia we're talking about here!

Already involved with the Slayerettes because, well, she knows Buffy is the Slayer and there are monsters and vampires and demons and...hey, she lives in Sunnydale too...Cordelia also begins to think Xander's not quite such a nerd after all. In fact, at the end of "Some Assembly Required," she thanks him for saving her life. Xander immediately rebuffs her, but observant viewers knew something was brewing in that exchange.

Despite her frequent collaboration in their efforts to save the world, it was difficult for Buffy and friends to accept Cordelia. But in the first part of "What's My Line?" she officially becomes one of them, with this exchange:

Cordelia: "I can't even believe you. You drag me out of bed for a ride? What am I, mass transportation?"

Xander: "That's what a lot of the guys say. But it's just locker-room talk. I never pay it any mind."

Cordelia: "Great, so now I'm your taxi and your punching bag."

Xander: "I like to think of you more as my witless foil—but have it your way. . . . Come on, Cordelia. You wanna be a member of the Scooby Gang, you gotta be willing to be inconvenienced now and then."

Cordelia: "Oh, right. 'Cause I lie awake at night hoping you tweekos will be my best friends. And that my first husband will be a balding, demented homeless man." **—"WHAT'S MY LINE? PART 1"**

And, of course, it's all cemented when, later in that same episode, Cordelia and Xander—under the duress of being attacked by a bug man—make out for the first time.

Cordelia Chase. Purposefully tactless. Materialistic. Sarcastic. Patronizing. Arrogant. And coming around.

The Puppet Show

WRITTEN BY Rob Des Hotel and Dean Batali; **DIRECTED BY** Ellen Pressman. **GUEST STARS:** Kristine Sutherland as Joyce Summers, Richard Werner as Morgan, Burke Roberts as Marc, and Armin Shimerman as Principal Snyder; with Chasen Hampton, Natasha Pearce, and Krissy Carlson.

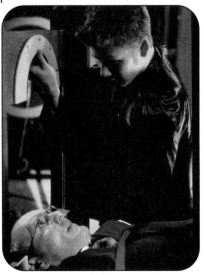

Giles faces a true horror—running the annual Talent Show—at the instruction of Principal Snyder, Flutie's somewhat militant replacement. Snyder also instructs Buffy, Xander, and Willow to be in the Talent Show, and generally makes a nuisance of himself. To add insult to injury, one of the Talent Show entrants is found dead—with her heart cut out. At first the Slayerettes think it might be your basic serial killer, but Giles finds a text on the Brotherhood of Seven, a clan of demons who must obtain the heart and brain of a human youth every seven years to keep up their own guise as youthful humans.

Suspicion falls upon Morgan, the class genius, who seems to be talking to the wooden dummy he uses for his performance and who is also suffering from headaches—right up until Morgan is found dead with his brain removed, and Buffy realizes that Sid, his dummy, is alive. Could he be the demon?

Sid turns out to be a demon hunter who has been imprisoned in a dummy's body. Once he and Buffy realize neither is the demon, they pair up to find the demon, which proves necessary once they realize that Morgan suffered from brain cancer, and so his cranium would be useless. And the magician really wants to demonstrate his magic trick involving a guillotine to Giles.…

Willow's running off in terror at the end of the episode, midway through the drama piece that she, Buffy, and Xander are performing, was not part of the script. Though it seems prophetic, considering that in the next episode, "Nightmares," Willow's primary fear has to do with stage fright.

Quote of the week:

"That's the kind of woolly-headed liberal thinking that leads to getting eaten."

Principal Snyder, on the shortcomings of his predecessor

Love, Slayer style:

More foreshadowing of Xander and Cordelia's future, as Cordelia cries, "All I can think is, it could've been me!" prompting Xander's reply of, "We can dream."

POP-CULTURE IQ:

Xander has Sid-the-dummy crying "Red Rum!" a reference to a line from *The Shining*—it's "murder" spelled backward.

"Does anyone else feel like we've been Keyser Soze'd?"

Xander, in reference to the manipulative villain in the film *The Usual Suspects*

CONTINUITY:

The wild-dogs-ate-Principal-Flutie story from "The Pack" seems to be holding up. Sid mentions that the Slayer in the 1930s was a Korean woman, with whom he had some "good times."

As Xander is trying to convince Buffy and Willow that Sid is just a piece of wood, he operates the dummy's mouth and cries "Redrum! Redrum!" The reference to Stanley Kubrick's *The Shining* was added by actor Nicholas Brendon and was not in the original script.

The following two exchanges were cut from the script to "The Puppet Show" because of length:

Buffy: "And I don't think we'll be featuring Xander's special gift . . ."

Xander: "Okay, some people are jealous that they can't burp the alphabet."

Buffy: " . . . so we're back to drama. We'll just do it quickly. Get in, get out. Nobody gets hurt."

Buffy: "Pretty good. I never heard 'Flight of the Bumblebee' on the tuba before."

Lisa: "Most people aren't up to it."

Sid is just one in a long line of terrifying puppets and talking dolls in film and television, from "Talking Tina" in a classic episode of *The Twilight Zone* to the horrifying dummy in William Goldman's *Magic.*

DEEP THOUGHTS: A GUIDE TO SLAYER PHILOSOPHY

Buffy: "You know, it's just, like, nothing's simple. I'm constantly trying to work it out, who to hate or love . . . who to trust. . . . It's like the more I know, the more confused I get."

Giles: "I believe that's called 'growing up.'"

Buffy: "I'd like to stop now then, okay?"   **—"LIE TO ME"**

Giles: "To forgive is an act of compassion, Buffy. It's not done because people deserve it. It's done because they *need* it."

Buffy: "No. James destroyed the person he loved the most in a moment of blind passion. And that's not something you forgive. No matter why he did what he did. No matter if he knows now that it was *wrong* and *stupid* and *selfish*. He's just going to have to live with it."   **—"I ONLY HAVE EYES FOR YOU"**

> **"There's moments in your life that make you. That set the course of who you're gonna be. Sometimes they're little, subtle moments. Sometimes...they're not."**
> Whistler, in "Becoming, Part 2"

Buffy: "Does it ever get easy?"

Giles: "You mean life?"

Buffy: "Yeah. Does it get easy?"

Giles: "What do you want me to say?"

Buffy: "Lie to me."

Giles: "Yes. It's terribly simple. The good guys are always stalwart and true. The bad guys are easily distinguished by their pointy horns or black hats, and we always defeat them and save the day. No one ever dies . . . and everyone lives happily ever after."

Buffy: "Liar."   —**"LIE TO ME"**

Buffy: "And don't lie to me. I'm tired of it."
Angel: "Some lies are necessary."
Buffy: "For what?"
Angel: "Sometimes the truth is worse. You live long enough, you find that out."   —**"LIE TO ME"**

Buffy: "Life is short."
Willow: "Life is short."
Buffy: "Not original, I'll grant you. But it's true, y'know? Why waste time being shy, worry about some guy and if he's gonna laugh at you? Seize the moment. 'Cause tomorrow, you might be dead."   —**"WELCOME TO THE HELLMOUTH"**

"It was wrong to meddle with the forces of Darkness, and I see that now." Xander, in "Witch"

"We saved the world. I say we party. I mean, I got all pretty."
Buffy, at the climax of "Prophecy Girl"

"I think anyone who cuts dead girls into little pieces does not get the benefit of any doubt."
Buffy, in "Some Assembly Required"

"Love makes you do the wacky."
Willow, in "Some Assembly Required"

"'I aspire to help my fellow man.' Check. I mean, as long as he's not, like, smelly or dirty or something gross."
Cordelia, filling out a questionnaire, in "What's My Line? Part 1"

"Sorry, I'm an old-fashioned girl. I was raised to believe the men dig up the corpses and the women have the babies."
Buffy, in "Some Assembly Required"

Buffy: "Vampires are creeps."
Giles: "Yes, that's why one slays them."   —**"TED"**

"Loneliness is about the scariest thing there is."
Angel, in "Ted"

Nightmares

STORY BY Joss Whedon, **TELEPLAY BY** David Greenwalt; **DIRECTED BY** Bruce Seth Green. **GUEST STARS:** Mark Metcalf as the Master, Kristine Sutherland as Joyce Summers, Jeremy Foley as Billy Palmer, Andrew J. Ferchland as the Anointed One, Dean Butler as Hank Summers; with Justin Urich.

Everyone's nightmares start coming true in Sunnydale, with the only common element being the occasional appearance of a young boy. One student's recurring dream of spiders attacking him in class actually happens; Xander walks into a class wearing only his underwear; Willow is forced to sing onstage; Giles gets lost in the stacks and forgets how to read; Cordelia has *really awful* hair and loses her fashion sense; and then Buffy is told by her father she was the reason her parents divorced.

Things get worse when the Master is freed—a nightmare Buffy has in the teaser made reality—Buffy is killed (Giles's nightmare) and comes back to life as a vampire (Buffy's). The chaos is finally traced to a young boy in a coma who was beaten by his Kiddie League coach, and whose constant reliving of that nightmare has been made real by the power of the Hellmouth—unless Buffy can make him confront his fear.

Quote of the week:

> "So you're the Slayer. You're prettier than the last one."
>
> The Master's first comment upon finally meeting his nemesis

CONTINUITY:

The Master's instruction of the Anointed One ("Never Kill a Boy on the First Date," "Angel") continues. Buffy's nightmare of the Master attacking and killing her serves as a teaser of sorts for their confrontation in "Prophecy Girl."

From the original teleplay:

Material cut from the script because of length includes the following gem from Xander:

> "Okay, despite the rat-like chill that just crawled up my spine, I'm going to say this very calmly: Helllppp...."

Also cut was the following exchange:
Giles: "Are you all right? You look a bit peaked."
Buffy: "Hospital lighting. It does nothing for my fabulous complexion."
Giles: "Are you . . . sleeping all right?"
Buffy: "I'll sleep better when we find this guy. Nothing like kicking the crap out of a bad guy to perk up my day."

> This is the episode where Xander officially grows up and turns from nerd into hero. Not by saving anyone's life, exactly, but by facing his own childhood fears and punching out a clown he's had nightmares about for a decade.

Living on the Hellmouth, there's rarely a bright side to look on, still our stalwart heroes do their best to be optimistic about things.

Buffy: "We averted the apocalypse. You gotta give us points for that." —**"THE HARVEST"**

**"That is the thrill of living on the Hellmouth—
one has a veritable cornucopia of fiends, devils, and ghouls to engage . . .
[off their looks] Pardon me for finding the glass half full."**

Giles, in "Witch"

**"If it weren't for you, people would be lined up five deep waiting to get themselves
buried. Willow would be Robbie the Robot's love slave, I wouldn't even have a head,
and Theresa's a vampire!"**

Xander, as Theresa is reborn, in "Phases"

**"I'd give anything to be able to turn invisible—but I wouldn't use my power
to beat people up. I'd use my power to protect the girls' locker room."**

Xander, in "Out of Mind, Out of Sight"

Cordelia: "It's about time our school excelled at something."
Willow: "You're forgetting our high mortality rate."
Xander: "We're number one!" —**"GO FISH"**

Xander: "Hellmouth. Center of mystical convergence, supernatural monsters. Been there."
Buffy: "A little blasé there, aren't you?"
Xander: "I'm not worried. If there's something bad out there, we'll find, you'll slay, we'll party."
—**"NIGHTMARES"**

"We're still the undead's favorite party town."

Xander, on Sunnydale, in "When She Was Bad"

Giles: "Grave robbing. Well, that's new. Interesting."
Buffy: "I know you meant to say 'gross and disturbing.'"
Giles: "Yes, of course. Terrible thing. Must put a stop to it…dammit."
—**"SOME ASSEMBLY REQUIRED"**

Willow: "By the way, are we hoping to find a body or no body?"
Xander: "Call me an optimist, but *I'm* hoping to find a fortune in gold doubloons."
Buffy: "Well, 'body' would mean flesh-eating demon. 'No body' points more toward the
'army of zombies' thing. Take your pick." —**"SOME ASSEMBLY REQUIRED"**

**"I must admit, I'm intrigued. A werewolf. It's one of the classics.
I'm sure my books and I are in for a fascinating afternoon."**

Giles, in "Phases"

Out of Mind, Out of Sight

STORY BY Joss Whedon, **TELEPLAY BY** Ashley Gable and Tom Swyden; **DIRECTED BY** Reza Badiyi. **GUEST STARS:** David Boreanaz as Angel, Armin Shimerman as Principal Snyder, Clea DuVall as Marcie Ross, Mercedes McNab as Harmony, Ryan Bittle as Mitch, Denise Dowse as Ms. Miller, Mark Phelan as Agent Doyle, Skip Stellrecht as Agent Manetti; with Julie Fulton.

Cordelia is campaigning to be crowned Sunnydale High's May Queen. Mitch, her prospective date for the occasion, is clubbed in the locker room with a baseball bat—a bat seemingly acting of its own accord! Later, Cordelia's friend Harmony seems to fall down the stairs, but Harmony insists she was pushed. Everything points to an invisible person, and Buffy finds evidence of someone living in the ductwork: a girl named Marcie Ross whom nobody remembers, yet who has a Sunnydale High yearbook signed by most of the class, including Xander and Willow (*everyone* signed, "Have a nice summer").

Having been treated as if she were invisible for so long—especially by Cordelia and her "Cordettes"—she has become literally invisible, and is now wreaking havoc on Cordelia's life. Buffy manages to stop her—though not before Marcie attempts to kill Giles, Xander, and Willow and almost mutilates Cordelia—at which point some federal agents take her away to a special school with some other invisible students to "rehabilitate" her.

> The Giles/Buffy exchange about listening (Giles: "You may have to work on listening to people." Buffy: "Very funny." Giles: "I thought so") was not in the original script, and was added in postproduction as a transition voice-over.

Quote of the week:

"Being this popular is not just my right, it's my responsibility."

Cordelia, upon accepting the honor of May Queen, summarizing her approach to life

Love, Slayer style:

Angel and Giles meet for the first time, and they discuss Angel's feelings for Buffy. ("A vampire in love with the Slayer.

When Marcie arrives at her new school, the teacher has her open to Chapter 11. That chapter's title is "Assassination and Infiltration." The first case study: "Case Example D: Radical Cult Leader as Intended Victim."

That's rather poetic," says Giles, a line used regularly in the "Previously on *Buffy the Vampire Slayer*" montages.)

POP-CULTURE IQ:

"Monsters don't usually send messages. It's pretty much 'Crush! Kill! Destroy!'"

Buffy, referring to a famous line uttered by the robot in the television series *Lost in Space*

CONTINUITY:

The seeds of Cordelia's eventual induction into the Slayerettes are sown here, as she comes to Buffy and the others for help when she egotistically yet correctly realizes that the attacks are directed at her. Giles mentions *The Pergamum Codex* to Angel, which has various prophecies regarding the Master and the Slayer, which Angel obtains for him—said prophecies prove vital in "Prophecy Girl."

The philosophies of Principals Flutie and Snyder are very clearly at odds.
Here, for your edification, the words of wisdom
from these two titans of education.

**"We all need help with our feelings, otherwise we bottle them up,
and before you know it, powerful laxatives are involved.
I really believe if we all reach out to one another, we can beat this thing.
I'm always here if you need a hug—but not a real hug, because there's
no touching in this school. We're sensitive to wrong touching."**

Principal Flutie, to Buffy, in "Teacher's Pet"

**"My predecessor, Mr. Flutie, may have gone in for all that touchy-feely,
relating nonsense. But he was eaten. You're in my world now.
Sunnydale has touched and felt for the last time."**

Principal Snyder, in "The Puppet Show"

**"Kids today need discipline. That's an unpopular word these days.
'Discipline.' I know Principal Flutie would have said kids need
'understanding.' Kids are 'human beings.' That's the kind of woolly-headed
liberal thinking that leads to being eaten."**

Principal Snyder, in "The Puppet Show"

"A clean slate, Buffy. That's what you get here. What's past is past."

Principal Flutie, in "Welcome to the Hellmouth"

"Kids. I don't like 'em."

Principal Snyder, in "The Puppet Show"

"All the kids here are free to call me 'Bob.'"

Principal Flutie, in "Welcome to the Hellmouth"

Principal Snyder: "I mean, it's incredible. One day the campus is completely bare, empty
. . . the next, there are children everywhere. Like locusts. Crawling
around, mindlessly bent on feeding and mating, destroying everything in sight in their relentless, pointless desire to exist."

Giles: "I do enjoy these pep talks. Have you ever considered, given your abhorrence of
children, that school principal is perhaps not your true vocation?"

Principal Snyder: "Someone's gotta keep an eye on 'em. They're just a bunch of
hormonal time bombs. Why, every time a pretty girl walks by, every
boy turns into a jibbering fool." **—"WHEN SHE WAS BAD"**

"There are things I will not tolerate. Students loitering on campus after school. Horrible murders with hearts being removed. And also smoking."

Principal Snyder, in "The Puppet Show"

"Buffy, don't worry. Any other school, they might say 'watch your step' or 'we'll be watching you,' but that's just not the way here. We want to service your needs and help you to respect our needs."

Principal Flutie, in "Welcome to the Hellmouth"

Principal Snyder: "There are some things I can just smell. It's like a sixth sense."
Giles: "No, actually, that would be one of the five."
Principal Snyder: "The Summers girl? I smell trouble. I smell expulsion. And just the faintest aroma of jail."
Giles: "Well, before you throw away the key, you might consider giving her the benefit of the doubt. She may surprise you."
Principal Snyder: "You really have faith in those kids, don't you?"
Giles: "Yes, I do."
Principal Snyder: "Weird."   **—"WHEN SHE WAS BAD"**

**"That's the Buffy Summers I want in my school.
The sensible girl, with her feet on the ground."**

Principal Flutie, just before Buffy leaps the fence in "The Harvest"

**"A lot of principals tell students, think of your principal as your 'pal.'
I say, think of me as your judge, jury and executioner."**

Principal Snyder, in "School Hard"

Principal Snyder: "This is my school. What I say goes. And I say this isn't happening."
Joyce: "Well, then I guess the danger's over."
Parent: "I'm not waiting for them to break down the doors. I'm getting out."
Joyce: "Don't be an idiot."
Principal Snyder: "I'm beginning to see a certain mother-daughter resemblance."
—"SCHOOL HARD"

Prophecy Girl

WRITTEN AND DIRECTED BY Joss Whedon. **GUEST STARS:** Mark Metcalf as the Master, David Boreanaz as Angel, Kristine Sutherland as Joyce Summers, Robia LaMorte as Jenny Calendar, Andrew J. Ferchland as the Anointed One.

On the eve of the prom, Giles translates a rather devastating prophecy in *The Pergamum Codex:* "The Master shall rise and the Slayer shall die." Several portents—noticed by Giles, Jenny Calendar, and Buffy—point to the Master finally freeing himself from his imprisonment. Giles tries to keep the prophecy from Buffy, but she overhears him discussing it with Angel. Though at first she rejects both the prophecy and her continuing as the Slayer ("Giles, I'm sixteen years old—I don't want to die"), the news of two students' deaths at the hands of vampires on schoolgrounds makes her realize her duty, and she goes after the Master. Angel and Xander go after her, arriving in time to find Buffy drowned and the Master free. Use of CPR revives Buffy, and she, Angel, and Xander return to Sunnydale High to find that the Hellmouth is opening—right under the library—despite the best efforts of Giles, Jenny, Willow, and Cordelia. Buffy confronts the Master once again, and this time he is the one who dies. "We saved the world," says Buffy at the end of it all. "I say we party."

Quote of the week:

"By the way, I like your dress."
This is said by Willow, the Master, and Angel to Buffy at various times; Buffy's mother bought her the dress to wear to the prom

Love, Slayer style:

Xander finally comes out and expresses his feelings for Buffy in the form of a labored attempt to ask her to go to the prom with him. Buffy turns the offer down, not feeling that way about Xander, prompting a snide comment about how one has to be undead to get her attention. ("I don't handle rejection well. Funny, considering all the practice I've had.") Later on, Xander recruits Angel to follow Buffy in going after the Master ("You're in love with her," Angel says, to which Xander replies frankly, "Aren't you?").
Xander practices his pickup line to Buffy on

The moment Willow discovers the corpses of Kevin and his friends in the audio/visual room is a major turning point for the character. From that point on, Willow becomes more proactive about her involvement with the Slayer. In that moment, she grows up.

Both Willow and the Master compliment Buffy on her dress, but the final exchange (Angel: "I really like your . . ." Buffy: "Yeah, yeah. It was a big hit with everyone.") was added during production and was not in the original script.

The massive demon coming up out of the Hellmouth at the end of "Prophecy Girl" had to be frightening, but the budget didn't allow for computer-generated images. The masterminds at Optic Nerve ended up making tentacle "costumes." Each of the tentacles has a human being inside, manipulating it from within.

Willow, which is some comfort for her, though not enough for her to accept his post-Buffy's-rejection offer of the two of them going to the prom.

POP-CULTURE IQ:

"Calm may work for Locutus of Borg here, but I'm freaked and I intend to stay that way."

Xander, upset by Giles's maddening reserve, referring to the emotionless cyborg characters on *Star Trek*.

CONTINUITY:

The Master's imprisonment finally comes to an end, with the help of the Anointed One, and he makes his second attempt to open the Hellmouth ("Welcome to the Hellmouth"). For the second time, but not the last, Buffy has a prophetic dream ("Welcome to the Hellmouth," "Surprise," "Innocence"). Buffy and the Slayerettes finally realize that the vampire they killed in "Never Kill a Boy on the First Date" *wasn't* the Anointed One. Jenny reminds Giles of her help in destroying Moloch ("I Robot, You Jane") when she tries to pry some solid information out of him. Since "Witch," Cordelia has passed driver's ed and obtained a car. Unlike other vampires, the Master's bones remain intact upon his death, which proves important in "When She Was Bad."

From the original teleplay:

The following scene, right after Buffy has turned down Xander's request that she go to the prom with him, was cut from this episode's script because of length:

Xander bails, wandering off under the archway. Buffy sits by herself on the bench, bummed.

Which is when the hail of pebbles starts.

The first few get Buffy's attention, tiny hard pellets hitting the ground around her. She stands as more start coming down.

People—including Buffy—all run for cover as the real shower starts. Buffy stands under the archway, watching the hail come down.

ANGLE: XANDER

Walking away, not near Buffy. He hears:

Student (O.S.): "Check it out! It's raining stones!"
Xander looks back over his shoulder.
Xander: "Figures."

SECOND SEASON

EPISODE NUMBER	EPISODE NAME	ORIGINAL AIRDATE
1	When She Was Bad	15-Sep
2	Some Assembly Required	22-Sep
3	School Hard	29-Sepr
4	Inca Mummy Girl	6-Oct
5	Reptile Boy	13-Oct
6	Halloween	27-Oct
7	Lie to Me	3-Nov
8	The Dark Age	10-Nov
9	What's My Line? Part 1	17-Nov
10	What's My Line? Part 2	24-Nov
11	Ted	8-Dec
12	Bad Eggs	12-Jan
13	Surprise	19-Jan
14	Innocence	20-Jan
15	Phases	27-Jan
16	Bewitched, Bothered, and Bewildered	10-Feb
17	Passion	24-Feb
18	Killed by Death	3-Mar
19	I Only Have Eyes for You	28-Apr
20	Go Fish	5-May
21	Becoming, Part 1 (Season Finale)	12-May
22	Becoming, Part 2 (Season Finale)	19-May

★ STARRING ★

Sarah Michelle Gellar . . . . .Buffy Summers

Nicholas Brendon . . . . .Xander Harris

Alyson Hannigan . . . . .Willow Rosenberg

Charisma Carpenter . . . . .Cordelia Chase

David Boreanaz . . . . .Angel

Anthony Stewart Head . . . . .Rupert Giles

When She Was Bad

WRITTEN AND DIRECTED by Joss Whedon. **GUEST STARS:** Kristine Sutherland as Joyce Summers, Robia LaMorte as Jenny Calendar, Andrew J. Ferchland as the Anointed One, Dean Butler as Hank Summers, Brent Jennings as Absalom, and Armin Shimerman as Principal Snyder; with Tamara Braun.

Buffy returns from spending summer vacation with her father. Willow and Xander are relieved at first, as the summer has been exceedingly dull, though Buffy returns just in time to save the pair from a vampire—the first such they've seen since the Master was killed. The relief turns to concern, however, as Buffy is withdrawn, snappish, a little too eager to continue her training, and more rude to Cordelia than even she deserves. She also has a nightmare about Giles attacking her while Willow and Xander calmly look on.

When the Master's buried bones go missing, everyone is concerned. Giles learns of a revivification rite that requires those "closest" to the Master when he died. It turns out to be a bad translation from Sumerian to Latin, and by the time he realizes it means "nearest," he and Willow are taken, along with Cordelia and Jenny, all of whom were next to the Master when he was impaled. Buffy, Xander, and Angel must stop the Anointed One and his new deputy, Absalom, from completing the ceremony.

Quote of the week:

Snyder: "There are some things I can just smell. It's like a sixth sense."
Giles: "Actually, that would be one of the five."

Love, Slayer style:

The romantic entanglements kick into high gear in this episode. Xander and Willow come within microns of actually kissing each other in the teaser after Xander licks ice cream off Willow's nose—interrupted by the vampire attack and Buffy's return to Sunnydale. Willow's attempt to re-create that mood later in the Bronze fails miserably, as Xander has returned to full panting-after-Buffy mode.

Giles and Jenny return from their summer vacation and immediately begin flirting, with an oblivious Principal Snyder carrying on about how teenagers are driven by their hormones.

Buffy, still reeling from her experiences with the Master and refusing to outwardly deal with it, plays mind games with all her friends. She is cold to Angel. ("Could you contemplate getting over yourself for a second? There is no us.") She dances a hormone-tingling slow dance with Xander at the Bronze, which manages to make Willow, Angel, and even Xander himself squirm, prompting Cordelia, of all people, to tell her to get over it ("Spank your inner mop-pet, whatever"). It isn't until the climax, when she cathartically smashes the Master's bones with a sledge hammer, that she seems to come out of it.

BUFFY'S BAG OF TRICKS:

She makes excellent use of a torch to simultaneously stake one vampire and burn Absalom to a crisp.

POP-CULTURE IQ:

Xander and Willow's movie quote contest includes T*erminator, Planet of the Apes, Star Wars,* and *Witness:*

> **"I mock you with my ice cream cone, Amish Guy...."**

CONTINUITY:

The entire episode picks up from "Prophecy Girl" showing that it *wasn't* as simple as, "We saved the world; I say we party." Buffy's slow dance with Xander will continue to have consequences ("Some Assembly Required")

From the original teleplay:

The following exchange between Buffy's parents was cut from the script for "When She Was Bad" because of length:

Hank: "Oh, I'm spoiling her. Did I forget to mention that?"

Joyce: "What you forgot is that I'm gonna have to deal with another year of 'Daddy would let me buy that.'"

WRITTEN BY Ty King; **DIRECTED BY** Bruce Seth Green. **GUEST STARS:** Robia LaMorte as Jenny Calendar, Angelo Spizzirri as Chris Epps, Michael Bacall as Eric, Ingo Neuhaus as Daryl Epps, Melanie MacQueen as Mrs. Epps; with Amanda Wilmhurst.

Some Assembly Required

After Buffy slays a newly minted vampire in the graveyard, she and Angel find that a body has been dug up and removed from its grave. The body belonged to a student from another school—a girl who was killed in a car crash with two fellow cheerleaders. The gang digs up one of the other graves to find that body missing as well. Meanwhile, Angel, while looking for Buffy, sees Cordelia in the parking lot, and they both stumble across body parts that turn out to belong to the three dead girls—but not enough parts for three *whole* girls. And all three heads are present.

Cordelia's science-fair project, "The Tomato: Fruit or Vegetable?" is completed by Willow in three words. "It's a fruit."

It turns out that Chris Epps—the Science Club's prize student—and his friend Eric are trying to pull a Victor Frankenstein and create life from lifelessness. A disgusted Buffy tries to stop them and soon learns that the Frankenstein analogy is closer to the mark than she thought: Chris had already brought his football-jock brother Daryl back from the dead, albeit in a hideous form, and has now promised to give him a companion. But they need a freshly killed head to complete the body, and so they're going after Cordelia....

Quote of the week:

"I'm an old-fashioned gal. I was raised to believe that men dig up the corpses and women have the babies."

Buffy, on why she and Willow don't help Xander and Giles dig up a grave

Love, Slayer style:

Angel and Buffy argue in the teaser, with Buffy accusing Angel of being jealous of Xander—which Angel finally admits at the episode's end. Giles is found working on a pickup line for Jenny in the library, prompting both ribbing and advice from Xander and Buffy ("She's a technopagan, right? Ask her to bless your laptop"). His attempts to use it later are hesitant and befuddled, prompting Jenny to ask him out instead, to the football game.

The first real seeds of the Cordelia/Xander pairing are sown here, as Xander saves Cordelia from a fire while Buffy is fighting with Daryl. At the end, Xander discusses with Willow how everyone is "paired off" (Buffy with Angel, Giles with Jenny) except them. Interrupted by Cordelia trying to thank him for his bravery, he blows her off, then turns to Willow to ask what they were talking about. "Why we can't get dates," Willow replies dryly.

POP-CULTURE IQ:

"Sorry to interrupt, Willow, but it's the Bat-signal."

Buffy, summoning Willow to the library for Slayer research, referring to the signal used by Commissioner Gordon in DC's *Batman* comics to summon the dark knight

The episode sees the destruction of the "old science building," the only structure remaining of the original school after the earthquake of 1937.

CONTINUITY:

Buffy's slow dance with Xander ("When She Was Bad") continues to have ramifications, mostly with a jealous Angel, but also in ribbing from her friends.

STORY BY Joss Whedon and David Greenwalt, **TELEPLAY BY** David Greenwalt; **DIRECTED BY** John T. Kretchmer.

School Hard

GUEST STARS: Kristine Sutherland as Joyce Summers, Robia LaMorte as Jenny Calendar, Andrew J. Ferchland as the Anointed One, James Marsters as Spike, Alexandra Johnes as Sheila, Gregory Scott Cummins as Big Ugly, Andrew Palmer as Lean Boy, Juliet Landau as Drusilla, and Armin Shimerman as Principal Snyder; with Brian Reddy and Keith Mackechnie.

There are a couple of new vampires in town: Spike and Drusilla. The former is a rebellious sort who goes his own way rather than stick with the traditional vampire rituals; the latter is the love of his life, who is completely insane and very weak. They show up in time for the Festival of St. Vigeous, when vampires' powers are at their height. Before that, though, is a much greater horror for Buffy: Parent-Teacher Night, and she's scared to death of what her teachers (not to mention the misanthropic Principal Snyder) will say to her mother. However, Spike—a.k.a. William the Bloody—decides to jump the gun and attack the school on Parent-Teacher Night, two days prior to St. Vigeous.

Buffy manages to drive them all off, with some help from Angel, Xander, and, at the end, her mother, who clubs Spike with a fire ax. Spike runs off, and is then soundly criticized by the Anointed One and his cronies. Spike replies by throwing the Anointed One in a cage and exposing the boy to sunlight, then going to watch TV with Dru.

Quote of the week:

> "If every vampire who said he was at the Crucifixion was actually there, it would've been like Woodstock."
>
> Spike, debunking the claims of his peers

Love, Slayer style:

Spike and Dru are the first vampires who are shown to be in love with each other, and Spike is obviously completely devoted to Drusilla.

CONTINUITY:

Angel reveals that he knows Spike, and Spike refers to Angel as his sire in front of Xander (though Xander doesn't know what that means). Spike makes reference to Prague, which we later learn is where Drusilla was believed killed ("Lie to Me"). The reign of "the Annoying One," as Spike calls him, comes to a sudden end ("Never Kill a Boy on the First Date," etc.). The first hint that Principal Snyder and other authorities in Sunnydale know, at the very least, that *some* kind of weird stuff happens in this town are provided—Snyder and Bob the Sheriff discuss what to tell the media, and decide to say it was gangs on PCP, since telling the truth is considered ludicrous ("I Only Have Eyes for You," "Becoming, Part 2").

From the original teleplay::

There are several lines cut from the "School Hard" script for length, including Spike insulting Big Ugly ("Would it kill ya, a little mouthwash every couple hundred years?") and Xander talking about planning a good party ("The important thing in punch is the ratio of vodka to schnapps....That was obviously far too sophisticated a joke for this crowd"). Also cut was a humorous exchange between Buffy and Giles (Buffy: "I don't suppose this is something about happy squirrels?" Giles: "Vampires." Buffy: "That was my next guess").

Inca Mummy Girl

WRITTEN BY Matt Kiene and Joe Reinkemeyer; **DIRECTED BY** Ellen Pressman. **GUEST STARS:** Kristine Sutherland as Joyce Summers, Ara Celi as Ampata, Seth Green as Oz, Jason Hall as Devon, Danny Strong as Jonathan; with Samuel Jacobs, Kristen Winnicki, Joey Crawford, Bernard White, Gil Birmingham, and Henrik Rosvall.

Sunnydale's exchange program brings students from all over the world to the school, and Joyce Summers is among the parents who volunteered to house the foreign kids. Buffy is not relishing the thought of sharing her house—nor is Xander when he learns that Ampata Gutierrez from South America is a boy. After a field trip to a local

museum, a young student tries to steal the seal on an Incan princess's mummified remains, and breaks it. This awakens the mummy, allowing her to drain the life, first from her would-be grave robber, then from Ampata, who is waiting for the late Buffy to pick him up at the bus station. Assuming the identity of Ampata, the princess learns about the modern world—and she and Xander fall for each other, to Willow's chagrin. As Xander and "Ampata" share a slow dance at the Bronze, Buffy and Giles realize that the exchange student is an imposter, and that they must find her and put the seal back together.

Quote of the week:

"Oh, I know this one! 'Slaying entails certain sacrifices, blah blah bliddy blah, I'm so stuffy, give me a scone.'"

Buffy, anticipating one of Giles's lectures

Love, Slayer style:

Xander finds someone who loves him, only to learn that she must periodically drain the life out of people in order to survive. Willow spends most of the episode moping (not aided by her overhearing a conversation between Xander and Buffy, where the former makes it clear that he sees Willow as his best friend and no more than that), but still suggests to Xander that he invite "Ampata" to the dance. Cordelia is dating Devon, the lead singer of Dingoes Ate My Baby, in this episode.

POP-CULTURE IQ:

**"I am from the country of Leone.
It's in Italy, pretending to be Montana."**

Xander, explaining why he's dressed like Clint Eastwood in an old Sergio Leone–directed spaghetti western, for the World Culture Dance

CONTINUITY:

Oz and his band make their first appearance, and Oz notices Willow for the first time at the dance—though, as with "Halloween," his initial attempts to strike up a conversation don't quite work. Xander briefly wonders if "Ampata" is a praying mantis ("Teacher's Pet"). Some disturbing parallels are drawn between the Inca princess's life and that of the Slayer. At the end, Buffy tries to comfort Xander with how she felt when she heard the prophecy that she would die—when Xander points out that she made the sacrifice anyhow, Buffy reminds him that she had a friend (Xander) to bring her back ("Prophecy Girl").

The Natural History Museum, where the students go on a field trip in this episode, is in real life located at 900 Exposition Boulevard, near the University of Southern California, in Los Angeles.

The following exchange was cut from this episode's script for length:

Ampata: "He [Xander] has a way of making the milk come out of my nose."
Buffy: "And that's good?"

Ara Celi, who plays Ampata, and Nicholas Brendon each wolfed down eight to ten Twinkies for one scene.

SHOPPING WITH BUFFY

**"I am, of course, having my dress specially made.
Off-the-rack gives me hives."**

Cordelia, in "Out of Mind, Out of Sight"

Costume designer Cynthia Bergstrom puts just as much time and effort into Buffy's wardrobe as Buffy would herself. She buys the show's "contemporary clothes" (as opposed to historical costumes) in stores in Los Angeles. Some designers send her things directly, such as Cynthia Rowley and Vivienne Tam.

Here's a list of where she shops in Los Angeles for some of our heroes:

BUFFY

**Fred Siegel • Barney's • American Rag on La Brea •
Cynthia Rowley**

WILLOW

**Contempo Casuals • Rampage • Macy's • Chenille sweaters from Wuiff Design •
Fred Siegel • Barney's**

CORDELIA

**Neiman Marcus • Bloomingdale's • Barney's •
Tommy Hilfiger on Rodeo Drive**

ANGEL

**Cashmere wool duster from Hugo Boss • Traffic in the Beverly Center •
Barney's • Macy's**

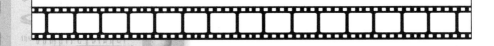

Reptile Boy

WRITTEN AND DIRECTED by David Greenwalt. **GUEST STARS:** Greg Vaughn as Richard Anderson, Todd Babcock as Tom Warner, Jordana Spiro as Callie Megan Anderson, Robin Atkin Downes as Machida, Danny Strong as Jonathan; with Coby Bell, Christopher Dahlberg, and Jason Posey.

In a period of relative inactivity for the Slayer, Buffy is feeling especially put upon by the demands of her duties. She also feels that her relationship with Angel is going nowhere fast. So when an older boy named Tom presents an opportunity to go to a fraternity party at the local college to Cordelia, she decides to take it.

Unfortunately, the frat worships a demon known as Machida and once a year has to sacrifice three teenage girls to it. Cordelia and Buffy turn out to be the second and third (along with a girl who has gone missing from another school). They are drugged and chained to a wall—leaving it up to Giles, Willow, Angel, and Xander to learn the truth and rescue them.

Quote of the week:

"This isn't some fairy tale: When I kiss you, you don't wake up from a deep sleep and live happily ever after."

Angel to Buffy in the graveyard. Her reply:

"When you kiss me, I want to die."

Love, Slayer style:

Buffy has been dreaming about Angel, and they argue in the graveyard over whether they can have a relationship. Cordelia also puts several moves on Angel, all the while trying to make an impression on college-boy Richard (she seems to have thrown over Devon, though she's sort of back with him in "Halloween"). Xander, meanwhile, is a teeming mass of jealousy regarding both Angel and Tom, and sneaks off to keep an eye on Buffy at the party.

The frat party is the first, and thus far only, time we have seen Buffy and Cordelia drink alcohol. (Xander was the first of the group to drink alcohol, in "Teacher's Pet.")

POP-CULTURE IQ:

"You could go on to live among rich and powerful men— in the Bizarro World."

Cordelia, dissing Xander, referring to the world in DC's *Superman* comics where everything is the reverse of what it is in our world

**"I, for one, am giddy and up.
There's a kind of hush all over Sunnydale."**

"A Kind of Hush" was originally a Herman's Hermits song,
although the Carpenters did cover it.

CONTINUITY:

Angel and Buffy at the end agree to go out for coffee, a date-like event which they
attempt to follow through on in "Halloween."

Halloween

WRITTEN BY Carl Ellsworth; **DIRECTED BY** Bruce Seth
Green. **GUEST STARS:** Seth Green as Oz, James Marsters
as Spike, Robin Sachs as Ethan Rayne, Juliet Landau as
Drusilla, Armin Shimerman as Principal Snyder, Larry Bagby III
as Larry; with Abigail Gershman.

It's Halloween at the Hellmouth—a slow time for vampires, but not for mischievous mystics. Ethan's Costume Shop is the newest store in town, and many buy their
costumes from there—including Buffy, who wants to dress up like the noble women
Angel would have known two centuries earlier, based on drawings she and Willow see
in a purloined Watcher diary.

However, the shop owner, Ethan Rayne, has other things in mind. Invoking the
Roman god Janus, he casts a spell that turns everyone who purchased a costume at his
store into the persona their costume represents. Xander becomes an army grunt (with
real machine gun), Willow becomes a ghost (the generic nature of her costume meaning she, at least, keeps her personality, but is physically completely insubstantial), Buffy
becomes an actual eighteenth-century maiden, and several little kids become demons.
Spike sees the resulting chaos—and the fact that the Slayer is now useless in that particular role—and decides to party.

Cordelia's lack of transformation reveals that only people who got their costumes at Ethan's were changed (Cordy obtained her cat costume elsewhere). A trip there
finds Giles confronted with old friend Ethan—and the ostensibly stuffy and befuddled
librarian proceeds to literally beat the method of
reversing the spell out of the costumer, just in
time to save Buffy from the business end of
Spike's teeth.

Quote of the week:

"This is...neat!"

Spike, on the chaos that results from Ethan's spell

Love, Slayer style:

Angel and Buffy's semi-date (planned in "Reptile Boy") is ruined by Buffy's lateness thanks to actual vampire slaying. Cordelia takes this opportunity to make a move on Angel, also later telling Oz that she's no longer interested in Devon. However, by the end, Angel and Buffy are actually necking in her bedroom, establishing the pair of them as a true couple at last.

In the denouement, Xander and Cordelia have a brief moment of bonding over Angel and Buffy, as Xander tells Cordy that there's no chance of getting between the two of them, as he knows from bitter personal experience.

As part of her distracting of Giles to allow Willow to swipe an old Watcher Diary, Buffy blurts out, "Ms. Calendar said that you were a babe!" This notion intrigues Giles, to say the least. ("A babe. I could live with that.")

Alyson Hannigan had makeup wiz Todd McIntosh do her up as a vampire for a Halloween party in 1997.

POP-CULTURE IQ:

"She couldn't have dressed up like Xena?"

Willow's plaintive cry after Buffy's shrinking-violet behavior goes into overdrive, referring to the tough title character of the TV series
Xena: Warrior Princess

BUFFY'S BAG OF TRICKS:

She uses a pumpkin-patch sign to stake a vampire, a bit of ingenuity noted by Spike, who had the fight videotaped by one of his cronies.

CONTINUITY:

The first hints of Giles's dark past are dropped here, to be picked up on in "The Dark Age." Cordelia is told that Angel is a vampire, but she doesn't believe it. (It is never revealed when Cordy learns the truth, though her lack of reaction when the vampiric demon inside Angel defeats Eyghon in "The Dark Age" indicates she found out some time prior to that.) Oz and Willow continue to fly by each other, first bumping into each other while Willow's in her ghost suit, then Oz passing her in the street later on, again wondering who that girl is.

According to set decorator David Koneff, "We would have found out a lot more about Oz if you had seen the inside of the van. It was just like a little sugar shack, a love shack, with black light and a mirror ball, black-light posters on the ceilings and a bean-bag chair, and the whole van was carpeted and wild."

Lie to Me

WRITTEN AND DIRECTED BY Joss Whedon. **GUEST STARS:** Robia LaMorte as Jenny Calendar, James Marsters as Spike, Jason Behr as Billy Fordham, Jarrad Paul as "Diego," and Juliet Landau as Drusilla; with Julie Lee and Will Rothhaar.

After observing Angel talking to a strange, attractive woman, Buffy starts moping—right until the arrival of Billy Fordham, "Ford" to his friends. Buffy's former crush and best friend for many years back at her old high school, Ford says he's transferred to Sunnydale High. In due course, Ford reveals that he knows that Buffy is the Slayer. A suspicious Angel has Willow check up on him, and they discover that he hasn't actually transferred and that he's part of a club that worships vampires and wishes to become like them. Ford's plan is to give Spike the Slayer in exchange for becoming a vampire—a preferred alternative to dying of a brain tumor, which is his expected fate. Buffy, however, manages to turn the tables on him and prevent the club members from being massacred by Spike and Dru.

The entire episode continues to turn on the theme of lies, and the title becomes particularly valid in the poignant conversation at the episode's end between Buffy and Giles, as she asks him to lie to her, to tell her that everything will be all right.

Quote of the week:

**"Things used to be pretty simple.
A hundred years, just hanging out, feeling guilty. I really honed my brooding skills.
Then *she*
comes along."**

Angel, describing to Willow how Buffy has changed his life

Love, Slayer style:

Buffy is jealous when she sees Angel with Drusilla and latches onto Ford as soon as he arrives, even hanging around with him to the exclusion of Angel at the Bronze. Later, though, she finally comes out and admits that she loves Angel.

Jenny and Giles go on their second date, which Jenny keeps a surprise; it turns out to be a monster truck rally.

POP-CULTURE IQ:

"It was terrible. I moped over you [Ford] for months. Sitting in my room listening to that Divinyls song, 'I Touch Myself.' [suddenly sheepish] Of course, I had no idea what it was about."

Buffy, getting herself into hot water

CONTINUITY:

Spike has one of his vampires steal the du Lac manuscript from the library (later used in "What's My Line?"). Buffy learns of Drusilla's existence; Giles had believed her killed in Prague ("School Hard"). Willow points out to Angel that he's acted jealous in the past ("Some Assembly Required"). Willow has also upgraded from a desktop to a laptop since "I Robot, You Jane" ("Passion"). Angel details how he tortured Drusilla and made her insane before he finally changed her into a vampire ("Becoming, Part 1").

From the original teleplay:

The following line of Angel's was cut from this episode for length:

> **"Yeah, I eat too. Not for nutritional value—
> it just kind of passes the time."**

DISSING THE BRITS

In the world of *Buffy*, there are many references to England and things English. Which makes sense: Joss Whedon lived in England, attending Winchester "public" boarding school for boys. Set designer Caroline Quinn is British, as is the show's producer, Gareth Davies. Anthony Stewart Head is English (although James Marsters and Juliet Landau, who play Spike and Dru, are not). Here are few bits from the scripts, which deal with lampooning the "matter of Britain"—all in good fun, of course.

> **"You could have just gone, 'Shhh.'
> Are all you Brits such drama queens?"**
>
> Xander, to Giles, in "Surprise"

> **"You know, raiding an Englishman's fridge is like dating a nun.
> You're never gonna get the good stuff."**
>
> Whistler, to Buffy, in "Becoming, Part 2"

In "Teacher's Pet," the following exchange took place:

Giles (gazing at the sky with loathing): "God, every day here is the same."
Buffy: "Bright, sunny, beautiful. How ever can we escape this torment?"

But the script provided for another version, if the typically sunny Southern California skies were overcast on the day the scene was to be shot.

Giles (gazing at the sky): "Reminds me of home."
Buffy: "Dark, dank, dreary. You must be so happy."

Here's another bit of dialogue from the original script that pokes fun at the Brits:
Buffy: "Do they know about 'fun' in England?"
Giles: "Yes, but it's considered very poor taste to have any." **—"LIE TO ME"**

And some bits that stayed in the episodes:

> **"Oh, I know this one. 'Slaying entails certain sacrifices, blah blah blah-bity blah, I'm so stuffy give me a scone.'"**
> Buffy, to Giles, in "Inca Mummy Girl"

> **"You also might want to avoid words like 'amenable' and 'indecorous.' Speak English, not whatever they speak in..."**
> Buffy, also to the long-suffering Giles, who replies, "England?" in "Some Assembly Required"

The Dark Age

WRITTEN BY Dean Batali and Rob Des Hotel; **DIRECTED BY** Bruce Seth Green. **GUEST STARS:** Robia LaMorte as Jenny Calendar, Robin Sachs as Ethan Rayne, Stuart McLean as Philip Henry; with Wendy Way, Michael Earl Reid, Carlease Burke, Tony Sears, Chris O'Hara, and John Bellucci.

Anthony Stewart Head visited an American high school library to prepare for his role as Rupert Giles.

A British gentleman comes to Sunnydale looking for Rupert Giles, but is killed by a dessicated creature he calls Dierdre. After the murder, the creature dissolves into blue goo. Giles later identifies the body as Philip Henry, and denies knowing what the tattoo on Philip's right arm is—though Giles has the same tattoo in the same spot on his left arm. Later, Philip awakens and leaves the morgue, obviously possessed by whatever had taken over Dierdre.

Buffy knows something is wrong when Giles misses a planned meeting, instead choosing to remain home and drink a lot. When Buffy finds Ethan Rayne lurking in the stacks, he informs her that it involves something called the Mouth of Eyghon. Giles tries to

keep Buffy out of it, but when the demon moves from Philip to Jenny, Giles realizes he needs Buffy's help. He explains that he and five friends summoned Eyghon; the demon then killed one of them. Now the demon's back. It is Willow who comes up with a solution—get the demon to move from Jenny to Angel, who already has a demon inhabiting his body, and one that is much older and stronger.

Quote of the week:

"Do you want me to answer that, or shall I just glare?"

Giles's dry response to Buffy's asking if she's ever let him down

Love, Slayer style:

Giles and Jenny share their first kiss after she returns a book he lent her and the planning of a weekend excursion. Said plans are derailed by the return of Eyghon, and Eyghon's possession of Jenny puts something of a damper on their passion. At the end, Jenny makes it clear that she needs some distance from Giles.

POP-CULTURE IQ:

"I'm not running around, wind in my hair, 'the hills are alive with the sound of music' fine, but I'm coping."

Jenny, after her possession by Eyghon, referring to the famous film

"I'm in a little restaurant [...in Florence, Italy], having ziti, and there're no more tables so they have to seat this guy with me, and it's John Cusack."

Willow, in "Anywhere But Here"

CONTINUITY:

The hints of Giles's past dropped in "Halloween" are expanded on here.

WRITTEN BY Howard Gordon and Marti Noxon; **DIRECTED BY** David Solomon. **GUEST STARS:** Seth Green as Oz, James Marsters as Spike, Eric Saiet as Dalton, Kelly Connell as Mr. Pfister, Bianca Lawson as Kendra, Saverio Guerra as Willy, Juliet Landau as Drusilla, and Armin Shimerman as Principal Snyder; with Michael Rothhaar and P.B. Hutton.

What's My Line? PART 1

The hold of the plane in which Kendra arrives was constructed on the set and later turned upside down and redesigned as a sewer tunnel.

It's Career Week at Sunnydale High School, which just drives home to Buffy that she can't possibly have a normal life. She proceeds to mope for some time, leading Angel to invite her to a skating rink. It cheers her up—right until she is attacked by a huge biker-dude type who is wearing a ring that identifies him as part of the Order of Taraka, a group of supernatural assassins. Three have been sent after Buffy by Spike, who doesn't want any distractions from curing Drusilla. The method for doing so is in the du Lac manuscript that had been stolen from the Sunnydale High library, which Spike eventually translates. Angel's attempt to find out what is

going on is interrupted by a woman who attacks him and locks him in a cage until sunup. The same woman then attacks Buffy, who has taken refuge from the assassins in Angel's empty apartment, and identifies herself as "Kendra, the Vampire Slayer."

Quote of the week:

"It's a statisstical impossibility for a sixteen-year-old to unplug a telephone."
—Xander

Love, Slayer style:

Angel is waiting in Buffy's bedroom when she returns from slaying, saying he's worried; she tells him, "You're the one freaky thing in my freaky world that still makes sense to me." They also neck at the skating rink (observed by Kendra, leading to the new Slayer attacking the old one at the episode's climax).

POP-CULTURE IQ:

"You wanna be a member of the Scooby Gang, you gotta be willing to be inconvenienced now and then."

Xander, to Cordelia, referring to the crime-busting kids who hung around with that famous cartoon Great Dane, Scooby-Doo

CONTINUITY:

The truth of the du Lac manuscript stolen from Giles in "Lie to Me" is revealed. Oz and Willow finally meet ("Inca Mummy Girl," "Halloween"), as both are chosen as recruiting fodder for a computer-software megacorporation in Seattle (never identified by name) during Career Week. Willow's fear of frogs is first mentioned ("Killed by Death").

WRITTEN BY Marti Noxon; **DIRECTED BY** David Semel.
GUEST STARS: Seth Green as Oz, James Marsters as Spike, Saverio Guerra as Willy, Bianca Lawson as Kendra, Kelly Connell as Mr. Pfister, and Juliet Landau as Drusilla; with Danny Strong.

Kendra and Buffy call a truce and realize that the former truly is a Slayer. When one Slayer dies, another is activated, and Buffy did die, however briefly. To Buffy's chagrin, Kendra seems more dedicated, more studious, and seems to get along better with Giles—but she also has had no life to speak of, and is long on duty but short on passion.

Meanwhile, Angel has been rescued from his cage by the slimy bartender, Willy, who hands him over to Spike. The two other Tarakan assassins attack, one going after Xander and Cordelia at Buffy's house, the other shooting at Buffy in school.

As the Slayerettes figure out for themselves, the ritual to restore Drusilla to full health requires the presence of her sire—Angel. Brutal questioning of Willy by the two Slayers reveals the location of the church where the ceremony will be performed, and they attack. Buffy manages to end the ceremony before Angel is drained of all life, then literally drops a church organ on Spike's head while the church burns around them. With the bad guys defeated and Angel saved, Kendra heads back home. But Drusilla has survived the church burning and rescued Spike—and she's stronger than ever....

Love, Slayer style:

While trapped in Buffy's basement by one of the assassins, Xander and Cordelia get into a knock-down, drag-out argument that culminates in a kiss, followed by a heartfelt, "We *so* need to get out of here." An attempt to redistance themselves at the climax fails miserably, and they wind up in each other's arms again, following yet another nasty argument, thus setting the tone for their relationship.

Oz and Willow make the first steps toward their eventual relationship, as Oz saves Willow's life from one of the assassins, then proceeds to flirt with her while discussing animal crackers.

Buffy tells Kendra to watch the movie on her flight home unless it's a "movie with a dog in it and Chevy Chase." This is a reference to *Funny Farm*, a 1988 movie starring Chase that Gellar had a small, uncredited role in.

POP-CULTURE IQ:

"Back off, Pink Ranger!"

Buffy, admonishing Kendra to not go off half-cocked, referring to one of the title characters in *Mighty Morphin Power Rangers*

"It's a little more complicated than that, John Wayne."

Buffy, once again admonishing Kendra,
referring to the legendary movie hero

CONTINUITY:

Kendra's activation as the Slayer apparently happened after Buffy died in "Prophecy Girl." Drusilla tortures Angel prior to the ceremony, reminding him of what he did to her ("Lie to Me," "Becoming, Part 1"). When Xander reveals that he and Cordelia encountered an assassin that is literally made of maggots, Buffy asks, "You and bug people, Xander—what's up with that?" ("Teacher's Pet"). Spike and Drusilla have their roles reversed at the end of the episode, as Spike is badly injured and Drusilla is at full strength.

The "Pink Ranger" line has additional significance beyond being a standard Buffy pop-culture reference: Sarah Michelle Gellar's stunt double, Sophia Crawford, used to play the Pink Ranger on *Mighty Morphin Power Rangers.*

From the original teleplay:

The following exchange was cut from the opening of this episode's script for length:

Kendra: "Your English is very odd, you know."
Buffy: "Yeah—it's something about being woken by an ax. Makes me talk all crazy."

Willow wears a backpack that has a little lion poking its head out from under a rainbow.

MOST OF THE RIGHT MOVES

Xander, the man, the myth, the dance machine. Xander does a lot of dancing, but where has it gotten him?
Aerobicizing at the Bronze:

Cordelia: "Ouch! Please keep your extreme oafishness off my $200 shoes."
Xander: "Sorry, I was just—"
Cordelia: "Getting off the floor before Annie Vega's boyfriend squashes you like a bug?"
—**"Angel"**

Then there was this scene from "Reptile Boy," which was expanded during filming. Although the shooting script called for a dark-haired wig, Xander actually wore a blond one. And he wore the bra over his bare chest:

A hideous wig of long, dark curls parked on [Xander's] head; an extremely large bra strapped over his shirt; a painful smile plastered on his face. Some of the guys swat him with paddles.

Linebacker: "Come on, dance, pretty boy! Come on, shake it! Don't break it!"
Xander: "Okay, big fun. Who's next?"
Tackle: "You are, doll face. Keep on dancing."
—**"Reptile Boy"**

Xander: "Aw, you just need cheering up. And I know just the thing [a few wild moves]. Crazed dance party at the Bronze!"
Buffy: "I don't know."
Xander: [restrained moves] "Very calm dance party at the Bronze." [no moves] "Moping at the Bronze."
—**"Lie to Me"**

Xander: "Having issues much?"
Buffy: "I am not!"
Xander points, with a mock-childish dance.
Xander: "You're having parental issues, you're having parental issues."
Willow: "Xander..."
Xander: "Freud would have said the exact same thing. Except he might not have done that little dance."
—**"Ted"**

Willow: [nailing crosses around her French doors], "I'm going to have a hard time explaining this to my dad."
Buffy: "You really think this'll bother him?"
Willow: "Ira Rosenberg's only daughter nailing crucifixes to her bedroom wall? I have to go to Xander's house just to watch *A Charlie Brown Christmas* every year."
Buffy: "Yeah, I see your point."
Willow: "Although it is worthwhile just to see Xander do the Snoopy dance." —**"Passion"**

Ted

WRITTEN BY David Greenwalt and Joss Whedon; **DIRECTED BY** Bruce Seth Green. **SPECIAL GUEST STAR:** John Ritter as Ted Buchanan. **GUEST STARS:** Kristine Sutherland as Joyce Summers, Robia LaMorte as Jenny Calendar; with Ken Thorley, James G. MacDonald, and Jeff Langton.

Buffy comes home to find her mother kissing a strange man. He is introduced as Ted, and he and Joyce have been seeing each other for some time. Buffy is leery of this new man in her mother's life. Xander and Willow disagree—sure, he talks like a '50s sitcom character, but he's a magnificent cook, and her mother seems happy. But Buffy is not convinced, especially after he threatens her during a miniature golf game when the pair of them are out of sight of the others.

When Buffy returns from a night of slaying, she finds Ted in her bedroom, having gone through her diary. She is justifiably angry at the invasion of her privacy, but her attempts to complain result in his striking her. That gives her the excuse she needs to wallop him—so much so that he falls down the stairs, dead. The police question her, and let her go for the time being.

Buffy is devastated at this abuse of her powers as the Slayer. But then, while Xander, Willow, and Cordelia dig deeper into Ted's life—finding drugs in his cookies, marriages dating to 1957, and odd things in his closet—Ted himself turns up alive at the Summers' house. He turns out to be a robot, and what's in his closet are his four previous wives....

Quote of the week:

"Buffy, I believe the subtext here is rapidly becoming text."

Giles, trying to find out what is irking Buffy

Love, Slayer style:

Giles makes an attempt to reconcile with Jenny, which she initially rebuffs. Later, when Giles is doing Buffy's rounds in her place following Ted's apparent death, Jenny attempts a reconciliation and proves that love means never having to say, "I'm sorry I shot you with a crossbow bolt."

Cordelia and Xander's tryst continues in secret (Xander later says pointedly, "I sometimes like things that are not good for me"), and Angel and Buffy indulge in smoochies while she helps him recover from his injuries.

In the final fight scene between Buffy and Ted, both Sarah Michelle Gellar and special guest star John Ritter were sick. Sarah had the flu, and John had food poisoning from the night before.

POP-CULTURE IQ:

In the teaser, Xander and Willow argue about the Captain &Tenille. At the episode's end, the Summers women want to rent a movie that has no horror and no romance, prompting Buffy to say, "I guess we're *Thelma & Louise*-ing it again."

CONTINUITY:

Cordelia mentions Giles's summoning of Eyghon after Giles talks about how hard it must be to be responsible for another's death ("Do let's bring that up as often as possible," Giles says tartly in response), and Eyghon's possession of Jenny continues to haunt both her and her relationship with Giles ("The Dark Age"). Angel is still recovering from Drusilla's revival ceremony ("What's My Line? Part 2").

WRITTEN BY Marti Noxon; **DIRECTED BY** David Greenwalt. **GUEST STARS:** Kristine Sutherland as Joyce Summers, Jeremy Ratchford as Lyle Gorch, James Parks as Tector Gorch, Danny Strong as Jonathan; with Rick Zieff, Eric Whitmore, and Brie McCaddin.

Bad Eggs

The Gorch brothers—who were a couple of lunatic hellraisers in the Wild West *before* they were turned into vampires—have arrived in Sunnydale. Buffy is busy helping Giles research them, and so misses health class, wherein the students are broken into pairs and given the responsibility of eggs to care for as if they were children. Buffy, having been absent, gets to be a single mother to "Eggbert."

However, these are not ordinary eggs, but the offspring of a bezoar that lives under the school and has now come to life. The offspring bond to human hosts, and several students and adults—including Willow, Cordelia, Giles, and Joyce—become drones for the bezoar. Only Buffy—who slays the offspring before it can bond with her—and Xander—who hard-boiled his "child"—escape unharmed. Of course, Buffy's attempts to stop the bezoar are hindered by the Gorch brothers deciding to attack.

Quote of the week:

"They're such a—oh, I don't want to say burden, but, uh...Actually, I kind of do want to say burden."

Joyce Summers, on children and parenting

Love, Slayer style:

Xander and Cordelia continue their tryst, complete with constant arguing, both in private and in public, the latter particularly in health class. (Xander: "This would work a lot better for me if you didn't talk." Cordy: "Well, it would work a lot better for me with the lights off.")

Angel and Buffy can't keep their hands off each other when they're supposed to be patrolling. When discussing possibilities of the future, Buffy says, "Angel, when I look into the future, all I see is you—all I want is you," which is fairly tragic in retrospect.

BUFFY'S BAG OF TRICKS:

She uses one of the pickaxs the drones are using to slay the monster.

Surprise

WRITTEN BY Marti Noxon;
DIRECTED BY Michael Lange.
GUEST STARS: Seth Green as Oz,
Kristine Sutherland as Joyce
Summers, Robia LaMorte as
Jenny Calendar, Brian Thompson as the Judge, Eric Saiet as Dalton, Mercedes McNab as Harmony; special guest stars Vincent Schiavelli as Uncle Enyos, James Marsters as Spike, Juliet Landau as Drusilla.

On the morning before her seventeenth birthday, Buffy has a dream that Drusilla is still alive and that she will kill Angel. This worries Buffy and the Slayerettes, but does not deter the latter from planning a surprise party for Buffy at the Bronze the following night. Meanwhile, a wheelchair-bound Spike and a restored Drusilla are planning to reconstruct the Judge, a creature whose purpose is to literally burn the humanity out of humankind, leaving only the evil to survive.

Though it cannot be killed "by any weapon forged," it was once dismembered, the parts spread to the four corners of the Earth—but now being brought to Sunnydale. Buffy intercepts the delivery of an arm, and Jenny and Angel agree that Angel should take it somewhere far away—a journey that would take months.

Buffy is reluctant to part with Angel, but as they kiss and say good-bye at the docks, vampires attack and retake the arm. Angel and Buffy brave the Factory to try and stop them, but the Judge is already assembled, and the pair barely escape with their lives. They return to Angel's apartment and find refuge in each others' arms, making love for the first time. But afterward, Angel feels strange....

Quote of the week:

"My boyfriend had a bicentennial."
—Buffy to Willow, re: Angel

Love, Slayer style:

Angel finally comes out and says he loves Buffy, though his feelings have been obvious since "Teacher's Pet." Before his planned departure, he gives Buffy a claddagh ring, which is as close to a wedding as these two are ever likely to get. After their abortive attack on Spike, Drusilla, and the Judge, they finally give in to their passion—with, as shown in "Innocence," devastating consequences.

Buffy convinces Willow to take a shot at dating Oz. The pair agree to go on a date in an adorable and hilarious scene. Xander makes an attempt to convince Cordelia to make their relationship public, but Cordy will hear none of it. And Spike and Drusilla are as devoted to each other as ever—indeed, the Judge smells the "stink of humanity" on them thanks to their affection for each other.

CONTINUITY:

The tent-like building where all the Buffy sets are constructed is called "the El Niño building."

Jenny Calendar is revealed to be Janna of the same Romany tribe that cursed Angel eighty years previous ("Angel," "Becoming, Part 1"), and she is warned by her uncle that Angel is becoming too happy. Buffy once again has prophetic dreams ("Welcome to the Hellmouth," "Prophecy Girl," "Innocence"). Oz finds out the truth about vampires and joins the ever-expanding Slayerettes.

From the original teleplay:

The following scene was cut from this episode's script for length:

Jenny: "I guess it makes sense. I mean, all of Buffy's senses are heightened. Why should her intuition be different?"

Giles: "Precisely. It's not unheard-of for the Slayer to start having prophetic dreams and visions as she approaches adulthood."

Jenny: "Adulthood? Buffy's seventeen tomorrow, Giles. Don't rush her."

Giles: "I'm not the one rushing her. While I'm loathe to say it, the fact is, the Slayer rarely lives into her mid-twenties. It follows that she'd exhibit signs of maturity early on. Her whole life cycle is accelerated."

Jenny: "Still, you should be careful about treating her like a grown-up. Like—this thing with Angel. Have you even talked to her about it?"

Giles: "I . . . I suppose I try not to pry."

Jenny: "Maybe you should, a little. The way she talks, it's clear she has intense feelings for him."

Giles: "Well, yes. They're friends. . . ."

Jenny: "They're more than friends, and you know it."

Giles: "I'm not her father, Jenny."

Jenny: "She looks up to you. She'll never actually say that, but she does. And I just think, at her age, it's easy to get in over your head. She could make some bad choices here. Trust me on this one."

Giles: "I'll keep an eye to it. Right now, I'm worried enough trying to think of the right birthday present."

> Spike's duster cost more than Angel's, a whopping $1,600. It was heavily "distressed" by the costume department.

> The docks sequence was filmed in San Pedro. The water was not as cold as anticipated, because of a warm, El Niño current.

WRITTEN AND DIRECTED BY Joss Whedon. **GUEST STARS:** Seth Green as Oz, Kristine Sutherland as Joyce Summers, Robia LaMorte as Jenny Calendar, Brian Thompson as the Judge; special guest stars Vincent Schiavelli as Uncle Enyos, James Marsters as Spike, Juliet Landau as Drusilla; with James Lurie, Carla Madden, Parry Shen, and Ryan Francis.

Angel's soul is again lost, and he has reverted to the same old vampire he was prior to the Romany curse. Spike and Drusilla are thrilled to find their sire back in the saddle, and invite him to join them in destroying the world with the Judge. Buffy, meanwhile, knows only that Angel has disappeared, and the Slayerettes are no closer to finding out anything useful about how to stop the Judge.

When Buffy finally finds Angel, he is standoffish and dismissive of her feelings. Then he attacks Willow at the school, though Xander and Buffy manage to drive him off. Jenny, under pressure from Buffy, reveals that she knew about the curse, that it was removed, and that she had been sent to Sunnydale to keep an eye on Angel. She takes Buffy to her uncle, but Angel has gotten there first and killed him. Xander, meanwhile,

comes up with a plan: to use a missile launcher, a weapon that is made, not forged, against the Judge. It works, but Buffy finds it impossible to kill Angel when she confronts him.

Quote of the week:

"My God! You people are all— Well, I'm upset, and I can't think of a mean word right now, but that's what you are, and we're going to the Factory!"

Willow, insisting, along with Xander, that they go after Angel and Buffy, who have not checked in since their attack on the Factory

Love, Slayer style:

Angel and Buffy obviously are on the outs; indeed, Angel is disgusted with the way he acted around the Slayer, and is determined to hurt her in much the same way he hurt Drusilla before he turned her into a vampire. His initial foray is a textbook example of the Insensitive Male After Sex, culminating with, "I'll call you." He also starts his campaign to come between Spike and Drusilla ("Bewitched, Bothered, and Bewildered," etc.).

Xander and Cordelia are caught kissing by a devastated Willow. ("It's against all laws of God and man!") Xander's attempt to explain that it doesn't mean anything fall on deaf ears, as Willow realizes that, "You'd rather be with someone you hate than be with me." Later, Willow asks Oz if he wants to make out with her, which he politely declines, knowing that she's only doing it to get back at Xander; the maturity of this response charms Willow.

The Giles and Jenny coupling comes to a screeching halt with the revelation of Jenny's true reason for being in Sunnydale.

> Often the scripts will contain some wry humor even in the stage directions. In the script for this episode, Joss Whedon wrote, "A couple of soldiers pass. Xander suavely nods to them. They nod back and pass without comment, because they are extras."

CONTINUITY:

Buffy continues to have prophetic dreams ("Welcome to the Hellmouth," "Prophecy Girl," "Surprise"). Xander's memories of his transformation into a soldier remain intact ("Halloween") and allow him and Cordelia to successfully break into an armory and make off with the missile launcher, and also allow Xander to instruct Buffy in its use.

From the original teleplay:

The following exchange was cut from this episode's script for length:

Gypsy Man: "You! Evil one!"
Angel: "Evil one? Oh, man, now I've got hurt feelings."
Gypsy Man: "What do you want?"

Angel: "A whole lot. Got a lot of lost time to make up for. Say, I guess that's kind of your fault, isn't it? You Gypsy types, you go and curse people, you really don't care who gets hurt. Of course, you did give me an escape clause, so I gotta thank you for that."

Gypsy Man: "You are an abomination. The day you stop suffering for your crimes, you are no longer worthy of a human soul."

Angel: "Well, that pesky little critter's all gone. So we can get down to business....Don't worry, it won't hurt a bit...after the first hour."

> The multiplex/mall set was in a closed Robinsons/May department store on South Grand Avenue in Los Angeles. A moat was built around the set to catch the water from the overhead sprinklers.

> Another Whedon stage direction, regarding Xander and Cordelia kissing: "They haben der big smootchen."

WILD KINGDOM

Angel: "I'm just an animal, right?"
Buffy: "You're not an animal. Animals I like."
—"ANGEL"

Animals are important to the denizens of Sunnydale, on and off the set. David Boreanaz has a dog named Bertha Blue, who has "one ear that goes up and one ear that goes down." Sometimes he brings her to his trailer, but she's run away a number of times. Still, they've always found each other again.

Nicholas Brendon rescued his dog from the streets, where a kid was feeding him bubble gum. David B. says, "Nick's a dog freak." In their spare time, David and Nicholas hang out together and sometimes take their dogs to the dog park together.

Alyson Hannigan keeps Alex, a Jack Russell terrier, in her trailer. When she walks him around the lot, she says to producer Gareth Davies, "This is a mythical dog," as animals are not officially allowed. At home, with her roommate, she has another dog, Zippy, and five cats: Dr. Seuss, Jupiter, Tear Drop, Rain, and Lucky.

Costume designer Cynthia Bergstrom has a beautiful Keeshond named Sammy, who spends the occasional day in the wardrobe department.

And Buffy—Sarah Michelle Gellar—also has pets, including a white Maltese named Thor.

As for the animals in *Buffy*, let's have a moment of silence for Sunnydale High's late (crunchy) mascot, Herbert the Pig. And for a dog named Spritzer, whose demise at the hands (and teeth) of demon Jenny Calendar was cut from "The Dark Age." And, finally, for Willow's fish, which Angel kills in "Passion."

And fish are not all that Angel kills:

Giles [reading aloud]: "Ah, here's another. Valentine's Day, yes, Angel nails a puppy to—"
Buffy: "Skip it."
Giles: "But—"
Buffy: "I don't want to know. I don't have a puppy. We can skip it."
—**"BEWITCHED, BOTHERED, AND BEWILDERED"**

Willow: "Thanks for having me over, Buffy. Especially on a school night and all."
Buffy: "Hey, no problem. Sorry about your fish."
Willow: "It's okay, we hadn't really had time to bond yet. I just got them for Hanukkah. Although, for the first time, I'm glad my parents didn't let me have a puppy."
—**"PASSION"**

On the lighter side and in happier times, Angel seemed to enjoy spending quality time with Buffy's stuffed-animal porker, Mr. Gordo.

And then there's that werewolf deal with the lead guitarist of Dingoes Ate My Baby:

> **"You're talking obedience school, paper training. Oz would be burying all their stuff in the backyard. And that kind of breed can turn on its owner."**
>
> Xander, in "PHASES"

Phases

WRITTEN BY Rob Des Hotel and Dean Batali; **DIRECTED BY** Bruce Seth Green. **GUEST STARS:** Seth Green as Oz, Camila Griggs as the gym teacher, Jack Conley as Cain, Larry Bagby III as Larry, Megahn Perry as Theresa, and Keith Campbell as the werewolf.

Xander and Cordelia are making out in Cordy's car when they are interrupted by the vicious attack of a werewolf. Giles is intrigued by the idea of a werewolf in Sunnydale—"one of the classics"—but intrigue turns to concern as he and Buffy encounter a hunter named Cain who wants to kill the werewolf for its pelt, and then a Sunnydale High student named Theresa is found dead. As the Slayerettes try to figure out who the werewolf might be—Xander's theory that it's Larry, one of the school jocks, turns out to be very erroneous—Willow tries to determine why Oz is acting so weird.

When she goes to his house to confront him, she finds him transforming into a werewolf. Buffy, Giles, and Willow manage to bring the werewolf down and keep Cain from killing their friend.

The pines outside Buffy's window are deodara pines.

"That's great, Larry, you've really mastered the single entendre."

Oz, after Larry makes a crudely sexual remark about Buffy and Willow

Love, Slayer style:

Oz and Willow have started dating (the episode begins with them discussing the movie they went to the previous night), but Willow is frustrated that he hasn't made a further move. ("But I want smoochies!") At the end, after Oz's lycanthropy is revealed, they decide to keep the relationship going, and they have their first kiss which Willow initiates.

Buffy is still smarting from Angel's reversion to type. When she learns that Theresa's death was caused not by the werewolf, but by Angel—confirmed when Theresa rises as a vampire and tells her that Angel says hi—Buffy finds comfort in Xander's arms briefly before leaving, causing the latter to mutter, "Oh, no, my life's not *too* complicated." Meanwhile, Xander and Cordelia's relationship continues apace, thus prompting a catty comment from Willow: "What's his number? Oh yeah: 1-800-I'm-dating-a-skanky-ho.'" Despite this, Willow and Cordy find themselves bonding in the Bronze over the inadequacies of the men in their lives.

Giles appears to be having trouble dealing with Jenny's apparent betrayal, as his behavior is slightly off throughout the ordeal—he even laughs at one of Xander's jokes.

BUFFY'S BAG OF TRICKS:

Not wanting to kill the werewolf, Buffy tries using a chain on it when they first clash at the Bronze. Later on, Giles employs a tranquilizer gun, which Willow actually wields in the end. Xander uses an easel in the funeral home to stake Theresa.

CONTINUITY:

Oz first discovers that he is a werewolf in this episode. Oz also notices the moving eyes of the cheerleader trophy ("The Witch"). Xander cites his temporary infusion with the spirit of a hyena as evidence that he understands where the werewolf is coming from ("The Pack"; by doing so, he also inadvertently reveals that he does, in fact, remember that entire experience, despite his claims at the end of that episode).

Seth Green and Alyson Hannigan, whose characters officially become boyfriend and girlfriend in this episode, also appeared as boyfriend and girlfriend in the film *My Stepmother Is an Alien*.

From the original teleplay:

The following exchange, during a self-defense class, appeared in the original script but not in the episode because of length:

Xander (to Cordelia): "Be gentle with me."
Cordelia (to Willow): "You first. I wouldn't want to be accused of taking your place in line."
Willow: "Oh, I think you pushed your way to the front long before this."
Cordelia: "Hey, I can't help it if I get the spotlight just because some people blend into the background."
Willow: "Well, maybe some people could see better if you weren't standing on the auction block, shaking your wares."
Cordelia: "Sorry, we haven't all perfected that phony 'girl next door' bit."
Willow: "You could be the girl next door, too. If Xander lived next to a brothel!"

WRITTEN BY Marti Noxon; **DIRECTED BY** James A. Conter.
GUEST STARS: Seth Green as Oz, Kristine Sutherland as Joyce Summers, Robia LaMorte as Jenny Calendar, Elizabeth Anne Allen as Amy Madison, Mercedes McNab as Harmony, James Marsters as Spike, Juliet Landau as Drusilla; with Jennie Chester, Lorna Scott, Kristen Winnicki, and Tamara Braun.

Bewitched, Bothered, and Bewildered

It's Valentine's Day, and all is not well. Giles is concerned for Buffy, given Angel's past history of tormenting people on this particular holiday, and Cordelia has noticed a downsurge in her own popularity since her relationship with Xander went public. As Angel leaves a box of roses for Buffy with a note saying, "Soon," Cordy breaks up with Xander just after he gives her a gorgeous silver locket as a Valentine's Day present. Now the laughingstock of the entire school, a heartbroken Xander turns to Amy—who has decided to take on her mother's calling of witchcraft—for a love spell that would make Cordelia love him and allow *him* to dump *her*, giving her a taste of the humiliation he's enduring. The spell backfires and instead makes every woman in Sunnydale *except* Cordelia fall for Xander. This leads to fierce jealousy and mob rage (Amy at one point transforms Buffy into a rat), as the entire female population of Sunnydale—including Drusilla and Joyce Summers—tries to kill both Xander (for not loving them) and Cordelia (for daring to break his heart). With Giles's help, Amy reverses the spell, and things revert to something resembling normal.

Buffy: "Slaying is a tad more perilous than dating."
Xander: "Obviously, you're not dating Cordelia."

Love, Slayer style:

Xander buys an expensive gift for Cordelia, which he gives to her just before she breaks up with him. Xander—who had asked Buffy to pick his clothes for the evening (she picks a wardrobe that looks like it comes straight from Angel's closet)—is devastated, to say the least, especially given that the breakup is on Valentine's Day. ("Were you running low on dramatic irony?") After learning the extent to which she broke Xander's heart, not to mention the realization that dumping Xander to satisfy her shallow friends was simply not worth it, Cordelia gets back together with him. ("I'll date who I want to date—no matter how lame he is.")

Oz and Willow's relationship continues apace (Willow gets to enthuse, "My boyfriend's in the band!" at one point), and when Willow's love-spelled heart is broken by Xander not returning her affections, she spends all night crying on the phone to Oz.

On the vampire side of things, the love triangle among the bad guys thickens: Spike gets Drusilla a piece of jewelry, but Angel gives her a heart—ripped from the chest of a "quaint little shop girl"—which she seems to like better, to Spike's annoyance.

POP-CULTURE IQ:

In the script, when Oz is searching for the Buffy rat, he's singing Michael Jackson's ode to rats, "Ben."

> Oz's guitar is inscribed with the words "Sweet J."

CONTINUITY:

Jenny makes two attempts to reconcile with Giles following the events of "Innocence," but the first is cut off by circumstances, and the second by Jenny falling victim to the love spell.

Passion

WRITTEN BY Ty King; **DIRECTED BY** Michael E. Gershman.
GUEST STARS: Kristine Sutherland as Joyce Summers, Robia LaMorte as Jenny Calendar, James Marsters as Spike, Juliet Landau as Drusilla; with Richard Assad.

Buffy wakes up to find a charcoal drawing of herself sleeping left on her bed by Angel, and Willow finds her fish dead in an envelope in her bedroom. At their behest, Giles searches for a spell that will uninvite the vampire from the Summers and Rosenberg residences. The spell comes from Jenny, meant as a reconciliation gesture. Angel, meanwhile, plays the stalking ex-boyfriend role on Joyce, complete with mention of the

Director Michael Gershmann is also the series' director of photography. The first two seasons of *Buffy* were shot on super 16mm film stock.

fact that they made love, which leads to a rather difficult conversation between Joyce and her daughter.

Meanwhile, Jenny is working to try and translate the spell that would return Angel's soul to him. Late one night, she finally does so, saving the file to a disk and printing it out. However, Angel has learned of this project, thanks to a prophetic vision from Drusilla, and destroys Jenny's computer and the printout, and brutally kills Jenny. He then places the body in Giles's bedroom, setting the place up with champagne and flowers, making it all the more devastating when he finds the corpse. The move backfires rather spectacularly, as Giles firebombs the Factory and manages to do some serious damage to Angel before the vampire gets the upper hand. Luckily, Buffy shows up and proceeds to pound Angel, though she is forced to cut it short in order to save Giles from the fire.

Quote of the week:

"You're supposed to kill her, not leave gag gifts in her friends' beds."
Spike, criticizing Angel's methods

Love, Slayer style:

Jenny has a few heartfelt conversations with Giles ("I know you feel betrayed." "Yes, well, that's one of the unpleasant side effects of betrayal"), even admitting she loves him. Despite Buffy's anger at Jenny, the Slayer does encourage Jenny to try to reconcile with Giles because he misses her, even if he won't admit it. Her death puts Giles in full "Ripper" mode.

The Angel-Drusilla-Spike triangle gets worse. Dru gets Spike a puppy that she names Sunshine, which makes Spike feel like he needs to be fed like a child, and Angel's jokes about Spike's wheelchair-bound condition grow crueler.

POP-CULTURE IQ:

"If Giles wants to go after the fiend that killed his girlfriend, I say, 'Faster, pussycat, kill, kill!'"
Xander, on Giles's course of action following Jenny's murder, referring to the title of a Russ Meyer movie

CONTINUITY:

The Slayerettes cast a spell that uninvites Angel from the Summers house ("Angel"), the Rosenberg house ("Lie to Me"), and Cordelia's car ("Some Assembly Required"). When Buffy warns her mother about Angel possibly coming around, Joyce remembers him as, "the college boy who's tutoring you in history" ("Angel"). Using a computer program, Jenny manages to re-create the spell that originally cursed Angel ("Angel," "Surprise," "Innocence"), but the only copy is on a disk that falls under her desk, where it remains until "Becoming, Part 1." At the end of the episode, Willow becomes the substitute computer-science teacher, a post she winds up retaining for the balance of the school year

("I Only Have Eyes for You," "Go Fish," "Becoming, Part 1"). The Factory, which has been vampire headquarters all season ("When She Was Bad," etc.), is destroyed by Giles, which will lead Angel, Spike, and Drusilla to take up residence in the mansion ("I Only Have Eyes for You").

From the original teleplay:

During the sequence just after Jenny is killed, we hear Angel in voice-over while we watch through the window of Buffy's home as the phone rings and she and Willow learn of Jenny's death. What follows is the dialogue the viewer can't hear:

Willow: "So was it horrible?" (referring to "The Talk" between Buffy and her mom)
Buffy: "It wasn't too horrible." [phone rings] "Hello?"
Giles (on the phone): "Buffy?"
Buffy: "Giles! Hey, we finished the spe—"
Giles (on phone): "Jenny... Ms. Calendar...she's been killed."
Buffy: "What...?"
Giles (on phone): "It was Angel."
Buffy drops the phone.
Willow: "Buffy?" [She picks up the phone] "Giles?"
Giles (on phone): "Willow. Angel's killed Jenny."
Willow: "What? No...oh...no..."
Joyce: "Willow! My God, Buffy! What's wrong? Has something happened?"

IN MY ROOM

Besides a desk drawer filled with stakes and holy water and a trunk with a false bottom loaded with communion wafers, yet more stakes, garlic, and holy water, what does today's Slayer keep in her bedroom?

With a framed picture of Xander and Willow by her bedside, Buffy's room looks very much like that belonging to any other seventeen-year-old girl. Here are some of the objects in the Chosen One's private abode:

- dolls and stuffed animals, including: a big Harlequin witch doll, a cow doll, a pink pig, a blue teddy bear, a black and white panda, and a green creature in a dress
- an umbrella with Chinese characters on it and a small dressing screen with a similar design
- a snow globe
- a straw hat and scarves hanging on the wall
- a black-light lamp

- two lamps with upside-down shades
- a purple and black pyramid candle
- celestial matters: a sun-and-moon art object with a face and a green-and-yellow moon box on the second shelf of her bookcase
- a wicker chair and a wicker shelf
- butterflies

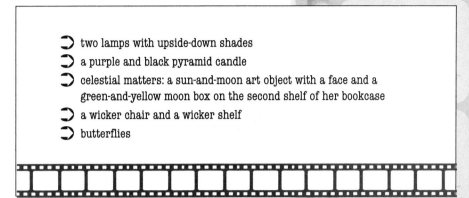

WRITTEN BY Rob Des Hotel and Dean Batali; **DIRECTED BY** Deran Sarafian. **GUEST STARS:** Kristine Sutherland as Joyce Summers, Richard Herd as Dr. Backer, Willie Garson as Don, Andrew Ducote as Ryan, Juanita Jennings as Dr. Wilkinson; with Denise Johnson as Celia, Mimi Paley as little Buffy, Robert Munic as the E.R. intern, and James Jude Courtney as Der Kindestod.

Killed By Death

Buffy is out patrolling, despite suffering from a flu bug. After a run-in with Angel, she collapses and is brought to the hospital. After she is stabilized and admitted, she has a dream about a strange-looking creature and a young boy—except the young boy is really in the kids' ward with a similar flu, and he has also seen the creature. The boy, Ryan, says that the creature is Death, informs her that children have died because of him, and then gives Buffy a drawing of the creature, which only kids can see. Initial research points to a more mundane source of the kids' deaths: Dr. Backer, who has used unorthodox cures in the past. However, Buffy discovers the slashed corpse of Dr. Backer, killed by an invisible creature that attacks Buffy.

Eventually, Giles and Cordelia discover that it's Der Kindestod—German for *child death*, a monster that can be seen only by children and also feeds on them. Buffy realizes that she can see it only when she's feverish and convinces Willow to give her a small dose of the fever to make her sick enough to see it. The question is, will she be too sick to fight it? Of course, the answer is no. She's the Slayer, after all.

Cordelia brings Xander Krispy Kreme donuts, considered by many to be elite among donuts. There is also only one Krispy Kreme in the Los Angeles area, so there's an implication that Cordelia went quite a ways to get Xander his breakfast.

Quote of the week:

"Tact is just not saying true stuff. I'll pass."

Cordelia, summarizing her character in ten words or less

Love, Slayer style:

Angel and Buffy's tête-à-têtes continue, first with his attack on a weakened Buffy in the graveyard, then in an attempt to visit her at the hospital, stopped by Xander, of all people. Xander spends most of the episode playing Buffy's White Knight, to Angel's amusement ("You still love her," he sneers. "It must eat you up that I got there first") and Cordelia's annoyance. Indeed, Xander and Cordelia snipe throughout the episode, with Cordy making a sweet peace gesture by bringing Xander—loyally standing guard at the hospital against Angel's returning—donuts and coffee.

POP-CULTURE IQ:

"If he asks you to play chess, don't even do it. Guy's like a *whiz*."

Xander, on Death, referring to the portrayal of Death in the Ingmar Bergman film *The Seventh Seal*, as well as *Bill and Ted's Bogus Journey* when the heroes meet Death.

It's also established that Buffy used to pretend she was the DC Comics superhero Power Girl as a kid—a character who is also blond, tough, and super-strong

CONTINUITY:

It's established that Buffy encountered Der Kindestod as an eight-year-old, when she saw her cousin Celia die in a hospital—that trauma would keep her hating hospitals ever since.

Joyce expresses her sympathy to Giles on the death of Jenny Calendar, and Giles later expresses concern that, in the wake of that murder ("Passion"), Buffy is making up the "death" creature to give her something to fight. Willow makes use of her fear of frogs ("What's My Line? Part 1") to distract hospital security. Xander tells Angel, "You're going to die and I'm going to be there," a semi-foreshadow of "Becoming, Part 2."

I Only Have Eyes for You

WRITTEN BY Marti Noxon; **DIRECTED BY** James Whitmore Jr. **GUEST STARS:** Chris Gorham as James, John Hawkes as the janitor, Meredith Salinger as Grace Newman, James Marsters as Spike, Juliet Landau as Drusilla, and Armin Shimerman as Principal Snyder.

On the night before the Sadie Hawkins Dance, Buffy is heading toward the library, only to encounter a boy about to kill a girl with a gun. As soon as Buffy knocks the gun from his hand, though, both of them regain their senses—the pair have no idea why they were fighting—and the gun disappears. Later, in Principal Snyder's office,

something knocks the 1955 yearbook off the principal's shelf in front of Buffy, and then, while bored to tears in history class, she gets a vision from the '50s of a Sunnydale High student named James and a teacher named Miss Newman, who seemed to have a relationship.

Strangeness continues as Xander is attacked by a dessicated arm in his locker, snakes start appearing in the school, and a janitor and a teacher play out the exact same scene as the two students did earlier—but without Buffy to interfere, the scene results in

> All the actors' shoes have rubber soles to cut down on noise that might be picked up while shooting.

the janitor shooting the woman. Willow discovers the story of James and Miss Newman, who had an illicit affair in 1955, and on the night of the Sadie Hawkins Dance, he killed her and then shot himself in the head. The Slayerettes figure it's a poltergeist: James's spirit trying to resolve the conflict. An attempt at an exorcism fails, and finally the spirits confront each other yet again—this time with James inhabiting Buffy and Miss Newman inhabiting Angel.

Quote of the week:

"Don't walk away from me, bitch!"

Said by James, the boy at the beginning, the janitor, and Buffy, and written on the blackboard at the poltergeist's urging by Mr. Miller

Love, Slayer style:

> Writer and story editor Marti Noxon loves ghost stories. She said of this episode, "I know my mom will cry when she sees it."

Willow gives Giles a stone that she found in Jenny's desk. "She told me it's rose quartz—that it has healing powers. I thought she'd want you to have it." Later, Giles convinces himself that the poltergeist is Jenny, even though there's no evidence to support it.

Buffy's unresolved issues over Angel color her judgment throughout the episode, both preventing her from accepting an invitation to the dance and in dealing with James's spirit, for whom she has no forgiveness.

POP-CULTURE IQ:

> Costume designer Cynthia Bergstrom is haunted by Jenny Calendar. She finds herself shopping for Robia LaMorte's character, though she's no longer on the series.

"Yeah, but if I see a floating pipe and a smoking jacket, he's dropped."

Xander, in an oblique reference to *The Invisible Man*

"Are you crazy? I saw that movie. Even the priests died!"

Cordelia, upon Willow mentioning an exorcism, referring to the movie *The Exorcist*

CONTINUITY:

Buffy has a dream with visions, but unlike her prophetic dreams ("Welcome to the Hellmouth," "Prophecy Girl," "Surprise," "Innocence"), this shows the past, is very specific in its imagery, and is provided by the ghost of James. Willow is still teaching Jenny Calendar's computer classes ("Passion," "Go Fish," "Becoming, Part 1"). Angel, Drusilla, and Spike move into the mansion following the destruction of the Factory ("Passion"), and Spike secretly gets up out of his wheelchair at the very end ("Becoming"). More hints that Snyder and the town authorities know more about the local weirdness are dropped ("School Hard," "Becoming, Part 2").

> Although the show has dealt with many a disturbing subject, this is the first one that has prompted a public-service announcement. Following the end of the final act, Sarah Michelle Gellar did a voice-over on the dangers of teen suicide and giving information on the American Association of Suicide Prevention.

Go Fish

WRITTEN BY David Fury and Elin Hampton; **DIRECTED BY** David Semel. **GUEST STARS:** Conchata Ferrell as Nurse Ruth Greenliegh, Wentworth Miller as Gage Petronzi, Charles Cyphers as Coach Carl Marin, Jake Patellis as Dodd McAlvy, Jeremy Garrett as Cameron Walker, and Armin Shimerman as Principal Snyder; with Danny Strong as Jonathon.

The Sunnydale High swim team has become the darling of the school, thanks to its actually winning several meets, putting it one up on the school's other teams. This extends to Principal Snyder's encouraging Willow to give a swimmer with an F a better grade and refusing to see Buffy's side of the story when she attacks another swimmer who tries to grope her. To make matters worse, the two best swimmers have apparently been killed by something that skinned them alive. Suspicion initially falls on Jonathon, a boy who was tormented by the team, but all he did was pee in the pool.

When Gage, the third-best swimmer, is attacked by Angel—who proceeds to spit out Gage's blood as if it were battery acid—they

> Though we knew there were docks nearby, this is the first time we find out that Sunnydale is actually a coastal town with a beach.

suspect steroid enhancement. When Gage transforms into a gill monster, leaving his skin behind, the slayerettes realize that none of them died, and it was more than steroids. Xander goes undercover, joining the swim team to get to the bottom of things. In the end, the newly mutated fish-men eat their coach and swim out to sea.

> Sunnydale High students have interesting reading tastes. Some of the magazines the school receives for its library are *Vegetarian Times*, *Women's Sports and Fitness*, *Upscale*, *National Geographic*, *PC World*, *Slam*, *Skin Diver*, *Sports Illustrated*, *ArtNews*, *Smithsonian*, *Bon Appetit*, and *Horseman*.

Quote of the week:

"That is wrong. Big, fat, spanking wrong. It's a slap in the face to every one of us that studied hard and worked long hours to earn our D's."

Xander, expressing outrage over Snyder's encouraging Willow to raise Gage's grade from an F to a D

Love, Slayer style:

Buffy finally gives in and decides to go on a date—with Cameron, who turns out to be stultifyingly dull and a pervert (and, later, a gill monster). Cordelia sees Xander wearing a Speedo and thinks that dating him isn't such an awful idea after all.

BUFFY'S BAG OF TRICKS:

She uses a lacrosse stick on two of the gill monsters.

POP-CULTURE IQ:

Giles: "He was eviscerated. Nothing left but skin and cartilage."
Xander: "In other words...'This was no boating accident!'"
—Referring to a famous line from the film *Jaws*

"Swim team. Hardly what I call a team. The Yankees. Abbott and Costello. The A. Those were teams."

Xander, bitter over the attention the swim team is receiving, referring to baseball, the classic comedy duo, and the '80s action series *A-Team*, starring Mr. T

CONTINUITY:

Willow is made a permanent substitute computer teacher through to the end of the term ("Passion," etc.).

> The long shots of the Bronze, which imply that it is on a block of warehouses, actually show the building that houses the sets where the series is filmed.

Angel's dimly lit apartment is rather sparse for someone who's 242 years old. Apparently, he enjoys a Spartan lifestyle. He has a striking chair upholstered in a blue feather design, a table with an antique ashtray and cigarette lighter, a statue in a glass case, and the many sketches he has drawn of Buffy and her loved ones. Also, a desk that looks as though he uses it, which begs the question, does Angel pay his own utility bills?

Becoming
PART 1

WRITTEN AND DIRECTED BY Joss Whedon. **GUEST STARS:** Seth Green as Oz, Kristine Sutherland as Joyce Summers, Max Perlich as Whistler, Bianca Lawson as Kendra, Julie Benz as Darla, James Marsters as Spike, Juliet Landau as Drusilla, and Armin Shimerman as Principal Snyder; with Richard Riehle as Merrick, Jack McGee, and Nina Girvitz.

The construction of a new housing project has unearthed the sarcophagus of Acathla, a demon that was turned to stone by a knight. Angel makes off with the sarcophagus and wishes to use the demon to bring about Hell on Earth, destroying everything. Meanwhile, Buffy and Willow discover the backup disk that Jenny Calendar had made with the translation of the spell to restore Angel's soul. Though Xander thinks re-cursing Angel is a mistake and Giles thinks Willow isn't ready to channel that kind of magic, Willow prepares to cast the spell.

Kendra reappears with the sword blessed by the knight who imprisoned Acathla, and a warning from her Watcher that something awful is about to happen. Angel's first attempt to make that something awful happen fails, and so he lures Buffy away from the library so Drusilla can lead a raiding party to kidnap Giles. That raid leaves Willow comatose with a nasty head injury, Xander with a broken wrist, Giles kidnapped, and Kendra slaughtered. Buffy returns to the library just in time for Kendra's dying breath—and the arrival of the cops, accusing her of the murder.

Quote of the week:

"It's a big rock. I can't wait to tell my friends. They don't have a rock this big."

Spike, less than impressed with Acathla's sarcophagus

Love, Slayer style:

In one of the episode's many flashbacks, Angel gets his first look at Buffy when Merrick first tells her she is the Chosen One, and it's obviously love at first sight.

BUFFY'S BAG OF TRICKS:

She is given a sword by Kendra to stop the demon, and Kendra also gives Buffy her favorite stake, which she has named "Mr. Pointy."

POP-CULTURE IQ:

Buffy mispronounces Acathla as "Alfalfa" (likely referring to the *Little Rascals* character) and "Al Franken" (referring to the comedian/writer/actor).

CONTINUITY:

This episode is festooned with flashbacks that detail important events in the lives of the characters: Darla turning Angel into a vampire ("Angel"), Angel torturing Drusilla ("Lie to Me"), Angel being cursed by the Romany people ("Angel," "Surprise," "Innocence"), and Buffy's first learning that she is the Slayer ("Welcome to the Hellmouth"). The disk with the spell to restore Angel is rediscovered ("Passion"), though Willow's attempt to cast it is interrupted; her next chance comes in "Becoming, Part 2." Angel's diversion of Buffy to get at the Slayerettes mirrors the similar stunt executed by the Anointed One and Absalom in "When She Was Bad," of which Angel reminds Buffy.

The stuntwoman who was set on fire for the vampiric "immolation-o-gram" is named Cindy Folkerson. She has been set on fire more times than any other stuntwoman in Hollywood.

From the original teleplay:

The following line was cut from the script for length:

Whistler: "There are three kinds of people that no one understands: geniuses, madmen, and guys that mumble."

Becoming
PART 2

WRITTEN AND DIRECTED BY Joss Whedon. **GUEST STARS:** Seth Green as Oz, Kristine Sutherland as Joyce Summers, Robia LaMorte as Jenny Calendar, Max Perlich as Whistler, James Marsters as Spike, Juliet Landau as Drusilla, and Armin Shimerman as Principal Snyder.

Joss Whedon's stage directions this time around included, "Yes, it's sunrise. Sue me." Sunrises and sunsets are almost impossible to film because they are so brief and difficult to schedule, much less capture on film.

Buffy runs from the cops before they can mistakenly arrest her for Kendra's murder. She later goes to the hospital to learn that Xander's arm is broken but fine and Willow's still in a coma. Whistler shows up and tells Buffy she has to know how to use the sword, but his importuning falls on frustrated ears. Spike then approaches Buffy with a proposal: a temporary alliance against Angel in exchange for Spike and Drusilla's being allowed to leave Sunnydale. Reluctantly, Buffy agrees. Meanwhile, Willow awakens from her coma and insists on trying to cast the spell again, and Angel is physically torturing Giles for information on how to awaken Acathla, which the librarian is handily resisting. However, Giles breaks when Drusilla creates the illusion of Jenny Calendar in his mind. Angel learns that his blood must be used to open the portal to Hell—and, as Buffy learns from Whistler, only Angel's blood can subsequently close it. She goes to the mansion, determined to free Giles and kill Angel, and unaware—through Xander's omission—that Willow is attempting the ritual again. With Spike's help, she does fairly well, but Angel manages to open the portal anyhow. When the curse takes effect and Angel's soul is restored, Buffy realizes that she has to impale the man she loves and send him to Hell in order to close the gate. She does so, and then departs from Sunnydale on a bus, leaving only a note for her mother.

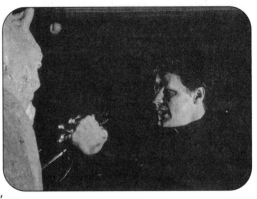

Exterior shots of the mansion are filmed in a residential neighborhood on a hill. The crew had to get special permission to drive a 6,000-pound crane on the street, and all filming had to be wrapped by 10 A.M. This is called the "taillights at ten" rule.

Quote of the week:

"I want to torture you. I used to love it, and it's been a long time. I mean, the last time I tortured someone, they didn't even *have* chain saws."

Angel, describing Giles's immediate future

Love, Slayer style:

Xander admits he loves Willow just before she awakens from her coma—so, naturally, the first thing she does upon awakening is call for Oz. Drusilla is able to use Giles's grief over Jenny Calendar's death to her and

The Factory set was torn down to make room for the mansion set on a *Buffy* soundstage.

Angel's benefit. The re-souled Angel and Buffy exchange a passionate kiss and declare their love for each other right before she is forced to stab him.

BUFFY'S BAG OF TRICKS:

She uses the sword Kendra brought for her.

CONTINUITY:

The police talk to Joyce regarding Buffy's possible involvement in Kendra's death, referring to her history of violence. After a vampire attacks Joyce, Buffy is forced to finally tell her mother that she is the Slayer—a concept Joyce has understandable problems facing. When Joyce asks Spike if they know each other, Spike reminds her that she hit him with an ax ("School Hard"). Spike's speech on how much he likes the world and doesn't want to destroy it ("Billions of people walking around like Happy Meals with legs") belies his actions with the Judge in "Surprise" and "Innocence." Buffy is expelled by Snyder, making Buffy two-for-two regarding high schools ("Welcome to the Hellmouth"). More hints regarding the apparent conspiracy among the authorities in Sunnydale are dropped via a phone call Snyder makes to the mayor ("School Hard," "I Only Have Eyes for You"). Spike and Dru leave Sunnydale the way they came in: driving in a fast car ("School Hard"). Again Angel is cursed with a soul ("Angel," "Surprise," "Innocence," "Becoming, Part 1"), but Buffy has to send him to Hell regardless.

To put himself in an "agonizing" frame of mind, Tony Head chopped chili peppers into small bits and popped them into his mouth before every take of Giles's torture scene.

121

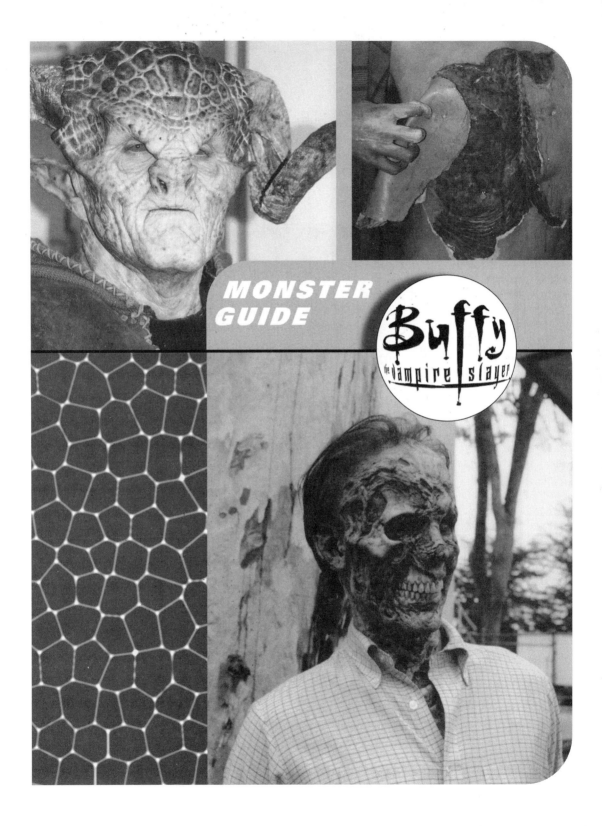

MONSTER
GUIDE

VAMPIRES

The legend of the vampire has existed, in one form or another, as long as there have been legends. From China to Ireland—in nearly every region of the world—there is some version of the vampire legend. There are those who believe that biblical references to a "screech owl" are actually comments about vampirism, since the word in Latin, *strix*, also means "vampire." The myths existed in ancient Babylon, and references have been found in ancient Assyrian and Chaldean tablets. Which, in a way, is disturbing. It makes absolutely no sense that similar ancient legends should exist in such diverse lands, unless there is some truth to those legends, some inspiration for them. Food for thought, at least.

From the horrifying tales of the Malaysian *penannglan,* to stories of the *nachzehrer* of Germany, belief in vampires seems to have always existed. It would be simple enough if we could distance ourselves from that mythology by placing it in a historical context. But, oddly enough, despite—or perhaps partially because of—the vibrant pop-culture existence of vampire mythology, belief in vampires actually thrives even to this day. There are groups of people around the world who still believe in, and in some cases believe themselves to be, vampires. A small "cult" of alleged vampires were responsible for several murders in the southeast United States in 1996. However, most modern "vampires" seem to be nonviolent and confine their blood-drinking to within their own circles. Thus far, none of them have exhibited any of the traditional powers or abilities of vampires, and there is no record of any modern vampire having died and come back to life.

Perhaps more so than any other supernatural legend, vampires owe much of their popularity, and certainly their endurance, to literature and the media. Though a number of writers had taken a crack at the vampire story before him, Bram Stoker certainly wrote the definitive vampire story in 1897—*Dracula.* For many decades thereafter, Stoker's work set the "rules" in place for vampire tales. Though the myriad legends from around the world each had their own wildly variant concepts about how vampires were created, what they actually did, what their weaknesses were, etc., there were now hard and fast rules.

Vampires could not be seen in mirrors. They cast no shadows. They could not cross running water, and direct sunlight could destroy them. They commanded the low creatures, bats and rats and wolves, and could transform themselves into those creatures. They slept on beds of their native earth. They had a powerful hypnotic gaze and could transform another person into a vampire by draining the blood from a living human, who would then, after death, rise from the grave. They feared the crucifix and garlic, and holy water could burn them. A stake through the heart and decapitation were the appropriate combination to kill a vampire once and for all.

Despite film and television creators and writers having worked their own twists on this basic formula for decades, the average consumer of Western pop culture still likely accepts Stoker's formula as an unassailable truth. Films such as *The Hunger* and *Near Dark,* among many others, have challenged those perceptions. Novelists such as Kim Newman, Dan Simmons, and particularly Anne Rice have radically altered those rules in creating their own vampire mythologies.

> "To make you a vampire, they have to suck your blood and then you have to suck their blood; it's like a whole big sucking thing. Mostly they're just gonna kill you, just take all your blood."
>
> **Buffy, in "Welcome to the Hellmouth"**

When it came time time for Joss Whedon to invent the mythology for *Buffy the Vampire Slayer,* he chose what suited him. The greatest diversion from Stoker's formula is that Whedon went back to an interpretation of ancient vampire mythology that few but scholars remember: some legends say that vampires are not humans at all, but demons who have taken up residence inside human corpses. From there, Whedon has built his own monsters. Built a better vampire, one might say, particularly since these vampires are not quite as all-powerful as their legendary and fictional forefathers.

> "Well, I've got a newsflash, braintrust. That's not how it works. You die. And a demon sets up shop in your old house. And it walks and talks and remembers your life, but it's not you."
>
> **Buffy, to Ford, in "Lie to Me"**

Vampires, in the world of *Buffy,* cannot fly. They cannot turn to mist. They cannot shape-shift at all. Though they cast no reflections in mirrors, they do cast shadows. In addition, they can be videotaped. While they do not actually need to breathe—at least not in the sense that humans do, with the intake of oxygen—their lungs do perform a function that simulates breathing. One possibility is that this process fouls whatever oxygen they do take in. It seems likely that the false act of "breathing" is somehow a comfort to them—and perhaps makes them feel less like the walking dead.

Whedon's vampires have a capacity for hypnosis, but some are much more skilled in its uses than others. Drusilla, for one, uses her hypnosis in Becoming, Parts 1 and 2 to great effect in the final episode of the second season, mesmerizing Giles into giving up valuable information and distracting Kendra long enough to cut her throat.

> "Xander, listen to me. Jesse is dead. You have to remember that if you see him. You're not looking at your friend. You're looking at the thing that killed him."
>
> **Giles, to Xander, in "The Harvest"**

> "A vampire isn't a person at all. It may have the movements, the memories, even the personality, of the person it takes over, but it is a demon at the core. There's no halfway."
>
> **Giles, in "Angel"**

Like Stoker's vampires, Whedon's cannot enter a private home without an invitation, but once they have been invited, they can return at any time. The traditional vampire cannot enter houses of worship or tread on hallowed ground, and they fear religious symbols, particularly the Christian cross.

> "We are defined by the things we fear. This symbol, these two planks of wood, it confounds me. Suffuses me with mortal dread. But fear is in the mind. Like pain, it can be controlled. If I can face my fear, it cannot master me."
>
> **The Master, about the crucifix, in "Nightmares"**

Whedon's creations have no problem entering a church, but touching actual consecrated earth causes them great suffering, and they do fear the cross. One thing Whedon's vampires share with Stoker's that many other creative imaginations have ignored over the years is the exposure to sunlight. In most recently created vampire mythologies, the sunlight will actually destroy a vampire. But for both Whedon and Stoker, in order for the sun to kill a vampire, it must be direct light. A heavily overcast day or some other kind of covering is sufficient to keep the creature alive for a period of time.

"I can't fly. There's no sure way to guard against the daylight."

Angel, on airline flight, in "Surprise"

In addition, vampires have frequently been portrayed as having almost instant healing abilities, save for the stake through the heart. Whedon's vampires can recover from just about anything, but it takes a lot longer to get there. Hence Darla's comment in "Angel" that "Bullets can't kill vampires. They can hurt them like hell...."

As to the origins of the vampires themselves, Whedon, through the character of the Watcher, Rupert Giles, has a very specific idea of their origins:

"This world is older than any of you know, and contrary to popular mythology, it did not begin as a paradise. For untold eons, demons walked the Earth, made it their home, their Hell. In time, they lost their purchase on this reality, and the way was made for mortal animals. For Man. What remains of the Old Ones are vestiges: certain magicks, certain creatures...."

"The books tell that the last demon to leave this reality fed off a human, mixed their blood. He was a human form possessed—infected—by the demon's soul. He bit another and another...and so they walk the Earth, feeding. Killing some, mixing their blood with others to make more of their kind. Waiting for the animals to die out and the Old Ones to return."

Toward the goal of returning their ancient ancestors to the Earth, the demons who reside within the vampires have created their own "families" and societies, tribes or clans of vampires who work and live together to further their chaotic impulses. As Buffy points out in "Lie to Me," however, "vampires are kind of picky about who they change." Frequently, a clan will include a group of vampires and their "sire," the vampire who turned them into vampires in the first place. The best-known vampire clan thus far in the *Buffy* mythology is the Order of Aurelius, which was led by the Master for centuries and whose Brethren, or adherents, have included Angel and Darla and, by implication, very likely Spike and Drusilla as well.

Indeed, Joss Whedon seems to have purposefully moved away from the vampire fictions of recent years, finding a middle ground between ancient legends, Bram Stoker's "rules," and his own unique twist on the subject. Witness, for example, the following exchange from "School Hard":

ANGEL: "I taught you to always guard your perimeter. You should have someone out there."
SPIKE: "I did. I'm surrounded by idiots. What's new with you?"

ANGEL: "Everything."

SPIKE: "Come up against this Slayer yet?"

ANGEL: "She's cute. Not too bright, though. Gave the puppy-dog, I'm-all-tortured act. Keeps her off my back when I feed."

SPIKE: "People still fall for that Anne Rice routine? What a world."

Without question, the vampires in *Buffy* are unique characters, and viewers are eagerly awaiting every new bit of information provided as the show moves forward.

ANGELUS

Without a doubt, Angelus is the most important vampire in the world of *Buffy*. He is both Buffy's great love and her worst enemy, the source of her greatest happiness and her deepest despair. Here in the Monster Guide, we will discuss the dark side of Angel, referring to him as Angelus.

As we learn in the first part of the second-season finale, in 1753, in Galway, Ireland, Angel was a drunken young scoundrel intent upon filching some of

his father's silver to buy himself a night of love at the local brothel. He is distracted in his purpose by the appearance of Darla, to whom he boasts:

"My lady, you will find that, with the exception of an honest day's work, there is no challenge I am not prepared to face."

Darla, amused, takes him at his word and not only invites him into her vampiric embrace, but sires him into eternal life as a vampire.

There is an interesting parallel between Angel's initiation into his new world and Buffy's, when, as a

shallow fifteen-year-old, she meets her first Watcher, Merrick. They share this exchange:

BUFFY: "You're not from Macy's, are you? 'Cause I meant to pay for that lipstick."

MERRICK: "There isn't much time. You must come with me. Your destiny awaits."

BUFFY: "I don't have a destiny. I'm destiny-free. Really." 	—**"Becoming, Part 1"**

But while Buffy becomes the heroic Slayer, the Irish lad Angel becomes Angelus, "the one with the angelic face," the scourge of Europe. The Master calls him "the most vicious creature I ever met."

One of his many evil deeds revealed thus far in the series was his insidious manipulation of Drusilla, a young English girl who is plagued by visions. The year is 1860. Her mother has told her that her clairvoyance is the work of the Devil, and the sadistic Angelus, posing as a priest in the confessional, takes full advantage of her confusion:

DRUSILLA: "My mum says I'm cursed. My seeing things is an affront to the Lord. That only He's supposed to see anything before it happens. But I don't mean to, Father, I swear. I try to be pure in His sight and do my penance. I don't want to be a thing of evil."

ANGEL: "Hush, child. The Lord has a plan for all creatures. Even a devil child like you."

DRUSILLA [mortified]: "A devil . . ."

ANGEL: "Yes, you're a spawn of Satan, all the Hail Marys in the world aren't going to help. The

Lord will use you and then smite you down. He's like that."

DRUSILLA: "What can I do?"

ANGEL: "Fulfill His plan for you, child. Be evil. Perform evil works. Attack the less fortunate. You can start small: laugh at a cripple. You'll feel better. Just give in . . . "

DRUSILLA: "No . . . I want to be good. . . . I want to be pure. . . ."

ANGEL: "We all do, at first. World doesn't work that way."

DRUSILLA: "Father, I beg you...help me."

ANGEL: "Very well. Uh, ten Our Fathers and an Act of Contrition. Does that sound good?"

DRUSILLA: "Yes, Father, thank you."

ANGEL: "The pleasure was mine." [She starts to go.] "Oh, and my child?"

DRUSILLA: "Yes?"

ANGEL: "God is watching you."
—"Becoming, Part 1"

Angelus drives poor Drusilla mad, exploiting her troubled mental state and killing everybody she loves. In desperation, she flees to a convent, and on the day she takes the veil, he turns her into a vampire.

He had also earlier killed his own family, and for over a century thereafter offers an ugly death to everyone he meets. "And I did it," he later tells Buffy, "with a song in my heart."

Eventually, Angelus leaves England—apparently in the company of his sire, Darla, with whom he is at least occasionally romantically involved—and they wreak havoc throughout Europe. In Budapest, they pluck human beings "like fruit off the vine." He delights in torturing both animals and people, as when he tells the captive Giles.

"I want to torture you. I used to love it, and it's been a long time. I mean, the last time I tortured someone they didn't even have chain saws."
—"Becoming, Part 2"

Angelus would probably have continued his career as "a vicious, violent animal"—to quote Giles—except that one fatal night, Darla brings him a Gypsy girl to feed on. Upon discovering her dead body, her clan, the Romany, decides to take its revenge against Angelus by returning his soul to him. As Angel explains to Buffy:

"When you become a vampire, the demon takes your body. But it doesn't get your soul. That's gone. No conscience, no remorse . . . it's an easy way to live. You have no idea what it's like to have done the things I've done, and to care."
—"Angel"

From that time until now, the Romany send clan members to spy on him, ensuring that their vengeance curse— "a living, breathing thing"—makes Angel's life a Hell on Earth.

But what Angel did not know that if he was ever completely happy, even for one second, his soul would once more be lost and he would revert to his evil state. After his night of passion with Buffy, in "Surprise," the curse is "lifted"—and Angelus howls into the night with pain as his soul leaves his body.

His first act as the newly restored Angelus is to feed upon a living human being—something he has not done in a century—and then he seeks out Drusilla and Spike to reassert his dominance over them. Engrossed as the couple are in their new toy, the Judge, it takes them a moment to realize what has happened when he strides boldly into their lair:

THE JUDGE [urged by Spike to burn all the good-
  ness out of Angel]: "This one cannot be burned.
  He is clean."
SPIKE: "Clean? You mean he's—"
THE JUDGE: "There's no humanity in him."
DRUSILLA: "Angel?"
ANGEL: "Yeah, baby, I'm back."   —"Innocence"

Angelus immediately sets about to establish himself as the head of "the family" that consists of
Drusilla, Spike, and himself. He taunts the weakened, wheelchair-bound Spike, calling him "roller-
boy" and "Sit 'n' Spin." He leers at Drusilla and
implies at every possible turn that he is sleeping
with her, instilling in Spike no end of jealous fury.

Angelus's next order of business is to destroy
anything and everything that had made him feel
like a human being when he was the brooding,
guilt-ridden Angel—most especially, the young girl
who had given him the first true happiness he had
known in over a hundred years—Buffy. First he
attempts to murder her friends, beginning with
Willow. He is thwarted only when Jenny Calendar,
knowing what has happened to him, distracts him
with a cross long enough for Buffy to attack him and
save her friend ("Innocence").

Hating the Slayer for making him feel love, yet
fearing her—she's the strongest Slayer he and
Spike have ever crossed—he wages a relentless
campaign of mind games against her—sneaking
into her bedroom and leaving sketches of her
asleep; killing Willow's aquarium fish; threatening to
harm Joyce Summers, then revealing to her that he
has slept with her daughter—with the same unre-
lenting cruelty that he once used on the hapless
Drusilla.

DRUSILLA: "You don't want to kill her, do you?
  You just want to hurt her. Just like you hurt me."
ANGEL: "Nobody knows me like you do, Dru."
SPIKE: "She'd better not get in our way."
ANGEL: "Don't worry about it."
SPIKE: "I do."
ANGEL: "Spike, my boy. You really don't get it, do
  you? You've tried to kill her, and you couldn't.
  Look at you. You're a wreck.... Force won't get it
  done. You gotta work from the inside. To kill this
  girl...you have to love her."
                                          —"Innocence"

But his plot backfires; the sheer magnitude of evidence that this is not some version of Angel on a
bad day but a different creature entirely, eventually
allows Buffy to accept that fact, and to resolve to
destroy him.

Around this time, Angelus realizes that Jenny
Calendar, the Gypsy woman sent to spy on him, is
trying to curse him once again—to restore his soul.
In one of the most chilling sequences in the entire
first two seasons, he comes upon her in the school,
smashes the Orb of Thesulah that was to house his
soul until it could be returned to him, and destroys
what he believes to be every copy of the incantation
itself. Then he hunts Jenny down and, with no passion, no hatred, just simple satisfaction, breaks her
neck.

Soon after, Angelus announces that he's done
with his personal vendetta against the Slayer. He
has decided that rather than bothering with her, he
will send every non-demon creature on Earth into
Hell by bringing the demon Acathla back to life. With
this decision, he has finally divested himself of
everything that once made him human—including
his passion, whether it be clothed as love or hatred,
for the Slayer.

Now Angelus, the one with the angelic face, is a
complete monster.

THE MASTER

This is what we know. Some sixty years
ago, a very old, very powerful vampire
came to this shore, and not just to feed."
That's the gospel according to Giles, from "The
Harvest," the second half of the two-hour premiere
of *Buffy the Vampire Slayer.* For the entire twelve
episodes of the first season, the Master, leader of
the Order of Aurelius, was Buffy's primary enemy,
the most evil creature in a town filled with them.
Though the Master's real name and history are
never revealed on screen, the true master of Buffy,
the show's creator, Joss Whedon, wrote in his script
of the pilot that the Master's real name was Heinrich
Joseph Nest. Whedon called him "the most powerful of vampires," and marked his age at roughly 600
years.

The Master was originally drawn to Sunnydale
because it is situated directly over the Hellmouth,

which Giles describes as "a sort of portal between this reality and the next." The next, obviously, meaning Hell. Based upon the basic mythology of the series, we know that this Hell is the dimension wherein the race of demons that walked the Earth before mankind currently reside. The worst and oldest of these demons are called the Old Ones, a term reminiscent of the Cthulhu mythos created by horror forefather H.P. Lovecraft.

As a worshiper of the Old Ones, the Master hoped to open the Hellmouth and allow the demons to walk the Earth once more. At the time of his arrival in Sunnydale, the evil one might well have succeeded with his plan if not for a horrible stroke of luck; bad luck for the Master, the good kind for the rest of the world. In 1937, an earthquake rocked Sunnydale, swallowing "about half the town," including an old church which, ironically, became the Master's lair. For it was in this shattered, now buried building that the Hellmouth began to open, only to be blocked by the earthquake and, it seems, by the Master. According to Giles, "Opening dimensional portals is tricky business. Odds are he got himself stuck. Like a cork in a bottle."

Thus, the Master remained stuck in an odd limbo between Earth and Hell from 1937 until 1997. He tried several times over the course of the first season to free himself. In fact, he was actually, very briefly, free during the episode "Nightmares," thanks to the reality-warping powers of a comatose boy named Billy Palmer. Fortunately for Sunnydale, when Billy awoke from his coma, the Master was returned to his limbo captivity.

Finally, however, in the last episode of season one, "Prophecy Girl," the Master did manage to get free. A prophecy in *The Pergamum Codex*—which Giles pointed out had never been wrong—predicted that the Slayer would face the Master and the Slayer

would die. At first, Buffy did not want to face him, but in the end, she descended into his underground lair. Little did she know, but that was exactly what the prophecy had meant. By entering the Master's lair, Buffy exposed herself to his attack. It was the power the Master received from tasting her blood in traditional vampiric fashion that allowed him to break free. After he had bitten her, the Master dropped Buffy in a pool of water, where she drowned and died. However, Xander was able to perform CPR and bring her back.

The Master had achieved his dream. The Hellmouth was open and the tentacled Old Ones were emerging when Buffy caught up with him. Their battle ended when the Master was impaled on shattered furniture in the school library and died. Over the intervening summer, Giles, Willow, and Xander buried the Master's bones in consecrated ground. In the second season opener, "When She Was Bad," the Master's remaining followers attempted to revive him, but Buffy stopped them, and then used a sledge hammer to pound the Master's bones to dust.

At this point, we can only assume that he is gone forever. But you never know.

SPIKE

Also known as "William the Bloody," Spike first appears in "School Hard," when he drives his car into the Welcome to Sunnydale sign on the outskirts of town. His first words as he reaches the Hellmouth, "home sweet home," are apparently a reference only to the idea that the Hellmouth is, de facto, home to all vampires, rather than any implication that he has ever been to Sunnydale before.

As the episode continues, the Anointed One holds court, and his followers argue over who will take the place of the Master, who will actually lead. A pair of vampires, referred to in the script only as "Big Ugly" and "Lean Boy," are arguing when Spike enters the Factory, wherein the Anointed One has set up shop.

BIG UGLY: "This weekend, the Night of St. Vigeous, our power shall be at its peak! When I kill her [the Slayer], it'll be the greatest event since the crucifixion. And I should know, I was there."

SPIKE: "You were there? Oh, please. If every vampire who said he was at the crucifixion was actually there, it would have been like Woodstock."

BIG UGLY: "I ought to rip your throat out."

SPIKE: "I was actually at Woodstock. That was a weird gig. Fed off a flower person, and I spent the next six hours watching my hands move. . . . So, who do you kill for fun around here?"

—**"School Hard"**

Spike goes on to brag that he has killed two Slayers in his life, one during the Boxer Rebellion. Then he brings Drusilla into the room. The two are obviously a couple, though Drusilla seems less than sane. She is a sickly vampire who also has prescient visions, and Spike's entire world seems to be about caring for her. That and his thirst for power. To prove himself, he vows to kill the Slayer.

Shortly, we see Spike and Big Ugly visit the Bronze. According to Spike's plan, Big Ugly draws Buffy out and into combat. Despite his bragging, he is easily dispatched by the Slayer as Spike watches, taking her measure. Later, Buffy and crew are discussing the arrival of Spike, and Angel reveals that he is familiar with the vampire. "Once he starts something, he doesn't stop until everything in his path is dead," Angel explains. Later,

Giles finds references to Spike in the Watcher diaries.

"Our new friend, Spike. 'Known as William the Bloody, earned his nickname by torturing his victims with railroad spikes....' Ah, but here's some good news: he's barely 200, not even as old as Angel." **Giles, in "School Hard"**

On Parent-Teacher Night, Spike and his hordes are defeated, and Spike himself is hit with an ax by Joyce Summers. He withdraws to consider an alternate plan. However, the Anointed One is less than pleased. Spike solves this problem quite simply: he kills the Anointed One. "From now on," he tells the other vampires, "we're gonna have a little less ritual and a little more fun around here."

The next time Spike appears is in "Halloween," when it is revealed that he has been videotaping Buffy fighting other vampires to watch her technique. Later that night, he makes his second attempt on Buffy's life, but once again, he is overpowered and forced to flee.

In "Lie to Me," Spike has yet another shot at the Slayer, but this time Buffy fends him off by threatening the weakened Drusilla's life. In the same episode, Spike begins to show the jealousy he feels over Drusilla's former involvement with Angel, a topic that later takes on a new significance. In the two-parter "What's My Line?" Spike finally manages to return Drusilla to health, only to become an invalid himself. After he is wheelchair-bound, Spike becomes quieter, almost morose. Even when he and Drusilla put the Judge together in "Surprise," Spike seems merely to be playing along because of his love for Dru. However, when Buffy and Angel make love at the end of that episode, causing Angel to lose his soul and revert to the demonic Angelus once more, the fire begins to burn in Spike again. For when Angel comes to stay with Spike and Drusilla, Spike's jealousy grows and grows. Of course, Angel's constant taunting doesn't help matters.

In fact, Angel's taunting, and Spike's anger continue to feed on each other, and Spike presses him time and again to kill Buffy and be done with it. However, at the end of "I Only Have Eyes for You," we begin to realize that Spike is not as docile as he has seemed. William the Bloody is up to something, for certain. In the last moments of that episode, when nobody else is around, Spike stands up out of his wheelchair, unaided, obviously strong again.

In the two-part season finale, "Becoming," his deceit takes on an entirely new meaning. Spike has decided that Angel's plan to destroy the world isn't exactly good for the vampire race. He's also realized that the only thing that really matters is that he gets Drusilla back. In order for that to happen, he allies himself with the Slayer, an unthinkable act for a vampire. He vows to Buffy that he will betray the others if she lets Drusilla live, that the two of them will leave Sunnydale and Buffy will never see them again.

"We like to talk big, vampires do. 'I'm gonna destroy the world'—just tough-guy talk, strutting around with your friends over a pint of blood. Truth is, I like this world. You got dog racing, Manchester United, and you got people. Billions of people walking around like Happy Meals with legs. It's all right here. But then someone comes along with a vision. A real passion for destruction. Angel could pull it off. Good-bye, Piccadilly, farewell Leicester bloody Square, you see what I'm saying?"
Spike, in "Becoming, Part 2"

Though events do not unfold as planned, Spike and Dru do manage to escape in that second season finale, driving off in the same car in which they first arrived, its windows blacked out against the sun. Though Spike vowed that Buffy would never see him and Dru again, the fact that in the final battle he abandoned her to Angel—decidedly not part of their bargain—chances are Buffy may have a very serious bone to pick with him if they ever do hook up again.

DRUSILLA

Like Spike, Drusilla first appears in "School Hard." She is perhaps one of the oddest characters in the *Buffy* mythology. She is also, interestingly enough, an intriguing parallel and foil to Buffy herself. When Dru is first introduced, she is sickly and weak. Spike caters to her every insane whim. And she does seem to be quite insane. She speaks in nonsense phrases and observations and has tea parties with her blindfolded dolls.

"Do you like daisies? I plant them, but they always die. Everything I put in the ground withers and dies. Spike, I'm cold."
Drusilla, to the Anointed One, in "School Hard"

"Miss Edith speaks out of turn. She's a bad example and will have no cakes today."
Drusilla, about her favorite doll, in "School Hard"

"You know what I miss? Leeches."
Drusilla, in "Halloween"

Drusilla also has prescient visions, seen through the kaleidoscope of her madness, and yet Spike never fails to interpret them. The Slayer has prescient dreams, and that is one trait they share.

The other thing, of course, is their feelings for Angel. In Drusilla's first appearance, we learn a bit about her past. She notes that she misses Prague, and Spike has to remind her that she was nearly killed by an "idiot mob" in Prague. Though she spends much of her time swooning and having visions, Drusilla does manage a late-night outing, during which she runs into Angel. It is here, in "Lie to Me," that we first get an inkling of their past. Later in that episode, Buffy grills Angel about Dru's identity.

ANGEL: "I did a lot of unconscionable things when I became a vampire. Drusilla was the worst. She was . . . an obsession of mine. She was pure and sweet and chaste."
Buffy: "You made her a vampire."
ANGEL: "First I made her insane. Killed everyone she loved, visited every torture on her I could devise. She eventually fled to a convent, and the day she took her Holy Orders, I turned her into a demon."　　　　　—"Lie to Me"

In the two-parter "What's My Line?" it is Angel's blood—as Dru's sire—and a ritual conducted by Spike that returns Drusilla to health. "Say 'Uncle,'" she says as she tortures Angel. "Oh, that's right, you killed my uncle." Ironically, at the end of that same episode, Spike is badly injured and is left confined to a wheelchair for a time, allowing Drusilla to take center stage.

"You've been a very bad daddy."
　　　　　Drusilla, to Angel, her sire,
　　　　　in "What's My Line? Part 2"

DRUSILLA: "My mummy ate lemons. Raw. She said she loved the way they made her mouth tingle. Little Anne, her favorite was custard . . . brandied pears . . ."
ANGEL: "Dru . . ."
DRUSILLA: "Ssshhhh. And pomegranates. They used to make her face and fingers all red. Remember little fingers? Little hands? Do you?"
ANGEL: "If I could, I . . ."

DRUSILLA: "Bite your tongue! They used to eat. Cake. And eggs. And honey. Until you came and ripped their throats out."
　　　　　—"What's My Line? Part 2"

In "Innocence," when Angel appears once more, now without a soul, Drusilla is thrilled. Spike, on the other hand, is less than pleased. Drusilla seems either ignorant of the tension or pleased with it, for she completely ignores Spike's jealousy and discomfort. It seems evident that Angel and Drusilla have become involved once again, although this is never confirmed, only implied. The tension continues to rise throughout subsequent episodes.

Perhaps Dru's most amusing appearance is when, affected by the love spell Amy Madison cast for Xander, she offers Xander eternal life in "Bewitched, Bothered, and Bewildered." In "Passion," she adopts a puppy whose owner has had a small accident—courtesy of her own fangs.

We get another look into Drusilla's past in a flashback sequence in the first half of the second season finale, "Becoming." It is an encounter in London in the year 1860, and apparently the first meeting between Dru and Angel. Angel begins to toy with Dru's mind, the beginning of the horrors he would later inflict upon her.

"I met an old man. I didn't like him. He got stuck in my teeth. And then the moon started whispering to me. All sorts of dreadful things."
　　　　　Drusilla, in "Becoming, Part 1"

It isn't until the end of "Becoming, Part 1" that we see Drusilla at her most evil, however. In that scene, she first hypnotizes Kendra, the *other* vampire Slayer. Then she cuts Kendra's throat. In part two, she also uses her hypnosis to convince Giles that she is Jenny Calendar to get him to reveal the last bit of information Angel needs to wake the demon Acathla and destroy the world.

During the final battle, however, Drusilla is overwhelmed by Spike, who has struck up an alliance with the Slayer, and she is forcibly removed from the battle. Spike and Dru then leave Sunnydale, presumably forever. But there is certainly a sense of unfinished business there.

Other than the Master and. of course, Angel, Darla is the most important figure in the vampire mythology from season one. A member of the Brethren of Aurelius, she is the first vampire we see in the series—when she kills a teenage boy in the opening teaser of "Welcome to the Hellmouth." In the same episode, she also becomes the first vampire to actually fight the Slayer in the series (Buffy is first attacked by Thomas, but she "dusts" him without any actual combat).

Darla is an interesting character because, while the Master habitually tortures or kills those who disobey him, Darla is able to be almost flippant, and, in fact, to disobey him without any obvious repercussions. Tasting Jesse's blood before handing him over to the Master in "The Harvest" is a good example of her disobedience. And yet, when Luke is killed in that very same episode, Darla takes Luke's place as the Master's primary acolyte.

The next time Darla appears is in "Angel." The Master has sent a trio of vampire warriors to kill Buffy, but "the Three" fail, and Darla gleefully kills them for the Master in punishment. In the same episode, a great deal is revealed during Darla's visit to Angel in his apartment. It is made quite clear that the two were involved for quite some time. In fact, the implication is that they were linked romantically, at least off and on, for the entire time that passed between Angelus becoming a vampire and the Gypsy curse that restored his soul. Darla brags that it was she who brought that very girl to Angel in the first place, and there is some suggestion that this took place in or near Budapest, about the time of an earthquake there.

It is also revealed that Darla was Angel's sire, that she was the one who turned him into a vampire in the first place.

Darla formulates a plan, hoping to bring Angel "back to the fold." If she can force him to kill Buffy, he will surely be evil again, she believes. To that end, she bites and bleeds Buffy's mother, Joyce, becoming the only vampire to bite any of Buffy's circle of family and friends (not including Buffy herself, of course). Darla then tries to frame Angel for this attack. In the long run, it does not work, and in the end of that episode, it is Angel who ends up killing Darla.

The Master mourns Darla's passing. "She was my favorite," he says. "For 400 years."

There will be a time of crisis, of worlds hanging in the balance. And in this time shall come the Anointed, the Master's great warrior. The Slayer will not know him, will not stop him. And he will lead her to Hell.

"As it is written, so shall it be . . .
Five will die, and from their ashes the Anointed One shall rise. The Brethren of Aurelius shall greet him and usher him to his immortal destiny. . .
"As it is written, so shall it be."

The Master, reading from the writings of Aurelius in "Never Kill a Boy on the First Date"

The Anointed One in mortal life was a sweet-looking little boy named Collin, whose last words as a human were, "I went on an airplane." When born into eternal life, he was to be the Master's greatest weapon against the Slayer.

He first appears in "Never Kill a Boy on the First Date," and he retains his angelic appearance, aside from a gravelly, echoing voice and soulless black eyes. Dropping stones into a pool of blood, holding hands with the Master and later with Buffy herself, he appears very much a small boy, save for his focused determination to rid the Master of the Slayer and his heartless assessment of various changes in the Master's situation. For instance, when Angel stakes Darla, the Master rages and sobs. Darla had been his favorite for 400 years, and Angel, the ultimate betrayer, was to have sat at the Master's right hand "come the day."

But, in "Angel," Collin calmly tells the grief-stricken Master in a flat, strong voice: "Forget her...she was weak. We don't need her. I'll bring you the Slayer."

Although he never physically attacks Buffy, it is he who leads her to the Master's lair in "Prophecy Girl." He also orchestrates the attempted resurrection of the Master (in "When She Was Bad"). After that fails, he serves as the leader of the Master's vampire family...until Spike and Drusilla arrive on the scene. Spike kills the "big noise" in "School Hard," by trapping him in a cage and exposing him to direct sunlight.

The coming of the Anointed One was prophesied in the twelfth century by one Aurelius, the founder of the Order of Aurelius. Aurelius foretold that the Brethren of his Order would come to the Master, to bring him the Anointed One. "Five shall die, and from their ashes shall rise" this very special vampire.

Giles's research indicates that the Anointed One will rise on the evening of the 1,000th day after the advent of Septus . . . that very night, in fact! The Master sends the Brethren out to fulfill the prophecy, which they accomplish by killing the passengers as well as the driver on an airport bus—five in all, including Andrew Borba, a lunatic who was sought by the police for questioning in a double murder. Giles, Buffy, and the Slayerettes all assume that Borba is the Anointed One when he rises from his slab in the Sunnydale Funeral Home as a full-fledged, very crazy vamp. After they dispatch Borba, Buffy and company assume all is well—unaware that little Collin is holding court beside the triumphant Master.

However, in "Prophecy Girl," Ms. Calendar tells Giles of "some crazy monk from Cortona" who has e-mailed her about some Anointed One. Giles later asks her if she managed to get in touch with him.

JENNY: "As far as I can tell, no one can. He's disappeared. He did send out one last global, though. Short one."
GILES: "What did it say?"
JENNY: "Isaiah 11:6. Which I dutifully looked up."
GILES: " 'The wolf shall live with the lamb, the leopard shall lie down with the kid, the calf and the lion and the fatling together, and a little child shall lead them.' "   **—"Prophecy Girl"**

When the Anointed One sees Buffy coming on the night she is prophesied to die, he begins to feign crying, a lost little boy. Buffy says, "It's all right. I know who you are."

She takes his hand, and he leads her to her destiny.

LUKE

The second vampire revealed to the audience is Luke. He is one of the Brethren of Aurelius, the Master's chief acolyte as the series begins, and is obviously quite powerful. In fact, his strength and prowess as a warrior is indicated by a conversation he has with the Master in "The Harvest":

THE MASTER: "A Slayer…have you any proof?"
LUKE: "Only that she fought me and yet lives."
THE MASTER: "Very nearly proof enough. I can't remember the last time that happened."
LUKE: "1843. Madrid. And the bastard caught me sleeping."

It is also a measure of Buffy's strength that she is the first opponent to survive a battle with Luke in more than a century and a half. Still, to be clear, none of Luke's opponents during that time were Slayers, since he later confesses that he had always "wanted to kill a Slayer."

In "The Harvest," the second hour of the premiere, it is explained that once every hundred years, the Master may gain power through a ritual or event called the Harvest. Luke is chosen as the Master's "Vessel." A symbol is painted on his forehead in blood, and a ritual is conducted, after which, according to the Master, "Every soul he takes will feed me. Their souls will grant me the strength to free myself."

Luke and the rest of the Master's minions attack the Bronze, and the Harvest begins. Unfortunately for the Master, and even more so for Luke, Buffy shows up to save the day. It isn't long before Luke is first outwitted, and then slain by the Chosen One, Buffy Summers.

DALTON

Unlike any other vampire we see in the first two seasons, Dalton seems quiet and bookish, almost like a demonic Willow. When we first see him, in "What's My Line? Part 1," Dalton is attempting to translate an ancient manuscript that Spike hopes will help cure Drusilla. Interestingly, despite his reserve, Dalton is willing to question Spike's judgment several times in this episode.

DALTON: "I'm not sure . . . it could be . . . *Deprimere ille bubula linter.*"

SPIKE: "'Debase the beef . . . canoe.' [beat] Why does this strike me as not right?"

—**"What's My Line? Part 1**

In that same episode, he is sent off to retrieve the cross of du Lac, which will allow him to translate the ritual for Spike. However, we don't see Dalton again until "Surprise," wherein he is helping Drusilla and the now wheelchair-bound Spike collect the pieces of the Judge. Drusilla nearly kills him at one point, but Spike stops her, suggesting instead that he rectify his error.

> "Dru, sweet. You might give him a chance to find your lost treasure. He's a wanker, but he's the only one we've got with half a brain. If he fails, you can eat his eyes out of the sockets for all I care."
>
> **Spike, on Dalton, in "Surprise"**

An interesting character, despite his few appearances, Dalton meets an untimely end as the Judge's first meal, in "Surprise."

THOMAS

Thomas is a relatively young, and not very bright, vampire who appears only in the very first episode of the series. He is also the first vampire Buffy actually spots in Sunnydale, ruffling Giles's feathers because she does so with her own teenage instincts rather than the instincts of the Slayer. Thomas dresses in '80s fashions, which is what tips her off in the first place, suggesting that vampires get stuck in the fashions of the time in which they "died." In the same scene, Thomas flirts with Willow and ends up convincing her to go get ice cream with him. Outside, he manages to lead her into the cemetery and to a large crypt that is an entrance to the Master's

underground lair. Shortly thereafter, Thomas thinks he can sneak up on Buffy and instead becomes the first vampire killed by the Slayer in the series.

CLAW

Claw, a.k.a. "Fork-Guy," was once a member of the Brethren of Aurelius, the Master's followers. Apparently, he "displeased the Master and cut off his [own] hand for penance." Claw then seems to have replaced the severed hand with a kind of metal claw or, to Buffy, a big "fork." Prior to the events in "Teacher's Pet," Claw apparently battled Angel, wounding him, but both of them survived the encounter. Angel tells Buffy, "Don't give him a moment's mercy; he'll rip your throat out."

In "Teacher's Pet," Claw is stalking people in Weatherly Park and fights Buffy early on, only to flee. Buffy follows and watches him stalk substitute biology teacher Miss French, who turns out to be the She-Mantis. Claw is afraid of her. Later, Buffy actually uses Claw's fear of the She-Mantis to track the creature and then "dusts" Claw without any obvious difficulty. Not as tough as we were led to believe.

THE THREE

In the opening sequence of "Angel," the Master reports to Darla that Zachary, a strong and careful member of the Master's vampire family, has been slain by Buffy. Supremely irritated, the Master decides to step up his war against the Slayer and summons the Three—much to Darla's delight.

The Three are a trio of imposing warriors, muscular, battle-scarred vampires who dress in leather and body armor. Without breaking stride, they clear Sunnydale's streets of terrified gangbangers in their search for the Slayer. Once they find her, they launch a brutal attack, and it's pretty clear that Buffy will lose this one—until Angel arrives on the scene. Still, despite the fact that he was once the most vicious vampire on earth, Angel and Buffy barely escape with their lives, and Angel is severely wounded.

Later, Giles tells Buffy, "You're really hurting the Master; he wouldn't send the Three for just anyone. We must step up our training with weapons."

Meanwhile, the Three, having failed in their mission, offer up their lives as penance. The Master dallies with them for a moment, allowing them to believe that he is going to spare them, while Darla circles behind them and, with great glee, stakes each one and they explode into dust.

LYLE AND TECTOR GORCH

These vampiric cowboy brothers appear in "Bad Eggs," arriving in Sunnydale for no apparent reason other than that the evil energy of the Hellmouth has drawn them there. Lyle tangles with Buffy first and decides that he and Tector should go after the Slayer when the moment is propitious. Originally from Abeline, Texas, they massacred an entire Mexican village in 1886...and that was *before* they became vampires. Not the sharpest tools in the shed, they finally attack Buffy while she is trying to deal with the Bezoar threat. The Bezoar kills Tector, and Lyle finally realizes that where this Slayer is involved, his wisest course is to head for the hills.

Lyle Gorch is still at large.

ABSALOM

Appearing in the second season opener, "When She Was Bad," Absalom is the mouthpiece for the Anointed One. Though the Anointed One is technically the leader of what remains of the Brethren of Aurelius, Absalom seems to be their spokesman

and the chief organizer of the effort to resurrect the Master.

ABSALOM: "Your day is done, girl. I'll grind you into a sticky paste. And I'll hear you beg before I smash in your face."

BUFFY: "So, are you gonna kill me? Or are you just making small talk?" —**"When She Was Bad"**

Of course, at the end of the episode, Buffy shoves a torch into Absalom's face, and he goes up in a blast of flame, cinder, and ash.

ST. VIGEOUS

St. Vigeous is a sort of patron saint of vampires. In ancient times, he led a vampiric crusade that swept through Edessa, Harran, and points east, destroying everything in its path.

The Feast of St. Vigeous is a time when the power of the vampire is at its peak. According to Giles, "For three nights, the Unholy Ones scourge themselves into a fury, culminating in a savage attack on the Night of St. Vigeous." In an expurgated bit of dialogue, Jenny Calendar refers to it as "a Holy Night of Attack."

DEMONS

Even more so than with vampires, entire volumes can and have been written on the subject of demons. The concept is a broad one, but rises out of a mixture of religious world views, as well as popular and cultural myths, folklore, and superstitions. The idea of a lord of an underworld is found in many hierarchies of gods and goddesses: the Romans had Pluto, the Greeks Hades, and the Norsemen had Hel, to name a few. In addition, a vast array of mischievous spirits, faeries, wood sprites, poltergeists, and so on populate the religious and mythological landscape.

In the Judeo-Christian system, Satan (or Lucifer) has his subordinate demons, whose purpose is to harry humanity with aggravation and temptation. In the Old Testament, Satan was an angel whose occupation was to test humanity's loyalty to God. Only later do we have the tale of Satan's rebellion against God and the casting out of Satan and the angels who had sided with him. After which, of course, they became known as demons.

Later in the history of the Christian church, around the twelfth and thirteenth centuries, there was a general consensus that demons were actually all the old gods and goddesses, not only the lords of the underworld, all of whom had animal incarnations of some kind. At baptism, Christian souls were commanded to renounce "Thor and Odin and Saxnot and all evil beings that are like them." But the older notion that demons were fallen angels serving Lucifer is the belief that proved more resilient and became the more traditional definition of demons in Christian teachings.

As noted in the vampire section, however, in the mythology of *Buffy the Vampire Slayer*, the traditional story of creation is considered a myth. The demons in this series are based not on Judeo-Christian and Western tradition, but are more influenced by Eastern traditions, and to some extent by the works of prominent horror forefather H.P. Lovecraft, whose own mythology seems to have been based largely on ancient Sumerian demonology. Lovecraft's fiction included references to a race of "Old Ones" or "Ancient Ones," who existed on Earth before humanity and who were constantly trying to regain control of our world. Various acolytes and half-demons (for instance, the human twin in *The Dunwich Horror*) labored to open the gates and let the Old Ones through.

Also, as previously discussed, the vampires in *Buffy* are corpses inhabited by demons, and thus it follows that in the *Buffy* mythology demons are more often described by their function than by the form they have currently taken:

MS. CALENDAR: "I knew this would happen sooner or later. It's probably a mischief demon, you know, like Kelkor or—"
GILES: "It's Moloch."
MS. CALENDAR: "The Corruptor."
—"I Robot, You Jane"

And from "Killed by Death":

CORDELIA: "*Ew. What does this do?*"
GILES: "It, um, extracts vital internal organs so that it can regenerate its own mutating cells."
CORDELIA: "Wow. What does this one do?"
GILES: "It elongates its mouth to engulf the head of its casualty between its teeth."
CORDELIA: "Ouch. What does this one do?"
GILES: "It asks endless questions of those with whom it's supposed to be working but they're not getting anything done!"
CORDELIA: "Boy, there's a demon for everything."

This stated function is generally some kind of static goal, from a mindless reflex to lash out and destroy to a more sophisticated need to dominate and control. This is a limitation of demons, as opposed to the more fluid and multidimensional "living of a life" that humans engage in. As Spike says to Angel in "School Hard":

ANGEL: "Things change."
SPIKE: "Not us! Not demons."

As demon-inhabited corpses, vampires are evil, and they remain evil, despite the assertion of the Judge, who says of Drusilla and Spike that they stink of humanity, sharing affection and jealousy (in "Surprise.") In a sense then, what makes them human is their *capacity* for feeling emotion; what makes them demons is their inability to change; their emotions don't grow or lead to good as human emotions can. They are what they are, and they remain that way. And if evil is the inability to choose good, or feel love, for instance, then perhaps that explains the fury Angelus exhibits when he contemplates how completely he was changed when his soul was restored.

However, there are also good—or perhaps a better word is "neutral"—demons in the *Buffy* universe. Whistler is one such demon, and even he describes himself in terms of his function:

ANGEL: "You're not a vampire."
WHISTLER: "A demon, technically. But I'm not a bad guy—not all demons are dedicated to the destruction of all life. Someone has to maintain balance, you know. Good and evil

can't exist without each other, blah blah blah. I'm not like a good fairy or anything. I'm just trying to make it all balance—do I come off as defensive?"

—**"Becoming, Part I"**

The introduction of a character like Whistler suggests that in Whedon's universe, at least, there seems to be a continuum running between the opposite poles of human and demon; in other words, some demons are more human than others, and some humans behave like demons. Or, to put it another way, what makes us human is our capacity to change, to feel emotions, to choose good over evil. As Buffy herself says to Ford, the terminally ill young man who wants to become a vampire so he won't "die":

"You have a choice. You don't have a *good* choice. What's behind door number three is pretty much a dead fish, but you have a choice. You're opting for mass murderer here and nothing you say to me is gonna make that okay."

Buffy, in "Lie to Me"

Having chosen such a versatile approach to the demon, Joss Whedon has provided vast opportunities for more stories about demons, what makes them different from and similar to humans, and the choices they make or fail to make in the ongoing battle between good and evil.

ACATHLA

cathla, the demon, came forth to swallow the world. It was killed by a virtuous knight who pierced the demon's heart before it could draw breath to perform the act. Acathla turned to stone, as demons sometimes do, and was buried where neither man nor demon would be wont to look. Unless, of course, they're putting up low-rent housing." —**Angel in, "Becoming, Part I"**

The entombed demon Acathla has been unearthed during the construction of low-income housing outside Sunnydale. He is stolen by Angel, Drusilla, and their henchmen and taken to their mansion. The lid of his coffin is opened, and the

vampires react to the sight of the grimacing demon, a stone sword sticking out of his chest:

DRUSILLA: "Ooh, he fills my head.… I can't hear anything else.…"
Angel approaches Acathla slowly, reverently.
SPIKE: "Let me guess. Someone pulls out the sword—"
DRUSILLA: "Someone worthy—"
SPIKE: " . . . the demon wakes up and wackiness ensues—"
DRUSILLA: "He will swallow the world."
ANGEL: "And every creature living on this planet will go to Hell. My friends, we're about to make history...end." —**"Becoming, Part 1"**

As explained by Giles, "The demon universe exists in a dimension separate from our own. With one breath, Acathla will create a vortex, a kind of whirlpool that will pull everything on Earth into that dimension, where any non-demon life will suffer horrible, eternal torment."

As is true of demons in the world of *Buffy the Vampire Slayer*, then, Acathla exists to serve a purpose. He is almost like a machine, with an on-off switch that, when pressed, will finally cleanse the Earth of humanity once and for all. His threat lies not in what he is, but in what he can do. And in the second-season finale, that threat is very real. In fact, only by sacrificing Angel does Buffy finally defeat Acathla.

EYGHON, THE SLEEPWALKER

n his twenties, Giles rebelled against his inevitable destiny to become a Watcher, and together with Ethan Rayne, he organized a circle that dabbled in the occult for their own amusement. "And then," Giles explains, "Ethan and I discovered something a little bigger."

This was Giles's "Dark Age" when he and Ethan learned how to summon the ancient Etruscan demon Eyghon. They would put someone into a deep sleep and the others would summon the demon to inhabit the sleeper's body. According to Giles, the possession induced "an incredible high." However, Eyghon asserted control over one of the sleepers—Randall—and they could not send it back.

Each member of the circle—including Giles—bears a tattoo called the Mark of Eyghon, and this mark acts like a homing beacon to the demon as it searches out the people who tried to kill it, possessing each and destroying each in turn. As Willow tells her friends, reading from one of Giles's books, in "The Dark Age":

> "Eyghon, the Sleepwalker, can only exist in this reality by possessing an unconscious host. Temporary possession imbues the host with a euphoric feeling of power....Unless the proper rituals are observed, the possession is permanent, and Eyghon will be born from within the host....Once called, Eyghon can also take possession of the dead, but its demonic energy soon disintegrates the host and it must jump to the nearest dead or unconscious person to continue living."

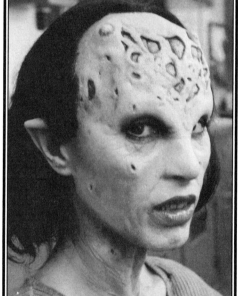

In the opening of the episode, Eyghon is wearing the decaying corpse of Deirdre as it shambles after Philip Henry, intent upon killing him. "She" easily snaps his neck, and then she liquefies into a pool of ooze. This is Eyghon, as it rolls down an incline and washes over the dead hand of Philip, into whom it now enters.

Using Philip's corpse to pursue its next victims—two of them are in Sunnydale, namely Ethan Rayne and Giles—Eyghon jumps next into an unconscious person—Jenny Calendar, whom it attacked as Philip. During her possession, Jenny becomes more and more grotesque, until she resembles the demon in its natural state—an ugly, horned creature. Filled with Eyghon's rage and aggression, she beats Giles in anticipation of killing him, until Buffy arrives on the scene. Then the demon jumps through a window to escape.

Eventually, the demon is tricked into jumping from Jenny into Angel—it believes that Angel is trying to kill it by choking Jenny—a chilling foreshadowing of what is to come. Once inside Angel, it wrestles with the demon already in residence there...and loses. As Angel explains:

BUFFY: "You [Willow] knew that if the demon was in danger, it would jump into the nearest dead guy."
Willow nods, even smiles.
ANGEL: "I put it in danger."
WILLOW: "And it jumped."
ANGEL: "But I've had a demon inside me for a couple hundred years just waiting for a good fight."
BUFFY: "Winner and still champion."

Eyghon, the demon within, serves as a metaphor for the dark secrets and longings that we wish to hide from others. Buffy and her friends have always seen Giles as a steadfast, stuffy Brit with most, if not all, of the answers to every question they ask. Now, however, he has been revealed as less than perfect:

GILES: "I never wanted you to see that part of me."
BUFFY: "I'm not gonna lie. It was scary. I'm used to you being, you know, the Grown-Up. And then I find out that you're a person."
GILES: "Most grown-ups are."
BUFFY: "Who would've thought?"
GILES: "Some of them are even very short-sighted, foolish people."
BUFFY: "So after all this time, it turns out we do have something in common. Which, apart from being a little weird...is kind of okay."

It's telling that now that Buffy has seen this side of Giles, she, too, bears the Mark of Eyghon. But with the resilience of youth, she complains about the expense of having it removed—she was saving up for some "very important shoes."

THE JUDGE

The Judge is a hideous blue demon (in fact, nicknamed "Big Blue" by Spike) that was brought forth to rid the Earth of the plague of humanity. "He would separate the righteous from the wicked...and burn the righteous down," Angel tells the others. In his last visit to Earth, it proved impossible to kill him, but an army finally managed to dismember him. The pieces of his body were scattered to the far corners of the Earth, each piece buried separately. In a scene expurgated from the episode for length, Xander quips: "Do you think they left his heart in San Francisco?" Oz replies, "I had that thought, too."

In "Surprise," the Judge's living arm nearly chokes Buffy to death when she opens the box containing it at her surprise birthday party—a gift originally meant for Drusilla, from Spike. Unsure if this is the only piece of the Judge in town, Angel is elected to take it far, far away, possibly Nepal, possibly somewhere even more remote.

Unfortunately, Spike's henchvamps steal back the box, and at the climax of Drusilla's party, the last piece of the Judge is put in place—his head. Energy surges around him. He's enormous, dressed in armor, with a horned head and solid black eyes.

His "righteousness radar" activated, his first impulse is to burn Drusilla and Spike who "stink of humanity." In their place, he is given the nebbishy Dalton, who is burned to a cinder because of his love for books. However, it's clear that the Judge needs to recuperate from his long ordeal—for now, he must touch his victims in order to burn them. But with each life he takes, his strength will increase. In time, he promises Spike, he will not need direct contact. In an expurgated sequence from "Innocence," the second half of the two-parter, he explains to Spike: "I fought an army. They hacked me to pieces. For 600 years, my living head lay in a box buried in the ground. I've learned to be patient."

It is because he isn't fully recovered that he briefly touches the Slayer and yet she lives.

It is the Judge who reveals to Spike and Drusilla that Angel has become Angelus once more, stating that "this one is clean." There is nothing human inside to burn.

Round-the-clock research yields no answer on how to destroy the Judge, until Willow's offhand comment, "Where's an army when you need one?" prompts Xander to come up with a plan to steal a rocket launcher. Since the Judge is a demon, an unchangeable being, modern warfare has caught up with him: an old-fashioned army may have had to physically hack him to pieces, but the Slayer, with one well-aimed shot with a rocket launcher, takes him out in a rain of blue fragments. The pieces are collected and kept separated...the implication being that the Judge will never be put back together again.

MOLOCH, THE CORRUPTOR

There's a demon in the Internet."
Giles to Jenny, in "I Robot, You Jane"

In these, the latter years of the century, there has been much concern over the awesome potential for harm afforded by misuse of the Internet. Story after story appears on TV news shows and in the papers about pedophiles luring young children into tragic situations and shady characters of every stripe preying on the shy, the lonely, and the trusting by involving them in long on-line conversations that grow increasingly more familiar and intimate.

Add to this the strong public fear over the wealth of data available about individuals—credit-card numbers, medical histories, and supposedly private e-mail messages—and you have the ingredients for the rich subtext of "I Robot, You Jane."

In the Middle Ages, it was books and reading that were generally regarded with suspicion, an occupation better left to monks hidden away in shadowed monasteries. So it follows that it was believed, as Giles states (in a section expurgated from the script):

> "There are certain books that are not meant to be read. Ever. They have things trapped within them....In the Dark Ages, demons' souls were sometimes trapped in certain volumes. The demon would remain in the volume, harmless, unless the book was read aloud."

In medieval Italy, the horned demon Moloch, the Corruptor, held sway over a group of devoted disciples, to whom he promised love, wealth, and power. Despite his leathery, distorted features and clawlike hands, he was eerily elegant in his velvet clothes, moving among his followers like a Borgia prince. His standard way of thanking them for their devoted service was to summarily break their necks.

Finally, he was bound by a group of monks, sucked into a large book, and shelved.

Since the essence of a demon is an entity, not necessarily a form, Moloch has dwelled for centuries within the infernal volume. When the book arrives in a shipment for Giles, he is too distracted to take much note of its distinctive cover, directing instead that it be placed on "Willow's pile." To his intense unease, his library has been invaded by Jenny Calendar, the beautiful computer-science teacher, and she is presiding over the wholesale scanning of the library's holdings into the "idiot box," i.e., the school computer system.

While Giles sequesters himself "in the Middle Ages" section of the library, Willow innocently opens the book and scans the strange characters within into the computer's memory. Intent upon her work, she doesn't see the single question that appears across the computer screen, signaling that Moloch has been freed: "Where am I?"

"A very deadly and seductive demon," Moloch's specialty is preying upon "impressionable minds." As soon as he realizes that he's been released into the Internet, he begins a campaign to enlist a new army of followers. Sensing that the computer-literate Willow is also lonely, he presents himself as a boy named Malcolm Black and begins to send her a series of friendly e-mail letters, ostensibly from his hometown of Elmwood, eighty miles away. Willow, who has never had a real boyfriend, is flattered by his attention and begins an on-line romance with him that gives Buffy pause and makes Xander jealous.

Moloch also connects with Dave and Fritz, two Sunnydale High computer nerds. Dave is shy and quiet, while Fritz is more aggressive and intense about his opinions: "The printed page is obsolete," he says. "Information isn't bound up anymore, it's an entity. The only reality is virtual. If you're not jacked in, you're not alive."

Moloch soon manages to hold Dave and Fritz in his thrall, and they join with other computer experts at a shut-down computer facility to create a robot body for the incorporeal Moloch. A body of his own is the thing the demon craves: "To be able to walk...to touch...to kill."

He also wishes to give Willow the world, or so he says:

MOLOCH: "You created me. I brought these humans together to build me a body, but you gave me life. Took me out of the book that held me. I want to repay you."

WILLOW: "By lying to me. By pretending to be a person. [weakly] Pretending . . . you loved me."

MOLOCH: "I do."

In a mirroring of the unquantifiable capacity of the Internet, once Moloch inhabits the robot body his minions have created for him, he is capable of being bound. Working with Ms. Calendar and her Internet circle of fellow technopagans, Giles traps Moloch in his robot body and Buffy electrocutes him. The question remains: if he had remained within the Internet, could he have ever been destroyed?

WHISTLER

As previously mentioned in the general overview on demons, Whistler describes himself as "technically" a demon whose function is to maintain the balance of good and evil. He is young and very badly dressed, "like a low-ranked mafioso." He tells Angel, whom he approaches in Manhattan in 1996, that his real name is hard to pronounce "unless you're a dolphin."

In "Becoming, Part 1," Whistler offers the half-sane vampire a choice: "You could become an even more useless rodent than you are right now, or you could become . . . someone. A person. Someone to be counted." Whistler then brings Angel to the spot where he sees Buffy for the first time, as she discovers she is the Slayer and must learn to fight the forces of evil. He is giving Angel a purpose—to help the frightened young girl—and he is giving Buffy an ally, for he says of her: "She's gonna have it tough, that Slayer. She's just a kid. And the world is full of big bad things."

Angel replies that he wants to help her. Whistler's impressed, but reminds Angel that this will not be an easy road. Angel asserts that he wants to learn from Whistler.

But he doesn't want to dress like him.

The demon next appears to Buffy, in "Becoming, Part 2." She guesses who he is—"an immortal demon sent down to even the score between good and evil"—but she's not impressed:

BUFFY: "Why don't you try getting off your immortal ass and fighting evil once in a while? 'Cause I'm tired of doing this by myself."
WHISTLER: "In the end, you're always by yourself. You're all you got. That's the point."
BUFFY: "Spare me."

Whistler's function, then, is not to actively even the score between good and evil, but to inspire others to do so. He can also give information, telling Buffy that using the sword blessed by the knight who slew Acathla isn't enough to thwart Angel's plan to send every non-demon being on Earth to Hell. As with all demons, he has limitations, and he cannot change.

But he can make bad jokes: "You know, raiding an Englishman's fridge is like dating a nun. You're never gonna get the good stuff."

MACHIDA

Also known as "Wormy," "the One We Serve," and "Reptile Boy," Machida appeared in the episode of the same name. Machida is an enormous demon snake-monster which inhabited the dungeon-like basement of the Delta Zeta Kappa fraternity house on the Crestwood College campus. Accompanied by subsonic rumbling as he shoots from a pit in the basement floor, Machida's "terrible countenance" is terrible indeed as he towers high above his worshipers and their victims. In the words of "Reptile Boy" writer-director, David Greenwalt:

> "Machida is half man, half snake. He has a muscular body (from the waist up) and the enlarged and frightening head of a man with the fangs and horrible eyes of a snake. His skin has the diamond pattern of a snake—thus the diamond carvings on his "people." From the waist down, he is all snake—and a big 'un, too, his snake body trails behind him into the depths of the pit: God knows how long this guy is."

Once a year, the frat brothers of the DZK "psycho cult" lure unsuspecting high school girls to wild parties, drug them, and offer them as sacrificial offerings to the "enhungered" Machida. In return, Machida showers the fraternity members with riches and power. This has gone on for over a century, until Buffy slices Machida in two and she and the Scooby Gang—plus Angel—bring the DZKs to justice.

Originally, Machida was supposed to survive Buffy's attack, but according to Greenwalt, there was not enough time in the production schedule to shoot the sequence, and so Machida met his untimely end. This is the section of the shooting script that was cut to make this adjustment.

(from scene 86):
Tom comes to near the altar. And, unbeknownst to any of our heroes, the snake body begins slowly moving. Until it joins up with the torso. A squooshy sound of flesh and protoplasm meeting and the two halves rejoin!

(cont'd)

CORDELIA (to Tom): "And you, you're going to jail for about 15,000 years. Oh, God, it's over . . . it's really . . ."

That's when Machida, rejoined, suddenly pops up again. Angel takes a threatening step forward next to Buffy, growls. Machida towers over Tom:

MACHIDA: "For a hundred years I have given your forebears wealth and power. And this is how you repay me? From this day forth, you are alone in the world."

Machida slides back down. Cordelia is afraid to breathe. With good reason. Machida pops back up, grabs Tom.

MACHIDA: "Li'l somethin' for the road."

Machida disappears into the pit with Tom. We hear Tom's screams, a quick couple of chomps and then silence.

THE KINDESTOD

$\mathcal{A}$t first glance, the monster in "Killed by Death" appears to be a hallucinatory projection of the Slayer herself, as she thrashes feverishly in a hospital bed, suffering from both the flu and severe injuries sustained in a battle with Angelus. But that's not it at all.

At the age of eight, Buffy was the lone witness to the bizarre and violent death of her little cousin Celia, who was in a hospital at the time. Now, at seventeen, Buffy is still terrified of hospitals and begs her mother not to make her stay despite her condition.

Adding to the air of menace is the fact that Angelus attempts to "visit" her. Xander blocks his entry and serves as sentry during Buffy's hospital stay.

Buffy's fever dream of a bizarre figure dressed "like a nineteenth-century undertaker" but with a pasty white face, beaky nose, and a mouth full of very ugly, sharp teeth propels her to investigate the hospital. In the children's ward, two doctors quarrel over the proper course of treatment for the children afflicted with the same virus Buffy has. As she observes them, a small boy and girl approach her, and the boy solemnly explains to her that the monster was with Tina, and he will come back for the rest of them.

The monster, he continues, is Death.

In the morning, Tina's sheeted body is wheeled out of the children's ward, and Buffy tries to explain to Giles and the others what Ryan told her. With her usual tact, Cordelia says what everyone else seems to be thinking:

"So this isn't about that you're afraid of hospitals 'cause your friend died and you wanna conjure up a monster that you can fight so you save everybody and not feel helpless?"

And despite the obvious truth that Don, the creepy security guard, shares with Cordelia—sometimes children die—Xander offers to help Buffy investigate Tina's death.

For a time, the doctor with whom Buffy's own doctor quarreled over treatment for the children—Dr. Backer—is suspected of being the culprit. But Buffy is eyewitness to his murder by an invisible assailant, who slashes his body and drags him down the hall. She is thrown against the wall by the unnamed, unknown force.

Ryan has given Buffy a picture of the monster, and she in turn hands the childish scrawl over to Giles to serve as a mug shot. At last he takes her seriously and heads to the library to do research. It is Cordelia, serving as his assistant, who pinpoints the monster:

CORDELIA: "It's called 'Der Kindestod.'. . . The name means 'child death.' This book says that he feeds off children by sucking the life out of them. *Blech.* Anyway, afterward, it looks like they died because they were sick."

BUFFY: "So it *did* kill Tina?"

CORDELIA: "Yeah. That's my take. 'Cause it would be looking at the children's ward as basically an 'all-you-can-eat' kind of thing, you know."

BUFFY: "Backer was curing the kids—and taking away the Kindestod's food."

CORDELIA: "Hence the slice-age."

Buffy puzzles over why she could at one time vaguely make out the figure of the Kindestod but since then he has been invisible. She finally realizes that she was sick—near Death—when she saw him. Ingesting a live virus, she faces him at last, to discover that he is a fearsome opponent. His method of killing the children is gruesome—worth every one of Cordelia's *"ews"* as she reads about him to Buffy: "His eyes bulge and protrude out of their sockets. Then they extend downward and push into the forehead of his victim." It's no wonder that Buffy's cousin Celia thrashed and screamed as she died.

Buffy is weak from the fever from the virus, and for one terrifying instant she finds herself on the receiving end of the Kindestod's terrible method of killing...until she manages with her last bit of strength to grab his head and break his neck.

It really doesn't look like we'll be seeing Der Kindestod again.

THE BROTHERHOOD OF SEVEN

The "seven" in their name reflects both the number of demons, as well as the length of the cycle of their evil. The Brotherhood of Seven originally were seven demons who had the capacity to take the form of young human beings.

"Every seven years, these demons need human organs—a heart and a brain—to maintain their humanity. Otherwise, they revert back to their original form, which is slightly less appealing."
Giles, in "The Puppet Show"

In "The Puppet Show," there is a series of murders relating to the Sunnydale High Talent Show. Due to the missing organs, Giles surmises that one or more of the Brotherhood of Seven is responsible. He is, of course, correct. However, at first, Buffy, Giles, and company believe the demon is a student named Morgan, a budding ventriloquist. Later, they come to believe that one of the Seven inhabits his dummy, named Sid, and for good reason.

"On rare occasions, inanimate objects of human quality, such as dolls and mannequins, already mystically possessed of consciousness, having acted upon their desire to be human by harvesting organs." **Giles, in "The Puppet Show"**

To everyone's surprise, it becomes evident that, although Sid is indeed mystically alive, he is not the demon. In fact, Sid was a demon hunter, cursed to live the rest of his life in the form of that dummy by the Brotherhood of Seven. By the time this story takes place, Sid has already dispatched six of the seven. When the last has been killed, his curse will be lifted. In the end, the seventh demon turns out to be a student magician named Marc. When Sid finally does kill that demon, his soul passes on to the next world at last, and the Brotherhood of Seven is destroyed forever.

WITCHES
AND
SORCERERS

The subject of witchcraft has become, particularly over the past two decades or so, a controversial one. For although the presence of a tribal shaman, magic user, "witch," or the equivalent, was a pivotal position in many ancient cultures, the rise of "New Age" groups, societies, communes, and "alternative religions" has brought new awareness and attention to old practices. Consequently, witches are once again in the news. Of course, much of what is popularly referred to as "New Age" is not new, but instead is an outgrowth of shifts in political, social, and cultural thinking. The feminist and civil rights movements, changes in health care, and educational programs are but a few of the influences leading to a revival of interest in "the old ways." Modern paganism is one example of a type of "new" religion which prides itself on its relationship with ancient Druidic styles of worship. Some members prefer to be known as "witches" or devotees of the goddess Wicca. Sadly, they must battle the pop-culture impressions of witchcraft, which have their foundations in Christian theology, dating to the beginning of the twelfth century.

Over the subsequent six centuries, Christian doctrine would be completely altered, and Europe itself would be changed forever. The idea that Satan had gathered his forces and was systematically attempting to corrupt Earth and subjugate humanity had really not developed until this time. Nor had there been a literate population across the continent, joined by religion and communication for the first time, that would have been able to mount the horrors of what would come to be called the Inquisition.

The Inquisition consisted mainly of Christian "investigators" and "judges," whose mission was to weed witches out of society. Sadly, we have no space for a detailed examination of this era and phenomenon here. Suffice it to say that the majority of those killed—and the numbers were horrifying— were not witches at all (and, of course, we point out that witches themselves were hardly the Satanic agents the Inquisition portrayed them as, but rather members of oppressed religious sects). If you were accused as a witch, you would be tortured until you either died or confessed. And, if you confessed, you would likely be burned to death. Therefore, accusation alone was a death sentence. Of course, this quickly became a political tool. Want to get rid of an enemy? Accuse them of witchcraft!

The madness of the Inquisition spread to America in 1692, in Salem (now Danvers) Massachusetts, where many women in the town were hanged as witches. Amazingly, there were people burned as witches in Europe as late as the 1780s. Popular culture—particularly in the form of film and television—kept alive the Inquisition's image of the witch for most of the twentieth century. Only now have we begun to separate the myth from the reality.

The relationship between modern witches and actual magic, or spellcasting, is something we will not address here. In fact, even attempting to define magic beyond the popular-culture image of it is not what we're after. In that, we are little different from the creators of *Buffy the Vampire Slayer*. Witches, in *Buffy* parlance, seem to be powerful female magic users. Little else of their nature is explained. However, a line is clearly drawn between witchcraft and paganism, because Jenny Calendar is specifically referred to as a pagan, but the two witches (mother and daughter) discussed in the series so far are never portrayed with any kind of religious belief. At one point, Giles actually asks Jenny if she is a witch, and she replies: "I don't have that kind of power," suggesting that the "source" of power—or the use of that power—is a distinguishing factor. Also, both Giles and Willow use magic at one point or another, and are not classified as witches. So what else is necessary to make one, in the world of this series, a witch? We'll just have to watch and see.

We get very little solid information on witches in the two episodes in which the craft is used. However, Giles does discuss a test that reveals Amy/Catherine as the culprit in "Witch." The test requires some of the witch's hair, mercury, nitric acid, and...eye of newt. "Heat ingredients and apply to witch. If a spell has been cast in the previous forty-eight hours, witch's skin will turn blue." Simple as that. The beauty of it, of course, is that it works. At least on television.

GILES: "Witchcraft. Blinding your enemy to disable and disorient them is a classic."

XANDER: "First vampires, now witches. No wonder you can still afford a house in Sunnydale."
—"Witch"

"Intent has to be pure with love spells."
Amy, in "Bewitched, Bothered, and Bewildered"

"People under the influence of love spells are deadly, Xander. They lose all capacity to reason."
Giles, in "Bewitched, Bothered, and Bewildered"

One particular spell cast by Catherine as Amy is the Bloodstone Vengeance Spell, which, according to Giles, "hits the body hard, like drinking a quart of alcohol, then eradicates the immune system." In fact, it is with this spell that Catherine nearly kills Buffy.

We also learn in that episode that a witch's spells can be reversed with the use of the witch's "spell book," which seems to be some kind of journal of the witch's activities—or by cutting off the witch's head. To cast spells, the witch needs "a sacred space with a pentagram, a large pot . . ."

Also, the presence of a black cat guarding the witch's spell book in "Witch" would indicate at least a passing acknowledgement of the concept of "familiars" in the *Buffy* mythology. Familiars are animals with whom the witches can communicate.

CATHERINE MADISON

In the episode aptly titled "Witch," the Slayer faces her first witch. Technically, this is the first use of magic on the series as well. Catherine Madison was the homecoming queen and cheerleading star of Sunnydale High when she was a teen. But when her own daughter didn't show an interest in such things, Catherine did something horrible. She used her witchcraft to actually switch bodies with her daughter, Amy.

No matter how hard Catherine worked to get Amy's body into shape, the change of bodies was too much for her, and she could not perfect the moves necessary to become a cheerleader. Instead, she made only the "alternate" list. To make the squad,

Catherine used magic to eliminate the competition. She caused Amber Grove to spontaneously combust, made Lishanne's mouth disappear, and nearly killed Cordelia Chase by blinding her.

In the end, Giles managed to return Catherine to her own body, after which an enraged Catherine tried to use her witchcraft to destroy first her daughter and then Buffy. Buffy was able to put a mirror between herself and Catherine, reflecting the magic back at the witch. Ironically, to this day, Catherine remains trapped in a trophy case in the high school's front hall, inside the small cheerleading trophy she had won for the school when she was a teen cheer queen.

AMY MADISON

Though Amy is not evil, she is, indeed, a witch. After being trapped for some time in her mother's body, one would have thought Amy would have learned not to toy with magic. Instead, it becomes obvious in "Bewitched, Bothered, and Bewildered" that Amy has been studying witchcraft. She casts a spell on one of her teachers to make the woman believe she has handed in homework that she never did. Amy is also coerced by Xander into casting a love spell on Cordelia, but the spell backfires with hysterical and discomforting consequences.

ETHAN RAYNE

Ethan Rayne is a sinister friend from Giles's youth in London. As leaders of a circle that dabbled in the occult, they were responsible for the death of one of their associates who was possessed by the demon Eyghon. Ethan stands for everything Giles has repudiated, and it seems that he has come back into Giles's life only to cause him misery.

Ethan first appeared in "Halloween" as the proprietor of a shop filled with costumes, which he cursed by praying to the two-faced god Janus. His second appearance comes in "The Dark Age." He and Giles are being stalked by Eyghon. Giles suffers from paralyzing remorse over having summoned the demon in the first place and orders Buffy as her Watcher—his highest mantle of authority—to stay out of it. Ethan tattoos Buffy with the Mark of Eyghon and destroys his own tattoo with acid so that the demon will come after her instead.

Ethan has a dry wit, which may be one of the reasons he and Giles became friends:

BUFFY: "I know you, you ran that costume shop."
ETHAN: "I'm pleased you remember."
BUFFY: "You sold me that dress for Halloween and nearly got us all killed."
ETHAN: "But you looked great."

But he's also an immoral dilettante, explaining why Giles has repudiated that friendship:

ETHAN: "What? No hug? Aren't you pleased to see your old mate, Rupert?"
GILES: "I'm surprised I didn't guess it was you. This Halloween stunt stinks of Ethan Rayne."
ETHAN (proud): "Yes, it does, doesn't it? Don't want to blow my own horn, but—it's genius. The very embodiment of 'be careful what you wish for.'"
GILES: "It's sick. Brutal. And it harms the innocent."
ETHAN (wry): "Oh, and we all know that *you* are the champion of innocence and all things pure and good, Rupert....This is quite a little act you've got going here, old man."
GILES: "It's no act. It's who I am."

In both "Halloween" and "The Dark Age," Ethan Rayne disappears into the night. We can only wonder when he'll turn up next....

WEREWOLVES, SHAPE-SHIFTERS, AND PRIMALS

The origins of werewolf and shape-shifter myths are intertwined heavily with those of vampire legends. Vampires could, according to some legends, change their shapes,

including transforming themselves into wolves. However, the best-known pieces of the mythology of lycanthropy, or werewolfism, are predicated on the fact that the werewolf or shape-shifter is a living human being somehow cursed or gifted with the ability to alter his or her form.

Like vampires, werewolf legends are found throughout history. Unlike vampires, however, stories about lycanthropy abound in the works of the most respected ancient historians. Herodotus, Pliny, Petronius, Virgil, and even, in his *Metamorphoses,* Ovid, discuss the transformation of men into werewolves, though in the majority of these cases the change is either permanent or it is an annual rather than a monthly event.

Indeed, werewolf stories or stories of similar shape-shifting, are to be found throughout ancient history and mythology, and into the nineteenth century. Norse mythology and Scandinavian folklore are rife with references to wolf-men, apparently in conjunction with the legend of the berserkers (literally, "bear-shirts," warriors cloaked in the skins of bears). Although in this case, rather than bear skins these wolf-men would wear wolf skins, and many had the power to make an actual change. Of course, this is but one example of a phenomenon found in folklore from around the world.

There are countless examples throughout history of man-beast creatures, and man-into-beast transformations, of which the traditional werewolf is only one. The *azeman* of South America is a human woman by day and a savage beast by night. There are legends of were-hyenas and were-lions in Africa, were-jaguars and were-boars in South America and kindly were-seals, or selkies, on the coastal islands of Scotland. Navajo legends discuss "skinwalkers," men who would wear the skins of wolves and thereby literally transform themselves into faster, more savage wolves. And these are merely a few examples.

"I must admit, I'm intrigued. A werewolf. It's one of the classics. I'm sure my books and I are in for a fascinating afternoon." **Giles, in "Phases"**

In the mythology of *Buffy the Vampire Slayer,* there seems to be no end to the variations upon the lycanthropic or shape-shifting theme. Each time the subject has been touched upon, it has been in a manner entirely different from the others, and completely in keeping with the program. Boys transformed by science into giant sea creatures. An ancient half-human, half-insect shape-shifter. Demonic hyenas able to possess the souls and minds of human beings. And werewolves, of course.

GILES: "A werewolf is such a potent, extreme representation of our inborn, animalistic traits that it emerges for three consecutive nights—the full moon and the two nights surrounding it."
WILLOW: "Quite the party animal."
GILES: "Quite. It acts on pure instinct, no conscience, predatory and aggressive." —**"Phases"**

Interestingly, the werewolf concept presented in the series is much closer to its traditional representation than the vampires and demons in the series are. A werewolf, in Buffy's world, is a human being who had the misfortune to have been bitten by a werewolf and survived. This person will, from that day forth, transform into a wolf for the three nights of the full moon, every month. A werewolf can be killed only with weapons made of silver—most commonly a silver bullet.

One major departure for the series, however, is that the presentation of the werewolf is a sympathetic one. The werewolf is the victim of a curse and is not responsible for his or her actions while in the wolf state. Which makes things wonderfully complicated, of course.

OZ

Oz is a werewolf. Apparently, he was bitten on the finger by his toddler cousin, Jordy, only to discover later on that Jordy was a werewolf. Jordy's parents, Uncle Ken and Aunt Maureen, may or may not be werewolves as well. This subject has yet to be addressed. However, Oz did seem strangely stoic about the revelation that he had become a *loup garous*.

"Is Jordy a werewolf? Uh-huh…and how long has that been going on? Uh-huh…no reason.
Thanks. Love to Uncle Ken."
Oz, in "Phases"

For the three nights of the full moon each month, Oz chains himself up to stop his wolf-self from hunting the nighttime streets of Sunnydale. The chains were supplied by Buffy's Watcher, Rupert Giles. The Slayer and all her friends are aware that Oz is a werewolf. Even his girlfriend, Willow Rosenberg, is sympathetic.

"Well, I like you. You're nice, and you're funny and you don't smoke, and okay, werewolf, but that's not all the time. I mean, three days out of the month I'm not much fun to be around, either." **Willow, in "Phases"**

As a werewolf, Oz has yet to take a human life. In wolf-form, he is huge and quite powerful. His only known natural enemy is the werewolf hunter, Gib Cain, who was forced to leave town without the werewolf pelt he wanted so badly. Cain hunts werewolves to skin them and sell their pelts in Sri Lanka. Chances are, we may see Gib Cain again, particularly with Oz taking a more prominent role in the series' third season.

THE PACK

In high school, as in any jungle, there always seem to be those mean kids who run together and pick on other, more timid classmates. They practice a kind of brinksmanship, rarely crossing the line into overt cruelty (for which they could be punished), but still satisfying some inner need to dominate.

Joss Whedon has commented that his high school years were difficult and that much of *Buffy the Vampire Slayer* springs, at its core, from those memories and experiences. They certainly resonate with the show's audience, which might explain why the viewership is so varied. All of us can remember a time in school when we felt put on the spot, laughed at, or misunderstood.

Four of the five "monsters" of "The Pack," begin the show as just this sort of bullying group. Kyle, Tor, Rhonda, and Heidi spend the field trip to the zoo picking on shy, bookish Lance, an easy and tempting target. They intimidate him into joining them on a forbidden tour of the Hyena House and half-threaten to throw him to the quarantined animals.

Xander arrives on the scene to help Lance. He and Kyle are practically on the verge of blows when the hyenas' eyes flash yellow…and the eyes of each member of the pack glow in turn. As do Xander's. Now he is possessed by the spirit of the hyenas.

Xander begins to change, subtly at first—he seems more aggressive, a little rude, and he starts sniffing his friends. The four other hyena-people seem to respect him in some way, perhaps even to include them in their sphere of influence.

The changes grow more pronounced, until Buffy appeals to Giles, certain that something is wrong. He responds by tut-tutting her concerns:

GILES: "Xander's taken to teasing the less fortunate?"
BUFFY: "Uh-huh."
GILES: "There's been a noticeable change in both clothing and demeanor?"
BUFFY: "Yes."
GILES: "And otherwise all his spare time is spent lounging about with imbeciles?"
BUFFY: "It's bad?"
GILES: "It's devastating. He's turned into a sixteen-year-old boy! Of course, you'll have to kill him."

It's not until Xander and the other members of his pack devour the school mascot that Giles does his research, and he recalls the story of a sect of animal worshipers called Primals. Their goal is to become possessed by the spirits of the most predatory animals—hyenas, for example:

"The Masai of the Serengeti have spoken of animal possession for generations. I should have remembered that….They believe that humanity, consciousness, the soul—is a dilution of spirit. To them, the animal state is holy. They were able, through trans-possession, to pull the spirit of certain animals into themselves."

As the possession continues, the victim, or host, takes on the characteristics of the animal that is possessing him or her, until they are little more than a savage beast. The hyena-people devour the principal, and Xander attacks Buffy. The stakes upped, Giles visits the zookeeper in charge of the hyenas and discovers that he knows of the legend of the Primals. He explains that the transference requires a predatory act and the presence of a totemic symbol. One of

which, Giles notices, is drawn on the floor of the hyena house.

In his own case—for the zookeeper is revealed as a Primal believer—the predatory act is Buffy's attack on him as he threatens to cut Willow's throat. The hyena-people burst into the Hyena House, intent upon devouring Buffy in a scene reminiscent of William Golding's *The Lord of the Flies,* a novel about British schoolboys who "revert" to savagery when they are marooned on an island.

The zookeeper chants sacred words, and the spirits inside the hyena-people leap into him all at once, completely obliterating his humanity. As Xander and Buffy fight to protect Willow from him, he falls to his death inside the hyena enclosure, devoured by the very animals he wished so desperately to commune with.

ZOOKEEPER: "A Masai tribesman once told me that hyenas can understand human speech. They follow humans by day, learning their names. At night, when the campfire dies, they call out to a person. And once that person is separated . . . the pack devours him."

SHE-MANTIS

Though she took on the identity of an aging substitute teacher named Natalie French when she came to Sunnydale, the true name of the She-Mantis is not revealed during her single appearance, in "Teacher's Pet." The creature is either a "perception-distorter" or possessed of the power to alter its physical mass between a human form and its true form, that of a giant praying mantis which has a taste for young male virgins. In "Teacher's Pet," it first dispatches biology teacher Dr. Gregory, so that the school will have need of a substitute. Then it sets its sights on and abducts a pair of young male students, Blayne Mall and Xander Harris. The She-Mantis is a terrifying creature, fierce enough that it frightens even vampires.

Like her tiny cousins, the She-Mantis is a cannibal who eats her mate's head during the act of mating. She "lays her eggs and then finds a mate to fertilize them." She can turn her head 180 degrees, even in human form.

"No, no, I'm not saying she craned her neck. We are talking full-on *Exorcist* twist."

Buffy, in "Teacher's Pet"

Giles has a former associate, Dr. Ferris Carlyle, who, according to the Watcher, "spent years transcribing a lost, pre-Germanic language," wherein he first read of the She-Mantis's existence. When several teenage boys were murdered, Carlyle went hunting for the creature.

"This type of creature, the Kleptes-Virgo or virgin-thief, appears in many cultures: the Greek Sirens, the Celtic sea-maidens who tore the living flesh from the bones of…"

Giles, in "Teacher's Pet"

Dr. Carlyle was committed to an insane asylum after his run-in with the creature. When Giles contacted him, Carlyle recommended that Buffy cleave all its body parts with a sharp blade. Which is, of course, what she did in the end. It is Buffy, however, who pointed out that they would be able to use the recorded sounds of bat sonar to distract the creature so that she could get close enough to kill it.

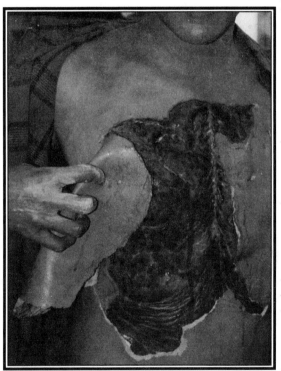

(with whom Buffy goes on a date early in this episode), and another swimmer, named Sean, lose their humanity, thanks to a type of steroid experimentation by Coach Marin and Nurse Greenleigh. On an interesting note, Buffy begins to suspect something is wrong with the swimmers when Gage is attacked by Angel, only to have Angel spit out the swimmer's blood.

BUFFY: "It's all here in their school medical records."
WILLOW: "All symptomatic of steroid abuse."
XANDER: "But is steroid abuse usually linked with 'Hey, I'm a fish'?"

—"Go Fish"

When Xander goes "undercover" and joins the swim team, he discovers that the "steroids" are being given to the swimmers as part of their steam bath. They're breathing them in. When Nurse Greenliegh tries to talk Coach Marin into abandoning the treatments, the coach feeds her to the fish-men. All that matters to the coach is that they win. When Buffy presses him, he reveals the source of these mutations.

"After the fall of the Soviet Union, documents came to light detailing experiments with fish DNA on their Olympic swimmers. Tarpon, mako shark—but they never cracked it." **Coach Marin, in "Go Fish"**

FISH-MEN

𝕴n "Go Fish," it at first appears as though the swim team is being attacked and devoured by huge fish monsters. However, over the course of the episode, it is revealed that the members of the team are actually evolving into these enormous fish-men. Dodd McAlvy, Gage Petronzi, Cameron Walker

Though the "team" has already eaten, Coach Marin ends up dropping Buffy down into the grotto where the fish-men are waiting. They aren't hungry, but the coach apparently has decided they can use Buffy to satisfy other needs. "This is just what my rep needs," she quips. "That I did it with the entire swim team." In the end, Coach Marin ends up down in the grotto, where the fish-men tear him apart. Finally, they are seen swimming out into the Pacific, and it is implied that this is home to them now and they won't be back.

GHOSTS

The words "ghost" and "guest" spring from the same source, the Germanic "Geist." In northern England, the words are still pronounced identically. In most early belief systems, ghosts were the spirits of dead ancestors invited to tribal events, ceremonies, and feasts, such as Samhain (Halloween). In Europe, the heads or skulls of the dead were preserved and decorated, and the spirits of the deceased were considered to be present when these objects were displayed. They were also consulted as oracles after being given an offering.

As Christianity established itself as a religious and political force, these customs were discouraged because the church's doctrine of the resurrection of the body insisted that a buried body be kept as whole as possible. Thus, the hanging of the heads of executed traitors on pikes or gates represented a direct threat against any kind of life in the hereafter. Yet the custom of preserving heads continued well after the establishment of the Christian church: in the days of Henry VIII of England, the daughter of Sir Thomas More retrieved the head of her executed father and rather than burying it, is reputed to have kept it with her until she died.

This concern is no doubt the source of many ghost stories in which the phantoms carry their heads under their arms—"The Headless Horseman," by Washington Irving, comes to mind.

Other beliefs attached to ghosts are that they are the restless spirits of people who died violently or committed suicide, were buried in unconsecrated ground, or had been possessed by evil spirits. They haunt the places where they dwelled as living beings or where they met their untimely ends.

In an expurgated sequence in "Out of Mind, Out of Sight," Giles talks about having seen a ghost:

"...in Dartmoor. A murdered countess, very beautiful. She used to float along the foothills, moaning the most piteous..."

In a sequence left in the episode, he explains that he has never touched nor been touched by a ghost, and they make the deduction that what they're dealing with is not a ghost:

GILES: "From what I've read, having a ghost pass through you is a singular experience. It's a cold, amorphous feeling, makes your hair stand on end."

BUFFY: "Okay, this is my problem. I touched the thing. It didn't go through me, it bumped into me. And it wasn't cold."

XANDER: "So this means, what— That we're talking about an invisible person?"

Though different cultures have adopted different "takes" on ghost lore—for example, Japanese ghosts are said to have no feet and are drawn to water—there seems to be universal agreement that they are the spirits of someone, or something, who has died.

JAMES STANLEY AND GRACE NEWMAN

In Western belief, a variant of the standard ghost is the poltergeist, or "noisy ghost." In the episode "I Only Have Eyes for You"—thus far the only episode that deals with ghosts—Giles deduces that the malevolent force at work within the school is a poltergeist. It seems that in 1955, a Sunnydale High student named James Stanley was in love with a teacher named Grace Newman. Though she loved him in return, she knew their affair must end and tried to tell him so on the night of the Sadie Hawkins Dance. In a blind panic at the thought of losing her, he shot and killed her. Then, filled with remorse, he turned the gun on himself.

Now, in present day, as the dance draws near (and, one assumes, the Hellmouth charges the situation with its energy), individuals who pass through the same part of the school where James and Grace fought and died become possessed by their spirits and reenact the tragedy. Buffy breaks up a fight between two quarreling students (who are reciting, we later learn, the last conversation James and Grace had before he shot her) and is sent to the principal's office for her trouble. While there, a yearbook from 1955 falls from the shelves, apparently moved by a ghostly hand.

In history class, she dreams of James and Grace during their tragic romance, and when she drowses awake, discovers that her teacher, Mr. Miller, is scrawling, DON'T WALK AWAY FROM ME, BITCH, on the blackboard, apparently without realizing it.

Concerned, Buffy talks to Xander, who replies: "I'm not trying to poo-poo your wiggins, but a domestic dispute and a little case of chalkboard Tourette's? Sounds like 'Hellmouth Lite' to me—"

His tune changes when a blue decaying arm bursts from his locker and tries to drag him inside. They hurry to Giles:

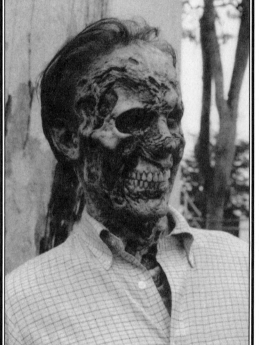

GILES: "Fascinating. It sounds like paranormal phenomena."

WILLOW: "A ghost? Cool!"

XANDER: "Oh, no, not cool. This was no wimpy chain-rattler. This was more like—'I'm dead as hell and I'm not gonna take it anymore.'"

GILES: "Exactly. Despite the Xander-speak, that's an accurate definition of a poltergeist."

XANDER: "I defined something? Accurately? Check me out. Guess I'm done with the book learning!"

BUFFY: "So we've got some bad boo on our hands?"

GILES: "Well . . . A poltergeist is extremely disruptive—and what you described certainly fits the bill."

WILLOW: "But why is it here? Does it just want to scare people?"

GILES: "It doesn't know exactly what it wants. That's the problem. Many times the spirit is plagued by all manner of worldly troubles. But, being dead, it has no way to make its peace. So it lashes out. Growing ever more confused, ever more angry."

BUFFY: "So—it's like a regular teenager. Only dead."

WILLOW: "What can we do? Is there any way to stop it?"

GILES: "The only tried-and-true way is to figure out what unresolved issues keep the spirit here—and resolve them."

BUFFY: "Great. So now we're Dr. Laura for the deceased."

GILES: "Only if we can find out who this spirit is. Or...was."

Giles, in a radical departure from his usually cautious approach to the presence of any kind of supernatural phenomenon, jumps to the conclusion that this troubled spirit is Jenny Calendar. Even after the school janitor shoots and kills Miss Frank, a teacher, Giles clings to this belief...a false hope at best, a poignant testament to his love for Jenny. Meanwhile, Buffy and company do the research that Giles usually does and discover the story of James and Grace. They conclude that the violent spirit is the ghost of James, in terrible need of forgiveness.

What is particularly interesting about this interpretation of a poltergeist is that not only can it wreak havoc, but it can possess individuals and move them to repeat the act which doomed it in the first place. And while the suffering spirit of James enters Buffy, who herself is burdened with guilt over the change in Angel—a change she feels entirely responsible for—the gentle ghost of Grace, who wishes to forgive James, manages to infiltrate the demonic Angel, completely obliterating—at least temporarily—his savage and brutal nature.

REANIMATED CORPSES

Legends and myths abound the world over about people coming back from the dead. The vampire myth itself is very much about life after death, or "undeath," as it is often called. So are ghost stories. But reanimated corpses are slightly different. These are people whom, for one reason or another, rise up from death in their own bodies, with their own minds (for the most part), usually for some sinister purpose or another. Once upon a time, our popular culture was able to make the distinction between a zombie—a human being raised from the dead, usually by magic or voodoo, and bound to obey the person responsible for their revival—and a ghoul, a person raised by some malevolent purpose and driven by the urge to eat human flesh. After George A. Romero's *Night of the Living Dead*, in 1968, however, the two became almost inextricably joined. Zombies and ghouls were, essentially, one and the same.

There are, of course, other theories about ways to reanimate a corpse. Primary among them is through scientific means. Mary Shelley's legendary novel *Frankenstein* introduced that enduring piece of mythology to the world. The mad scientist playing god, the corpse brought back to life, and the tragedy that ensues, have been portrayed by writers and filmmakers time and again, inspired by Shelley.

But how do these things translate into the world of *Buffy the Vampire Slayer*?

ZOMBIES

Zombies do exist in Buffy's world, although technically, we have yet to actually see one. However, there are several discussions about them in "Some Assembly Required." The specific mythology of zombies in the series has few established facts, but Giles does tell Xander that "zombies don't eat the flesh of the living." That, of course, leaves the door open for ghouls down the road, although

ghouls were usually thought to frequent gravesites and eat the flesh of the newly dead.

It also implies that zombies, according to the series, do eat the flesh of dead humans.

In addition, in the same episode, when Giles discovers that someone has been robbing graves, he suggests that it might be a voodoo practitioner. When Xander asks him if he means somebody might be "making a zombie," Giles replies, "...or zombies. For most traditional purposes, a voodoo priest would need more than one."

Thus far, this is all the information we have on zombies in Buffy's world.

DARYL EPPS

Some Assembly Required" is clearly, in part at least, an homage to Mary Shelley's *Frankenstein*. In this instance, however, the mad scientists in question happen to be two high school boys, Chris Epps and his friend Eric. Their monster is Chris's older brother, Daryl, who died in a fall, "rock climbing or something," according to Willow. But Chris wasn't content to let his brother stay dead. With Eric, he sewed his brother back together and, through some unrevealed scientific process, brought Daryl back from the dead.

Daryl remained in his family's basement, while his mother grieved endlessly upstairs. He needed a companion, and he asked Chris and Eric to make him a woman who was like him so he wouldn't be alone. When their plans were ruined by Buffy's interference, Daryl died a final death because he refused to leave the partially constructed companion to burn in the old science building where the experiments were taking place. Daryl Epps is one monster we can reasonably expect to never see again. Except, perhaps, as a ghost. On this series, you never know.

AMPATA GUTIERREZ, A.K.A INCA MUMMY GIRL

Five hundred years ago, the Incan people chose a beautiful teenage girl to become their princess ..." so that they could sacrifice her to the gods. Mummified and imprisoned in a tomb in a state of living death, the mummy was bound in that state by a ceramic seal clasped between her withered hands.

When Rodney, a Sunnydale High student, tries to steal the seal, the mummy rises from her sarcophagus, kills Rodney, and leaves his freeze-dried corpse in her place. In the process, the protective seal is broken.

Ampata is actually the name of the South American exchange student who is slated to stay with Buffy and her mother. By the time Buffy is to pick him up at the bus station, the mummy has sucked the life out of him, renewing her own once more. She introduces herself to Buffy as Ampata.

Ampata's hunger not only for the life force of others but for the experience of life itself, makes her one of the most sympathetic monsters to appear in the first two seasons:

"She was sixteen. Like us. She was offered as a sacrifice and went to her death. Who knows what she gave up to fulfill her duty to others. What chance at love?"
    Ampata, to Buffy, in "Inca Mummy Girl"

She is a tragic figure, given no choice in her fate. She is even described as the Chosen One by the Peruvian man who hunts her, seeking to stop her from taking the lives of others and return her to her hellish existence inside her cramped, dark tomb.

She also is the first girl other than Buffy to attract Xander, who cannot believe his good fortune that the beautiful, exotic girl seems to return his affection ("You're not a praying mantis, by any chance, are you?"). She grows to love him, and though desperate, struggles not to take his life away from him. She tries to deflect her need onto others—Jonathan and even Willow:

XANDER: "If you're going to kiss anybody, it should be me."
AMPATA: "Xander, we can be together. Just let me have this one."
XANDER: "That's never gonna happen."
AMPATA: "I must do this *now*, or it is the end. For me and for us."   **—"Inca Mummy Girl"**

And it is not until she is almost completely decayed that she approaches Xander with her fatal kiss.

After the mummy is destroyed, Buffy underscores

the tragedy of "Ampata's" life, while Xander emphasizes Buffy's heroism when confronted by a similar destiny:

BUFFY: "She was gypped. She was just a girl, and she had her life taken from her. I remember when I heard the prophecy that I was going to die. I wasn't exactly obsessed with doing the right thing."
XANDER: "But you did. You gave up your life."

OTHER MONSTERS

INVISIBLE PEOPLE

Though it's reasonable to assume that in the *Buffy the Vampire Slayer* mythology there are many different ways for someone to become invisible, we're going to concentrate on the one documented brand of invisibility.

"Greek myths talk about cloaks of invisibility, but they're usually just for the gods....Research boy comes through with the knowledge."
    Xander, in "Out of Mind, Out of Sight"

In "Out of Mind, Out of Sight," there is a series of attacks on unsuspecting students by an invisible person. At first, Giles considers several possibilities, including ghosts and telekinesis, but it's soon obvious that they are dealing with a living human capable of invisibility.

Soon, Buffy discovers the identity of the "invisible girl." Marcie Ross was a student at Sunnydale High—a student nobody spoke to, or remembered. Even Xander and Willow, kind to a fault, seem to have been oblivious to her existence. This leads Giles to the astonishing revelation that Marcie is not invisible because of any supernatural event, but rather because of a scientific one. In a line cut from the script, Giles explains that "reality is shaped, even created, by our perception of it." The answer lies in quantum mechanics, according to Giles, who realizes that Marcie was perceived as invisible, and so she became invisible.

Marcie is understandably angered, and perhaps even slightly insane, due to her condition. She attempts to get her revenge, and, in the end, plans to carve up Cordelia's face as an example to everyone and a lesson to Cordelia. Of course, Buffy manages to save the day, but in the end, Marcie is spirited away by FBI agents Doyle and Manetti. "This isn't the first time this has happened, is it?" Buffy asks. "This has happened at other schools." Of course, Doyle and Manetti don't bother answering the question. Marcie is taken to an FBI compound and into a classroom filled with invisible people who are learning about "assassination and infiltration" in their textbooks. Obviously, Marcie and a lot of others like her are still out there.

THE ORDER OF TARAKA

The Order of Taraka first appears in the two parter, "What's My Line?" Spike, desperate to cure Drusilla and fearing Buffy's interference, decides that extraordinary measures are required. As such, he calls in the Order, to the surprise of his followers.

DALTON: "The Order of Taraka? I mean, isn't that overkill?"
SPIKE: "No. I think it's just enough kill."
—"What's My Line? Part 1"

At this point, the only hint as to the nature of the Order is a single reference, when one of the vampires, Dalton, refers to them as "the bounty hunters." But they are far, far more than bounty hunters. They are, in fact, a "society of deadly assassins dating back to King Solomon," or so Giles informs us.

"Their credo is to sow discord and kill the unwary....They're a breed apart....Unlike vampires, they have no earthly desires except to collect their bounty. They find their target and eliminate it. You can kill as many of them as you like. It won't make any difference—where there

is one, there will be another. And another. They won't stop coming until the job is done. Each one of them works alone. His own way. Some of them are human. Some are not. We won't know who they are...until they strike."
Giles, in "What's My Line? Part 1"

Members of the Order of Taraka also wear a particular ring that identifies them as assassins of the Order. They are, according to Kendra, also discussed in detail in volume six of the *Writings of Dramius*. In this two-part episode, we are exposed to three of the Order's assassins. First is a woman known only as Patrice, who disguises herself as a police officer and attempts to shoot Buffy during Career Week at school. Patrice ends up living longer than the others, though she seems in many ways less frightening. The first to attack Buffy, and also the first to die, is Octarus, whom the original script described as "a GIANT. Seven feet tall in boots and a hard 400 pounds. A thick milky cataract covers one eye. His other eye is set deep in the fleshy mask of assorted scars and carbuncles he calls a face." Fortunately, the Octarus that reached the final version of the episode was just as horrifying. Unfortunately, he doesn't last very long.

The most disturbing assassin from the Order of Taraka, at least that we have seen thus far, is Mr. Pfister. Probably a demon of some kind, Pfister is a being who looks human but is actually composed entirely of maggots and other bugs. In an unfortunately expurgated moment from the second half of this two-parter, Xander says it best: "You know, just when you think you've seen it all, along comes a worm guy."

BUFFY: "You and bug people, Xander. What's up with that?"
XANDER: "No, this dude was different than praying-mantis lady. He was a man *of* bugs, not a man who *was* a bug."
—"What's My Line? Part 2"

In the end, while Octarus and Patrice are defeated in straight combat by Buffy and Kendra, respectively, Mr. Pfister takes a bit more ingenuity. He can be killed only when he is in his disassembled state. Thus, Xander and Cordelia taunt him, then hide behind a door so that he must break up into his true self, the horde of bugs. When they crawl under the door, they find themselves trapped in a pool of white paint that Xander and Cordelia have spread there . . . and they stomp him to death.

"Hey, larva boy! That's right. I'm talking to you, the big cootie!"
Xander, in "What's My Line? Part 2"

After the finale, we don't hear anymore about the Order until the next episode, "Ted," where Buffy tells Willow and Xander that "Angel's sources" say the contract is off. However, since the Order of Taraka is made up of all kinds of creatures—human, demon, vampire and otherwise—chances are, we may well end up seeing them again.

BEZOAR

From "Bad Eggs" little Bezoar grow....
A Bezoar is a prehistoric parasite. The mother hibernates underground, laying eggs that look identical to chicken eggs. While still in the egg, the Bezoar sends out long tendrils that spread over the intended host's face, preparing its prey for subjugation. The Bezoar hatchling is an ugly creature that looks like a chicken breast riding on crab legs, reminiscent of the early stages of the Alien in the *Alien* film series.

Buffy, the gang, and the other students in their Teen Health class accidentally (?) receive Bezoar eggs to "parent" in a section on sex ed. As the eggs hatch, the offspring attach themselves to the unsuspecting students, taking control of their minds and bodies through "neural clamping." Cordelia and Willow, as well as their health teacher, Mr. Whitmore, Giles, and Buffy's mother are all taken over. Xander is spared because he boiled his egg to lessen the chances that it would break while he was parenting it, and Buffy catches her Bezoar hatchling as it breaks out of its shell and kills it.

The mother Bezoar is "a slimy expanse of black that moves and breathes below the cave" that lies beyond the school's boiler room, opening one sole eye to observe her surroundings. Her hatchlings are directing their human hosts to break open the floor under which she lies and free her. The hosts are directed to kill any humans who have not been subjugated, which they attempt without hesitation. With

a whiplike tentacle, the mother Bezoar lassos the vampiric cowboy Tector Gorch and pulls him down into the pit, apparently consuming him. Tector's brother, Lyle, tries to feed Buffy to the monster, but the Slayer destroys the creature and then emerges from the Bezoar's pit covered in the blue goo that is the Bezoar's blood.

THE UGLY MAN

The Ugly Man is a fascinating monster, in that he exists only as a construct of the imagination of young Billy Palmer. After a Kiddie League baseball game in which he missed a critical play, twelve-year old Billy was attacked and brutally beaten. Billy was comatose after the attack, and his attacker remained unknown to the authorities. Only after Billy had regained consciousness did Buffy, Giles, and the others realize that it had been Billy's baseball coach who had attacked the boy.

While comatose, Billy suffered horrible nightmares, and somehow his mind interacted with the Hellmouth to reach out to others in the town and bring their own nightmares to life. While all of this was occurring, however, Billy's own nightmare, "the Ugly Man," was also running free in the town. The Ugly Man was Billy's nightmare version of the man who'd beaten him. As an interesting aside, it seemed that Billy was also astrally projecting an image of himself into the real world, an image which only the Slayer could see. Giles postulates that it is this projection that has caused Billy's nightmares to "leak" into reality.

The first actual appearance of the Ugly Man is at the end of the first act of "Nightmares." A student named Laura ducks into the school boiler room for a cigarette and is attacked and savagely beaten by the Ugly Man, who says only "lucky nineteen." This turns out to be a reference to Billy's jersey number on the baseball team—it was what the coach called him, at least before he missed an important catch. The Ugly Man also has a thick club arm, and is, hence the name, hideous to look at. For most of the rest of the episode, he hunts Billy and Buffy, and in the end Buffy not only defeats him, but helps Billy "unmask" him. Billy wakes, and all returns to normal. A short time later, his coach, the real-life inspiration for the psychically created

Ugly Man, enters the room. When he realizes his crime has been discovered, he attempts to flee, but Xander and Giles stop him.

TED BUCHANAN

Ted Buchanan would have been enough of a monster if he'd been human. In the episode simply titled "Ted," Buffy comes home to find her mother "Frenching a guy" in their kitchen. This turns out to be Joyce's new boyfriend. To everyone else, Ted seems to be the perfect father figure. He's a great cook, obviously has great values, and gets along well with everyone. But…

BUFFY: "So far, all I see is someone who apparently has a good job, seems nice and polite, and my mother really likes him.…"
XANDER: "What kind of a monster is he?!?!"
—"Ted"

Needless to say, Buffy's friends don't take her concerns very seriously, even though Ted, in a private moment, actually threatens to slap Buffy. Later, he reads her diary, and when they argue over it, he does finally hit her. She fights back, and as the Slayer, overpowers him. Ted ends up falling down the stairs and apparently dying.

Later, however, Buffy's suspicions are proven correct: Ted comes back to life, psychotically obsessed with Joyce. We quickly discover that Ted was never what he seemed, particularly after Xander, Willow, and Cordelia visit his address and find his four previous wives or, rather, their preserved corpses.

"Feels like home. If it's the '50s and you're a psycho."
Cordelia, on visiting Ted's abode, in "Ted"

As it turns out, "Ted" isn't Ted Buchanan at all, but a robot that the brilliant but mad Buchanan built when he was dying. To put it in terms Xander could understand:

"'I'm Ted the sickly loser; I'm dying and my wife dumps me. I build a better Ted. He brings her back. She dies in his little love bunker, and so he keeps bringing her back over and over.' That's creepy on a level I hardly knew existed."
Xander, in "Ted"

In the end, Buffy destroys Ted. Later, she tells Joyce that she is certain he's on the "scrap heap." But anyone who's seen *The Terminator* will tell you that you can't keep a good robot down. After all, there's no telling how many "Teds" the original built.

SPELLS, CHANTS, AND INCANTATIONS

"The sleeper will awaken. The sleeper will awaken. And the world will bleed."

Luke, chanting in "Welcome to the Hellmouth"

"And like a plague of boils, the race of Man covered the Earth. But on the third day of the newest light will come the Harvest, when the blood of men will flow as wine, when the Master will walk among them once more, the world will belong to the Old Ones, and Hell itself will come to town. Amen."

Luke, quoting from "the sacred text" in "Welcome to the Hellmouth"

MASTER: "My blood runs with yours. My soul is your province."
LUKE: "My body is your instrument."

—preparing the Vessel, in "The Harvest"

"The center is dark. *Centrum est obscurus.* The darkness breathes. *Tenebrae respiratis.* The listener hears. Hear me. Unlock the gate, let the darkness shine. Cover us with holy fear. Show me. Corsheth and Gilail, the gate is closed. Receive the dark, release the unworthy....Take of mine energy and be sated! Be sated, release the unworthy!"

Giles, casting the spell to switch Amy and Catherine back to their own bodies, in "Witch"

"I shall look upon my enemy. I shall look upon her and the dark place will have her soul. Corsheth! Take her!"

Catherine, trying to zap Buffy into oblivion, in "Witch"

"For the Old Ones, for his pain, for the dark."

The Brethren of Aurelius, chanting for the Master's resurrection in "When She Was Bad"

"St. Vigeous, you who murdered so many, we beseech you, cleanse us of our weaknesses: mercy, compassion, and pity."

Lean Boy's prayer to St. Vigeous, in "School Hard"

"Diana, goddess of love and the hunt, I pray to thee. Let my cries bind the heart of Xander's beloved. May she neither rest nor sleep until she submits to his will only. Diana! Bring about this love and bless it!"

Amy's love spell in "Bewitched, Bothered, and Bewildered"

"Goddess Hecate, work thy will. Before thee let the unclean thing crawl!"

Amy, turning Buffy into a rat, in "Bewitched, Bothered, and Bewildered"

"Diana! Hecate! I hereby license thee to depart! Goddess of creatures great and small, I conjure thee to withdraw!"

Amy, turning the rat back into Buffy, in "Bewitched, Bothered, and Bewildered"

"Eligor, I name thee. Bringer of war, poisoners, pariahs, grand obscenity! Eligor, wretched master of decay, bring your black medicine. Come restore your impious, murderous child. From the blood of the sire she is risen! From the blood of the sire shall she rise again.... Right, then. Now we let them come to a simmering boil, then remove to a low flame."

Spike, intoning the du Lac ritual, which will restore Dru to health, in "What's My Line? Part 2"

"Diana, goddess of love, be gone! Hear no more your siren's song!"

Giles, breaking the love spell, in "Bewitched, Bothered, and Bewildered"

"And there will be a time of crisis, of worlds hanging in the balance. And in this time shall come the Anointed, the Master's great warrior. And the Slayer will not know him, will not stop him. And he will lead her into Hell. As it is written, so shall it be. Five will die, and from their ashes the Anointed shall rise. The Brethren of Aurelius shall greet him and usher him to his immortal destiny. As it is written, so shall it be."

The Master, reading from the writings of Aurelius, in "Never Kill A Boy on the First Date"

"By the power of the Circle of Kayless, I command you, demon. Come!"

Thelonius Monk, binding Moloch into the book, in "I Robot, You Jane"

"By the power of the divine...by the essence of the word, I command you. By the power of the Circle of Kayless, I command you! Demon, COME!"

Giles, speaking and Jenny typing, getting Moloch "off-line," in "I Robot, You Jane"

YOUNG MAN: "I pledge my life and my death...."
RICHARD: "To the Delta Zeta Kappas and to Machida, whom we serve."
YOUNG MAN: "To the Delta Zeta Kappas and to Machida, whom we serve."
RICHARD: "On my oath, before my assembled brethren."
YOUNG MAN: "On my oath, before my assembled brethren."
Richard: "I promise to keep our secret from this day until my death."
YOUNG MAN: "I promise to keep our secret from this day until my death."
RICHARD: "In blood I was baptized, in blood I shall reign, in His Name!"

YOUNG MAN: "In blood I was baptized, in blood I shall reign, in His Name!"
RICHARD: "You are now one of us."
YOUNG MAN: "In His Name!"

—initiation ceremony into the DZK fraternity house, in "Reptile Boy"

TOM: "Machida...We who serve you, we who receive all that you bestow, call upon you in this holy hour."
OTHERS: "Machida."
TOM: "We have no wealth, no possession, except that which you give us. We have no power, no place in the world, except that which you give us."
OTHERS: "Except that which you give us."
TOM: "It has been a year since our last offerings . . . a year in which our bounty overflowed....We come before you with fresh offerings . . . we hope you find them worthy. Accept our offering, dark lord, and bless us with your power, Machida! Come forth and let your terrible countenance look upon servants and their humble offerings! We call you, Machida!"
OTHERS: "In his name! Machida!"
TOM: "For he shall rise from the depths and we shall tremble before him. He who is the souce of all we inherit and all we possess. MACHIDA!"
OTHERS: "Machida!"
TOM: "And if he is pleased with our offerings, then our fortunes shall increase."
OTHERS: "Machida, let our fortunes increase."
TOM: "And on the tenth day of the tenth month, he shall be enhungered and we shall feed him. Feed, dark lord."

—ritual for feeding Machida, in "Reptile Boy"

"The word that denies thee, thou inhabit. The peace that ignores thee, thou corrupt. Chaos, I remain, as ever, your faithful, degenerate son. [Then, in Latin] Janus, hear my plea. Take this as your own. Come forth and show us your truth. The mask is made flesh. The heart is curdled by your holy presence. Janus, this night is *yours*."

Ethan Rayne, incantation to enchant the wearers of his costumes, in "Halloween"

"...his verbes, consesus rescissus est. [By these words, consent repealed.]"

Willow, repealing Angel's invitation to enter Buffy's home, in "Passion"

"I shall confront and expel all evil...out of marrow and bone—out of house and home—never to come here again."

Willow, Cordelia, Xander, and Buffy performing a ritual of exorcism, in "I Only Have Eyes for You" (Cordy adds "totally")

In Rumanian: *Nici mort nici al flinçtei*
Te invoc, spirit al trecerii
Reda trupului ce separa omul de animal
Cu ajutorul acestui magic glob de cristal.

"Not dead, nor not of the living. Spirits of the interregnum, I call. Restore to the corporal vessel that which separates us from beast. Use this orb as your guide."

Gypsy woman, chanting the Spell of Restoration of the Soul, in "Becoming, Part 1"

"I will drink...the blood will wash in me, over me, and I will be cleansed. I will be worthy to free Acathla. [to Spike and Dru]: Bear witness as I ascend. As I become."

Angel, reciting the ritual to awaken Acathla, in "Becoming, Part 1"

"*Quod perditum est, in venietur.*" [What was lost, shall be found.]

Giles, reciting the Spell of Restoration of the Soul in Latin, in "Becoming, Part 1"

"Not dead, nor not of the living. Spirits of the interregnum, I call. Let him know the pain of humanity, gods—reach your wizened hands to me, give me the soul of—" [she's interrupted]

Willow, reciting the Spell of Restoration after Giles, in "Becoming, Part 1"

"Gods bind him, cast his heart from the demon...realm...return his...I call on...I...*Te implor Doamne, nu ignora accasta rugaminte! Lasa orbita sa fie vasul care-i va transporta sufletul la el!* [I call on you, gods, do not ignore this supplication! Let the orb be the vessel to carry his soul to him!] *Este scris, aceasta putere este dreptul poporuil meu de a conduce...* [It is written, this power is my people's right to wield...] *Asa sa fie! Acum!* [Let it be so! Now!]"

Willow, attempting the Spell of Restoration one more time, in "Becoming, Part 2"

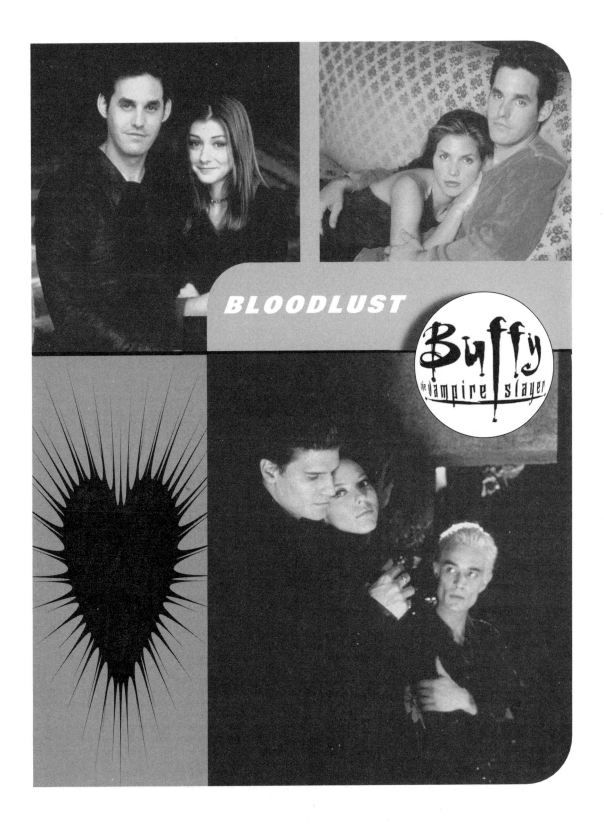

BLOODLUST

Buffy
the vampire slayer

Love may make the world go round, but in Sunnydale, it can kill you. Do the wacky with the wrong vampire, demon, robot, or bug woman and you may be the next to die. Maybe it's the Hellmouth and maybe it's hormones, but Sunnydale is one smoldering berg when it comes to 'der big smootchen.' Thrill, therefore, as the fireworks go off—and the smoke alarms—for these...

Sunnydale Love Connections

Buffy and Angel

For ne'er was there a tale of more woe . . .

The course of true love has never run less smoothly than for the Slayer and the tormented Angel. Introducing himself as "a friend" (though not necessarily *her* friend) in the premiere episode, "Welcome to the Hellmouth," Angel's earliest meetings with Buffy generally consisted of warning her about impending danger...neither of them dreaming that he would ultimately pose the greatest threat of all the evil forces she has ever faced.

In the second episode, "The Harvest," he takes a risk by telling her his name. After all, her Watcher may eventually make the connection between Angel and Angelus. But apparently his courage has limits...or could it simply be that he understands that the Slayer has a sacred duty, while he does not?

Buffy: "If this Harvest thing is such a suck-fest, why don't **you** stop it?"
Angel: "Because I'm afraid."
Angel: "They'll be expecting you."
Buffy: "I've got a friend down there—or, a potential friend. [joking] Do you know what it's like to have a friend?"
He doesn't answer.
Buffy (gently): "That wasn't supposed to be a stumper."

In "Teacher's Pet," the fourth episode of the first season, it is established that Angel has made it a practice to come to Buffy when he has heard of possible dangers in her midst:

Buffy: "Well, look who's here."
Angel: "Hi."
Buffy: "I'd say it's nice to see you but we both know that's a big fib."
Angel: "I won't stay long."
Buffy: "No, you'll just give me a cryptic warning about some exciting new catastrophe and then disappear into the night, right?"
Angel: "You're cold."
Buffy: "You can take it."
Angel: "I mean you look cold."
Angel takes off his leather jacket.

Nevertheless, this mysterious man—"dark, gorgeous, in an annoying sort of way" (as she decribes him to Giles)—continues to intrigue her. A solitary figure, he seems haunted and lonely. Perhaps she is drawn to him because of aloneness...something she shares, for although she has good friends in Willow and Xander, she alone in all her generation is the Slayer.

Yet Angel has revealed to her a shared sense of purpose—"to kill them, kill 'em all—" which bonds them to each other almost before Buffy realizes what is happening. This man, this guardian Angel, has become important to her, though she knows very little about him. And though she tries to be "a real girl," having real crushes on boys and going out on dates, the importance of all they share overshadows everything else:

Angel: "Buffy. I was hoping I'd find you here."
Buffy (a little flustered): "You were hoping—?"
Angel: "There's severe stuff happening tonight. You need to be out there."
Buffy: "Oh, no. Not you too."
Angel: "You already know?"
Buffy: "Prophecy, Anointed One, yada yada yada."
Angel: "So you know. Fine. I just thought I'd warn you."
Buffy: "Warn me?" [indicating Owen] See that guy over at the bar? He came here to *be* with me."
Angel: "You're here on a date?"
Buffy: "Yeah. Why is that such a shock to everyone?"

—"NEVER KILL A BOY ON THE FIRST DATE"

The next episode Angel appears in is the one that bears his name, promising revelations. Buffy has not been successful in her bid to be a regular girl:

Willow: "It's a lot of fun [the Bronze fumigation party]. What's it like where you are?"
Buffy: "I'm sorry. I was just...thinking about...things."
Willow: "So we're talking about a guy."
Buffy: "Not exactly. For us to have a conversation about a guy, there would have to be a guy for us to have a conversation about. Was that a sentence?"
Willow: "You lack a guy."
Buffy: "I do. Which is fine with me, most of the time, but . . . "
Willow: "What about Angel?"

Buffy: "Angel. I can just see him in a relationship. 'Hi, honey, you're in grave danger. I'll see you next month.'"

Willow: "He's not around much, it's true."

Buffy: "When he's around, I think it's like the lights dim everywhere else. You know how that happens with some guys?"

—AT THE BRONZE, IN "ANGEL"

Later, when he joins in her battle against the Three and they escape together into her house, the tension builds. He takes off his shirt; they stand close as she tends to his wound; still, attracted though she is, the Slayer tries to stay in control of the situation:

Buffy: "I was lucky you came along. How did you happen to come along?"

Angel: "I live nearby. I was just out walking."

Buffy: "So you weren't following me? I just had this feeling you were...."

Angel: "Why would I do that?"

Buffy: "You tell me, you're the Mystery Guy who appears out of nowhere—I'm not saying I'm not happy about it tonight—but if you *are* hanging around, I'd like to know why."

Meanwhile, Joyce Summers has told Buffy to go to bed, and Angel can't leave because "the Fang Gang" may be loitering nearby. And so together they climb the stairs to her bedroom, as the tension rises.... "So, uh-oh, two of us, one bed—that doesn't work—" And the next evening, when she returns from her life in the daylight, he confesses: "I did a lot of thinking today. I can't really be around you...because when I am...all I can think about is how badly I want to kiss you—"

Unable to conquer his passions, he does kiss her, fiercely, until, bloodlust upon him, he pulls back and reveals his true face:

He is her enemy.

He is a vampire.

> "I can't believe this is happening....One minute we're kissing, the next minute
> [to Giles]...can a vampire ever be a good person? Couldn't it happen?"
>
> **Buffy, in "Angel"**

Still, Buffy wavers in her duty as the Slayer: "He's never done anything to hurt me." And she and Willow talk about him pretty much as they would talk about any boy they were interested in:

Willow: "Okay, here's something I gotta know: when Angel kissed you, I mean before he turned into....How was it?"

Buffy: "Unbelievable."

—"ANGEL"

Willow: "And it is kind of novel how he'll stay young and handsome forever—although you'll still get wrinkly and die—and ooh, what about the children—I'll be quiet now."

—"ANGEL"

Then, in what for her is the ultimate betrayal, Buffy is horrified to find Angel bent over her mother, his fangs lowered near the bleeding puncture wounds in her neck. Still, Buffy does not stake him. She throws him through the window and calls 911. But later, at the hospital, she realizes that the time has come to destroy Angel.

Showdown, as terrible truths are revealed:

166

Buffy: "Why? Why didn't you just attack me when you had the chance? Was it a joke? To make me feel for you and then....I've killed a lot of vampires. I've never hated one before."

Angel: "Feels good, doesn't it? Feels simple."

Buffy: "I invited you into my home. And then you attacked my family."

Angel: "Why not? I killed mine."

This is a pivotal moment, because it shows the depth of Angel's remorse. Rather than correct her false conclusion—his sire, Darla, attacked Buffy's mother, in order to both frame him and get him to feed on a living human, thus returning to the vampire fold—he tells her more horrible things about himself: "I killed their friends and their friends' children. For a hundred years, I offered an ugly death to everyone I met. And I did it with a song in my heart."

When he does admit that he didn't attack her mother, he makes another confession: "I wanted to. I can walk like a man, but I'm not one. I wanted to kill you tonight."

Buffy sets down her weapon—a crossbow—walks to him, and offers him her neck, saying, "Go ahead." When he only looks at her, they reach an understanding: it's not as easy as it looks. Their relationship is deeper and more complex than that.

When they meet again, agreeing that they must part, they tenderly kiss...the Slayer's cross-shaped brand searing the heart of Angel.

Angel vanishes for three episodes, and when he returns, in "Out of Mind, Out of Sight," he is avoiding Buffy:

Giles: "Is that why you're here? To see her?"

Angel (shakes his head): "I can't. It's . . . it's too hard for me to be around her."

Giles: "A vampire in love with the Slayer. It's rather poetic, in a maudlin sort of way."

In the first season's finale, "Prophecy Girl," the joy Buffy feels upon seeing Angel is wrenching...once she knows that he's discussing the fact that she will die in less than twenty-four hours. "You think I want anything to happen to you? You think I could stand it?" he asks her.

And though Angel loves her, it is Xander who forces him to go down into the tunnels with him to rescue Buffy. And it is Xander who brings Buffy back to life with CPR. But it is Angel who finally, publicly attacks his own kind as the Hellmouth opens. And Angel who is finally accepted as Buffy's companion...at least for this evening...as they set off for the prom.

In the second-season opener, "When She Was Bad," Buffy is having a hard time dealing with her own fate at the hands of the Master...as well as her destiny as a Slayer. She is cold and cruel to all her friends, including Angel:

Buffy: "Is that it? Is that everything? 'Cause you woke me up from a really nice dream."
Angel: "Sorry. I'll go."
He heads for the window. Stands facing it as Buffy hunkers down in bed, facing away from him.
Angel (quietly): "I missed you."
She can't reply, but the hardness in her face melts away. After a couple of beats, she turns, her true emotions about to spill out.
Buffy: "I missed—"
But he's gone. She stares at the window, unhappy. **—"WHEN SHE WAS BAD"**

"Uh, could you contemplate getting over yourself?
There's no 'us.' I'm sorry if I was supposed to spend the summer
mooning over you, but I didn't. I moved on. To the living."
Buffy, to Angel, in "When She Was Bad"

Angel: "Why are you riding me?"
Buffy: "Because I don't trust you. You're a vampire. Or is that an offensive term? Should I say 'undead American'?"
Angel: "You have to trust someone. You can't do this alone."
Buffy: "I trust me."
Angel: "You're not as strong as you think."
Buffy: "You think you could take me."
Angel: "What?"
Buffy: "Come on, you must have wondered . . . a vampire, the Slayer, I know you've thought about it. If it came down to a fight . . . could you take me? Why don't we find out?"
Angel: "I'm not gonna fight you."
Buffy: "No? Big strong vampire like yourself?"
Angel: "Buffy..."
Buffy: "Come on. Kick my ass." **—"WHEN SHE WAS BAD"**

When Buffy finally grinds the Master's bones into dust, she collapses into Angel's arms, sobbing out her fear, her frustration, and her victory to the one she loves best.

In the next episode, "Some Assembly Required," they move on, becoming more of a twosome. Which includes quarreling:

Buffy: "Are you jealous?"
Angel: "Of Xander? Please, he's just a kid."
Buffy: "Is it 'cause I danced with him?"
Angel: "'Danced with' is a pretty loose term. 'Mated with' might be a little closer...."
Buffy: "Don't you think you're being a little unfair? One little dance, which I only did to make you crazy, by the way; behold my success!"
Angel: "I am not jealous!"
Buffy: "Oh, you're not jealous. What, vampires don't get jealous?"
Angel: "See? Whenever we fight, you always bring up the vampire thing."
Buffy: "I didn't come here to fight."

—"SOME ASSEMBLY REQUIRED"

By the end of the episode, Angel can laugh at himself a little and make an admission:

Buffy: "Love makes you do the wacky."
Angel: "What?"
Buffy: "Crazy stuff."
Angel: "Oh. Crazy like a 241-year-old being jealous of a high school junior?"
Buffy: "Are you fessing up?"
Angel: "I thought about it. Maybe he bothers me a little."
Buffy: "I don't love Xander."
Angel: "But he's in your life. He gets to be there when I can't. Take your classes, eat your meals, hear your jokes and complaints. He gets to see you in the sunlight."
Buffy: "I don't look that good in direct light."
Angel: "It'll be morning soon."
Buffy: "I should probably go…. I could walk you home."　　**—"SOME ASSEMBLY REQUIRED"**

And they have their miscommunications, the same as any other new couple:

Angel: "You said you weren't sure if you were going."
Buffy: "I was being cool. C'mon, you've been dating for what, 200 years, you don't know what a girl means when she says maybe she'll show? Work with me here."　　**—"SCHOOL HARD"**

Things go from bad to worse in "Reptile Boy":

Buffy: "I was just thinking, wouldn't it be funny to see each other sometime when it wasn't a blood thing? Not funny ha ha."
Angel: "What are you saying, you want to have a date?"
Buffy: "No—"
Angel: "You don't want to have a date?"
Buffy: "Who said 'date'? I never said 'date.'"
Angel: "Right. You just want to have coffee or something."
Buffy: "Coffee?"
Angel: "I knew this would happen."
Buffy: "Really? And what do you think is happening?"
Angel: "You're sixteen years old, I'm 241."
Buffy: "I've done the math."
Angel: "You don't know what you're doing, you don't know what you want."
Buffy: "Oh, I think I do: I want out of this conversation."
Angel: "Listen. If we date, you and I both know one thing's going to lead to another."
Buffy: "One thing's already led to another. It's a little late to be reading me the warning label."
Angel: "I'm just trying to protect you. This could get out of control."
Buffy: "Isn't that the way it's supposed to be?"

Angel: "This isn't some fairy tale; when I kiss you, you don't wake up from a deep sleep and live happily ever after."

Buffy: "No. When you kiss me, I want to die."
—**"REPTILE BOY"**

In "Halloween," Buffy hopes to please Angel by dressing as a noblewoman after seeing a sketch of one in a Watcher's Diary about him. After their misadventures, they debrief:

Angel: "I don't get it, Buffy. Why did you think I'd like you better dressed that way?"

Buffy: "I—I just wanted to be a real girl, for once. The kind of fancy girl you liked when you were my age—what?"

Angel: "I hated the girls back then. Especially the noblewomen."

Buffy: "You did?"

Angel: "They were just incredibly dull. Simpering morons, the lot of them. I always wished I could meet someone...exciting. Interesting."
—**"HALLOWEEN"**

But the lightness of this interlude is shattering in "Lie to Me," when Buffy must learn more bitter truths about Angel. As she had to accept that he had been sired by Darla in "Angel," she now must learn that the beautiful girl she has seen him with is not only a vampire and Spike's "paramour," but someone Angel hideously wronged:

Angel: "I did a lot of unconscionable things when I became a vampire. Drusilla was the worst. She was...an obsession of mine. She was pure and sweet and chaste."

Buffy: "You made her a vampire."

Angel: "First I made her insane. Killed everybody she loved, visited every mental torture on her I could devise. She eventually fled to a convent, and on the day she took her Holy Orders, I turned her into a demon."
—**"LIE TO ME"**

Buffy absorbs this shock as well, and their love continues to grow. In "What's My Line? Part I," as it hits home to Buffy that no matter what the results of the school Career Fair, her destiny is unalterable, she assures Angel of her love:

Buffy: "Angel, it's not you. You're the one freaky thing in my freaky world that makes sense to me. I just get messed up sometimes. I wish we could be regular kids."

Angel: "I'll never be a kid."

Buffy: "Okay, then. A regular kid and her cradle-robbing, creature-of-the-night boyfriend."
—**"WHAT'S MY LINE? PART 1"**

Later, after Angel takes Buffy skating in an effort to recapture her lost girlhood dreams, they do battle with an assassin from the Order of Taraka. Angel is still wearing his vamp face when she tends to his wounds, even as he's urging her to flee:

Angel: "I—you shouldn't have to touch me when I'm like this."

Buffy: "Like—what?"

Angel: "You know. When I'm . . . "

Buffy: "Oh. I didn't even notice."
—**"WHAT'S MY LINE? PART 1"**

In "Bad Eggs," Buffy prophetically speaks the line that foreshadows their doom: "Please. Like Angel and I are just helpless slaves to passion. Grow up."

But their passion is growing as their relationship matures past the dating stage and into serious love. And while Angel, as the older and more mature of the two of them, begins to look at their future and worry, Buffy struggles to hold onto her dream with the hopefulness of any seventeen-year-old:

Buffy: "Like, I'm really planning to have kids anytime soon. Maybe someday, when I'm done having a life. But I think a kid would be a little too much to deal with."
Angel: "I wouldn't know. [then, carefully] I don't . . . Well, you know, I can't."
This sinks in.
Buffy: "Oh. [regrouping] "Well, it's totally okay. I figured there are all kinds of things vampires can't do, like, you know, work for the telephone company, volunteer for the Red Cross. Have little vampires."
Angel (skeptical): "So you don't think about the future?"
Buffy: "No."
Angel: "Never?"
Buffy: "No."
Angel: "How can you say that? You really don't care what happens a year from now? Five years from now?"
Buffy (with difficulty): "Angel. When I try to look into the future, all I can see is you—"
—**"BAD EGGS"**

Now their relationship has reached the apex of its growth: they have faced many dangers together; Buffy has discovered and accepted the terrible truths that lie behind her beloved's face. She loves him completely...and she is pondering her next step...to love him utterly. She has accepted that death stares her in the face each night—her death, but perhaps Angel's death—as she has a terrible dream, only to be reassured by his loving presence when she runs to him:

Buffy: "...I like seeing you first thing in the morning—"
Angel: "It's bedtime for me."
Buffy: "Then I like seeing you at bedtime...I mean...you know what I mean. That I like seeing you. And the part at the end of the night where we say good-bye, it's getting harder."
Angel: "Yeah, it is." —**"SURPRISE"**

It's a more reflective, thoughtful Buffy who discusses her feelings with Willow:

Buffy: "Want isn't always the right thing...to do. To act on want can be wrong."
Willow: "True."
Buffy: "But, to not act on want. What if I never feel this way again?"
Willow: "Carpe diem. You told me that once."
Buffy: "Fish of the day?"
Willow: "Not carp. Carpe. It means seize the day."
Buffy: "Right." [a long beat] "I think we're going to . . . seize it. Once you get to a certain point, then seizing is sort of inevitable." —**"SURPRISE"**

Buffy has had many things taken from her: she comes from a broken home; she has been essentially exiled from Los Angeles. Nightly, while other girls are gossiping on the phone and trying out new nail polish colors, she is keeping those same girls safe until another sunrise. As the Slayer, she cannot look forward to a normal future. Loving Angel, she cannot hope for a white picket fence and a yard full of kids.

171

So when it appears to her that Angel might be taken from her in "Surprise," and he is given back to her one more time, it makes sense that Buffy would do everything in her power to claim him. To claim her love for him, and for life.

Buffy gives herself to Angel. They make love.

And their world shatters.

For in that one moment of true happiness, Angel loses his soul and Buffy's nightmare begins.

Angel: "Lighten up. It was a good time. Doesn't mean we have to make a big deal."
Buffy: "It is a big deal! It's—it's—"
Angel: "Fireworks. Bells ringing. A dulcet choir of pretty little birdies. Come on, Buffy, it's not like I haven't been there before."
Buffy: "Why are you saying these things to me?"
Angel: "I should have known you wouldn't be able to handle it."
Buffy: "Angel...I love you."
Angel: "Love ya too. I'll call ya."
                                                                    —**"INNOCENCE"**

Buffy: "Angel...there must be some part of you inside that remembers who you are...."
Angel: "Dream on, schoolgirl. Your boyfriend is dead. You're all gonna join him."
Buffy: "Leave Willow alone and deal with me."
Angel: "But she's so cute and helpless. It's really a turn-on."   —**"INNOCENCE"**

As she realizes that the beautiful gift she gave to him—her complete and unconditional love, forsaking all others, cleaving to him, has made him into a monster.

He hounds her, terrifies her with threats toward her mother and her loved ones, delighting in her fear as he sits beside her bed, stroking her hair as she sleeps, leaving portraits and roses in his wake....

Yet with each morning, her resolve strengthens: this is not the man she loved. This is the final, terrible truth: her love killed that man.

Angel: "You know what the worst part was? Pretending that I loved you. If I'd known how easily you'd give it up, I wouldn't even have bothered."
Buffy: "That doesn't work anymore. You're not Angel."
Angel: "You'd like to think that, wouldn't you? Doesn't matter. The important thing is, you made me the man I am today."   —**"INNOCENCE"**

He begins to taunt her, as in "Phases," when he "sends his love" by turning a schoolmate into a vampire. Or as Valentine's Day nears:

Giles: "There's a disturbing trend. Around Valentine's Day, he's prone to rather brutal displays of...what he would think of as affection, I suppose."
Buffy: "Like what?"
Giles: "No—no need to go into detail."   —**"BEWITCHED, BOTHERED, AND BEWILDERED"**

Giles: "He's doing this deliberately, Buffy. He's trying to make it harder for you."
Buffy: "He's only making it easier. I know what I have to do."
Giles: "What?"
Buffy: "Kill him."   —**"INNOCENCE"**

With the murder of Jenny Calendar—the person the Watcher held most dear, the Slayer is compelled to act against the murderer . . . he demon who has taken the place of her beloved: "Because I know now that there's nothing that's ever going to change him back to the Angel I fell in love with."

And yet, there is an odd resonance to the discord of his actions:

Buffy: "It's so weird....Every time something like that happens, my first instinct is to run and tell Angel. I can't believe it's the same person. He's the complete opposite of what he was."
Willow: "Well...sort of, except...."
Buffy: "Except what?"
Willow: "You're still the only thing he thinks about." —**"PASSION"**

Angel proves this to her, in "Killed by Death," when he tries to "visit" her and Xander staves him off. Then, in "I Only Have Eyes for You," Buffy cannot forgive herself for sleeping with Angel and tearing his soul away from him. She is awash in misery, and yet, as the ghost of someone who desperately needs to be forgiven fills her spirit and Angel and his demon are possessed by the one who was wronged and who needs to forgive, there is a moment—brief and gossamer—where grace descends.

Finally, in the climactic season finale, Angel is saved...only to be damned. When, as the demon, he decides to send the entire world to Hell, he believes that he has lost his passion for Buffy. And she, having loved him through the first shock of his vampirism, through the sins he committed as a demon, to the realization that she must sacrifice him just as he has regained his soul, becomes the ultimate tragic hero. Their last words:

Angel: "What's happening, Buffy?"
Buffy: "Sh....It doesn't matter."
She pulls away to look at him. Kisses him passionately.
Buffy: "I love you."
Angel: "I love you . . ."
Buffy: "Close your eyes."

And then the Slayer sends Angel, a redeemed soul and her one true love, straight to Hell. For never was there a tale of more woe...

Three Strikes...

BUFFY AND FORD: Buffy "loved" Billy Fordham in the fifth grade, but he was a manly sixth-grader who had no time for younger women. When "Ford" arrives in Sunnydale, he tells Buffy that his father has been transferred and that he'll be attending Sunnydale High.

He's lying. Terminally ill, he doesn't even bother with registering in school. Instead, he meets as soon as possible with Spike and offers him a deal: if Spike will agree to turn Ford into a vampire, Ford will lure the Slayer to the Sunset Club, a private Goth hangout, and Spike can come to collect her.

Buffy is devastated when she discovers Ford's betrayal, moved though she is by his revelation that he is dying. When he rises as a ravening, mindless vampire, she stakes him without reaction; the Ford she knew and loved had already died.

BUFFY AND OWEN THURMAN: Buffy did not choose to be the Slayer. By some whim of fate yet unknown to us, the universe did the choosing, and Buffy must deal with the consequences. But having a crush and getting asked out on a date, as any normal sixteen-year-old would love to do, are "problematic at best" (to quote Giles) for Buffy. When shy, handsome Owen finally asks her out, Buffy is delighted...until he becomes involved in a vampire battle at the Sunnydale Funeral Home and she discovers that he has a yen for danger. Realizing that her world is too dangerous for Owen, she breaks up with him...unable to tell him the real reason why, nor to say that she still cares for him just as much.

BUFFY AND CAMERON WALKER: Initially, Buffy is interested in Cameron, a member of the Sunnydale swim team. He waxes poetic about the ocean and he's good-looking...and he seems equally interested in her. However, the bloom is off the rose by the end of the first date: he's boring and self-absorbed. When he won't take no for an answer, she breaks his nose...and gets blamed for leading him on. And, of course, any hope Cameron might have had with Buffy is dashed when he becomes a giant fish-guy...

And one more:

TOM WARNER: Tom is the fraternity brother of Cordelia's love interest, Richard Anderson. The fraternity, Delta Zeta Kappa, worships Machida, a giant demon-snake, and Tom is their leader. He lures Buffy to a fraternity party for the express purpose of feeding her to Machida as a sacrifice. Naturally, this relationship was doomed from the start.

Love Is Strange.
Very, Very Strange.

Xander has likewise had his share of bizarre romances. If, as Willow says, "Love makes you do the wacky," it can also make you date the wacky. *Par exemple*—as they say in France—with regard to:

XANDER AND MISS NATALIE FRENCH: Miss French murders the science teacher, Dr. Gregory, and takes his place as a substitute teacher. Sexy and mesmerizing, she is actually a huge praying mantis intent upon mating with young male humans in order to fertilize her eggs. Her first two targets are Blayne Mall—who has been bragging about his many conquests to Xander—and Xander himself, who has been bragging back. Of course, once the She-Mantis is dispatched and the two are rescued, it comes out that the She-Mantis only selected young male *virgin* humans as her potential mates....

XANDER AND AMPATA: Ampata is actually the name of a male South American foreign-exchange student who is to live with Buffy and her mother for two weeks. However, the millennia-old mummy of a sixteen-year-old Inca princess has been freed from her sleep and literally sucks the life out of Ampata when she kisses him. He becomes a shriveled corpse. As the female foreign-exchange student Ampata, the mummy falls in love with Xander. At first she finds she cannot kill him, even to per- petuate her own life, and in desperation attacks Willow. When Xander stands between Willow and Ampata, it appears that in her hunger for life, she may actually take his. But with Buffy's intervention, the once-beautiful Inca princess decays and falls to pieces before his very eyes.

BEHOLD THE WEIRDNESS: XANDER AND CORDELIA: What's up with that? Astute *Buffy* viewers of season one may have sensed that beneath the caustic remarks and rapid-fire banter, Cordelia and Xander were racking up passion points. But for the rest of us, it was quite a shock when, facing death from Mr. Pfister, the Tarakan bug- man assassin in "What's My Line? Part 2," they clung to each other in an embrace that can only be described as it is in the shooting script:

A beat. They FALL INTO A KISS. A kiss of steel-melting, ground-shaking intensity. It just goes on and on and on....

Finally, they break. LEAP apart as if they've been electrocuted....

Naturally, Cordelia wants to keep this strange lust connection a secret, and perhaps she is right: for when Willow finds out, she is devastated:

Willow: "I knew it! I knew it! Well, not 'knew it' in the sense of having the slightest idea, but I knew there was something I didn't know. You two were fighting way too much. It's not natural."
Xander: "I know, it's weird...."
Willow: "Weird? It's against all the laws of God and man! It's *Cordelia!* Remember? The 'We Hate Cordelia Club,' of which you are the treasurer?"
Xander: "I was gonna tell you. . . . "
Willow: "Gee, what stopped you? Could it be *shame?*"
Xander: "All right! Let's overreact, shall we?"
Willow: "But I'm—"
Xander: "We were kissing. It doesn't mean that much."
Willow (softly): "No. It just means you'd rather be with someone you hate...than be with me."
—**"INNOCENCE"**

If the course of true love never ran smooth, the course of unadulterated passion has practically no chance for pothole-free driving, as Xander and Cordelia quickly discover.

Xander: "You know, it's really better for me if you don't talk."
Cordelia: "Well, it's really better for *me* with the lights off."
Xander: "Are you saying you can't *look* at me when we . . . whatever we do?"
Cordelia: "It's not that I can't. It's more that I . . . don't want to."
Xander: "That's great. That's just dandy. We're repulsed by each other. We hide from our friends—"
Cordelia: "I should hope. Please."
Xander: "All and all. This thing is not what I'd call a self-esteem booster." **—"BAD EGGS"**

They struggle to define what it is they have; if it's only lust, why are they jealous of other people?

Cordelia: "Excuse me. We did not come here to talk about Willow. We came here to do things I can never tell my father about because he still thinks I'm a good girl."
Xander: "I just don't trust Oz with her. He's a senior, he's attractive. Okay, maybe not to me, but . . . oh, and he's in a band. We all know what element that kind attracts."
Cordelia: "I've dated lots of guys in bands."
Xander: "Thank you!"
Cordelia: "Do you even want to be here?"
Xander: "I'm not running away."
Cordelia: "Because when you're not babbling about poor, defenseless Willow, you're raving about the all-powerful Buffy."
Xander: "I do not babble. I occassionally run-on. And every now and then I yammer..."
Cordelia: "Xander, look around. We're in my daddy's car. Just the two of us. There's a beautiful, big, full moon out tonight. It doesn't get more romantic than this....So shut up!"
—"PHASES"

But are they even dating?

Xander: "So, you're going. And I'm going. Should we—maybe—go?"
Cordelia: "Why?"
Xander: "I don't know. This thing. With us? Despite our better judgment—it keeps happening. Maybe we should just admit that we're dating."
Cordelia: "Groping in a broom closet isn't dating. You don't call it a date until the guy spends money."
Xander: "Fine. I'll spend—then we'll grope. Whatever. I just think it's just some kind of whacked that we feel we have to hide from all our friends."
Cordelia: "Well, of course you want to tell everybody. You have nothing to be ashamed of. I, on the other hand, have everything to be ashamed of."
Xander: "Know what? 'Nuff said. Forget it. Must have been my multiple-personality guy talking. I call him Idiot Jed, Glutton for Punishment." **—"SURPRISE"**

And then, the payoff . . . finally:

Cordelia: "Me? I'm not the one who embraced the black arts just to get girls to like me. Well, congratulations, it worked."

Xander: "It would have worked fine! Except your hide's so thick not even magic can penetrate it!"

Cordelia: "You mean, the spell was for me?" —**"BEWITCHED, BOTHERED, AND BEWILDERED"**

As Cordelia realizes how much Xander cares about her, she courageously takes a stand that could bring her down socially until the end of time:

Cordelia (to Harmony): "I'll date whoever the hell I want to date, no matter how lame he is! [she walks away] Oh, God...oh, God."

Xander: "It's gonna be okay. Just keep walking."

Cordelia: "Oh, God, what have I done? They're never gonna speak to me again."

Xander: "Oh, sure they are. If it helps, when we're around them, you and I can fight a lot."

Cordelia: "You promise?"

Xander: "You can pretty much count on it." —**"BEWITCHED, BOTHERED, AND BEWILDERED"**

XANDER AND THE ENTIRE FEMALE POPULATION OF SUNNYDALE

"Dammit, Xander, what is going on? Who died and made you Elvis?"
Cordelia, on Xander's sudden irresistibility to all but her, in "Bewitched, Bothered, and Bewildered"

In "Bewitched, Bothered, and Bewildered"—an episode rewritten to give Sarah Michelle Gellar more days off for her appearance on *Saturday Night Live*—Xander blackmails Amy Madison, the witchly daughter of Catherine Madison, into casting a love spell on Cordelia. As mentioned above, Queen C is crumbling under peer pressure: the Cordettes are snubbing her because she is dating the lamest of the lame...Xander. In an attempt to regain her hard-won popularity, Cordelia dumps him, although it is clear to us, the viewing audience, that she still cares about him.

Xander retaliates. But the spell goes awry: instead of enchanting Cordelia, the spell works on every *other* female in Sunnydale . . . including Jenny Calendar, Buffy, Joyce...and, in a lucky misadventure that saves Xander's life . . . Drusilla!

As Angel grabs him and prepares to kill him, Drusilla steps in and saves Xander's life:

Drusilla: "If you so much as harmed one hair on this boy's precious head—"
Angel can't believe his ears.
Angel: "You've got to be kidding? Him?"
Drusilla: "No, now. Just because I finally found a real man...."
Angel shakes his head, uncomprehending.
Angel: "A real man? I guess I really *did* drive you crazy."
—**"BEWITCHED, BOTHERED, AND BEWILDERED"**

Drusilla: "Your face is a poem. I can read it."
Xander: "Really? It doesn't say 'spare me,' by any chance?"
Drusilla: "Ssshhhh. How do you feel about eternal life?"
Xander: "We couldn't just start with a coffee? A movie, maybe?"
—**"BEWITCHED, BOTHERED, AND BEWILDERED"**

Xander discovers that it's not wonderful to be the object of mass obsession, as the women of Sunnydale literally attack him in a mob of possessive, love-crazed Xander groupies. Armed with axes, knives, and sheer *need*, they trap him and Cordelia in Buffy's basement.

When things go back to as normal as they get, Cordelia takes her place in the sun once more...on Xander's arm.

XANDER AND...KENDRA? One can only speculate about Kendra's flustered reaction around Xander. It's true that she hasn't had a lot of contact with boys her own age, but in "What's My Line? Part 2," she's clearly unsettled by him:

Xander: "Welcome. So you're a Slayer, huh? I like that in a woman."
Kendra can only look at her shoes. Totally flustered.
Kendra: "I—I hope. . . . I thank you. I mean, sir... I will be of service."
Xander: "Good. Great. It's good to be a giver."
Xander looks to Buffy—what's with her? Buffy shrugs.

When Xander and Kendra meet again, there's no time for such exchanges. But one wonders what might have been, if only Kendra had had more time....

LOVE IS CRUEL: XANDER AND BUFFY From the first moment he sees her, Xander is attracted to Buffy. Oblivious to the fact that he's wounding Willow, who has carried a torch for him ever since they were five and he stole her Barbie, he discusses his feelings about the new girl with his best buddy on an almost constant basis. It takes the entire first season for him to ask Buffy out, with less-than-sterling results:

Xander: "You know, Buffy, Spring Fling is a time for students to gather and...oh, God. Buffy, I want you to go to the dance with me. You and me. On a date."
Buffy: "I don't know what to say...."
Xander: "Well, you're not laughing, so that's a good start. Buffy, I like you. A lot. And I know we're friends, and we've had experiences, we've fought some bloodsucking fiends, and that's all been a good time, but...I want more. I wanna dance with you."

Buffy: "Xander…you're one of my best friends. You and Willow . . ."
Xander: "Hey, Willow's not looking to date you. Or, if she is, she's playing it pretty close to the chest."
Buffy: "I don't want to spoil the friendship that we have."
Xander: "I don't want to spoil it, either. But that's not the point, is it? You either feel a thing or you don't."
Buffy: "I don't…Xander, I'm sorry. I just don't think of you that way."
Xander: "Well try, I'll wait."
Buffy: "Xander…"
Xander: "No, forget it. I'm not him. I guess a guy's gotta be undead to make time with you."

—"PROPHECY GIRL"

The "him" that Xander is referring to is Angel, of course. It really hurts Xander that Buffy prefers "Dead Boy," and Xander stands alone in his continuing mistrust of the "good" vampire, even when other people chalk up his concern to jealousy.

"Hey, it's *me*. If Angel's doing something wrong, I need to know.
'Cause it gives me a happy."
Xander, in "Lie to Me"

As previously mentioned, it is Xander, not Angel, who insists that the two of them go down into the tunnels to rescue Buffy in "Prophecy Girl." And Xander often acts as the leader of the group when mobilization is required, assigning tasks for himself and the others. Despite the fact that when Angel's not in the picture Buffy goes out or hangs with other boys—Owen, Ford, Tom, Cameron—and that when she is desperately angry and unhappy, she flirts with Xander only to provoke reactions in others ("When She Was Bad"), Xander's yen for Buffy never diminishes:

"Buffy. My Lady of Buffdom. The duchess of Buffonia. I am in awe.
I completely renounce spandex."
Xander, upon seeing Buffy in her costume, in "Halloween"

Still, Xander, Buffy, and Willow continue to be a special threesome, spending idle hours together, watching Indian TV, sharing their lives. Not even Xander's strange new relationship with Cordelia can lessen his love for Buffy. Cordelia repeatedly accuses him of being obsessed with the Slayer, pouting that while he would die for his beloved Buffy, he would never die for *her* ("Innocence"). And on occasion, Willow still tests the wind, even though she eventually moves on to Oz:

Willow: "When Buffy was a vampire, you weren't still, like, attracted to her, were you?"
Xander: "Willow, how can you . . . I mean, that's really bent, she was grotesque."
Willow: "Still dug her, huh?"
Xander: "I'm sick. I need help."
Willow: "Don't I know it."

—"NIGHTMARES"

Angel, reborn as Angelus, taunts him:

Angel: "Buffy's white knight. You still love her. It must just kill you that I got there first."
Xander: "You're gonna die. And I'm gonna be there."

—"KILLED BY DEATH"

There are moments when it seems that Xander's faithfulness will be rewarded, as in "Phases," when Buffy destroys the vampire Theresa, created and sent by Angel as a token of his own "affections":

> "Oh, no, my life's not too complicated."
> **Xander, after a too-long embrace with Buffy, in "Phases"**

Now, after the second-season finale, Buffy has sent Angel to Hell and left town. Will Xander ever see her again? Will she ever return his loyal and lasting love? At this point, we can only speculate.

And the Torch Is Passed, Sputtering at First

WILLOW AND MOLOCH: In her sweet, wry, and unsure way, Willow has yearned after Xander nearly all her life. Encouraged numerous times by Buffy to make the first move, Willow demurs. "No speaking up. That way leads to madness and sweaty palms" ("Angel").

Xander makes it very clear that Buffy is the girl he wants, and so Willow tries to move on. In "I Robot, You Jane," she meets "Malcolm Black" on the Internet, and they begin a romance via e-mail that deeply concerns Buffy, much to Willow's disappointment:

Willow: "You're having an expression."
Buffy: "I'm not. But if I was, it would be saying...this just isn't like you."
Willow: "Not like me to have a boyfriend?"
Buffy: "He's...boyfriendly?"
Willow: "I don't understand why you don't want me to have this. I mean, boys don't chase me around all the time—I thought you'd be happy for me."
Buffy: "I just want you to be sure. To meet him face-to-face. In daylight in a crowded place— with some friends. You know, before you get all obsessive."
Willow: "Malcolm and I really care about each other. Big deal if I blow off a couple classes."
Buffy: "I thought you said you overslept."
Willow (Turning away): "Malcolm said you wouldn't understand."
Buffy: "Malcolm was right." —**"I ROBOT, YOU JANE"**

Unfortunately, this being Sunnydale and all, it turns out that Malcolm is not what he seems. Rather, he's a demon Willow inadvertently freed into the Internet when she scanned the book he was bound in into the school library computer system. Now housed in a terrifying robot body, Moloch, the Corruptor, used to tempting humans into his service with promises of love and riches, has Willow kidnapped and brought to him:

Willow: "I don't understand. What do you want from me?"
Moloch: "I want to give you the world."
Willow: "Why?"

Moloch: "You created me. I brought these humans together to build me a body, but you gave me life. Took me out of the book that held me. I want to repay you."

Willow: "By lying to me. By pretending to be a person. [weakly] Pretending...you loved me."

Moloch: "I do."

But of course he doesn't, and when Willow tries to "break up" with him, he prepares to kill her. And in the last scene of the episode, the immortal wisdom of the three friends—Buffy, Xander, and Willow—is laid bare:

Willow: "The one boy that's really liked me, and he's a demon robot. What does that say about me?"

Buffy: "It doesn't say anything about you."

Willow: "I mean, I thought I was really falling—"

Buffy: "Hey. Did you forget? The one boy I've had the hots for here turned out to be a vampire."

Xander: "Right! And the teacher I had a crush on: giant praying mantis."

Willow (brightening): "That's true...."

Xander: "Yeah. It's life on the Hellmouth."

Buffy (cheerfully): "Let's face it. None of us are ever going to have a normal, happy relationship."

Xander (laughing): "We're doomed!"

Willow: "Yeah!"

They all laugh together. Then it kind of sputters out, and they all sit there, incredibly depressed.

Burning Bright

WILLOW AND OZ   In "When She Was Bad," the second-season opener, just as it seems that Xander may indeed finally notice Willow—kissing the ice cream off her nose—Buffy shows. And the moment is lost. Forever—for Willow tries vainly to recapture it and must admit defeat.

But on the horizon for this brave little boat sails a conquistador: Oz, the equally wry, very laid-back lead guitarist of Dingoes Ate My Baby. For two episodes—"Inca Mummy Girl" and "Halloween"—Oz admires Willow from afar with but a single question: "Who is that girl?!" Then in "What's My Line? Part 1," they discover they are the two students singled out by a hush-hush computer organization, and he utters his first word to her: "Canapé?"

In "What's My Line? Part 2," they discuss their feelings about being candidates for the computer company, then move on to Oz's real ambition: to play the manly chord of E-flat, diminished ninth.

Then the spark is definitely ignited:

Oz: "Oh, hey, animal cracker?"

Willow: "No, thank you. How's your arm?"

Oz: "Suddenly painless."

Willow: "You can still play guitar okay?"

Oz: "Not well, but not worse."

Willow: "You know, I never really thanked you."

Oz: "Please don't. I don't do thanks. I get all red and I have to bail. It's not pretty."

Willow: "Well then forget—that thing. Especially the part where I kind of owe you my life."

Oz pulls a cracker from the box, hoping to change the subject.

Oz: "Look. Monkey. And he has a little hat. And little pants."

Willow: "Yeah. I see."

Oz: "The monkey is the only cookie animal that gets to wear clothes, you know that.... You
have the sweetest smile I've ever seen.... So I'm wondering, do the other cookie animals
feel sort of ripped? Like, is the hippo going, 'hey man, where are my pants? I have my
hippo dignity.' And you know the monkey's just, 'I mock you with my monkey pants,' then
there's a big coup at the zoo....'"

Willow: "The monkey's French?"

Oz: "All monkeys are French. You didn't know that?"   **—"WHAT'S MY LINE, PART 2"**

Then Willow musters up the courage to invite Oz to Buffy's surprise birthday party in
"Surprise"—and he is immediately initiated into the Scooby Gang when he sees a vampire
explode into dust. He joins in the heist of the rocket launcher without so much as batting an
eye: "So, do you guys steal weapons from the army a lot?" he asks. And he makes it very
clear where he stands:

Oz: "Sometimes when I'm sitting in class, I'm not thinking about class, 'cause you know that
could never happen, I think about kissing you and then it's like everything stops. It's
like, freeze frame. Willow kissage...but I'm not gonna kiss you."

Willow: "What? But...freeze frame..."

Oz: "Well, to the casual observer, it would appear like you want to make your friend Xander
jealous. Or even the score or something. That's on the empty side. See, in my fantasy,
when I'm kissing you...you're kissing me. It's okay, I can wait."   **—"INNOCENCE"**

So Willow has clearly connected with a wonderful guy. But—this being Sunnydale and
all—the course of true love never runs smooth for anyone. In "Phases," Willow discovers
that Oz has a secret:

Willow: "What am I supposed to think? First you buy me popcorn, then you put the tag in my
shirt, and then you're all glad I didn't get bit. But I guess none of that means anything, because instead of looking up names with me, here you are all alone in your
house doing nothing by yourself."

Oz: "Willow, we will talk about this tomorrow, I promise."

Willow: "No, darn it, we will talk about this now! Buffy told me that sometimes what the
girl makes has to be the first move, and now that I'm saying this, I'm starting
to think that the written version sounded pretty good, but you know what
I mean!"

Oz: "I know. It's me. I'm going through some . . . changes."   **—"PHASES"**

Oz is a werewolf. A bit shocking at first, but in the end, sort of okay:

Oz: "You mean . . . you'd still . . ."

Willow: "Well, I like you. You're nice, and you're funny and you don't smoke, and okay, werewolf, but that's not all the time. I mean, three days out of the month I'm not much fun to be around, either."

Oz: "You are quite the human."

Willow: "So I'd still if you'd still."

Oz: "I'd still. I'd very still." —**"PHASES"**

And at last, Willow has not only a boyfriend, but a very cool boyfriend:

> "My boyfriend's in the band!"
> **Willow, in "Bewitched, Bothered, and Bewildered"**

Clearly, there is more...much more...to Oz than meets the eye. At the end of the second season, we can only imagine the adventures he and Willow will share.

WILLOW AND XANDER: Willow and Xander have been best friends for years . . . and through those years, Willow has come to love Xander in a more-than-best-friends kind of way. Xander, of course, has no clue. In a section cut from "Angel," he sums up the situation perfectly, without the slightest idea that with every word, he's wounding Willow:

Xander: "Love sucks. Ever since I was in grammar school, it's the same old dance...you dig someone, they dig someone else. And then that someone else digs someone else."

Willow: "That's the dance."

Xander: "I mean, I'm right for her. I'm the guy. I know it. She's so stupid! She's not stupid. But . . . it's too much. We're such good buds, I'm *this* close to her, and she doesn't have a clue how I feel. And wouldn't care if she did. It's killing me."

He exits into class. She stands alone a moment.

Willow: "Gee, what's that like?" —**"ANGEL"** (expurgated)

Willow struggles with her feelings, trying to replace Xander in her heart with someone else. But it's difficult at best when your one prospect turned out to be a demon, and no one else is beating down your door.

Willow: "Well, you know, I have a choice. I can spend my life waiting for Xander to go out with every other girl in the world before he notices me, or I can just get on with my life."

Buffy: "Good for you."

Willow: "Well, I didn't choose yet...." —**"INCA MUMMY GIRL"**

Finally, Oz arrives on the scene. And maybe that's the wake-up call Xander finally needed . . . or maybe he realizes his love for her far exceeds the boyfriend/girlfriend thing:

> "Come on, Will... [he takes a moment, continues.] Look, you don't have a choice
> here. You gotta wake up. I need you, Will. How am I gonna pass trig? Who am I
> gonna call every night to talk about what we did all day. You're my best
> friend, you've always . . . [He leans in close.] "I love you."
>
> **Xander, in "Becoming, Part 2"**

And Willow wakes up, speaking Oz's name.
What will happen here?
Only time will tell.

The Many, Many Loves of Cordelia Chase

CORDELIA AND THE ENTIRE Y-CARRYING POPULATION OF SUNNYDALE HIGH: Cordelia has always prided herself on her fine taste in men. She knows what she wants: the best. She knows what she deserves: the best. Anything less would be...less. As she explains to the Cordettes in "Welcome to the Hellmouth":

> "Senior boys are the only way to go. They're just a better class of person.
> The boys in our grade? Forget about it. They're children. Like Jesse—
> did you see him last night? The way he follows me around?
> He's like a little puppy dog: you just want to put him to sleep.
> Senior boys have mystery, they have...what's the
> word I'm searching for? 'Cars.'"

But being Cordelia's boyfriend can be bad luck of the worst kind: in the first two seasons, Cordelia racks up more dead or severely injured boyfriends than a black widow spider:

CORDELIA AND DARYL EPPS: Former all-state champion football star Daryl appeared in "Some Assembly Required." He was severely injured in a rock-climbing accident and presumed dead. But his science-fair-winning younger brother, Chris, stitches him back together a la Frankenstein and his monster, and now Daryl dwells, quite alone, in their basement. As with the original *Frankenstein*, Daryl prevails upon Chris to build him a mate. And Cordelia will be the crowning achievement . . . the head.

CORDELIA AND MITCH FARGO: Mitch is Cordelia's "hunk du jour" in "Out of Mind, Out of Sight." He is to reign beside Cordelia as May King, preferably in a lot of pancake makeup after Marcie Ross, the insane, invisible girl, takes a baseball bat to him.

CORDELIA AND KEVIN: Kevin was to have escorted Cordelia to the prom, but vampires attack and kill him in the school's AV room...also nixing his ability to help Cordelia with the sound system at the Bronze.

CORDELIA AND RICHARD ANDERSON: Richard is a fraternity brother of the Delta Zeta Kappas, a cult that sacrifices beautiful young high school girls to their demon lord, the giant snake-man, Machida. Initially, Richard goes after Cordelia; then, needing more girls, the cult leader, Tom, invites Buffy to their party.

> "The Zeta Kappas have to have a certain balance at their party—Richard
> explained it all to me but I was so busy REALLY LISTENING to him that
> I didn't hear much—anyway, the deal is they need you to go.
> And if you don't go... [her eyes moisten] I can't! I'm talking about Richard
> Anderson, okay? As in Anderson Farms, Anderson Aeronautics...
> [she can no longer hold back the tears] and Anderson Cosmetics!"
> **—Cordelia, in "Reptile Boy"**

In the end, Buffy kills Machida and she and Cordelia are rescued by the Scooby Gang, pretty much putting the kibosh on this romance.

CORDELIA AND JONATHAN: Jonathan has appeared in four episodes thus far: "Reptile Boy," "Inca Mummy Girl," "Bad Eggs," and "Go Fish." In "Inca Mummy Girl," the Incan princess/mummy Ampata nearly sucks the life out of him in a stolen kiss. In "Reptile Boy," Cordelia favors him with her presence (although he scarcely deserves it, having forgotten the extra foam on her cappuccino). He is neurally clamped by a Bezoar hatchling in "Bad Eggs." He escapes becoming a gill-man in "Go Fish," but so far, Jonathan has more lives than Catherine Madison's black cat.

CORDELIA AND DEVON: Devon is the lead singer for Dingoes Ate My Baby. He first appears in "Inca Mummy Girl," when Oz first notices Willow. By "Halloween," Cordelia is dating him—and it appears that he's been standing her up. Still, she hovers at the edge of the stage—even though she informs him not to expect her there.

CORDELIA AND ANGEL:

> "Hel-lo! Salty goodness. Pick up the phone. Call 9-1-1. That boy's going to need
> some serious oxygen after I'm through with him."
> **Cordelia, spotting Angel, in "Never Kill a Boy on the First Date"**

> "Oh. He's a vampire. Of course. But the cuddly kind. Like a Care Bear with
> fangs....You know what I think? You're trying to scare me off because you're
> afraid of the competition. Look, Buffy, you may be hot stuff when it comes to
> demonology or whatever, but when it comes to dating, *I'm* the Slayer."
> **Cordelia is told that Angel's a vampire, in "Halloween"**

Just like any other girl who has eyes would attest to the fact that Angel is a honey, Cordelia attempts several times to attract/distract him from Buffy. She never gets anywhere, despite the fact that Buffy's own insecurities lead her to assume that Cordelia could pose a serious threat, and Cordelia takes advantage of that when it suits her:

Buffy: "I'd say it's about time for you to mind your own business."
Cordelia: "It's long past. Nighty-night....I'll just go see if Angel feels like dancing."
—"WHEN SHE WAS BAD"

Incredibly, Angel never starts dating her, despite the fact that she showers on a regular basis and spends as much time on her hair as Marie Antoinette.

CORDELIA AND OWEN: Owen Thurman also prefers Buffy, even though, technically, Cordelia asks him out first:

Cordelia: "Owen, a bunch of us are loitering at the Bronze tonight. You there?"
Owen: "Who's all going?"
Cordelia: "Well, I'm going to be there."
Owen: "Oh. Who else?"
Cordelia (genuinely confused): "You mean besides me?"
Owen: "Buffy, what about you?"
Buffy: (caught off guard): "What?"
Cordelia: "No, no, no. She doesn't—like—fun."
Owen (to Buffy): "How about we meet there at eight?"
Cordelia glares at Buffy.
Buffy: "Yeah. Eight. There."   **—"NEVER KILL A BOY ON THE FIRST DATE"**

CORDELIA AND XANDER: And then, there is "the weirdness of them," as she discovers her one true passion:

Cordelia: "I can't believe that I'm stuck spending what are probably my last moments on
              Earth with you!"
Xander: "I hope these are my last moments! Three more seconds of you and I'm gonna…"
Cordelia: "You're gonna what? Coward!"
Xander: "Moron!"
Cordelia: "I hate you!"
Xander: "I hate you!"
(Then big smoochies, and then…)
Xander: "We so need to get out of here!"   **—"WHAT'S MY LINE? PART 2"**

In an expurgated section from "Surprise," Cordelia tries on new clothes as Xander's girlfriend:

Cordelia (too casual, to Harmony): "Hello. I'm having, like, a totally random thought. [then]
              Xander Harris. Is it just me, or does his shirt almost match his pants?"
Harmony looks. Shrugs.
Harmony: "Almost. Why do I care?"
Cordelia: "Well. If you look at him a certain way—is he vaguely…cute?"
THEIR POV
As XANDER does some spazzy dance for Willow's amusement.
RESUME
Harmony: "Oh, yeah. I'm hot for spaz boy. Are you tripping, Cordelia?"
A beat. Cordelia laughs a little too loud.
Cordelia: "You thought I was serious? Please. I was just testing you. Ha. [Sighs.] I'm hot for
              spaz boy. Good one."   **—"SURPRISE"**

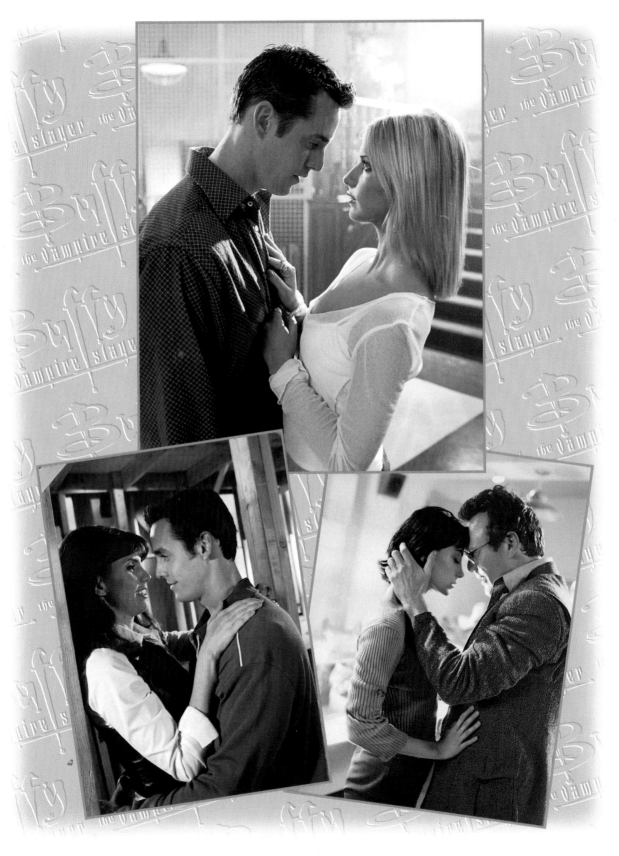

Angel's Demon Lovers

ANGEL AND DARLA: In her human form, Darla is a beautiful young blonde who can pass herself off as a high school student. She sired Angel in Galway in 1753:

Angel: "God, but you're a pretty thing. Where are you from?"
Darla: "Around. Everywhere."
Angel: "Never been anywhere, myself. Always wanted to see the world, but..."
Darla: "I could show you."
Angel: "Could you, then?"
Darla: "Things you've never seen. Never even heard of."
Angel: "Sounds exciting."
Darla: "It is. And frightening."
Angel: "I'm not afraid. Show me. Show me your world."
Darla: "Close your eyes."   **—"BECOMING, PART 1"**

Angel is involved with Darla at least periodically for the next century. But when his soul is restored, he forsakes all other vampires—including Darla—and lives alone. Darla flourishes as the reigning favorite of the Master, presiding with joy over the executions of those who fail her demon lord. When it comes to light that Angel is keeping company with the Slayer, Darla concocts a plan to pit Buffy and Angel against each other. Either Buffy will kill him, or Angel will kill Buffy . . . and hopefully, return to the vampire fold.

Unfortunately for Darla, her plan backfires. After she taunts Buffy with her past relationship with Angel—"There was a time when we shared everything"—Angel kills Darla. Her last word—his name—is uttered with shock and astonishment, as if, to the last, she cannot believe she has lost her hold over him.

ANGEL AND DRUSILLA:

Angel: "I did a lot of unconscionable things when I became a vampire. Drusilla was the
worst. She was...an obsession of mine."   **Angel, in "Lie to Me"**

Angel sires Drusilla in London in or around 1860. In the full glory of his demonic existence, he torments her in the confessional as she speaks tremulously of having visions. Her mother has told her this is the work of the Devil, and she turns to the Church for absolution. But Angel gives her no release, only more pain, as he tells her she is the spawn of the Devil.

Angel kills all her family and drives her completely insane. When she is left with nothing and no one—not even her own identity—he enfolds her in the vampire's kiss.

When his soul is restored, his agony over seeing Drusilla again in "Lie to Me" is palpable. If vengeance is a living thing, as Jenny Calendar's Gypsy uncle posits, so is remorse. And it is a hungry living thing, demanding constant feeding....

Angel: "Drusilla, leave here. I'm offering you that chance. Take Spike and get out."
Drusilla: "Or you'll hurt me? [looks down.] No. No, you can't. Not anymore."
Angel: "If you don't leave...it'll go badly. For all of us."
Drusilla: "My dear boy's gone all away, hasn't he? To her."

Angel: "Who?"

Drusilla: "The girl . . . the Slayer. Your heart stinks of her. Poor little thing. She has no idea what's in store."

Angel: "This can't go on, Drusilla. It's gotta end."

Drusilla: "Oh, no, my pet . . . [She leans in for what looks to Buffy like a kiss, whispers in Angel's ear.] This is just the beginning."

DRUSILLA AND SPIKE:

The Judge: "You two stink of humanity. You share affection and jealousy."

Spike: "Yeah, what of it?"   —"SURPRISE"

Drusilla and Spike are an adoring couple when they burst upon the Sunnydale scene. Drusilla is incredibly weak and wraithlike, having barely survived an angry mob in Prague. She and Spike set up shop in Sunnydale, joining the Anointed One's court while they plan their strategy. Which is: to get rid of the Slayer and restore Drusilla to health in "Sunnyhell."

Spike clearly worships Drusilla. When she enters the Factory for the first time ("School Hard") to greet the Anointed One and his court, Spike loses his vampire face and turns to her with the adoring eyes of a young human man.

They discover that Angel is in town ("School Hard"), and the audience learns that Angel sired Drusilla, who, in turn, sired Spike—which makes Angel Spike's grand-sire. Now the jig is up: the vampire couple knows that Angel has somehow become good, that he is the Slayer's lapdog...and their enemy.

On occasion, Drusilla uses her madness to manipulate Spike:

Spike: "You, uh, meet anyone? Anyone interesting? Like Angel?"

Dru: "Angel."

Spike: "It's a little off, you two so friendly, him being the enemy and all that."   —"LIE TO ME"

When he flares up on learning that she has indeed seen Angel, impatiently pointing out to her that the bird she is coaxing to sing for her is dead because she forgot to feed it, Drusilla begins to keen. Spike is immediately contrite, dropping entirely the subject of her clandestine meeting with Angel.

> "I'm sorry, baby. I'm a bad, rude man."
> **Spike, to Drusilla, in "Lie to Me"**

Spike's world revolves around Drusilla and getting her well again. But even in that effort, foreshadowing of things to come darken his finest hour as he allows Drusilla to torture Angel before performing the ritual that will cure her and kill Angel:

Spike: "I've never been much for the pre-show."

Angel: "Too bad. That's what Drusilla likes best as I recall."

Spike: "What's that supposed to mean?"

Angel: "Ask her. She knows what I mean."

Spike: "Well?"

Drusilla: "Ssshhh. Bad dog."

Angel: "You should let me talk to him, Dru. Sounds like your boy could use some pointers. She likes to be teased...."

Spike: "Keep your hole shut!"

Angel: "Just take care of her, Spike. The way she touched me just now.... I can tell when she's not satisfied."

Spike: "I said, shut up!"

Angel: "Or maybe you two just don't have the fire that we did." —**"WHAT'S MY LINE? PART 2"**

When Angel finds true happiness in the arms of Buffy, he loses his soul, and in that moment, Drusilla cries out in "orgasmic pain." Then:

Spike: "Are we feeling better, then?"

Drusilla: "I'm naming all the stars."

Spike: "Can't see the stars, love. That's the ceiling. Also, it's day."

Drusilla: "I can see them. But I've named them all the same name, and there's terrible confusion. I fear there may be a duel." —**"INNOCENCE"**

She is so very right....

ANGEL AND DRUSILLA AND SPIKE

When Angel changes, he goes immediately to the Factory to reunite with Spike and Drusilla, who are delighted.

Angel: "It's really true."

Drusilla: "You've come home."

Spike: "No more of this 'I've got a soul' crap?"

Angel: "What can I say? I was going through a phase."

Spike: "This is great! This is so great."

Drusilla: "Everything in my head is singing. We're family again. We'll feed, and we'll play...."

Spike: "I gotta tell you, it made me sick to my stomach, seeing you being the Slayer's lapdog—"

Drusilla: "How did this happen?"

Angel: "You wouldn't believe me if I told you."

Spike: "Who cares? What matters is, now he's back. Now it's four against one, which are the kind of odds I like to play." —**"Innocence"**

But soon the invalid Spike's pleasure turns to acute discomfort and jealousy as Angel taunts him with suggestions that he has taken Spike's place in Drusilla's arms:

Angel: "Well, maybe next time I'll bring you with me, Spike. Might be handy to have you along if I ever need a really good parking spot."

Spike: "Have you forgotten that you're a bloody guest in my bloody home?!"

189

Angel: "And as a guest, if there's anything I can do for you. . . . Any. . . responsibility I can assume while you spin your wheels [purposeful leer toward Dru], anything I'm not *already* doing, that is...."
                                                                        —"PASSION"

Spike attempts to give as good as he gets, but Angel is an old hand at cruelty in the matters of the heart:

Spike (re: Angel)**:** "All hat—no cattle."
Angel: "I don't know about that."
Drusilla: "Oh, Angel's got cattle all right. *Mooooo.*"
Angel: "Yeah. I think this whole Buffy thing has run its course. I'm ready to focus my energy elsewhere."
Spike: "Really?"
Angel: "Oh, yeah. What with you being special-needs boy, I figure I should stick close to home. You and Dru can always use another pair of hands...."
                                                        —"I ONLY HAVE EYES FOR YOU"

Spike [to Dru]**:** "I won't have you feeding me like a child, Dru!"
Angel: "Why not? She already bathes you, carries you around, and changes you like a child."
                                                                        —"PASSION"

Angel: "I know Dru gives you pity access, but you have to admit, it's so much easier when I do things for her."
Spike: "You'd do well to worry less about Dru and more about that Slayer you've been tramping around with."
Angel: "Dear Buffy. I'm still trying to decide the best way to send my regards."
Spike: "Why don't you rip her lungs out. That might make an impression."
Angel: "It lacks poetry."
Spike: "It doesn't have to. What rhymes with 'lungs'?"
                                                —"BEWITCHED, BOTHERED, AND BEWILDERED"

When Angel decides to send the non-demon beings in this world to Hell, Spike frets:

Spike: "Darling, if this works, everything changes. Think about it. In this world, we can be kings. In the next . . ."
Drusilla: "My Spikey's getting cold feet. Don't you worry about the next world. You'll always have me."
Spike: "Will I?"   **—"BECOMING, PART 1"**

And it is really because of his fear of losing Drusilla, and not so much of bidding a final farewell to Piccadilly, that Spike betrays Angel by forming an alliance with Buffy.

> "I want Dru back. I want it like it was before he came back.
> [Disgusted] The way she acts around him . . ."
> **Spike, to Buffy, in "Becoming, Part 2"**

In the end, Spike betrays Angel and Buffy both, thinking only of saving himself...and getting Drusilla as far away from Angel as possible.

The Sorrow and the Pity: Jenny and Giles

GILES AND JENNY: Jenny Calendar, the beautiful technopagan and Sunnydale computer-science instructor, makes her first appearance in "I Robot, You Jane." Although she is lovely, at first Giles seems more put off by her invasion of his library with her book scanners than interested in the woman herself.

Giles: "I'm just going to stay and clean up. I'll be back in the Middle Ages."
Jenny: "Did you ever leave?"   **—"I ROBOT, YOU JANE"**

Once he learns that she's a "technopagan" who not only knows what he's talking about when he tries to tell her there's a demon in the Internet, but helps him cast the demon out of the Net, he's smitten...and intrigued.

Jenny: "Well, you really are an old-fashioned boy, aren't you?"
Giles: "Well, it's true I don't dangle a corkscrew from my ear."
Jenny: "That's not where I dangle it."   **—"I ROBOT, YOU JANE"**

He determines to ask her out . . . but finds himself tongue-tied and shy. Buffy and company are more than happy to offer him advice:

Buffy: "You also might want to avoid words like 'amenable' and 'indecorous.' Speak English, not whatever they speak in..."
Giles: "England?"
Buffy: "Yeah. Just say, 'Hey, I got a thing, you maybe have a thing, maybe we could have a thing?'"
Giles: "Well, thank you so much."
Buffy: "I'm not finished. Then you say, 'How do you feel about Mexican?'"
Giles: "Mexicans."
Buffy: "Mexican! Food. You take her for food. For which you then pay."
Giles: "Right."
Xander: "So this 'chair' woman? We are talking Ms. Calendar, right?"
Giles: "What makes you think that?"
Xander: "Simple deduction: Ms. Calendar is reasonably dollsome, especially for someone in your age bracket; she already knows you're a school librarian, so you don't have to worry about how to break that embarrassing news to her...."

Buffy: "And she's the only woman we've ever actually seen speak to you. Add it all up, it spells 'duh.'"

Xander: "Now, is it time for us to talk about the facts of life?"

Giles: "I am suddenly deciding that this is none of your business."

—**"SOME ASSEMBLY REQUIRED"**

The sweetness of their budding romance is underscored by her more matter-of-fact approach. He wants to lead, but it's really best if he just gets out of her way.

Giles: "I just think it's rather odd that a nation that prides itself on its virility should feel compelled to strap on forty pounds of protective gear just in order to play rugby."

Jenny: "Is this your normal strategy for a first date: dissing my country's national pastime?"

Giles: "Did you just say...'date'?"

Jenny: "You noticed that, huh?"

—**"SOME ASSEMBLY REQUIRED"**

"Nothing's safe in this world, Rupert. Don't you know that by now?"

—**Jenny, in "The Dark Age"**

Their romance continues. And then bitterness overshadows the sweetness: Giles's past is brought to light, and Jenny is possessed by the demon Eyghon. Giles is overcome with guilt, which makes Jenny's dishonesty all the more difficult to excuse, once it's revealed that she has been sent by the same Gypsy clan that cursed Angel over a century ago. Because she did not speak up, Angelus has returned, Buffy is bereft, and there's a good chance the Judge will cleanse the Earth of mankind.

She attempts to apologize, but to no avail.

Jenny: "Rupert, I know you feel betrayed."

Giles: "Yes, that's one of the unpleasant side effects of betrayal."

Jenny: "I was raised by the people Angel hurt the most. My duty to them was the first thing I was ever taught. I didn't come here to hurt anyone. I lied to you because I thought it was the right thing to do. I didn't know what would happen. I didn't know I was going to fall in love with you." —**"PASSION"**

But no one can hold anger toward the kind and well-meaning Jenny of the Kalderash people for very long, not even Buffy:

Buffy: "Look, I know you're feeling bad about what happened and I want to say...good. Keep it up."

Jenny: "Don't worry. I will."

Buffy: "Wait. I, uh ... He misses you. He doesn't say anything to me, but I know he does. I don't want him to be lonely. I don't want anyone to." —**"PASSION"**

And when she thinks that she can restore Angel's soul—an act of redemption not only for Angel, but for her, she plans to share the wonderful news with Giles first. These are the last words between Giles and Jenny:

Jenny: "I spoke to Buffy today."
Giles: "Yes."
Jenny: "She said you missed me."
Giles: "She is a meddlesome girl." [But the truth of it is on his face.]
Jenny: "Rupert, I don't want to say anything if I'm wrong, but I may have some news....
   I have to finish up—can I see you later?"
Giles: "Yes. You could stop by the house."
Jenny: "Okay."
Giles: "Good."

—"PASSION"

Other Lovers:

LOVE IS FOREVER: JAMES AND GRACE: In 1955, James Stanley was a Sunnydale High student who fell in love with Grace Newman, a teacher. Realizing that their love was wrong, Grace attempted to break off their affair on the night of the Sadie Hawkins Dance. In desperation, he shot and killed her, and their ghosts have haunted the school ever since, doomed to repeat their tragedy.

James (in many guises, possessing many people, including Buffy): "Come back here! We're
   not finished. [He grabs her arm. Stops her.] You don't care anymore? Is that it?"
Grace (also in many guises, possessing many people,
   including Angel): It doesn't matter. It doesn't
   matter what I feel."
James: "Then tell me you don't love me.
[She's silent. He burns. Shakes her—hard.]
Say it!" [She starts to cry.]
Grace: "Will that help? Is that what you have to
   hear? [lying] I don't. I don't. Now let me
   go!" [James is devastated—disbelieving.]
James: "No.... A person doesn't just wake up one
   day and stop loving somebody. [Now he
   raises his gun.] Love is forever."
   —"I ONLY HAVE EYES FOR YOU"

When James possesses Buffy and Grace possesses Angel, they play out this scene and the ensuing one, where Grace finally appears to James and forgives him. Released from his unending cycle of guilt, James is finally freed, and the school is cleansed of his self-hatred. Buffy is not quite as lucky; she still blames herself for Angel's loss of his soul. But at some deep level, she has experienced, perhaps, a lifting of some of the burden she carries.

The poignant subtext of this episode is that Giles so wants the spirit haunting the school to be Jenny that he virtually ignores any detail that undermines his assertion. He misses her terribly.

He is haunted by her.

DADDY DEAREST: JOYCE AND TED: Joyce Summers has a difficult life at best. The single mother of a daughter she doesn't understand at all, forced to move from Los Angeles to some tiny, strange town called Sunnydale...it's frightening and lonely. Still, Joyce is more than a match for the task, giving voice to the notion that the fruit never falls far from the tree. After all, she is the mother of a Slayer.

When she falls in love with Ted Buchanan, it seems like a dream come true. He's kind, thoughtful...and he cooks! In fact, he makes pizzas and cookies people can barely stop scarfing.

Yet there is discord between Buffy and Ted, which hurts and disappoints Joyce.

Buffy: "I mean so far all I see is someone who apparently has a good job, seems nice and polite, my mother really likes him. . . ."
Xander: "What kind of monster *is* he?!"   —**"TED"**

A robot monster, it turns out, who tries to reinvent the perfect wife and family he never had in life. Before this is known, Buffy is hauled up on a murder charge when she sends him hurtling down the stairs, quite by accident...severely testing the limits of her mother's love for her. And yet, Joyce comes through when Ted comes back as if from the dead:

> "Oh, my God, Buffy.... Ted, I swear she never meant to hurt you;
> you have to believe me."
> **Joyce, to Ted, in "Ted"**

Though she loves this man, she loves her daughter more.

BEHIND THE SCENES

∎INTRODUCTION∎

Joss Whedon says of the world of *Buffy the Vampire Slayer:* "At the core, it's an emotionally safe place to be." The main characters care deeply about one another (yes, even Cordelia), and when the chips are down, they can count on one another. They share a common vision, and they serve a common purpose. They are loyal and true, and yes, they would die for one another.

What all that is, is love.

The entertainment industry as a whole is not about sharing vision, purpose, or love. It's not a safe place to be. Despite the proliferation of TV channels, networks, a new appreciation for independent film, and quirky, risk-taking films in general, as well as the current new trend of putting short QuickTime movies on the Net as "job applications" for new directors, it is still incredibly easy to be pushed off whatever mountain you have managed to scale. Shows are canceled after three episodes, or they're never picked up in the first place. Beautiful movies that took years to make it to the screen fail because they are released at the same time as a cynical, commercial blockbuster.

(Frankly, book publishing is not a safe place to be, either, but that's neither here nor there.)

Yet, there exists within the arts a place where the heart and soul are safe: in the knowledge that you had your chance to do your best on a project you care deeply about.

Welcome to the Hellmouth.

An emotionally safe place to be?

No way.

Because on the lot, and in the interviews, and through the day-to-day encounters we had with the cast and crew, we came to understand the dedication everyone connected with *Buffy* brings to their craft.

They talked about having to spar with their agents over accepting positions at *Buffy* ("the vampire what? Are you nuts?"). They shared with us the painful truth that when the twenty-minute presentation of *Buffy* was shown to "the suits" around town, no one wanted it. *It was passed over. It was not picked up.* And then, finally, twelve episodes were ordered so that *Buffy* could serve as a mid-season replacement series. Hardly a sign of enthusiasm or confidence.

It was the critics who found *Buffy* first, and then the fans. And it was a huge, diverse audience of fans: horror devotees, teenagers, Boomers—anyone who watched the show and realized this wasn't just about icky things that go bump in the night. This was a show about the heart...by people who were pouring their hearts and souls into it.

A shared vision.

SARAH MICHELLE GELLAR

Wandering around the set, conducting on-site interviews, and in later phone interviews, we hear the same things about Sarah over and over again. She's a true professional. She was a child prodigy. Her natural ability as an actress is astonishing. She tends to mother cast and crew alike, taking an interest, solving a problem.

She works too hard.

That's something that is echoed time and again. Indeed, between her last day of work on *Buffy's* second season and the first day of work on the third, she'll have something like three days off. In the meantime, she'll be filming two movies, a *Dangerous Liaisons* update called *Cruel Inventions*, and a romantic fantasy called (for the moment) *Vanilla Fog*. When does she sleep?

Does she need to sleep?

Apparently not, because, despite the concerns of her coworkers, this is a pace Sarah seems to have been on since birth. Or, at the very least, since she began making television commercials at the age of four. From that moment on, she was the kind of girl, the kind of actor, who got noticed.

Marcia Shulman, casting director for the first two seasons of *Buffy*, remembers Sarah from her days as a child actor in New York City. In fact, she cast Sarah and Seth Green in a commercial together when the two were barely old enough for kindergarten. She stood out from the crowd. Even more so when, at the age of four, she was sued by McDonald's for a Burger King ad in which she, just a little girl, had teased the other company about its allegedly less substantial burgers.

Marcia is also the one who reveals that the producers had a very good idea of what they wanted in the actress who would play the title role—until Sarah came along. When they knew she was what they had been looking for all along, they revised their ideas about the character slightly to accommodate the actress they had found. As has been said, Sarah was there to audition for the role of Cordelia. To her incredible good fortune, Joss Whedon and the other producers saw her in another role.

Julie Benz, who played Darla, remembers screen-testing along with Sarah for the role of Kendall Hart in *All My Children*. They were in the same small audition group. She knew Sarah was going to get the part, she says. Just knew.

Sarah, by the way, is apparently meticulous about keeping a record of her career. The ad she did with Seth Green? When Marcia reminded her of it, she knew right where to find a copy. Same with her *All My Children* screen test. And the blooper reel for *Buffy the Vampire Slayer*? Last seen in Ms. Gellar's hands, perhaps never to surface again.

Sarah grew up in Manhattan, where she attended the Professional Children's School. She has appeared in countless commercials. Her TV credits include the series *Swan's Crossing* and the miniseries *A Woman Named Jackie*, in which she played a teenage Jacqueline Kennedy. As the world knows by now, Sarah won an Emmy for her stint on *All My Children*. Her film credits include *Funny Farm, Scream 2,* and *I Know What You Did Last Summer*. And all of that was before she kicked it into total overdrive.

Driven doesn't even begin to describe her.

While we're on the set, Sarah jokes with producer Gareth Davies and story editor Marti Noxon, and frightens away a crew member who offers to relieve her of her not-quite-finished yogurt before grinning wickedly. Before she has to run back over to hit James Marsters again, she quickly tells a story about her recent trip to the Blockbuster Movie Awards. There are workmen doing some renovations on her house. On that day, they were completely redoing her driveway. In her gown and heels, Sarah couldn't figure out how to get out to her limo with-

out ruining her outfit. Fortunately, the blue-collar heroes offered to carry her out to the waiting car. She's surprised at how nice these guys were…as if this chore were actually a hardship in some way.

Her current social status is as mysterious as ever, but then, a woman with this kind of schedule likely doesn't have much time for romance. Or much else, for that matter.

Indeed, Sarah must be very pleased. It wasn't all that long ago, September 1994, that she was modeling back-to-school fashions on *Regis and Kathie Lee*. Things have changed considerably since then. Sarah bought her first house and her first car, among other things, including her much-talked-about tattoo.

Her own life reflects Buffy's dilemma quite dramatically, though Sarah's mission is one she herself chose, rather than being the Chosen One. Due to her work habits, it seems that Sarah has never really had time to kick back and just be "a kid." In fact, she sometimes has to ask Joss Whedon what some of the slang in the scripts means.

When she has a few moments when she isn't being filmed or photographed or interviewed, Sarah does spend time with other members of the cast, particularly Alyson Hannigan. In fact, Sarah credits the addition of Alyson to the cast (another actress was originally cast as Willow) as the final ingredient needed to make the rapport among the main characters truly click. When Sarah does hang out with the cast, a typical get-together might be like the night Sarah, Alyson, and Charisma Carpenter went to the Hard Rock Café and then to the movies to see *Scream*.

Where would Sarah find the time? What she does find the time for is her dog, a white Maltese named Thor, after the Norse god of thunder. Also John Cusack movies. And, sometimes, vanilla wafers.

How busy is she? Well, let's just say she made no secret of the day she drove to work in knee-high boots and a slip—but forgot to wear her dress. It's a story she's told several times, and the busier she gets, the more likely it becomes that it might happen again! But maybe next time she won't be in a convertible.

Ever since the series premiered, Sarah's star has been skyrocketing. She hosted *Saturday Night Live*, appeared on the covers of *Entertainment Weekly, Rolling Stone, Seventeen, YM, Cinefantastique*, and just about every other magazine out there. Her "Got Milk?" ad ran everywhere from mainstream publications to the backs of Marvel comic books. *Entertainment Weekly* called her star turn in *Buffy* one of the great performances of 1997.

Sarah, and the show in which she stars, are big enough that when asked by *EW* to define the level of pop-culture excitement over the release of *Scream 2*, director Wes Craven said, "The idea that Buffy the Vampire Slayer has a relatively minor role shows you how big this thing is."

As Buffy, Sarah is far more afraid of emotional wounds than physical ones. But in her two horror films, the tables were turned, and she became a more traditional "scream queen." What is Sarah herself afraid of? Not much, but she has admitted a terror of an intruder in her home, as well as a fear of cemeteries and the idea of being buried alive. And, as far as being a scream queen is concerned, as Sarah told *YM* magazine, "Some of the best work for girls my age is in this genre."

NICHOLAS BRENDON

Nicholas Brendon isn't Xander. Right off the bat, that's clear. He's quick-witted, a bit mischievous, yes. But where Xander is open and spur-of-the-moment, Nicholas seems more guarded and contemplative.

We meet outside his trailer. These "Star Wagons" are split into two compartments, and Nicholas shares his with Alyson Hannigan. While we talk, he sits in a rocking chair he brings out of the trailer (though he first offers it to us: a gentleman). Alyson comes out walking her little dog. Charisma comes and wants to talk about plans for them to hang out after shooting is completed for the day.

We talk about auditioning in general first, and the way he has of delivering his lines so they sound natural, rather than like "acting."

"If I have to go in and read for something, [I try to] use an unusual but natural beat. Take a breath where I shouldn't be taking it. It also helps you slow down; in real life people think about what they are saying."

It is perhaps impossible to turn auditioning into a formula—otherwise a casting director could choose anyone for a part. But something of Nicholas's philosophy and strategy must work. For an actor with a relatively short resumé, he snagged the role of Xander more quickly than anyone could have expected.

"I met with [casting director] Marcia Shulman," he recalls. "She brought me back that day. I met Joss and Gail and did my thing and got a phone call about an hour later saying I was going to Fox to test. I went to Fox and was very nervous and tested. They allowed me to go to Warner Brothers the following Monday. There were two of us, and then Tuesday I found out that I got the role."

Four days. That's fast.

And acting was not Nicholas's first career choice. Born and raised in Granada Hills, California, he attended College of the Canyon, where he played baseball. That was his dream: the majors. A dream that ended when he broke his arm in a manner which would impede his baseball performance.

It wasn't long before Nicholas was working in TV commercials. Unsatisfied with the way things were going, he switched to the other side of the camera, becoming a production assistant on the series *Dave's World*. After acing an audition for a guest spot on that series, his luck started to change. Nicholas also appeared in a recurring role on the daytime soap *The Young and the Restless,* as the lead in a pilot called *Secret Lives,* in a guest spot on *Married...With Children,* and as a homicidal corn worshiper in *Children of the Corn 3: Urban Harvest.*

Then came *Buffy.*

"My twin brother, Kelly, dyed his hair blond because he was sick of people coming up to him [for autographs]," he says in wonder.

Hmm. Nicholas has a twin brother. While that thought will send many a female fan's mind whirling, it also makes one wonder how long it can be before the "evil doppelganger" episode of *Buffy.*

"You never know," Nicholas says. "The show's been sold into syndication already. They're going to need to do about a hundred episodes. So you never know what's going to happen down the road. And you've *got* to have a doppelganger episode. But we've got to find a doppelganger for each individual."

The differences between Nicholas and Xander aren't limited to just personality, either. There are some, well, physical differences as well.

"I had my belly button pierced for three or four years," he says. "I took that out because of the show. I had to have my shirt off a few times and Joss said, 'Xander wouldn't have a belly-button ring.'"

Do you have any scars, tattoos or other distinguishing marks?
NICHOLAS: "The scar on my elbow from my baseball injury. And as my girlfriend just said, there are scars all over my heart because she's broken it so often."

Are you expecting Speedo backlash over your performance in "Go Fish"?
NICHOLAS: "I'm not looking for backlash. I'm looking for forward lash."

Do you have any skills or talents you haven't showcased as Xander yet?
NICHOLAS: "I *discover* new talents. Like dancing. Whatever comes up, I'll do it. I've done a lot of pratfalls and stuff like that."

What were you afraid of as a child?
NICHOLAS: "I'm afraid of that question. I don't talk about my childhood that much."

Which isn't all that unusual for actors.
NICHOLAS: "That way you know there's a reason we're acting."

Which member of the Scooby Gang are you?
NICHOLAS: "I'm both Scooby and Shaggy. Maybe a little bit of Fred in there as well."

You have a great love for old movies. Your favorite actor is Jack Lemmon, your favori film is *Some Like It Hot.* What else do you like, and where does that love come from?
NICHOLAS: "Cary Grant. Looking at his whole body of work. Most of those actors were vaudeville-trained. Cary Grant was one of those and was great at physical comedy but had leading-man looks. If anyone ever said of me that 'he's like a poor man's, '90s, Cary Grant' I would be very, very happy about that. Jimmy Stewart, of course. Ernest Borgnine in *Marty* is one of the best performances I've ever seen. Hollywood was so different. Some ways better, some ways worse. But not being born in that era, you fantasize. Everything seems so epic."

During season two, Alyson pantsed you on the set. You still haven't gotten her back.
NICHOLAS: "I can't do it. Instead, I'll take that anger out on some guy driving the car. Road rage. Someone's goin' down."

Do you have a favorite moment, on or off camera, from your tenure on the series?

NICHOLAS: "Probably the day I did my Speedo stuff. The crew was so supportive. I was so terrified of it. When we finally did my scene it was four minutes of sheer hell. Walking in, doing my dialogue, then diving into the pool. Then, coming up from the water, I heard this weird smattering, and then I emerged and the whole crew was applauding. It was really nice. Everyone was very supportive."

Even David [Boreanaz]?

NICHOLAS: "Heh. Dave wasn't there. Yeah, he's a wiseguy."

You've kissed or been in some intimate situation with each of the female cast members. Is this the best job you've ever had?

NICHOLAS: "It's not bad. I'm sure I can get paid to do worse things."

Everyone on the set seems to think that *Buffy*'s success, and the team that came together to make it happen, was almost destiny. Do you share that feeling?

NICHOLAS: "It's one of those things where everything worked. When you're creating a successful show, it's ninety percent luck. Joss has the talent, but when it comes to casting, it's all luck. It was my first pilot season, and I kind of won the lottery."

ALYSON HANNIGAN

She isn't Willow. That's patently obvious. The veteran actress, who has been working since the age of four, is confident and outgoing, funny and mature. But then again, there's that smile, those expressive eyes, the warmth and sincerity. And then you have it. This is what Willow might be like when she grows up.

Born in Washington, D.C., Alyson spent years working in commercials in Atlanta before moving to Los Angeles at the age of eleven. She has appeared in several TV series as a guest star, including *Picket Fences*, *Roseanne*, and *Touched by an Angel*, and was a regular on the short-lived *Free Spirit*. Her feature films include *Dead Man on Campus* and *My Stepmother Is an Alien*, in which she first performed opposite Seth Green, who played her boyfriend in that film, just as he does in *Buffy*.

On the question of how much she's like Willow, Alyson, of course, has her own opinions. So does her boyfriend. When asked, he replied that Willow was "one of her personalities."

"I love that," Alyson says happily.

Though, unlike Willow, Alyson has not achieved computer nerd-dom just yet.

"I have a computer, and I'm signed onto the net," she says. "I'm not nearly as literate as Willow but definitely can make my way around the computer and programs and everything. I have a Packard Bell. It is kinda slow now; in fact, it discourages me from going on the Net, because my modem is not very fast. I think I need to upgrade my computer."

Like many of the actors on the series, Alyson loves animals. She has, in her words, "an army of pets," including two dogs, and, together with her roommate, a total of five cats in the house. Her dog Alex, who is a Jack Russell terrier, is on the set with her, though officially pets aren't allowed. Alyson insists that Alex is a figment of the imagination of anyone who might see him running about. The other dog is named Zippy, and the cats are Dr. Seuss, Jupiter, Tear Drop, Rain, and Lucky.

One has to wonder, given Willow's naivete, if playing such an innocent character has made Alyson want to act, well…naughty.

"No," she says dismissively. "You know, we sort of dabbled in the different wardrobe with the *Halloween* episode. Perhaps if the character were completely different…but to be Willow in that outfit, I was self-conscious. But if I were playing a different character that was just evil, then I could be more comfortable with the wardrobe. But, no, I don't ever want to be evil. I love Willow as she is."

The way she is. Interestingly enough, Alyson figured out "the way she is" by instinct, and the way she read her lines in her audition has defined the character ever since. We like to call it "the Willow cadence."

"I was sitting in the parking lot in my car waiting for the audition," she recalls. "I was reading the lines, and it was just sort of depressing. She was saying, 'Oh, boys don't like me, and this and that, and I can't really speak around guys.' I just didn't want to feel sorry for her. How are [viewers] going to like her if they're saying, 'Oh, look at her feeling sorry for herself'?

"There was a scene between Buffy and Willow, and in the beginning of the scene Willow says, 'Xander and I went out when we were four or five, and then we broke up.' Buffy says, 'Why?' 'Because he stole my Barbie.' It changed once we got to [shoot] the actual scene, but in the [original version] Buffy says, 'Did you ever get your Barbie back?' And Willow's line was: 'Most of it.' And so I thought, you know what, I'm gonna make that a really happy thing. I was so proud that I got most of my Barbie back. And then that clued in how I was going to play the rest of the scene. It defines the character. That was the one line that triggered it. Then I went back and said, 'Okay, now how can I play the whole scene like that?' And it really helped me. And Joss said later, 'Oh, yeah, *most* of it!' It was a funny line, and he didn't even know there was a joke there. I made the right choice."

Do you have any scars, tattoos, or other distinguishing marks?

ALYSON: "I have all of the above. I have a bunch of scars. Let's start with the one on my nose from a dog ripping it open when I was two. He was kissing me, and then his tooth got caught in my nose, and he was trying to get it out, and he just ripped my nose apart. And then I have a scar in my eyebrow, from— I was in the bathroom with my friend when we were little kids. We were about to take a bath, and for some reason, I don't understand why, my foot went into the waste basket, and I tripped, and my head fell onto the track from the sliding door. I also have a scar on my chin that I got when I was a little baby. I was running around with a glass bottle, and I fell.

"Then I have a scar under my chin from— The story my mom knows is I just fell on the chain-link fence, but the real story is that I was playing Marco Polo with my friend, and my mom said, 'Go get the mail.' I said, 'I can't, I'm playing Marco Polo.' I was the one with my eyes closed, I guess that's Marco. So I decided, 'Okay, fine, I've got to go get the mail, but I still want to play the game. I'll do both.' So, I decided I'd walk to the mailbox from the backyard swimming pool with my eyes closed. I was doing quite a good job, I thought, until I was in the carport, and I was walking through, and we had just gotten the chain-link fence removed from the front yard, and the people just put it into the carport. I guess I forgot about that, so I tripped over it, and my chin landed on the top part of it. I was probably about seven. You know, that's just my face. I guess I wasn't a very graceful child.

"As for tattoos, I have tribal dolphins on my ankle, and I have a Japanese *kanji* on the lower part of my back."

Tribal dolphins?
ALYSON: "They're black, and they are in more of the tribal form. It's not like Flipper or something."

And what does the *kanji* say?
ALYSON: "It's the *kanji* for luck and happiness."

Do you have any skills or talents you haven't been able to use on the show that you'd like to showcase?
ALYSON: [laughter] "No. I don't think so. I can't think of anything right now."

You worked with Seth on *My Stepmother Is an Alien.* Do you have any other connections with any other cast members or crew members from previous jobs?
ALYSON: "I worked with Seth on a couple of things actually. The other was *Free Spirit,* this sitcom that I did."

Were you interested in horror and fantasy growing up?
ALYSON: "Yeah. I mean, I was a chicken. I still pretty much am, you know. I'm the screamer in the theater, but it was always fun to get spooked."

What were you afraid of as a child?
ALYSON: "Tests that I hadn't studied for? I was sort of afraid of my spelling teacher. She was mean. Obviously, you go through the phases of, 'Okay, there are monsters moving under my bed,' so I was obviously afraid of anything that could be under there. That's why I kept all of my toys under my bed. You know, my mom thought I was just messy. No, no, it was protection."

CHARISMA CARPENTER

Just out of makeup, Charisma Carpenter is wearing a long overcoat that covers whatever Cynthia Bergstrom has dressed her in for this episode. She has only a few minutes before she'll be called to the set, so while we sit at a picnic table, Charisma enjoys a light lunch. The picnic table is located on a patch of lawn in the middle of the parking lot. A patch of lawn which also sports portions of a cemetery set.

The first thing that comes to mind upon meeting Charisma is, of course, "How much is this girl like Cordelia?" The immediate answer is "not at all." It is evident that Charisma Carpenter is intelligent, focused, and thoughtful, three things her television counterpart has never been accused of being.

Charisma was born and raised in Las Vegas, Nevada, where she lived until she was fifteen, at which point her family moved to Mexico. Charisma's interest in the performing arts was evident from childhood. At the age of five, she began to study classical ballet. She continued to dance through high school, during which she commuted between Mexico and San Diego to take classes at the School of the Creative and Performing Arts.

After her high school graduation, and a jaunt through Europe, Charisma entered junior college in San Diego and worked the usual jobs in restaurants and video stores, and was also an aerobics instructor. In 1991, she spent a brief period as a cheerleader for the San Diego Chargers—experience that would come in handy later as cheer-queen Cordelia.

Eventually, the actress moved to Los Angeles.

"I was working in a restaurant, saving my money to go back to college," she recalls. "I wanted to be an English teacher. When I was working in this restaurant, a lot of people would ask, 'Are you an actress? Are you a model? Why don't you consider that?' Finally, one person specifically said, 'I know somebody. I want you to meet them.'"

Then she met a commercial agent who recommended several acting schools. After visiting the most reputable on the list and auditing classes, she wound up at the well-known Playhouse West, where she studied for eighteen months.

"That was when I discovered how much I enjoyed acting and what an outlet it was—and that I could actually make a living at it," Charisma notes. "It gave me a lot of confidence. That school made me feel like 'This is possible; if I worked hard, I could really do this.' This is what I want. I love doing this."

Still, despite her blossoming career, Charisma hasn't forgotten her interest in teaching.

"I'm sure I would be a good teacher, and maybe down the road, that [could] happen," she says. "I mean, I love children, and I love the aspect of giving and loving and nurturing in an educational environment. It would be great. But it's not me right now."

While attending Playhouse West, Charisma began to do commercials. She appeared in more than twenty before her first real break came in the form of a guest shot on *Baywatch*. Shortly thereafter, Charisma auditioned for Aaron Spelling, who cast her in the role of Ashley in his short-lived NBC series *Malibu Shores*.

It was while she was working for Spelling that Charisma first found out about *Buffy the Vampire Slayer*.

"Working with Aaron Spelling was a great experience," Charisma says fondly. "But I was working on his show, and the vibe was that it wasn't 'going.' Thankfully, my agent sent me out on the *Buffy the Vampire Slayer* audition."

Charisma first auditioned for the role of Buffy.

"I was wearing overalls and these bright orange flip-flops and a jacket, and I was just kind of hanging, you know, because I felt that Buffy could really just be herself," she remembers, a wry smile playing at the edges of her mouth. "She could wear the flip-flops, and she could be low-key and still be very—it wasn't about looking as cute as I could to get the part. It was about just being cool, just being fun with your identity. And that's how I felt. The other girls in the room were really dressed up, and they were wearing very high school trendy clothes with knee-high stockings and short skirts."

To Charisma's surprise, however, the producers asked her to audition for the role of Cordelia as well. To say the least, the actress was unprepared. She had, after all, come to read for *Buffy*.

"I was thinking, *I'm never going to get this part because of the way they're seeing me.* Sometimes you have to show people. Cordelia is definitely a character to dress for. You have to kind of give it to them and let them work on that. It was an interesting experience, because I had about fifteen minutes to go outside and prepare for Cordelia when I had spent all this time on Buffy."

Obviously, it went well. The producers soon had Charisma scheduled for a screen test for Cordelia. All did not go as smoothly as one might imagine, however.

"I was super, super late for the screen test, because I was working all the way down on the beach for *Malibu Shores,* and I had to go to Burbank, which was on the opposite end of the city. I was late, and there was traffic, and it was raining," she remembers. "My agent called me right when I was at the exit, paged me, 911, and I went 'Oh, gosh, I better answer this.' So I pulled over, even though I was tremendously late. I said, 'What? I'm on the exit right now.' She tells me, 'They're going to leave, you'd better hurry up.'"

Most actors would have been in a panic by that time. Not Charisma.

"I said, 'You tell them that they'd better order a pizza or something, because I did not drive an hour and a half in all this traffic to not go in there and at least audition.' Obviously, I was panicked."

Fortunately, when she finally arrived, the audition went well. The producers were "laughing, really responsive," Charisma recalls. She left with a rush of confidence. "After it was over and they had all left, I called my agent and said, 'I got this part.' She said, 'No, don't say that, you don't know.' But I knew I had the part, I could tell."

She was, of course, absolutely correct. During the first season, the character of Cordelia seemed little more than Buffy's snobby nemesis. But in the season finale, the character learned the truth about Sunnydale. From that point on, Charisma knew that her character was going to be much more involved with the Slayer's posse. Ironically, she admits that this news caused her some anxiety.

"I wasn't sure how I felt about it, because I didn't want to lose my edge. I didn't want her to be nice; I didn't want her to change because that's who she is," she says thoughtfully, although she notes that Cordelia's somewhat rough edges can make for difficult experiences with fans.

"Sometimes it's hard when they don't expect you to be anything but snobby. They don't necessarily want to approach you. Fan letters often ask, 'When are you going to be nice to Buffy?' Fans don't know how to take me, they don't know that I'm nice, they don't know that I'm normal, and Cordelia is just a character. People get confused. It's a TV show. I provide conflict, and that's what good drama needs."

Perhaps because of that element of conflict, Charisma didn't want her character to change too much. In fact, when discussing a moment of kindness Cordelia exhibits toward Xander in the second-season finale, Carpenter asserts in no uncertain terms that: "We don't want too many of those nice moments." In fact, she has often urged the producers to "make her meaner."

"It would be boring if she was too one-dimensional. It's a challenge for me to find that balance. That's why I enjoy playing her so much. She's got to be somewhat tolerable or why would they hang out with her? But I [try] not to lose her edge, her honesty."

Which brings us round to that first question: does Charisma Carpenter share anything with Cordelia Chase beyond her initials? Before our interview, she would have said absolutely not. Now, though, she's not so sure.

"Now that we're talking about it, in this context, I am kind of like her. That's the first time I ever realized it; that's how I am," she admits. "Sometimes I'll say things, but it's just the truth, you know? You kind of have to learn the balance, so you don't offend people. Sometimes I do get in that situation where I have said something outspokenly, and based on [somebody's] reaction, later wondered, *Ooh, how did that come across?* I have a good heart, I'm a good person, honest."

But what about in high school? Was she Cordelia in high school, or was she more like one of the other characters on the show?

"Well, I wasn't Willowish, I wasn't terribly academic," she says quickly. "I wasn't in the clique, either; I wasn't Cordy. I was kind of a loner, and nobody really is a loner in this cast."

Conversation eventually turns to the future, of course. But Joss Whedon, the series' creator, plays things very close to the vest. So close that cast members rarely know what will happen to their characters next season, or in some cases, even next month. Charisma will say only that she's "curious," and who can blame her?

Do you have a favorite moment, either off camera or on, since you've been on the show?

CHARISMA: "I have a lot of favorite moments, most with Xander. A lot of Cordy's conflict, and a lot of who she is, comes out around Xander. Because she is in love with him in spite of herself, or in spite of him. I have my best moments with Nicky (Nicholas Brendon)."

Are you more of a preparatory or an instinctual actor?

CHARISMA: "A little bit [preparatory]. But I leave room for whatever's going to happen instinctually. I read the scripts, and if I find something that I don't like, it's up to me to deliver it in a way that makes me happy and is true to [the character]. Fortunately, I have been working as Cordelia for two years, so I'm getting to know her really well, and that's a benefit of television."

Do you have any tattoos or distinguishing marks?

CHARISMA: "Just a beauty mark on the hip."

Scars?

CHARISMA: "I do have a scar, actually, a really nasty scar on my stomach. Do you want to see?"

Ow, that looks like it hurt. How did you get it?

CHARISMA: "I was five years old, and I had snuck into the backyard when I wasn't supposed to. The pool was being built. I guess the construction workers had left the gate open. So me and my adventurous friend were in the backyard. We ran around to the deep end, where he bumped me, so I fell forward, and I impaled myself on a rebar (one of those metal bars that stick up out of the cement in any new construction). It almost punctured my stomach. I don't know how I came to. I don't remember lifting myself off or any of that, but I must have, because nobody else did it. The next thing I remember is going into my downstairs bathroom and taking the toilet paper in both hands, just getting gobs and gobs of toilet paper and putting it on my tummy and going upstairs.

"My mom was getting ready in the bathroom and I came in and said, 'Mommy, I have a boo-boo.' She said 'Okay, let me kiss it better,' and she turned. I took [the toilet paper] off, and she started to freak out. That day my dad was at work, and the car was in the shop. So my mom was carrying me in her arms, pounding on the neighbor's doors to take me to the hospital. I got stitches, and that was a painful part. That was a drama.

"I almost died."

What were you afraid of as a child?

CHARISMA: "My brother. And that's not a joke."

Do you have any talents or skills that you haven't used on the show that you'd like to?

CHARISMA: "I dance. I love ballet. I sang [on the show], and that's not a gift. That is specifically why they had me sing, I think. 'Do you sing?' 'No.' 'Well great!' I did classical ballet all my life, growing up."

DAVID BOREANAZ

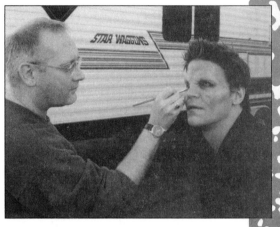

He's as arresting in person as he is on camera. Very kind, very gracious. He ushered us over to some overstuffed chairs and couches on part of the mansion set, but just as soon as we settled in, the grips started moving things around. So he suggested we move. As soon as we got settled into our new chairs, someone started vacuuming. David seemed apologetic, but we assured him everything was fine there.

David Boreanaz was born in Buffalo, New York, grew up in Philadelphia, and graduated from Ithaca College in New York before moving to Los Angeles to try his luck at acting. His luck, it must be noted, at first didn't seem to be all that good. He parked cars, painted houses, and handed out towels at a sports club. He did some local theater and managed to get a guest spot on a single episode of *Married...With Children*. But his big break is a story right out of 1940s Hollywood.

Casting director Marcia Schulman had seen just about every young actor in L.A. for the role of Angel. One day, she received a phone call from a friend, a manager, who had just signed a new client—a guy he had seen out the window of his home. David had been walking his dog when the man approached him. In no time, he was off to audition for the role of Angel. The moment he walked in, Marcia Shulman, who had already seen so many actors for the role, wrote in the margins of the casting sheet, "He's the guy."

He was the guy.

As an actor, he is intense and focused. Off the set, however, he has earned a bit of a reputation as a wiseguy. Both sides are in evidence during our visit.

Both sides, angel and devil. Or, if you prefer, Angel and Angelus. Which brings us round to the question of David's preference: which of his character's personae has he most enjoyed portraying?

"There are pluses and minuses to each," he points out. "With Angel's good side, I wasn't really exploring as much, as far as his being as outgoing as I wanted to be. But I know when I go back to being good, then I'll have learned from that. I think they both balance each other out pretty well....Yeah, I've done some bad things."

Bad things, perhaps, but that's Angel. David's intensity tells you he's capable of that, but mention his dog, Bertha Blue, and he turns into a softie, sad that he must leave her at home.

"It's terrible. Terrible," he says. "Sometimes I bring my dog on the set. It is hard: she's in the trailer and you don't want to bring her out and you are afraid that she might run away. But it is good to come home and see her all happy. [To know that] she is okay.

"I've had her about four years. She has her own house. She has one ear that goes up and one ear that goes down. She has been lost many times, but she has always found her way home or I've found her. She's got a collar on and tags; so she'll come up somewhere eventually. I just don't stress. I home in on her."

Not exactly brooding, is he? And yet, other than the subject of Bertha Blue, David does seem to have some of that Angelic demeanor to him. Let's face it, Angel is cool. But as for David—observations about the present aside, we want to know about the past. As a child, was the man who went from walking his dog to talking about his own television series, well, *cool?*

"Ahhh, was I cool?" he repeats, a bit mystified by the question. "I liked the Fonz. Arthur Fonzarelli [from *Happy Days*]. I thought he was cool. But I don't know. I felt good about myself, I guess that is being cool."

Moments before the interview, we had been watching David shoot several takes of a very intense scene. It can't be easy to prepare as an actor, particularly emotionally, for each new scene.

"It's tough," David admits. "You have to find a focus. You do your homework and you come to the set prepared and you [just] have to go out the door and see what happens. That is the most exciting thing. You've got everything down and you have it in your body and you let things happen. That is when it really starts to get fun. You get those magical moments where something goes wrong but it turns out good. That is the best thing about it."

Hmm. So, homework, then. What is an actor's homework, exactly? To David, the answer is: whatever it takes.

"Everything an actor goes through for a specific scene—whatever it calls for," he says. "And, no, I don't practice in front of a mirror. There are some secrets you have to keep; there is a fine line. And those are the things that you cherish. You go home, memorize your lines, get that over with, then you add to your character. You bring certain things to the rehearsal, and they either work or not. The director might like them, or he might not like them. Then when you are finished, you drive home and you think how you could improve. When I've finished a scene, there is always something more that I want to do. Even if it was great, that's fine, but there is always something more. You want to push yourself, to find a different level. It is tiring."

David admits that he is being recognized more and more frequently, but he is resolved to whatever may come.

"It goes with the territory. You kind of embrace it," he says. "More and more people are coming up to me to say they are enjoying the show or the character. It is pretty wild. It is nice to be recognized. You are doing work and you are on a good show."

As for the break between seasons two and three, David had no real plans.

"I'm just going to go on vacation and take some time to relax. When I come back from vacation, I'll see what happens. I'm a real patient person. I let things kind of happen. I'm young and I have my whole life in front of me. I want to enjoy this time. I really don't want to overindulge myself in work or push things, because you can really wear yourself out. And I don't want to do that. I want to kick back, have a margarita," he says with a smile.

"Also, I don't want to be overly exposed. I don't want to push anything. I don't want to be in a film or a project that I'm not passionate about and have it flop. Then where are you five years from now?"

On the subject of the future, the conversation turns to ways in which David would like to explore his character, if he could choose.

"I'd like Angel to be able to go to Las Vegas on road trips, spend the night with my vampire friends," he says. "You don't want to take your work home and think about the show, but you do inevitably because you are part of it and it is part of you. There is a lot to him that I would like to explore. He's got a good side, and he's got a bad side. How you keep that balanced is pretty interesting. Sure, he can mope around and be sad and brooding. Or he can try to make a difference, somehow, in somebody's life. You know what I am saying? Sure, you make your amends and go on with it."

How do you feel about being a sex symbol?

DAVID: "Oh, geez, I didn't know I was. Am I a sex symbol? I'd have to thank my mom and dad; they made me. That was pretty easy. Those are the two that started it. I was conceived in Toronto, too, did you know that? Yeah, my parents conceived me in Toronto."

It must be difficult for an actor to start a new series, for the cast to work together without knowing one another and yet still try to be an effective ensemble.

DAVID: "Well, you're thrown together. In my case, I've been blessed that things have been very, very good. I haven't had any problems with people I'm working with. My fellow actors have all been very giving. There are tense moments, but that is because of the time and because of the hours. You can catch somebody at a very vulnerable spot sometimes and they won't find that amusing and/or they just want to get the day over with. And you've got to respect that. So, I think it's all been pretty good. I can count on the cast. You don't really try to create that, I think it just happens."

What was your schedule today?

DAVID: "I got up at five. I had a six A.M. call."

Were you interested in the horror genre at all when you were growing up?

DAVID: "I remember being terrified by *Frankenstein* when I was a kid. The old *Frankenstein*. Boris Karloff. When he came and visited the little girl playing by the lake. Terrible, I couldn't watch it. That and I like Godzilla movies."

Do you want to direct?

DAVID: "Yeah, definitely. I love people. I studied film in college, so I understand it. I love moving the camera. I just need to understand a little bit more about the technical side of the camera."

Do you have a favorite moment, either on or off camera, from your work on the series?

DAVID: "There were a couple actually. When I had the scene in the Factory—just after I had changed—and I was striking the match off the brick table. That was a really cool moment. That whole scene seemed to really gel.

"Also, I work with Sarah a lot and there is good chemistry between the two of us. We are able to grasp each other's insights pretty easily. That's really pleasant. There have been a lot of moments with her that I would walk away and say, 'Wow, that was really great.' And there are moments where you say 'Wow, that was really bad,' but it comes out great. You can't really judge yourself. You've just got to do it. You learn from your mistakes; you grow from them."

ANTHONY STEWART HEAD

Anthony Stewart Head is at present the resident "grown-up" among the cast regulars. He portrays Rupert Giles, Buffy's Watcher, and the librarian at Sunnydale High School.

Born in Camdentown, England, he has enjoyed a long and successful career with roots in musical theater, following completion of his training at the London Academy of Music and

Dramatic Arts. His first break came playing Jesus in *Godspell* in the West End. He has also appeared in British theaters in *The Rocky Horror Show* as Frank N. Furter, *Julius Caesar, The Heiress, Chess,* Peter Shaffer's *Yonadab,* and *Rope.*

In America, he attracted attention as regular cast member Oliver Sampson on *VR5*. He has guest-starred on *Highlander, NYPD Blue,* and many BBC productions (including his first TV role, in *Enemy at the Door.*) He also appeared with Jim Belushi in the Showtime movie *Royce,* and in feature films, including *A Prayer for the Dying* and *Lady Chatterley's Lover.*

His long-lasting fame as the romantic and intriguing "coffee guy" on the long-running Taster's Choice coffee commercials is gradually being supplanted by his new image as the sexy librarian on *Buffy*. When he asked to visit an American high school library in order to research his role, the librarian he interviewed was thrilled at the prospect that a librarian would be featured so prominently in the show—and played by a handsome man, at that.

"She said it was really good to have a spokesman for librarians because somebody could finally tell the true story of the hard time that librarians have. For instance, she said, did I know that there were more libraries in state prisons than there were in schools? I promised that I would try to get that in a script somewhere."

Of his role as a heroic librarian, Tony adds, "I don't think Giles is a very good librarian, actually. No one ever comes into his library. The library's all over the place, and I think that's part of his charm."

He was surprised by the strong reaction to Giles as a sex symbol.

"I have played a number of types before now," Tony says, "but usually on TV I have played dark, the character himself quite sexy. Nice sort of thing. I have to thank Jeri Baker [of the *Buffy* hair department], because when I first sat down in her chair and we talked about what we were going to do, I suggested parting my hair on the side and flattening it down for a really, really geeky look.

"She said, 'No, please, don't do that. You're a good-looking man, and I promise you there are going to be women out there who would rather see you looking attractive.' So I said, 'All right, fair enough.' So I am thankful to her, because otherwise Giles wouldn't have had any fans at all."

Fans he does have, including his loyal GASPers on the net and members of the American Library Association. He is quite appreciative of their attention. They have sent him many gifts, including a T-shirt laden with "Buffyisms."

In addition to soliciting his input on his character's appearance, Tony has been consulted by the *Buffy* production staff about how to decorate his haunts: the library, his office, and his apartment. He and production designer Carey Meyer share a love of Art Deco, which shows in Giles's furnishings. Tony suggested having a bedroom loft. A support beam in the apartment reminded him of one of the tenets of Feng Shui, and he decided that Giles would probably be a devotee of the Chinese spiritual philosophy.

So Tony was quite charmed to discover that someone had added some hanging crystal prisms used in Feng Shui to his apartment set. In addition, he decided that Giles had at one time been an archeologist, and so there are photographs and memorabilia about digs in his school office. He based this part of his characterization on a friend from his youth, "who is or was" a librarian and an archeologist, and was fascinated by the occult.

"It always used to worry me," Tony confides. "I have always hated those Ouija boards and things. I've always thought they were dangerous."

His suggestions for his transportation—Giles drives a barely functional Citröen DS—were not heeded, however, as he explains, with a grin:

"I was severely pitching for a motorcycle and sidecar. With Sarah on the back of a 1950s, 1960s BSA. An English bike. You used to be able to get a double sidecar. Willow and Xander would ride there. I think I got the image from *The Aristocats.*

"But Joss says there are times for humor and times for seriousness, and rolling up like that in a moment of great urgency wouldn't work."

Tony comes from a theatrical family. His mother is an actress, probably best known for her role of Madame Maigret in the BBC television series, *Maigret.* His father , a documentary-film producer, founded the British production company Verity Films. And his brother sang the role of Judas in the original recording of *Jesus Christ Superstar.*

He's working on a script of a musical he's written with a collaborator, as well as talking to a stateside producer interested in reworking a project into an animated feature. He misses singing, "because it is a great means of self-expression, a completely different buzz" from acting. The only singing he does at the moment is at charity functions and the like. As he removes his makeup, he chuckles at the memory of a recent benefit casino night, where he sang one of his favorite songs, by the Police: "Every breath you take, every move you move, I'll be watching you," without making the connection to the fact that Giles is a Watcher, prior to selecting the song. The audience loved it.

However, he's very pleased with the acting opportunity that *Buffy* presents him: "It is a wonderful thing being able to do the story arc of a character. It is extraordinary. I thought I was pretty lucky in *VR5* to have the story arc that I had then, but this is even better."

Do you have a favorite moment, either off camera or on, since you've been on the show?

TONY: "There was a moment in 'The Dark Age.' Certainly as an English actor, real emotion is consummate to be discovered and looked for—not having to create an emotion, just finding an emotion there. I have always had great technique, but it is something to really break down and cry. There was a scene with Buffy, and my line was that I didn't know how to stop the demon without killing Jenny. I just wept. Ever since then I have not had any problem with emotions at all.

"It was a huge breakthrough, a lovely moment. Although they used a slightly less emotional take, it was still there."

Do you know why they used a less intense take?

TONY: "Joss's feeling is that you shouldn't push the emotion. The tear welling up is enough. The tear rolling down the cheek is too much. You have done the work for the audience, and the audience can move on. As another example, in 'Passion,' after I have assaulted Angel, I come out sobbing. It was dry sobbing. It was basically a man who is just spent of his emotion, at the end of his rope. They turned the sound down a little and muted it.

"A number of people on the set who saw the scene actually had to walk away because they said it was really embarrassing watching it. A grown man sobbing. The found the moment almost too powerful. You don't want to take the audience out of the story. You want to keep them with you. You don't want to turn them off.

"Joss walks a very fine line, but I have to say, I take my hat off to his instinct. He is a very sharp cookie."

Do you have any scars, tattoos, or distinguishing marks?

TONY: "When I was seven I fell off a coal bunker and broke my nose. This was in the 1960s; in England, it's cold, so you had coal. At least, some households did. We were playing in the garden and I jumped up on this thing, which is about five feet tall. I put my foot through the lid, went straight off the end, and landed on concrete. And so I have an interesting-shaped nose.

"Another time, I was playing a villain, running away from somebody. The scene was being filmed in three sections, and in each [my pursuers] were supposed to get closer. Like an idiot, I said to the director, "Why don't I turn around to look and see where they are?" Which obviously slows me down.

"The director thought it was a good idea. I completely lost my balance and found my legs running away from me, and just piled into the concrete. I tucked and rolled, as I had learned to do in drama school. So I dislocated my shoulder. I could have an operation, but I don't have the time to have my arm in a sling for two to three months."

Do you really wear glasses?

TONY: "I have astigmatism. I wear them for driving and for the theater and the movies. But in fact, I believe very strongly that you can tell when glasses are fake on TV and in the movies, and so it was important to me for them to be integral. I have prescription lenses and I wear them most of the time unless they reflect the lights during a shot, and then I will wear a flat, nonreflective pair. I try to avoid that as much as I can. I've been wearing my prescription lenses a lot."

Has it affected your vision?

TONY: "A little. I went bowling last night and bowled a few frames very badly. I thought maybe I should put my glasses on. Suddenly I could see everything. Not that it actually improved my game very much, but I could see.

"Actually, I have to pretend that Giles wears bifocals. My prescription is for shortsighted-ness, while Giles wears glasses to read. I saw somebody take his glasses off to read in a movie the other day, and I think that would have been quite cool, a nice bit of business. Real stuff that brings your life outside of the scene into the scene is what I find interesting; the reality outside the theater. The choices you make against the scene that make the scene live.

"There was a scene I did with Alyson and just off the top of my head, I thought I should be eating an apple, perhaps one a student left me. I was munching away and she gave me something of Ms. Calendar's, and so I suddenly forgot the apple and just put it down. It means the scene is about people and life and it is not just about what is written on the page."

So are you a method actor?

TONY: "I don't know what 'method' really is, but I just know there are things that you can do to help yourself. I tried something today [for a torture scene]. I wanted to cause myself some discomfort while I was being tortured. I asked Jeri [for advice] because she used to be a nurse. She came up with the idea of chili peppers.

"I got the hottest peppers I could. My fear then was that I was going to be kissing these girls and set their lips alight. I must admit that I was buzzing.

"I was able to use the discomfort and went into a bit of a shudder, which wasn't difficult, and I felt a bit sweaty. It made me feel right.

"But there are times when the director says, 'I want you over there. Find something to do.' Something I was pleased with the other day, was that they stuck me behind my desk because it looked good in the shot and I thought, 'What the hell am I going to do down here?' Everyone else was [on the other side of the library] and Buffy was coming in to say something big. I think it was in 'Passion,' when she comes to say that Angel has been in her room.

"I decided to stamp the school address in the library books. Then, because Buffy has said something earth-shattering, I wandered into the scene with the stamp in my hand. It was just a little thing, but those are the kinds of things that bring life into scenes. I don't look for props for their own sake."

How did it feel to do the scene when Giles discovers Jenny Calendar's body?
TONY: "Joss is a genius. I thought it might be better if we didn't see Jenny killed when Angel chases her. That we might leave it over the commercial break . . . did he or didn't he? Then you would see someone entering my apartment and think it was Jenny, and then you would get the big revelation: 'Oh, my God, she *is* dead.'

"But Joss knew the audience's discomfort would be that much increased knowing. It was really clever writing."

Tony smiles for a moment when we discuss Marcia Shulman's delight in casting him for Giles on her first day. He says, "When I went to audition, it felt very good. I remember going to the Fox [screen] test and seeing Joss there, and I knew that I was going to know him....[It's like] when you see somebody and you just know that you are going to know them for a long time and they are going to be a friend. I just knew it."

KRISTINE SUTHERLAND

Kristine Sutherland is the immensely talented actress who plays Joyce Summers (Buffy's mom), a role that has provided her with both heartbreakingly familiar moments of maternal tribulation, and some exceedingly odd ones as well. She's been bitten by a vampire, stricken by a love spell that caused her to lust for a seventeen-year-old, and romanced by the robot doppelganger of a long-dead mad scientist.

Without question, Kristine sounds like she's having the time of her life.

The actress, who has appeared in such films as *Honey, I Shrunk the Kids* and *Legal Eagles,* was born and lived most of her adult life in New York before moving to Los Angeles. She is married to *Mad About You* scene-stealer John Pankow, and the couple have one daughter, seven-year-old Eleanore. Kristine, who admits to feeling protective of her younger cast mates, is using her experience as the fictional mother of a teenage girl as preparation for the time when her own daughter comes of age.

"I look forward to someday being the kind of mother to an adolescent that allows that [process of growing up] to sort of happen in a good way. I really enjoy playing Buffy's mother, because it is kind of like a dress rehearsal. I get to explore these feelings and situations that someday will be mine because I have a daughter and I will go through that," Kristine reveals.

"Everyone says it is going to be awful, and I am sure it will have its moments, but I just think adolescence is such an interesting time," she says. "It was such a struggle for me, that in many ways I think I identify—personally, heavily—with adolescents. Some adults remember, and some don't."

Kristine is quick to note that series creator Joss Whedon "definitely remembers."

Interestingly, she feels protective not only of her real-life costars, but of their fictional counterparts as well.

"As a mother, I can't help but be concerned about Buffy not having a father figure and not having a father around. My parents were divorced, so I have some sense of what it is like to grow up in a divorced household. The dynamic, at least from my experience, was very different, because for me, when my parents got divorced, it was such an admission of failure on their part somehow, that they lost a tremendous amount of authority in the household. They both had their own emotional problems, which I suppose contributed to that, but as an adolescent you take that and you wedge it wide open: 'What would you know? You screwed up in such a big way, and *you* are going to tell me what to do?'

"That makes it difficult for a single parent to wield authority over an adolescent. Actually, I have gotten a number of letters from parents in their early thirties who write to me about their empathy with Joyce as a single mother and the struggles involved."

Gradually, the conversation turns back to her young cast mates, and Kristine notes that playing Buffy's mom, as well as working so closely with Sarah Michelle Gellar, has made her feel "very protective" of the young star.

"I worry about her working too hard," Kristine says. "You know, it's like, 'You should get an assistant; you shouldn't be doing that by yourself; you are working much too hard.'"

As for her character, Kristine thinks Joyce Summers is coming along very nicely, thank you.

"I think everybody was sort of finding their way, and there were other things to establish the first season," she notes. "I have been really, really thrilled with the writing and some of the stuff we have had to do this year. It has been really nice. I think one of my favorite scenes was the one at the end of her birthday, that two-part story ["Surprise" and "Innocence."]. When [Joyce and Buffy are sitting] on the couch. I thought Joss did something so wonderful in that scene with Joyce being her mother and *knowing* that something is going on that is very hard for her. Just being there and not asking what it is. Knowing that. You just have to be there and hope for the best for them. You can't say, 'Oh; let me be your best friend and tell me everything that is going on.' That's not your place; you're a mother."

Though she's biased, of course, Kristine is a very enthusiastic fan of the show.

"I get very caught up in the story," she says happily. "I remember so much of what it was like to be an adolescent, and it just rings so true in so many ways." And as for the second-season finale, she reports having been "stunned" by it.

"I read it in my car," she says incredulously. "I couldn't wait to read it and I had picked it up, but then I had to go to this morning voice-over thing. Well, the first free moment I had, I am sitting in my car, baking without air-conditioning, parked somewhere in Hollywood. I just had to find out what happens and I just sat there and read it. I was in shock. I mean when she gets on the bus and leaves. I was just sobbing in the car."

It should come as no surprise, at this point, that Sutherland loves her job. The beauty of it is that, as with many of the cast and crew members interviewed for this book, her participation in the series seemed to fall into place almost as though it were fate.

"I was actually kind of hiding," she recalls. "I had left New York and I had come back to L.A. and my daughter was out of school. I hadn't really told anybody I had left New York, and I hadn't really told anybody in L.A. I had gotten back. I was in limbo somewhere and thought they'd never find me. I was just sort of taking it easy and being with my daughter. It was August and nobody was around, and suddenly the phone rang and it was my agent. I thought *Damn it, how did they find me?* He said, 'Oh, Kristine, I'm so glad to find you, I have been calling everywhere looking for you because I have got this audition and I just think you are really right for this part.' He sent me the [script pages] and I just sort of toddled off to the audition. I walked in the room and it just immediately felt good. I had really loved the material. It was a very short scene, but I really enjoyed working on it and enjoyed auditioning with it. It was one of those weird things where you leave the room and go, 'Wow, I might actually get that job!'"

That feeling of destiny is strong on the *Buffy* set.

"I feel so privileged to be a part of that," Kristine says. "I really believe in the show. I think it has a great message for kids. I don't know if all parents would necessarily think so, because it is wrapped in the garb of kidspeak and trendy clothes. It is amazing how many parents who are older don't get it. It is so great because Buffy struggles. It is not all easy. She really has to struggle with things—her loyalty to her friends, issues of popularity. There are really wonderful messages in those stories."

By way of example, Sutherland points out "When She Was Bad," the second-season opener.

"How many times, when you are a kid, and even as an adult, do you have a day when you are just not proud of your behavior at the end of the day? Where you just don't feel like you acted as responsibly to your friends or your peers as you should have? At the end of the day, you review it and you think, *I really screwed up today. That wasn't cool what I did.* That had a lot of resonance for me as an adult, because all those issues that we grapple with as teenagers still resonate for the rest of your life. You never really completely grow up."

Were you a fan of horror or fantasy growing up?

KRISTINE: "I loved fantasy and science fiction, but I could never stomach horror. In fact, when I rented the movie *Buffy the Vampire Slayer*, I had to have my husband sit and watch it with me. I know it is funny and everything, but I am so terrified of horror films. I am waiting for Sarah to do a film that isn't a horror film so I can go see it. I don't know if I could even watch the show if I wasn't in it. I'm terrible. I get scared watching the show even when I'm in the episode and have seen most of it being shot."

What were you afraid of as a child?

KRISTINE: "Demons, strangely enough. I used to lie on my bed, and I used to think the whole room was just filled with evil spirits. I would break into an absolute sweat and be so terrified I couldn't talk, I couldn't move. I was convinced that there were demons under the bed. Demons and skeletons under the bed and—I think because I would be home with my mother and I didn't have a man in the house—I was always terrified that somebody was going to climb in the window. Intruders were going to come in and kill my whole family. To this day, I hate living on the ground floor. I am a New Yorker. I like to live on the eleventh floor, behind the doorman and ten locks."

Do you have a favorite moment, on or off the screen, from your work on the series?

KRISTINE: "It has been really fun for me this year, because last season almost all my work was just with Sarah, and I felt I didn't know the rest of the cast that well. So this year has been really fun, getting to know everybody else and feeling much more a part of the group. But my favorite day this year was Halloween. I was working Halloween day—which was a slight bummer because I didn't get to go trick-or-treating with my daughter—but what better place to be on Halloween than on the set of *Buffy the Vampire Slayer* with vampires running around? A lot of us came in costume, which was really fun. We were shooting the episode "Ted" that week. I came in a whole '50's garb as Ted's first wife. Sarah was Dorothy from *The Wizard of Oz,* and [her dog] Thor was Toto."

Did you have any professional history with any of the cast or crew prior to this series?

KRISTINE: "No, but I auditioned the day that David auditioned as well. I remember walking into the room. There were couches over in the corner. There were about five guys there—I figured out later that they were auditioning for Angel—and David was one of them. I saw these five guys, and he just leapt out at me. What a striking-looking guy. So it was so interesting when he showed up for Angel. I just happened to be there when they were auditioning, and I knew he had it."

Do you have any talents or skills you haven't been able to use on the show as yet that you would like to showcase? Just as a for-instance, by the way, Armin plays trumpet.

KRISTINE: "Well maybe we could do a duet. I play the piano. Actually, that was a big thing between me and my mother when I was a kid. I just hated taking piano lessons so much, and I thought it was just a curse that she put on me, just to torture me, of course. I had taken lessons since I was maybe seven, and I finally managed to quit when I was about fourteen. I picked it up again and started taking piano lessons again about a year and a half ago. Actually, just about the time that we started doing the first season of Buffy...and I love it. I love playing the piano. [Those lessons] actually turned out to be a marvelous gift."

Do you have any scars, tattoos, or other distinguishing marks?

KRISTINE: "Well, I do, but they are not that interesting. I'm riddled with scars. Fortunately, they are all small. But there are only two that are really interesting at all. I have a scar on my face, which you can't really see. You have to look very closely for it. My brother attempted to tear my eye out during one of our sibling battles. I have another scar high up on my forehead, which my hair covers, from me trying to do my brother in at a very early age. Sticking him in a wagon and going down a really, really steep hill...running off the road, over the bridge and into the creek."

The same brother?

KRISTINE: "Yeah."

Was this payback for trying to rip your eye out?

KRISTINE: "No, I think trying to rip my eye out was the payback."

Angel is a big-time sex symbol, but a lot of women we've spoken to seem to like Oz as well.

KRISTINE: "You know what it was? It was the scene in the van where she asks him to kiss her and he says, 'I don't want to kiss you until you want to kiss me.' That is the kind of man that every woman is looking for."

Your series and your husband's (*Mad About You*) air opposite each other. Any competition there?

KRISTINE: "We only have one TV. Sarah offered to take up a collection for a second one, but it's okay, we already ordered one."

What about you and John working together sometime?

KRISTINE: "We try to keep our lives and our careers separate, that works best for us. When we first came out here and he was doing *Mad About You*, they all said, 'Great we will get a part on it for Kristine.' I just didn't want to do that. It works great for some people, some people work together all the time, but we have always had different agents, different jobs, everything."

Does Joyce think that Giles is sexy?

KRISTINE: "Yeah, I think she does."

ARMIN SHIMERMAN

Once upon a time, Armin Shimerman planned to be a lawyer. To the relief of millions of fans, he scrapped that idea in favor of what some would call a similarly provocative profession. These days, he's one of the most in-demand character actors in Hollywood. But when he started, Armin had no real interest in television.

"I studied for and apprenticed in classical theater," he notes. "If you had asked me twenty years ago if I would be on TV, I would have answered with a big fat '*no!*' No, I was set on being a stage actor. Which I became. For many years, I appeared in regional theater and Broadway in classical plays. But I was seduced by the dark side of the force and moved to Hollywood. Even today, I always think of myself primarily as a classical actor on hiatus. In fact, should the TV work end for me, I will most assuredly go back to my first love. That is what I am trained to do. That is what makes me most happy. However, it may be that my classical training, that sort of larger-than-life approach to material, is what gets me parts in the fantasy programs I frequent.

"A classical approach to a fantasy show is required. You need an actor who is not going to just mumble and worry about an itch on the left side of his arm. You need somebody who is going to deal with larger issues—life and death issues—in both a serious way and sometimes in a comedic way."

Armin knows whereof he speaks. The actor has been a regular on several successful television series, including a number of popular fantasy and science fiction series. He spent two and a half years playing Pascal in *Beauty and the Beast* before moving onto a period series called *Brooklyn Bridge* (obviously not a fantasy series), in which he starred with *Happy Days* alum Marion Ross. He has played at least half a dozen different roles on the *Star Trek* franchise, most notably fan-favorite Quark, and has also appeared on *Alien Nation* and *Stargate SG-1.* Armin also regularly appears as a judge in both of David E. Kelley's lawyer series, *Ally McBeal* and *The Practice.*

The man gets around.

His path to *Buffy,* however, was not as direct as some might think. Originally, Armin had auditioned for the role of Principal Flutie, the first-season administrator who died in "The Pack."

"Ken Lerner got the part, but I suppose that months later, when they decided to kill off Principal Flutie, they remembered me from that audition. I am assuming that is how that happened. It could very well be that they knew me from *Star Trek* and requested me from my work there, but I am assuming it was from that audition I had for Principal Flutie."

Though he grew up on the other coast, Armin's hometown of Lakewood, New Jersey, is probably not very different from the fictional Sunnydale. "I had a very nice childhood, in a wonderful small town," he recalls. "It was an incredibly good childhood, except for the fact that I came from a very poor family. But when I look back and I hear about other people's growing-up process, mine was [idyllic] in comparison."

On the subject of the obvious conspiracy being conducted by Snyder, the mayor, and the police chief, Armin is in the dark, just like the rest of us.

"I have asked Joss once or twice," Armin admits. "He won't share. I don't know if Joss has decided where he is going or not, but it does *look* like it is definitely going somewhere and, of course, I appreciate that. It is great fun for me to play a role so different from Quark."

Other than the obvious differences in character, of course, Armin is also talking about the fact that, much to his relief, his *Buffy* character is (apparently) human. No full head mask or makeup! That's one aspect of the series that thrills him. In fact, when asked if he laughs silently as actors walk by in full makeup, he says, with obvious glee, "I laugh out loud! I just smile at them, and they probably don't understand why this guy is grinning at them. I look at all the vampires and say, 'Drink a lot of water,' because it is so much pleasure not to have to be in it. I am very pleased. I think one job with makeup is sufficient.

"I am sure for the rest of the cast and the crew, this is their job, they do it every day. It's hard work, but for me it is a vacation. I get to be with very nice people doing very creative things and playing a character that is normal. So going to work [on *Buffy*] is really a vacation for me. It is delightful, and it is different, and it is creative."

Juggling his schedule isn't easy, but Armin chalks it up to the cooperative efforts of *Buffy* producer Gareth Davies and *Deep Space Nine*'s unit production manager, Steve Oster.

"There was one day recently where Steve was able to get me out of *Star Trek* at about 11:00 and gave me two hours so I could drive to Malibu to be there at 1:00 for *Buffy*. It was a good day. It is a good day when an actor gets to do two jobs in one day," Armin says happily.

At least until the end of season three, when the cast will presumably graduate from high school, the series is immersed in high school culture. A large part of that, since his first appearance in "The Puppet Show," has been the foreboding presence of Shimerman as Principal Snyder. Surprisingly, Armin admits that there are certain traits he shares with the youth-hating Snyder.

"Principal Snyder bristles much more so than I, of course, but I am not particularly easy around children. I have a lack of communicative skills with people that age and younger. So that is what I draw upon. Some of the principals that I remember growing up were major authoritarian figures who had a disdainful aura about them.... And I draw upon that as well."

In fact, Armin believes that, to a point, Snyder is more threatening to the teen characters on the series than the vampires.

"He really holds power over their future," he explains. "If they get expelled from the school, then they'll really be screwed over. They can attack a vampire, but they can't attack a school record. To our younger viewers, that's a real threat."

What were you afraid of as a child?

ARMIN: "I was afraid of snakes, which I just had to recently deal with in *Buffy*—not as close as Charisma did, but close enough. I was afraid of chickens, because I grew up on a chicken farm and they constantly pecked at me, and that was pretty unnerving. And certainly, as far as the show is concerned, I was certainly afraid of not being liked. That is probably what endears the show to me the most. Here are teenagers who are desperately dealing with the angst of growing up amidst a group of people that they are not a part of."

Do you have any scars, tattoos, or other distinguishing marks?

ARMIN: "*Ah-h-h,* that is an interesting question. I never have been asked that. I have no tattoos. I adore scars, by the way. I love scars on people. I find them fascinating. I, indeed, do have a scar. Little noticed but there it is. It is over my right eye. It was acquired when I was six years old. I was hanging onto my dog, Brownie, and I was sitting on a trash can. My father was a painter, and there were several open paint cans below. The dog pulled me and I landed on the edge of one of these paint cans, which required about seven stitches. I have always been fascinated by scars. I find them very erotic."

Do you have any talents or skills you haven't been able to use on either *Star Trek* or *Buffy* that you want to showcase?

ARMIN: "Yeah, I want to play trumpet. I do play trumpet a little, not very much anymore and not very well, but it would be kind of a hoot to play trumpet somewhere. Any other skills? I juggle, but I can't picture Principal Snyder juggling."

Do you have a favorite moment, on or off screen, from your tenure on *Buffy*?

ARMIN: "It happened the very first day. I knew that I wanted my new character to be something totally different from Quark and I wanted it to be serious and comic at the same time. I was blessed from the very start. It is the scene where Tony and I are walking down an aisle of the school auditorium. As it went on, I remember thinking, *This is exactly the character; this is exactly right; right off the bat this is working exactly right.* I was elated. When I did *Deep Space Nine,* it took six full episodes before I realized, *Ah, this is who Quark is!* But when I walked down that aisle with Tony in that first scene and talked with the four of them on my first day, I thought, *This is it.* It was a great feeling of achievement. Sometimes I try to re-create that specialness. Sadly, my acting moments aren't always as good as that first encounter. But that first meeting was just something magical for me; when I worked with those people for the first time and slipped flawlessly into character the first time. It was perfect."

ROBIA LaMORTE

The actress who plays Jenny Calendar has done a great many different things in her career, from dancing to touring with Prince, from music videos to major TV ad campaigns, from *Beverly Hills, 90210* to Sunnydale. Without question, it's only the beginning.

Robia was born in Queens, New York, but moved around a great deal growing up.

"I had kind of a gypsy childhood," she recalls. "I traveled all around the country. My mom is not a freaky gypsy, but she's kind of a nomadic type. I grew up everywhere. I lived in Aspen, Colorado. I lived in Maryland. I lived in a bunch of the [Florida] Keys, and then I lived in Connecticut right before I moved out here with my dad when I was fourteen."

Robia pursued her first love, dancing, vigorously upon her arrival in California. She had studied "back east," and then spent six months at the Los Angeles County High School for the Arts. She took the GED and left high school early to follow up on a scholarship offered to her by the Dupre Dance Academy. But by the age of sixteen, Robia was already making her first music video, Debbie Gibson's "Shake Your Love."

She has also appeared in videos by artists as diverse as Yanni and Donny Osmond ("nothing tacky or gross," Robia says), been in fashion shows around the world, and toured with various bands, including the Pet Shop Boys and, most notably, Prince.

Indeed, for many months, Robia traveled the world as "Pearl" in Prince's *Diamonds and Pearls* world tour. She appeared as Pearl in all the music videos tied to that album, and is also on the disc's holographic cover.

"That was the pinnacle of my dance career," Robia says. "I started out auditioning for one video. He was looking for a set of twins and they couldn't find any twins they liked. The dance circle is pretty small, and I knew a girl, Laurie. We thought the twins part would be not really featured, so we didn't even want to be the twins. They told us to dress alike, and we said, 'No, no, no.' We wound up getting hired for the twins, and we started rehearsing with him. We had great chemistry, and he loved us, and he got the idea, because the album was *Diamonds and Pearls,* that one would be Diamond and one Pearl. It turned into five, six, seven videos.

"We went on tour with him all around Europe, and that's when he wasn't speaking at all, so we did all the press for the album," Robia recalls. "I did *The Joan Rivers Show,* Howard Stern, *Hard Copy, Current Affair, Inside Edition.* We went all over the place signing albums. It was a pretty awesome thing. For a year and a half, that was basically my life. Flying back and forth to Minneapolis and shooting videos, flying around to the other side of the world and hosting parties and doing fabulous things.

"That was really the perfect time for me to make the transition. After I had done that, there was really nowhere else to go with dancing, and I was training as an actress. I thought, *Okay, this is the time."*

Robia quit dancing and quickly landed a several-episode guest shot on *Beverly Hills, 90210.*

"People still recognize me off the street, and this must have been four or five years ago," she says of her stint on the popular series.

Robia played Jill Fleming, a New York girl who was spending the summer in L.A. and was romantically involved with Ian Ziering's character, Steve Sanders.

"I think they were going to develop my story line, but then that's right where Brandon started to get involved with a teacher. That was that."

Robia has worked in a number of television commercials for companies such as Oil of Olay, GE, The Gap, and Budweiser. Most memorable, perhaps, is her Mitsubishi commercial. She is sitting in her car, using an audiotape to learn Italian, when a darkly handsome man pulls up beside her in an identical vehicle. Hearing her speak Italian, he believes she is Italian and speaks to her in that language.

Not long thereafter, Robia found herself working on *Buffy.* Already familiar with the fame game from her work with Prince and the *90210* gang, she realizes that *Buffy* has raised the bar a little higher. For one, she's likely to be attending conventions until she's ninety. For another, well, the fans are everywhere....

"A few months back, I was at 7-Eleven," she recalls. "It was ten at night. I pop out of my car. This homeless guy is sitting at 7-Eleven panhandling for money. He looks at me and says, 'Hey, you're a friend of Buffy's, aren't you?' I look at him, and I smile, and I say, 'Yeah.' And I'm starting to walk in the 7-Eleven and he says, 'Can we spare a little change, Ms. Calendar?' I've seen him a few times now, and I'm like, 'Hey, how are you?' And he says, 'I'm starstruck; I can't talk to you.' He never misses the show."

Though it seems like karma now, Robia came to the series through the usual audition process. But she knew right off that this was something different.

"Sometimes you get scripts, and you just know," she says. "The words just fit in your mouth a different way when you know you're supposed to speak them. And I kind of knew I was going to get it. I came in and auditioned, and they liked me, and I came back and met with everybody, and Tony [Head] came in to read with me. I think it was me and one other girl, so they wanted to see the chemistry. But I didn't know who he was. I thought he was a producer, so he was talking with me, and I was joking with him, and we walked into the room, and I was chewing gum, and I gave it to him, and said, 'Here, hold this.' I didn't even know. I was just playing around with him. They hired me, I think, the next day."

Do you have any scars, tattoos, or other distinguishing marks?
ROBIA: "No, I'm clean. [Pauses, then points to an attractive birthmark on her neck.] This is my only distinguishing mark. [Producers] either love it, or they hate it. Half the time when I do jobs, they cover it, and half the time they think it's great." [The *Buffy* producers didn't have it covered, by the way.]

What were you afraid of as a child?
ROBIA: [long pause] "A few things. Bugs. I grew up in Florida, and there were always bugs, and I don't like bugs. And, um, not really the dark, but what could happen in the dark. What might be there. Also, I've always been scared of sharks. I love to swim, though. I've never not gone in the water, but I have this crazy fear of sharks, even to the point where I dream I see a wave coming up, and I'll see the outline of the shark in the wave, and it's coming toward me. I have that dream all the time. So, one thing I would do when I was little, and this is crazy, I would just play with my mind. I would go into the swimming pool, and I would close my eyes, and I would swim around under there, and just see it all dark and oceany, and I could get myself so scared that there were sharks in there that I'd have to jump out of the pool. You know? I would freak myself out."

Do you have a favorite moment, on or off screen, from your time on the show?
ROBIA: "The moment I loved, loved, loved, is in the very first episode I did. As soon as I saw it on tape, I said, 'Praise God that I get to say this kind of line, because you don't get the chance to do it very often.' It's when Giles is returning her earring. I loved it on the page; I loved the way it came off. 'No, that's not where I dangle it.' Yeah, that's a classic."

Do you have any professional history with anyone else on the series?
ROBIA: "No, but you want to hear something crazy? You want to go all the way back. Last year, I was in my grandmother's house, and I was going through some jewelry. You know how grandparents always have all this crazy stuff in their drawers. There was a *TV Guide* in there. I opened up the *TV Guide*, and I'm thinking, it's from my *90210*. I open it up, and it is. There's my *90210*, with my name circled. I go to the front of the *TV Guide*, and there's a big picture of Sarah Michelle Gellar from an article on her about *All My Children*, and I thought, *Whoa, who would have thought five years later?*

Unlike many of the other characters, you didn't get much chance to kick butt. Are you disappointed?
ROBIA: "I have not gotten to kick as much butt as I would have liked, but I did get to do a little bit of stuff in my demon episode. I jump out the window, and I throw Giles. I got to slam his head into the table and throw him and do some stuff like that. That was a fun episode."

Is LaMorte your real name?
ROBIA: "Yes. 'The Death.'"

SETH GREEN

Like his cast mates Sarah Michelle Gellar and Alyson Hannigan—both of whom he had worked with prior to his stint on *Buffy*—Seth Green has pretty much grown up on camera.

Born in Philadephia, he began in New York City, making television commercials as a toddler. One of those commercials also featured a four-year-old girl named Sarah Michelle Gellar, a fact the actors didn't realize until Marcia Shulman—*Buffy*'s casting director and the woman who cast that commercial so long ago—reminded both of them.

Seth has gone on to appear in such television series and miniseries as *The X-Files*, *The Wonder Years*, *Beverly Hills 90210*, *Evening Shade*, and *Seaquest*. He had starring roles in *Stephen King's It* and *Byrds of Paradise*. Seth has also appeared in a number of feature films, including *Hotel New Hampshire*, *Radio Days*, *Pump Up the Volume*, *Austin Powers*, and *My Stepmother Is an Alien*, in which he played the boyfriend of a young girl played by...you guessed it: Alyson Hannigan. Even as this is being written, he has several films on the way, including *Can't Hardly Wait*, starring Jennifer Love Hewitt, *Stonebrook*, a con caper, and *Idle Hands*, a thriller.

In this interview, he's all over the place. He's driven, but he also seems like he's having a very good time. And who can blame him? On top of the movies he has coming up, he's just been offered a gig as a regular on *Buffy*, one of the hottest shows on television.

"In a way, I was kind of welcomed from the very start. I had someone that I have known a long time, who was already ingratiated into the fold. Alyson and I have stayed friends for the last ten years or so. I wasn't an outsider from the start. I was just kind of included. When things went on, I was invited. When everybody left the set to go to the service table, they asked me."

Interestingly, Seth is content to remain a background player on the series, though he'll be a regular cast member in season three.

"If you're there all the time and you're in the forefront, then it is so over, so fast. I would rather be a supporting player for the rest of my life. I would be very content with that," he says.

In fact, though most young actors (and older actors, come to think of it) seem to have a longing for the director's chair, Seth has no interest in directing. Instead, he'd like to produce and act in feature films and is working toward those ends with some close friends.

"Directors have to have a vision, and they have to have stamina, and I have neither," Seth says amiably. "I just want to take things from their very earliest points and I want to put the people into them and make them something special."

The conversation turns to Hollywood and politics, and Seth decides fairly abruptly that it's a tangent he doesn't want to go off on. Instead, we talk about fun stuff. Like Oz's van.

"It was carpeted, there were bean-bag chairs, there was a bench. It had black-light posters, there were shrunken heads, there was a disco ball, a dart board, a fridge. There was just all this stuff. They went all out. They so defined the van. It was really funny. They did a great job finding cool stuff."

Oddly enough, there is apparently an Internet group devoted solely to Oz's van. Seth has spent some time on the official *Buffy* posting board, and enjoys it, but he doesn't let the attention go to his head.

"It's just nice because the people who like the show, the fans of the show, are very, very supportive, and it is such little effort to show them that you appreciate it," he says of his chatting on the board. "So long as it doesn't take focus away from the work. Because if you get too wrapped up in your own ego, you stop working as hard. So as long as I avoid that, then, yeah, it is nice to know that people are into it.

"Somebody gave me a piece of advice a couple of years ago that I wasn't quite in the place to receive then. But it has resonated in my head ever since. That advice was to treat every audition like it's the Super Bowl and treat every day of your job like it is your first audition. Never lose the same commitment and intensity. If you just always try to do your best work every day, and never become complacent and never become satisfied, then you will always be successful."

Seth is looking forward to his promotion to "series regular" status.

"I'm very excited about it, and it's nice to know that I have a steady job. I look forward to developing the character. Also I think it makes everybody a little bit more comfortable knowing that we don't have to worry about making a deal show by show. We know that they can do longer character arcs and plan ahead. I also told them that I would just as soon sit in a scene without saying anything than say something that is uncharacteristic or some fluffy dialogue."

Not that he's expecting any fluffy dialogue. Not with the writers on this show.

"Between Joss and Marti and Rob and Dean and everybody else that has contributed, they have really helped me to find this character, and I want to make sure that we all keep sight of that. There is a tendency to forget where each character came from or all the things you are setting up. You have a scene and you want a character in that scene. You just want to give them something to say so that you don't forget that they are there. But at the same time, I feel that Oz is defined by a few specific moments.

"One of them is that scene [in *Innocence*] where we are stealing the weapons from the armory and I am sitting in the van with Alyson. I haven't said anything, this whole episode I haven't said a word. And then she says, 'Do you want to make out?' And I remember this so specifically: I say, 'Well, to the casual observer, it would appear that you are trying to make your friend Xander jealous, or even the score, or something like that, and to me that is on the empty side.' Right away, you get the impression that Oz knows what is going on. He pays attention, not only to what people are doing to him but to what people are doing to each other.

"He just takes things as they come and recognizes them for what they are. So, while I would love to explore the more emotional side of him, I think it is going to necessitate a huge and very powerful catalyst to even break through that. It's the werewolf thing. The way that his family has reacted to the whole thing, too, because no one else seemed too upset about their kid being a werewolf. He has been conditioned in one way or another, and while there is a little bit of an emotional reaction, it is pretty internal. It is so much more cerebral than that. He's like, 'Well, all right, how am I going to deal with that?'"

Of course, Oz wasn't always intended to be a werewolf. In fact, when Seth first came onto the show, it was with a three-episode commitment.

"Then they saw that Aly and I got along really well, and I saw the wheels spinning in Joss's head and he was like, 'I can work with this.' He came to me really early on and said...well actually Alison said it to me first....She said, 'If they asked you to be a regular, would you do it?' I was like, 'Hell, yeah...absolutely. Absolutely.' Then I talked to Joss and I said I just wanted to know what he was thinking, because that was integral in my decision whether this was the show that I was going to commit to.

"He said, 'Well, there is talk of making him into a werewolf, but we don't know exactly how we would handle that.' I said, 'Okay, let's keep our minds open and see where it goes.' He told me a couple of weeks later to read episode fifteen. 'That is what I am going for. If you like that, we will go into negotiations.' Fifteen was "Phases," the werewolf episode, and I loved it. It was perfect."

Soon, we discover a little-known piece of trivia. Seth is connected to the series through Alyson and Sarah and Marcia Schulman. But he's also connected to it in a more direct way. He's the only member of the series cast who was in the movie.

Yes, really.

"I was cut out of the film, but I'm on the back of the video box," he says. (Go on, check it.) "I was awful in it, and I really hope the footage never surfaces, because in retrospect I realize how bad I was in it. At the time, I was very excited. You see me really early on as sort of a geeky guy that Sasha kind of makes fun of in passing, like knocks books out of my hands or something like that....And then he is walking through the woods toward the merry-go-round.

"The way it goes in the movie now, Sasha says, 'I'm going to turn around, and when I do, you are not going to be there.' When he does, it is Paul Reubens on the merry-go-round. There are five minutes cut out of that, where he turns around and I'm standing there and I have the face of a vampire, and I call him by name, and he says, 'What are you doing here?' and he comes over and I just start laughing, and he picks me up. He lifts me up threateningly, gripping my collar, and he lets me go and I stay floating in the air. I start laughing like crazy, and I grab him and I bite him.

"It was terrible. For some reason, I told them I had a thirty-two-inch waist, so the harness they gave me was five sizes too big. I just look like I'm wearing a diaper....It was impressive," Seth concludes with a dry chuckle.

Were you interested in horror and fantasy growing up?

SETH: "Absolutely. There was a time when I was very into vampire mythology and things like that. Then it got a little spoiled for me. It is difficult for it not to be spoiled when there are all these people running around with dyed black hair and Marilyn Manson T-shirts talking about how they suck blood. Quite frankly, when you have something that you take relatively seriously, just made so laughable by a few ignorant people, it is difficult to still hold it with the same amount of respect. That is why I am glad there is a show like *Buffy*, where even though the show is a little tongue-in-cheek sometimes, they take their monsters seriously and it is scary. It is not a joke. Like *Buffy* the movie was just on TV a couple of times, and I always get that kind of sadness when I see it."

Oz is the lead guitarist for Dingoes Ate My Baby. Do you play guitar?

SETH: "I can fake it, can't I?"

That's not what I asked.

SETH: "No, I sure can't. I can strum. I know where notes are on the guitar, but I really don't have any dexterity when it comes to it. But our music coordinators on the show [help], and my friends who do play guitar. I get the tapes well in advance and I sit and practice and practice and practice, and it is all for naught because you really never see me playing guitar on the show."

Do you have any scars, tattoos, or other distinguishing marks?

SETH: "I have two scars on my head in the same place. I was five years old and my sister and

I were running around our living room. I just dove headfirst into the corner of our coffee table and split my head right open. And then, this is the best part, about two years later I was playing super-jock football with my dad and I go to run out of my room, and I hit my head on the protruding corner of the wall, right in the same place. Split my head right open again."

There you have it. The question is sort of another version of something Cordelia says in one episode: 'What is your childhood trauma?'

SETH: "My childhood trauma was when I realized I was going to Hell very early on in my life because I saw an old lady fall when she was trying to get off the bus and I laughed. It was bad, man. It was a very slight fall, and we helped her up, mind you. We raced to help her up, but at that moment I realized I had laughed at an old woman falling off a bus. I was going straight to Hell. As a result of that, I have lived my life with the theory that I'm already going, so I might as well live it up."

What were you afraid of as a child?

SETH: "I don't know...stupid stuff. When I was four years old, there was this episode of *Starsky and Hutch* on TV and they opened up a closet and there was a decaying body inside, and that scared me. But I never had an ongoing fear....Then, over the course of my life, I have seen so many horror films I am conditioned to not jump at the big scare, and as a result, I don't jump. Creepy is so much better than the big scare."

What other actors do you admire?

SETH: "Breckin Meyer, who I think is one of the best young actors around. Definitely one of the most underused talents around. He is up and coming, just a huge sex symbol. And if there were a man that I was going to be in love with, it would be Breckin Meyer."

Is he standing right there next to you?

SETH: "Kinda."

So you have to say that?

SETH: "Well, Breckin and our friend Ryan and I intend to produce stuff, and we're trying to work toward that. If I could sound any more arrogant and pretentious."

Do you have a favorite moment from your tenure on the series?

SETH: "There was a day when we were making "Innocence." They had built that whole mall in this warehouse in downtown Los Angeles, and we had a kind of mini-revolt, and Aly and Charisma and Nick and Tony and I all went to the mall across the street and we ate lunch there. It was so bad, we were told there was a Chinese place and they wouldn't serve us. They were like, 'We're only doing lunch orders now.' We said, 'Yeah, we want lunch.' 'No, no bulk orders for delivery,' and they wouldn't give us food. So we wound up eating at McDonald's or something, and then we started scouring the mall for board games, and we wound up buying TVopoly, which is like TV monopoly. It was just like a long time between setups. Juliet and David and Sarah were all on set; they were working. We didn't have anything to do, so we just sat in Charisma's trailer playing board games. It was so much fun."

JAMES MARSTERS

It's just after dusk. James Marsters comes over to say that he has a short break while the lighting setup is changed. We go and sit on the steps in front of the trailer he shares with Juliet Landau, and he lights a cigarette. In full Spike costume, the smoking is eerily appropriate. But other than that, James is about as unlike Spike as you could imagine. He's a genuinely nice, enthusiastic man with undying affection for the theater, for his craft, and for *Star Trek*. He jokes freely, comfortably chuckles at his own humor, and—it seems—at the very idea that he's being interviewed.

James is originally from Modesto, California. He has appeared in several films and as a guest star on several TV series, including *Northern Exposure*. James studied at Juilliard and came to Los Angeles in 1997 after spending more than ten years on the regional-theater circuit. The decision was based on a conversation about pragmatism that he had with an idol.

"I was talking to Michael Winters, who I think is the best actor in America. Primarily stage. He's been my idol since I was ten years old," James says. "I was lucky enough to do table readings of *The Cider House Rules* in Seattle with him, which Tom Hulce was directing.

"I was driving Michael home and he was saying that his car was on the fritz and he didn't have enough money to fix it and he was damn tired of being poor. Michael is fifty years old. He told me that everyone told him if he pursued stage acting he'd end up poor, and he never believed them. For the first time in my life, there was something about Michael that I didn't want for myself.

"He went down to L.A. and got a recurring role in *The Single Guy*. He's got a TV movie coming out, and he's doing quite well. He's a marvelous actor. So I decided to come down here and try to make enough money to stow away so that I wasn't poor. I came down here willing to be the new ALF if I needed to, to do about anything. I didn't want to be one of those stage actors who came down here and who whined about not doing Shakespeare.

"The irony of it is, I think I'm working on a show with better scriptwriting than many of the original plays that I worked on in theater. I'm very lucky. It doesn't hurt to be known first as 'cool sexy killer guy.' You can't overstate enough how lucky it is to be cast in a project with good writing and good producing and good actors. Quite frankly, the other good thing about this is that I've been learning film acting. There's a lot about stage acting that you take years to learn which is of absolutely no use at all [on film]."

Interestingly, when James auditioned for the role of Spike he had dark wavy hair, not unlike David Boreanaz, who plays Angel. In order to cast him, the producers had to look at his performance alone and imagine what he might be like as Spike. Obviously, his audition went well.

"Juliet and I hit it off really well, and I thought I auditioned really well," he remembers. "But I have to say that the people around here realize that the look of a character is really malleable. They really want to cast off of who fits the part internally. They trust that they'll be able to make the visuals of the character work the way they want them to work. I think the casting office is more in tune with acting than with 'type.'"

Particularly since Spike is British, and James couldn't be more American. The accent didn't intimidate him, though.

"I've done lots of plays with different accents," he explains. "When I got the call for the audition I was doing a production of *The Tempest* with Shakespeare Festival L.A. There was a gentleman from North London playing Caliban, so I asked him if he could go over some lines with me. Tony Head's been very helpful as well. He doesn't want his friends in England being embarrassed."

One thing James did have to adjust to early on (though it wasn't as much of an issue in the latter half of his run on the series) was the vampire prosthetic.

"I have to say that the advances they've made in both the foams they've used to create the appliances and the adhesives they use to glue it onto you are so much improved in the last ten years that it's actually comfortable," he says. "The foam is so pliable that it moves with your face. You can almost forget that it's there."

That doesn't mean, however, that an actor can use his or her free range of facial expression with the prosthetic on.

"I learned very quickly to let the mask have its own expression and not try to add too much to it. It's damn scary, and [you should] act with your eyes. At first I was practicing what expressions would be good through the mask. And that's called bad acting [smile]. Pre-planning what you're going to do is just not good. The mask makes me scary and Joss's words make me funny, and that's all there really has to be."

Do you spend time with any of the other cast members off the set?

JAMES: "Yes, very much. We get along really well. In fact, David and Nick and Todd McIntosh and Seth Green and I all went over to Todd's for dinner. He's a great cook. We had a marvelous time. Todd wanted us to get on-line, and we were all like, 'What are we going to say?' By the time we actually got in there, they couldn't put us out.

"Last Halloween, Alyson and I got made up as vampires and went out. She's hot as a vampire.

"I have to say, the people who do the hiring around here really understand how important it is that people work well together. A lot of people would sacrifice that for other things, but I think it makes it a nice place to work."

Do you have a favorite moment, on or off screen, from your tenure on the series?

JAMES: "By far, my favorite moment was in the first episode I did when I put my vampire henchman's head through the glass of the fire extinguisher. I love playing Spike because I get into fights and no one has to go to the police station, and no one has to go to the hospital."

And unless it's against Buffy, you get to win!

JAMES: "Yes. Which is very nice. But I have to say the stunt guy was just incredible with that. He put his head through inch-thick candy glass three times, and I was the one who looked like the tough guy. He really sold it. My favorite parts are always the violent parts."

Any idea what's to come for Spike and Drusilla?

JAMES: "He realized that Dru is drawn to Angel like an alcoholic is drawn to booze. And for their relationship and her health, he needed to get her the hell out of Sunnydale. There's a lot of jealousy, but there's also a lot of understanding. He's her sire. It makes it easier for Spike to forgive her for going with him, since it's a sickness more than an attraction."

Were you interested in horror growing up?

JAMES: "Very much. I grew up on *Creature Feature*. I think fantasy and horror have the ability to use metaphor to a much better extent than shows that are more tied to realism. You often find issues that are taboo in any other realm except for horror and science fiction. It's kind of like the jester in the old medieval courts. He could say whatever he wanted, as long as it was a joke. I think it's quite important, actually. Most television, movies, and stage are in the death grips of naturalism. I'm quite happy not to be doing it. Robert Heinlein said 'In good science fiction, you ask your audience to suspend their disbelief once. The rest should follow from there.'"

Do you have any scars, tattoos, or other distinguishing marks?

JAMES: "I have a scar on my left leg that I got in fifth grade playing a game called Hot Box or Pickle. I was sliding downhill and caught my leg just below my knee on a sprinkler head. It ripped my flesh to the bone two-thirds of the way around my leg. My leg slid down my bone like a sock. The only thing holding it was about an inch and a half of flesh on the back. They had to take a skin graft from my left thigh, and put it there because my skin wasn't growing back. I was off my feet for almost a year. So all the hair on my lower left knee grows sideways, because they took the skin and rotated."

Do you have any talents or skills you haven't used on the series?

JAMES: "Yeah, I play guitar and sing. I paint. I write."

What do you do with your spare time?

JAMES: "I have a little house near the beach. I like to spend time down there. I have a girlfriend I've been with for about eight months. Actually, I don't enjoy time off."

What were you afraid of as a child?

JAMES: "Not getting everything done. I did a lot of stupid things in my youth, because I didn't have enough fear. But I'm better now. I'm recovered. With my leg, I found out that it's possible for the worst thing in the world to happen to you and you still live. And I also found out that if you're in a position where you can get away with whining and you don't, you score big brownie points with everyone."

JULIET LANDAU

As Drusilla, Juliet Landau portrays a slightly insane, slighty clairvoyant, British vampire torn by her attraction to two other vampires. Needless to say, it's an odd role. Which, for an actor, is a little bit like gold.

Juliet is a second-generation star, the daughter of the inimitable Martin Landau and Barbara Bain, neither of whom were strangers to television themselves. In an era when many actors and producers are just beginning to accept the idea that actors can work successfully on both large and small screens, it should be remembered that Juliet's parents were among those who paved the way.

In a very short time, however, this young actress has made a name for herself. Aside from her role on *Buffy the Vampire Slayer*, she is perhaps best known for her role in the quirky Tim Burton film *Ed Wood*. Juliet has also appeared in *The Grifters, Pump Up the Volume,* and *Neon City,* among others.

We're fortunate enough to catch up with her for a few minutes on one of her final days of shooting. While the crew is changing the lighting for the next scene, we sneak away to an abandoned set, with Juliet in full Drusilla makeup and costume. A true professional, she seems at first distracted—loath to break from character. But after only a moment or two, Juliet relaxes and it's obvious she is warm and open, quite unlike the Hollywood stereotype.

She is a unique actress, an observation borne out by the fact that, unlike nearly everyone else in this cast—and nearly everyone else in Hollywood making less than ten million a picture—Juliet did not actually audition for her role in the series.

"Joss had seen my work in *Ed Wood.* He called my agent, and they sent over a reel, and I came in for a meeting with Joss and David Greenwalt, Gail Berman (both executive producers), and [casting director] Marcia Shulman. It was an incredibly creative meeting. It was great. All I had read was a couple of pages in the script about Spike and Drusilla, and the character description. And I got a real strong sense from what was written about what I felt about the character. Joss apparently had these characters running around in his brain for years. So it was this amazingly creative meeting, and then I left, and within half an hour they called my agent and said that they wanted me to do it."

Apparently, as part of that meeting, on the spur of the moment, Juliet began to go into what we would now call her "Drusilla mode," with fluttering hands and distant stares. The producers loved it. So did Juliet. When Drusilla first appears, in a weakened state, she is reminiscent of classical opera heroines, dying of consumption or some other debilitating disease. But the idea that she would start this way and become strong really appealed to the actress.

"There are so many colors to this character: going from weak to strong; being a villain. There's also this sweet sort of love story in a way between Spike and Drusilla. It's a little kinky and strange, but it's also sweet. You just have these different dynamics. She's evil, but there was a side to her when she was ill that was sort of fragile. Ethereal. Joss described us as Sid and Nancy as vampires. And the look of Drusilla is fun, this sort of cross between Victorian period heroine and Kate Moss."

Interestingly enough, Juliet does not think of Drusilla as evil.

"I'll say that to Joss, and he just says, 'Yeah, and I can tell that you think so, and it shows.' She's so creepy, but she doesn't think of herself that way. 'And so I eat a few people, it's no big deal.'"

Indeed, from Drusilla's perspective, it's perfectly reasonable to kill people and suck their blood.

Juliet makes a point of discussing how fortunate she and the rest of the cast are to be working on this series, where characters do develop and change over time.

"It evolves," she says appreciatively. "Angel goes from being the good guy to where he's come to be with Spike and Drusilla. Then there's my character's whole journey, and the fact that the second I become healthy, I have to take care of Spike while *he's* in a wheelchair."

Conversation turns to the subject of Juliet's British accent. American by birth, she did spend four years in London as a child. It paid off.

"There was an Englishman who was the double for the Judge (in "Surprise" and "Innocence"). That day I guess I had been speaking mostly in dialect. He came up to me afterward and asked where I was from. I said, 'Actually, I'm from here,' and then he said 'Oh, my God, I can't believe you fooled me.' And I thought, that was really good."

Do you have a favorite moment, on or off screen, from your time on *Buffy*?

JULIET: "After they hired me, they paired me with their two final choices for Spike. James [Marsters] came in and immediately we just bounced off each other. There was a moment during his audition—it was our very first scene of our first episode, and [Spike and Dru] are talking to the Anointed One. James came up to me as if we were going to kiss, and then we didn't and we turned [away from each other]. And we ended up doing it in that scene, and it was kind of fun that it came from that initial meeting. Then they actually used it in the promo—'Evil has a few new faces.' They used that actual thing."

Were you interested in horror as a child?

JULIET: "No, actually, not really. But it's funny, because the show doesn't feel like horror to me. The dark forces are used to show the high school experience to the absolute extreme. High school is a horror movie, which we all can relate to. It's got this humor and this dark edge, and it bounces between being scary and funny and tragic."

Drusilla is the most powerful female villain we've seen on television in a long time. How come Buffy has never beaten the crap out of you?

JULIET: "Actually, what's been interesting with Buffy and me is that [my character has] these visions and sees things, and her character has these dreams and premonitions. It's been sort of mind-to-mind [combat], women battling with their minds. It's been interesting."

JULIE BENZ

Things are really taking off for Julie Benz. Not only did the actress have a role in the smash comedy *As Good As It Gets,* which had her in nearly every commercial for the film, but she's recently gotten married, and has a new film, *Jawbreakers,* with Rebecca Gayheart, Rose McGowan, and Pam Grier, on the way.

Julie has also appeared in *Inventing the Abbotts, Black Sheep,* and *Two Evil Eyes,* as well as making guest appearances on such series as *Diagnosis Murder, Step by Step, Married…With Children, Sliders,* and *Fame L.A.* She also had a recurring role on *All My Children.*

For the woman who played Darla, the vampire who sired Angel into the "nightlife," it's been a very good year. Still, no matter how busy she's been, she was more than happy to return to the series for the two-part second-season finale.

"I was very excited, especially when I found it was set in 1760 Ireland," she says. "I had never done a period piece before, so I was very happy to return to the show. They sent away to London for my costume."

Julie was a bit surprised when she found out that Darla would be back. After all, the powerful blond vampire girl was…well, dead.

"I *was* really surprised, even though when I died, they kept saying, 'Oh, we will bring you back somehow. We want to have you come back at some point.' They can't ruin the reality of how vampires die. I was cooked," she says. "When you are cooked, you are dead. You have to stick to that reality because they have killed about a hundred vampires that way. So I was really surprised when they actually did bring me back, and in the way that they did."

As things go forward and Angel's past is delved into, there will likely be many opportunities for Darla to appear. If that comes up, no matter how high her star rises, Julie will be there.

"Our characters have an interesting past," she notes. "It would be so interesting to flash back to different time periods when we were together. It is very fun and creative as an actor to have that. I love the show."

Interestingly enough, Julie originally read for Buffy, and it wasn't the first time she tried out for a role that eventually went to Sarah Michelle Gellar. But we'll get to that.

"Like every actress in Hollywood, I had originally gone in and read for the role of Buffy," Julie says. "Sarah is just so wonderful as Buffy. When they were doing the pilot, they came to me and asked if I would play the vampire, and I was like, 'Sure, sure, okay.' It was interesting. I had never played a vampire before. I didn't have to audition for it, which makes me glad because I don't know if I would have gotten it.

"So I did the pilot for them, and then they wrote me into a couple of episodes, which was really nice. I honestly thought that I would just be in the pilot and that would be it. I would never see those people again."

Unlike some of the other actors who have appeared on the series, Julie is rarely recognized in public from her *Buffy* work. She suspects it is because most of Darla's scenes involve her being in full-vamp mode. Although, interestingly enough, people do sometimes recognize her by her voice alone.

Though she's always enjoyed horror films, Julie admits that even the bad ones frighten her. It was a nice opportunity to turn the tables by working on this series.

"In the first or second episode, we were sitting in this really creepy cemetery late at night. I had on full vampire makeup and it was pretty scary. It freaked me out. I mean, here I was supposed to be scaring everybody else."

What were you scared of as a child?

JULIE: "The dark. I was terrified of the dark, and I was also terrified that there were people under the stairs. In the dark, I would creep up the stairs, and I always thought somebody was under there ready to grab my legs. I was always afraid that someone was in my closet, so my closet was always a mess as a kid. I would never hang up clothes and stuff to make sure that nobody was there. And the closet door had to be open. Because if it was closed, somebody was in there."

Do you have a favorite moment, on or off camera, from your work on *Buffy*?

JULIE: "David and I had a lot of fun working together. In the episode where I get killed, he stabs me in the back with the stake. I turn, and I look at him and I realize it is Angel. We had the giggles. We could not stop laughing, and it was so hard to do that scene. I would turn and look in his eyes and I would just bust up laughing and so would he. I mean, here we were in the whole vampire faces and we had the giggles. The whole thing seemed absurd. And then in that moment, I am supposed to fall out of frame onto a mattress but I missed the mattress and hit the floor. We felt like kids. 'Oh, no, we can't stop laughing.' And the more you try to stop laughing, the more you laugh."

Do you have any scars, tattoos, or other distinguishing marks?

JULIE: "Well, I have two tiny little scars on my chin, two little ones. I was an ice skater growing up. When I was a kid, I accidentally tripped over my own skate and split my chin open on the ice. I was in first grade when it happened, and I had to go get two stitches, and I thought it was the ugliest thing in the world. Then I got the stitches out, and two weeks later I did the exact same thing and reopened the exact same part of my face. I had to get two stitches again."

Did you have any professional history with any of the cast and crew prior to working on Buffy?

JULIE: "Actually, Sarah and I both tested for the role of Kendall Hart in *All My Children*. It was a long time ago, but we tested together. She went first. I actually remember what order we were in. She went first, and I was fourth; there were six of us there. When I went to work on the pilot, I told her we had tested together. [I reminded her that] I had short hair then, then she remembered me. Then she went back and watched the audition tape....I was really embarrassed to find that out because it was a long time ago. She was very sweet. I remember watching her test and knowing right away she was going to get it. She is really amazing: her work ethic, being as young as she is and working as hard as she does. It is really an admirable thing. I admire her."

What's your latest film, Jawbreakers, about?

JULIE: "It's about three high school students. We kidnap our best friend on her birthday and we accidently kill her. It's a very dark comedy, like in the vein of *Heathers*."

If you have the opportunity to play Darla again...

JULIE: "Darla is one of my favorite characters ever. It is so much fun playing a vampire, because you can do so many different things and you have a freedom there to play. I love it even though the sight of blood makes me faint. I love Darla, and the great thing is that they don't use blood on the show. Even fake blood makes me want to faint."

BIANCA LAWSON

She was there to die.

Bianca had come to the set just to die. The actress, who played Kendra the Vampire Slayer for four episodes of the second season, had returned to film her last scene. Her death scene.

The scene, shot on the library set, was directed by co-producer David Solomon. Makeup master Todd McIntosh was there, overseeing every moment, as Juliet Landau, playing Drusilla, slashes Bianca's throat. Bianca holds in her hand a small sponge filled with stage blood. When she is "slashed," she slaps the sponge to her throat, and blood drips down her neck.

Bianca has appeared in many television series as a guest, including *Sister Sister, In the House, Saved by the Bell: The New Class,* and *Parenthood* (coincidentally, a series Joss Whedon wrote for). Bianca began her acting career at the age of nine in a Barbie commercial, and she's been working ever since. She had a small role in the John Travolta film *Primary Colors*.

When Bianca was cast for Kendra, the scripts for the two-part "What's My Line?" were still being written. The night they called to tell her she had the part, they asked her what accents she could do. Eventually, they went with Jamaican.

"I have a friend who is a dialect coach, and I ran through it with him. But some people had ideas of what they wanted that were a little bit different. Do I want to be upper class? Do I want to be, like, smart but upper class? Sounds very British. So it was like the lower class, with a heavier patois."

Once they had determined what her accent would be, it was up to Bianca to get it down right. She worked hard with her dialect coach and, in fact, the producers weren't certain exactly what her accent would be until she showed up to start shooting. Obviously, they were pleased enough to bring her back for two more episodes. Her hard work paid off.

As far as the impact *Buffy* has had on her, Bianca was very pleasantly surprised.

"It was only one two-parter," she says with wonder. "I wasn't even in the previews for it. I was surprised that so many people saw it, so many different kinds of people. All these adults in the mall, married women, mothers; they're like "Oh, my God, you were so good, I saw you last night."

Do you have a favorite moment, on or off camera, from your work on the series?
BIANCA: "I have a lot of fun doing the fight scenes. That was when I knew I really enjoyed being here. In the past, I have done a little bit of kickboxing and a little bit of boxing, but it was never anything I did consistently. It's been so much fun."

ARA CELI

One of the first things you notice about Ara Celi is her laugh: a beautifully lilting and infectious sound that instantly dispels the glamour of Hollywood. This is a laugh, it is easy to believe, that springs not from managers and agents and image-makers, but from the heart of a real person. The pleasant, inclusive laughter one hears among friends.

No surprise, then, that Ara, the exotic-looking young actress who portrayed the "Inca Mummy Girl" in the episode of the same name, is quickly making plenty of friends in Hollywood.

In fact, the *Buffy* role came as the result of a conversation between casting director Marcia Shulman and ultra-hot, maverick director Robert Rodriguez. Rodriguez was considering Ara as the title character in *The Hangman's Daughter*, the *From Dusk 'Til Dawn* prequel (a role she eventually won), and recommended that Schulman see her. On her third audition, she met with the series' producers and later that day learned she had the tragic role of a sixteen-year-old girl who died for her peoples' beliefs, cursed for eternity. In fact, of all the monsters on *Buffy*, the "Inca Mummy Girl" is perhaps the most sympathetic. Certainly according to Ara's fans.

"Everybody says, 'We didn't hate you. Usually we hate the bad guys on that show. Even though you were the villainess, we liked you, and we didn't want to see you die. We wanted to see you and Xander get together.' It's funny."

And clearly, fans were not the only ones who didn't want to see Ara go.

"It worked out well. I mean, everybody really liked the show. People kept saying, 'I wish there was some way, why do we have to kill you off? Why do we have to kill you off?' Really, the cast was great to me—everybody was great. They were trying to figure out a way they didn't have to kill me so that they could bring me back on."

The actress is a former Miss Texas, originally from El Paso. In addition to *The Hangman's Daughter*, Ara also has the lead in a film scheduled for release in late '98 titled *Looking for Lola*. Her career is taking off quickly, but she promises that no matter how successful she might be, she would never turn down a chance to reprise her role as Ampata. Her experience on that episode was overwhelmingly positive, thanks in large part to Nicholas Brendon, with whom she shared most of her scenes.

But it wasn't until after the episode aired that Ara realized that her feelings about the show were echoed by millions of fans.

"I'll tell you when it hit me," she says. "The day after the first time that episode aired, I went to the movies. My friends and I were walking up to the movie theater and a crowd of about ten or twelve guys said, 'Oh, my gosh, it's her.' And we were looking around, thinking, Who are they talking about? And they said, 'You were great on *Buffy* last night.' And my friend, Ally, said, 'Dude, they're talking about you.'

"I did not believe it. I promise you. The guys were like, 'You were awesome.' I just said, 'Thanks,' and I waved, and I could not believe it. And then I was at the Super Bowl in San Diego, and there was this huge party in the Gas Lamp District. They close off the street. There were 130,000 people. I cannot tell you how many people rushed me asking for my autograph. 'That's Ampata, that's Ampata!' and yes, that is when it became pretty relevant. I mean, one episode! So, yeah, I think it's great. I don't know. People pray for stuff like this. You do one thing, and everybody knows you."

Do you like Twinkies?

ARA: [laughter] "That is such a classic question. As I child, I used to love, love Twinkies. They were my favorite snack. I mean I loved Twinkies. Well, I'll tell you what, shoving eight to ten in my mouth at one time, ooh…but I do still like Twinkies!"

Is that how many you ended up having to eat?

ARA: "Yeah, we did about ten, myself and Nicholas. And after every take, we turned yellow. We both turned yellow in the face. It was wild. We laughed a lot."

Do you have a favorite moment, either off camera or on, from your adventures on *Buffy*?

ARA: "My favorite moment was the part where Xander and I were dancing. It was just like a fairy tale come true, because we're like standing around, and we're lost in each other's eyes at the dance. I just love that moment, because it was really magical. I forgot about every-thing. I forgot about the cameras. I forgot about acting. I was really, really in that moment, and just staring into his eyes. It was unbelievable."

And he didn't even call the next day.

ARA: "Actually, he was great. We did exchange numbers as friends. He's really, really a nice guy. He's wonderful."

Were you ever a horror fan?

ARA: "You know what, I'd never even seen the show before I was booked on it. What I did know was, when I read the character, about this Inca princess, I liked it, I liked her. I liked the way she was naive, and I liked the fact that she never really had the chance to fall in love, and I thought that was kind of fun."

Very sad, though.

ARA: "Yes, it was sad, but she got kind of lucky. At least she got a little taste of it."

What were you afraid of as a child?

ARA: "As a child, I was afraid of the dark. I was afraid of being alone. I didn't like to be anywhere, even in my front yard, alone."

Do you have any scars, tattoos, or other distinguishing marks?

ARA: "Oh, I have a great scar."

See, this is the weirdest thing. It must be actors, I don't know.

ARA: "It must be. I don't have any tattoos, but I do have a scar over my top lip. It's clearly visible. It looks like a little Frankenstein scar. When I was very small, I wanted to get out of my crib, and my mom wouldn't get me out, so I decided to jump. I leapt out of my crib and hit the floor, and I had to get stitches. I think I got seven or eight stitches across my lip. The funny thing about this scar, which is so beautiful, is that when I was a little baby, my mother said to my grandmother, 'I can't believe she did this, she ruined her face.' My grandmother said, 'Oh, it doesn't matter, it's not like she is going to be an actress or a beauty queen or anything.' And then I was Miss Texas. And of course, I act, so my grandmother constantly tells me that story. Over and over again. But I love my scar. When I first moved out here to Hollywood, this man lived with me who's a casting agent, and he said, 'You know, if you just had that scar removed off of your face, your face would be flawless.' And I said, 'I like it, it gives me character, I'll never remove it.' And he said, 'You're going to do fine in this business with that attitude.' I like it. I don't think I'll ever get rid of it."

You know all the female viewers are going to want to know if Nicholas is a good kisser.

ARA: "Yeah, actually I've been asked that quite a bit. And yes, he was a wonderful kisser."

You kind of have to say that.

ARA: "Yeah, I know. No, he was really great."

JOHN RITTER

One of the best-loved sitcom stars ever, for his roles on *Three's Company* and *Hearts Afire*, John Ritter also starred in such films as *Skin Deep, Problem Child, Hero At Large,* and *Sling Blade.* In the episode "Ted," he plays Buffy's mother's new boyfriend, a man who isn't what he appears to be. It afforded him an opportunity to play against his image, and it gave *Buffy* one of the best ratings it had received up to that point, not to mention an opportunity for the show to explore the series' mother/daughter relationship in more detail.

As for John, he had a great time. Even better because he was already a fan of the show.

"It was so much fun," he says. "And it was interesting because my agent said, 'Do you want to do *Buffy the Vampire Slayer*?' I had really liked the movie, but when the TV show came on, I liked the TV show so much better because there was a quality to it that I hadn't seen on TV before. It was stylized and so funny and so hip. They were creating teenage jargon that I hadn't heard before. Very sarcastic and intelligent dialogue, as opposed to that kind of *Beavis and Butt-Head* thing.

"And there was a real sexiness to it, and it was scary and action-packed. The fights were thrilling and creative. Not just exchanging punches but using the environment around the combatants. I took a couple of years of karate—I'm so old it was when Bruce Lee was alive. These guys have come up with so many creative things. The way the vampires explode, and the makeup....I would say, they can't possibly do this every week. I sat down with my three kids to watch the first episode, and we were hooked.

"So when my agent called and said, 'They want you for *Buffy the Vampire Slayer*,' I said, 'Absolutely. I'd love to see the script.' Well, when I called my agent and said, 'What happened to that script?' they said, 'Oh, the *Sabrina, the Teenage Witch*?' I said, 'Wait a minute, I thought it was *Buffy*.' Then I got the script. Usually you have a suggestion, but I just thought it was really well written and well worked out. It was a really fun turn."

Doing the show also scored big points for John with his children.

"My kids visited me as much as they could," he says with a chuckle. "I've always said, 'I'm going to do this and this. Do you want to come down to the set? Do you want to come to the theater?' 'No, that's okay, Dad.' Then it was, 'I'm doing *Buffy*.' 'All right, we'll be there at lunch, and then when we get out of school.' That was the one thing that really impressed them."

But John's appearance on the series impressed a lot of people besides his kids.

"Garth Ancier from Warner Brothers said, 'John, it was the highest-rated *Buffy* we ever had.' So many people have come up to me and said, 'Do that thing with your head.'"

"Aside from the adventure and everything else, it's a girl and her friends going through all the teenage angst that normal kids go through, except there are vampires and monsters and creepy things. It's such a metaphor," John observes. "Some of the worst times you can have—at least it feels that way—are when you're a teenager. The greatest upsets, the highest highs, [then] you can't get out of bed. You're so sad because of a heartbreak or something.

"'Ted' fed on the fear of being somewhat abandoned by your mother for a stepdad or a step-parent. It turned out that I was *reaaaally* bad. Everybody else really liked Ted, as long as they kept eating the cookies and brownies with drugs in them."

And, as Ted, John was very effective, very disturbing, even for *Buffy*'s creator.

"Joss's one note to me every day was, 'John, that was just a little too creepy.' He said, 'Be as normal as possible. You've got to really take the audience by surprise.' I was just looking, staring with too much subtext. He asked me to lighten it up a little bit," John says, amused.

The other thing that made this a unique experience for John was working with the series' talented young actors.

"I'm really knocked out by that cast," he says. "They're really good. There's a technique to acting for camera. A lot of people treat every line like it was handed out by your professor in college and you've got to say every word clearly or Homer, who wrote the *Iliad* and the *Odyssey*, will come out of his grave and tear you apart. There's a way of throwing away dialogue, like people do in real life. There's a kind of nonchalance, or planned casualness, that is really appealing sometimes. This kid Nicholas Brendon and Alyson Hannigan just really knocked me out. They're all so good.

"Sarah is such a professional. She's just adorable, but you assume someone that young can do one or two things, but she can do it all. She's been around since she was a zygote. I think she started acting as a fetus. She was really fun to act with. At the dinner table, which was done the first day, I think that's where I went, 'This little girl is a major talent.' You see a whole lot of subtext in her eyes. She's always thinking. The camera is the one invention by man that can record thought as it's taking place. Actors who know that are off to a great start.

"Then she went off and did *Scream 2* and *I Know What You Did Last Summer* and then she comes right back to the TV series with nary a break in between. I think that's smart of her. When I did *Three's Company* and it started to be a hit the first year, I got very busy during my hiatuses because I knew that I didn't want to just sit on my laurels. That introduced me to different casts and crews, and the idea that I could do things other than sitcoms. I thought that was really smart, when I was young enough to do three things at once."

Unfortunately, though he persevered, it wasn't all good times on the set for John.

"It turned out that Sarah and I both got the stomach flu on the last day," he remembers. "We were both saying 'excuse me' and visiting our respective toilets in our trailers. I was in really bad shape. Then we had to do the fight scene. The most convincing thing I did that day was be dead, 'cause that's how I felt. But the thing is, I've been around and I know there are some days you feel good and some days you feel bad. If you're freezing cold, you can't show the audience. I have a way of shutting down."

Conversation comes round, almost inevitably, to some of the films John has done, including the average-joe turned superhero flick, *Hero At Large*.

"That was the first major film that I did," he says. "I think that was released in late '79 or early '80. That was one of the things I did during hiatus from *Three's Company*. The author was this guy, A.J. Carruthers, this sweet guy, a real optimist. He wanted it to be a Capra film. The film was so sweet."

Though many readers might not remember that film, John went on to make the *Problem Child* films, as well as a film that combined drama and comedy called *Skin Deep*.

"That was a dream of mine—to work with Blake Edwards. I just love him. He and I became really great friends after *Skin Deep*. I don't remember how we got through some of those days. I've never worked with a director who encourages you to break up, and might do something in the middle of a scene to make you laugh. Like tell another actor to give you a false line to see how you'll respond. Many, many times I've ruined takes with my laughing out loud or his laughing out loud. To me that was so helpful, because I felt there was an underlying sadness to that film."

We hear that you're a hell of a ball player. You saved the cast and crew of *Buffy* in their game against *Seventh Heaven*.
JOHN: "Where's a stake when you need one? No, it was really a fun thing. I love playing."

What were you afraid of as a child?
JOHN: "Unrequited love."

That's an adult fear, too.
JOHN: "I was very mature for my age. Early on I realized that's my problem. Unrequited love, and in a totally unrelated matter, quicksand. Actually, that's sort of a metaphor for unrequited love, but let's not get into my psyche."

Do you have a favorite moment from your *Buffy* adventure?
JOHN: "I think it was throwing the baseball around with Nick Brendon. I knew I could really dig being a part of this company. Also, I have three really, really nice and loving kids, and I just remember taking them around the set. The whole place is just Buffyland. I would take them to wardrobe and makeup and props, and I remember showing off the set and the cast to my children. It was just really family-friendly, even though it's about vampires. They're trying to make an hour show under Herculean challenges, and they make it. And they still have time to be friendly. I think that reflects Joss and the deep respect everybody has for what he's trying to do, and that incredible, extraordinary crew they have over there."

Did you have any previous professional experience with any of the cast or crew?
JOHN: "No, but I had worked with Tom Whedon, Joss's father, years ago. And my son Jason had done a one act play by Zack, Joss's brother."

Would you like to do it again?
JOHN: "I really had a wonderful week with those folks. We were talking about how I could get back. Willow, being a computer genius, said, 'Well, I just kept a little bit of him.' She could accidentally build one or something."

ROBIN SACHS

Born in London, England, Robin Sachs is, to all appearances, everything his character, Ethan Rayne, is not. Good natured. Courteous. Decidedly not a wizard. His background is in London theater, but he has appeared in many films and TV series in Britain and America. His

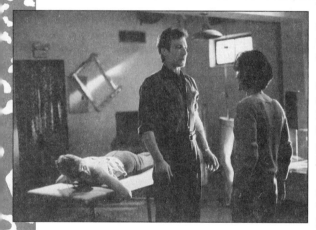

TV work includes guest stints on *Diagnosis Murder, Nowhere Man, Nash Bridges, Walker Texas Ranger, Brideshead Revisited, Babylon 5,* and *Murder, She Wrote.*

As for his work on *Buffy,* Robin was already familiar with the series when his agent put him up for the part of Ethan Rayne. "I had seen it before, and I thought it was a very good show, well written, well produced, well directed," he recalls. "I liked it."

Though he has no special affinity for horror, Robin has always been intrigued by it, "so long as it is well done. I have always loved watching TV, and I have loved going to the movies, and all parts of the visual media appeal to me in any form. I used to watch Boris Karloff when I was a kid, and wonderful horror movies that seemed horrifying at the time, they are nothing compared to what we do now."

The subject of Hammer Studios, the classic British horror production company, comes up, and Robin notes that he was in a Hammer film called *Vampire Circus,* now a cult classic.

As it is for Armin Shimerman, working on *Buffy* is a pleasure to Robin, who has frequented *Babylon 5.* At the moment, he has just completed an episode of the series in which he recurs "occasionally as people wearing latex heads." The actor has also done a number of voice-over projects.

And what about the character's future? While it seems likely we will eventually encounter Ethan Rayne again, Robin has his own version of the character worked out all too well.

"I have the feeling his mother didn't like him too much and left him in the broom closet when she went shopping," he says. "It certainly has something to do with childhood."

Did you have any professional history with any of the cast or crew before working on the series?
ROBIN: "I knew Tony Head briefly back in England."

Assuming Ethan will return, which, as we said, we all hope, do you have any particular talents or skills that you would like to see them work into the character?

ROBIN: "I have a lot of talents and skills outside of acting that I would love to see worked into characters, but you know, I am delighted to work with whatever they have. I am a black belt in karate. I have boxed; I play tennis; I ride horses. I would love to ride horses on screen. I haven't done that since I was in England. I suppose the likelihood of my playing a cowboy is pretty minimal. It would be great. I would love Ethan to come back as a cowboy."

Do you have any scars, tattoos, or other distinguishing marks?

ROBIN: "I have scars all over myself. I ripped my arm open on a metal railing when I was eight. I have scars in my eyebrows from playground fights. I have a recent scar, two scars that happened just before I started filming *Buffy*. I was putting in a new air conditioner on an old window and there was no one around to help. I was taking the old one out by myself, and as I took the old one out, of course, the window fell apart and I went through it with the air conditioner. So I ripped open my shoulder and my neck, just on my Adam's apple.

"I bled a lot. It doesn't usually bother me too much, but after I sort of mopped up and put the air conditioner in, I went to look in the mirror and one of my shoulders was okay, but it needed stitches. The one on my neck was very clean, right across the Adam's apple. Every time I bent my head back, it looked like a little mouth. I was filming in two days, so I decided to go to the hospital, and they stitched it up with clear stitches, which didn't show on film. I have this British thing about not going to doctors or hospitals too often. I am glad. Actually, my wife persuaded me to go.

Giles and Ethan have this horrible dark past of something really, really stupid that they did when they were younger. What have you done that has come back to haunt you, if anything?

ROBIN: "Me, personally? Oh, God. Nothing major. Nothing huge. When I was in my early twenties, I had a set of head-shot photos done. I was extremely buff at the time, or so I was told, and so the photographer said, 'Well, why not do some bare top shots, just in case they come in useful for later?' And I did them, and I sent them to my agent to pick out and he obviously kept one because it got circulated."

JOSS WHEDON

We were fortunate enough to be on the set while Joss was directing the two-part second-season finale. Though he was on an insanely tight schedule, as always, he used several of his breaks to sit down and chat with us about his creation. Strangely, the greatest testament to what Joss has created did not come from the modest writer/director/producer, but from the rest of the cast and crew.

And they all know the vision that he brought to the show. This isn't really about vampires and demons, though Joss loves those things. It's about personal demons. It's about high school. As David Greenwalt said, "If Joss Whedon had had one happy day in high school, none of us would be here."

Indeed, that has been the magic of the show from the beginning. People can relate to Buffy and company not because they face the forces of Darkness, but because they are also facing the horrors that we all face growing up. In fact, the monsters are frequently metaphors for things teens have to face as they mature.

It's one of the hottest series on television. It almost single-handedly put the WB Network on the map. And yet *Buffy the Vampire Slayer* made an unlikely journey from Joss's original script to a movie that never became more than a cult hit, to a television series that is both hugely popular with mass audiences and a critical darling. The movie varied greatly from his original story. The series, though, is right on target, because Joss is at the controls.

But to do that, he had to take a detour from his burgeoning career as one of the hottest feature-film writers in Hollywood.

Joss is a third-generation television writer. His grandfather wrote for such programs as *The Donna Reed Show* and *Leave It to Beaver,* and his father, Tom Whedon, for *The Dick Cavett Show, Alice,* and *Benson,* among others. Before moving on to major success, writing such features as *Alien: Resurrection,* and *Toy Story*—for which he was nominated for an Oscar—Joss wrote for the hugely popular sitcom *Roseanne* and for *Parenthood,* a series adapted from the eponymous film.

He grew up in Manhattan and attended high school at Winchester, an all-boys school in England, before returning to the States to attend Wesleyan College, in Connecticut. After a year writing "a sickening number of spec scripts," Joss was hired by the producers of *Roseanne.* As he has said, he literally went from "working at a video store on a Friday to work-ing on *Roseanne* on Monday."

Still, after all the things he has achieved, Joss says that *Buffy* "is the most personal work I've ever done. Which is funny. The opportunity to mythologize my crappy high school expe-rience makes it extremely personal, but also sort of exorcises it. It isn't just reliving it, it's sort of reinventing it, so it moves me more than anything I've ever done. The opportunity to keep developing the characters and finding out what's going to happen to them and how they're going to grow apart or together is…the more it goes on, the more personal it gets."

With all that soul-searching, one would think that Joss would begin to change his feelings about his high school years. Joss disagrees. He also notes that, contrary to popular opinion, "my high school years were not all terrible. There was that Thursday…." He laughs.

"No, I did have a couple of friends, and I had a lot of good times, but all the bad high school stuff definitely went down. This lets me come to peace with that. But really, I'm at enough of a distance, and it's not like 'That girl, and I'll get her….' There's nobody I harbor any particular malice toward from high school.

"I think that's part of why I like doing the show so much. I'm able to look at high school and say, 'There's the dumb jock who was mean to me. Well, what's his perspective? He's going through something, too. There's the teacher who flunked me.' I suppose in that sense, it is sort of revelatory. It's nice because I can go to the pain, but at the same time, I have a much more pleasant view of it, because I am seeing it from a bit of a distance."

That pain, in fact, has become almost more important to the series than the horror or the humor of the characters.

"When we realized how much we could really live these characters' lives, we found that we could go to that dark place," Joss says. "I made a joke that, 'The key to the show is to make Buffy suffer.' Sarah said, 'Why do you do this to me? Another crying scene? Do you know what I go through here?' and I said, 'America needs to see you suffer, because you do it really well.'"

Joss laughs, but he isn't really joking.

"We're doing these sort of mythic-hero journeys in our minds," he says. "A lot of times, the story doesn't make sense until we figure out who's suffering and why. Including the bad guy. If the bad guy's not hurting, not relating to her, then it's just a cardboard guy to knock down. And the same thing goes for the audience. If they're not feeling it, if her relationship to what's going on isn't personal, and if ours isn't, then it's just guys with horns running around and some good jokes, but it's not going to resonate."

It's amazing, given how personal a project this is, that Joss ever got to do it at all. The film was not what he had originally envisioned, and he thought he'd had his chance. Then Gail Berman and Fran Kuzui came to him to ask if he wanted to do the TV series.

"I had never thought of doing it myself, but I was like, 'Oh, wow, that's sort of neat!' And I thought about it, and the more I thought about it, the more I realized how many stories there were to tell and how excited I was," he recalls. "I was pretty much out of TV completely at that point, and my agent asked me, 'Now, come on, really, what do you want to do?' I said, 'I'm already writing scenes for this in my head,' and he said, 'Fine, I'll make the deal.' I did not expect it to take over my life like this. I did not expect it to move me as much as it did."

And, though he loves horror and always has, it isn't really the horror that moves him.

"I love invoking all those [old horror] movies, but at the same time, the core of this series, emotionally, is a very safe place. These are people who care about one another and when their world is upset, *you* care about it. Whatever horror is out there is not as black and terrible as what is already within and between us. A lot of my friends never watch horror, and they get scared and don't like that part. But they respond to the show."

With the wonderful cast on the series, one can't help but think of the adage that writers are frustrated actors. Joss goes one step further.

"I'm a frustrated writer, I'm a frustrated actor. I'm frustrated at everything I don't do. But that is why I love this so much, I get to do everything, including some set dressing and some costume work. That is the fun thing about producing television, you're doing all of that," he says.

Still, horror has and will always have a special place in Joss's heart. His knowledge of films, comic books, and movies is encyclopedic, and his influences are many and varied.

"I have a lot of influences," Joss says. "So many, in fact, that I can't even think of them all. I've sort of hodge-podged together my favorite bits of everything. I take what I need for the series. For example, vampires look like vampires part of the time, because I want to see demons so you don't have a high school girl just stabbing people. At the same time, I want her to see people that [the viewer] doesn't know if they're vampires or not. They turn to dust because it's cool, but also so we don't have to have twenty minutes of body-cleaning-up at the end of every show.

"I read *Tomb of Dracula,* and I'm a huge *Blade* fan and a fan of [comics artist] Gene Colan. I always loved Morbius, and I loved anything that smacked of the undead and tortured souls. I just rock on that stuff. The old horror comics.

"The movies? Well, *Lost Boys* is in there, obviously. Their vampires change, they get ugly-face when they feed. And *Near Dark,* because it's just so important. The Langella *Dracula,* which I actually saw onstage. *Night of the Comet* is an underrated flick. The remake of *The Blob,* too. I really loved that movie. I actually have a picture of Shawnee Smith with an M-16 on my desk. She was a big inspiration."

Do you have a favorite moment, on or off the screen, from the series?

JOSS: "At the end of 'I Robot, You Jane,' when they're all sitting there realizing how pathetic their love lives are, that was my favorite ending. That was very nice. For me, there have been a bunch of things. I think one of them was definitely when I shot 'Innocence.' Things came together for me. That's when everything just completely fell into place. And I thought we had created something that is more than the sum of its parts. And I'd always been proud of its parts, but that was the first time the thing really just completely talked back to me.

"That was really neat, and then, everyone was like, 'You must be so happy you did well?' And I would say, 'Oh, yeah, but I was so happy before.' I didn't even notice the ratings because I was already on such a high.

"There was a moment when we were shooting that scene in 'Innocence' with the rocket launcher: the guys are flying, a big explosion, and I was quite literally jumping up and down. I was so happy. And the next day, we shot the last scene with Buffy and her mom, and I was watching the two shots of Kristine and Sarah, and I thought, *Yesterday, I had the rocket launcher, and this is better.* They were so good in that, and it looked so beautiful, and it felt so right, and that to me was just . . . we had everything. We had the kitchen sink on this show, but it's still the small stuff that holds it together."

Has the cast ever inspired the evolution of their characters?

JOSS: "Oh, absolutely. They certainly inform the way the characters behave and the way they talk. They can't help but bring some of themselves to it. Although I'm still pretty strict about what they have to do. But the more we write the characters, the more Willow becomes like Aly...all of them. As I get to know them more as people. They bring so much more depth to it. They all become the heroes to their own stories because I know them as people."

Are the vampires in the *Buffy* mythology organized as clans?

JOSS: "I don't really think of them as clans. I think of them more like people. There are religions, there are religious leaders, different sects. What do they say in C.S. Lewis books, 'We all worship the same god, we just call it different names'? Well, they all worship evil, they just call it different names. It's not so much clans where different vampires have different appearances or powers. What you have are certain charismatic figures who find themselves surrounded by stuntmen."

Carey Meyer
ne Quinn
d Koneff
ustafson
Brennan
on Webb
Starlight

ve West
ecauwer
on Hight

ngblood

Wilson
Grastein
he Barry

rgstrom
osenthal
Shapiro
n Dunn
uzdernik

Is there a Council of Watchers?

JOSS: "There is an actual little Watcher Bureaucracy based in England that Giles works for. But they're very loose and pretty incredibly inefficient. Since nobody ever seems to know what anybody else is doing. But so much of finding the Slayer and training her and figuring out who's going to be next is magic and luck. And nowadays, people are just not that dedicated. Giles tried to get out of it. It's a little bit muddy. Things get balled up at the head office."

Are you prepping Willow to be a Watcher?

JOSS: "No, I'm not. I've never thought of Willow as a Watcher. I've got something else in store for Willow."

What were you afraid of as a child?

JOSS: "I'm going to have to go with standard-issue dark and monsters, and pretty much my older brother. I was sort of terrified of my father, too, but he turned out to be a really nice guy, so I got over that. And *Horror Hotel*. That stuff was scary. Witches in cowls, hooded figures walking through graveyards chanting…every time I get scared."

Do you have any scars, tattoos, or other distinguishing marks?

JOSS: "I have a scar on my wrist. I always like to pretend I tried to commit suicide, but I really didn't. It was a rusty nail."

We saw you wolfing Hershey's Kisses on the set. Are you a chocolate fiend?

JOSS: "I wouldn't call myself a chocolate 'fiend.' I'm a friend to chocolate. Occasionally, I eat a lot of chocolate, but I'm not one of those scary people who eat it all the time."

Everyone involved with this show seems to think of it as some kind of destiny. Does that spook you?

JOSS: "It's only spooky when I think, Jeez, *I'm going to work on other shows where this doesn't happen.* It does feel like Manifest Destiny. It's such luck and chance that everybody from our D.P. to David Greenwalt to the entire cast just happened upon this project. And if they hadn't…I break into a cold sweat thinking about what I would do without any of them. Let alone Sarah. It does have a kind of inevitability to it. It seems like it just flowed into being."

AcIntosh
ldonado

Kenney

ri Baker
kpatrick
ermaine

Vankum
C. King
s Kimble
Kim Ray
Domald

oodman
Saldutti
ryl Cain
an Casas
hip Hall

L. Perez
Mendez
li Flores

bert Ellis
ath Culp

AcEntyre
AcEntyre
AcGivern

arry Fee

DAVID GREENWALT

If you saw him walking around the set, you'd swear he was one of the actors. Actually, though, David Greenwalt is the series' co-executive producer, and has written more than his share of episodes. He works hand in hand with Joss Whedon each day and may well be the only member of the staff besides Whedon who truly knows where Buffy's destiny lies.

David is a Hollywood veteran who has worked as a screenwriter, a producer, and a director for more than twenty years. Series that have been positively influenced by his work include *The Wonder Years, The Commish, Shannon's Deal, Doogie Howser M.D.*, and *Profit*, which he co-created.

We met with David in his office, and he was kind enough to give us all the time we needed. We started off talking about Angel, whom David said "was tortured, and then he's good when he comes back, and then eventually he will probably go his own way."

Accordingly, there will be some very serious reservations among the other characters about Angel's return. At first, David says, "Buffy will keep him secret for a while."

As far as the quality of the series itself, David modestly deflects any praise to *Buffy*'s creator. He's one of several people who refer to Joss Whedon as a "genius."

"This stuff just pours out of him," David says. "He is very, very emotionally connected to all of these characters. He has an excellent idea of who they are, and he has a pretty good idea of where they are all going at any given time in the universe. The world [of *Buffy*] has become more complex, which is all part of his master plan. These are adolescents becoming young adults. It's a lot about the veils dropping from your eyes and realizing these essential facts of life, which is what happens. Next year they'll graduate from high school, and some of them will go to college, and some of them will go away, and they'll go on with their lives.

"Now some things, like Jenny being a Gypsy, we're seeing develop sort of after the fact. We're saying, 'Wouldn't it be cool if she had an agenda?' because everybody has some kind of agenda. Then there are other elements, like Angel turning bad. Most shows like to just choose the same person every week, doing the same thing. There's a certain comfort level in that. But Joss takes a lot of risks. He gives the audience what it wants, but he also gives the audience what it needs: a deep emotional connection to the characters and the knowledge that anything can happen in the show. Regular characters can die, people you love and trust can turn completely evil, and there's a good metaphor for that, too. That whole arc of Buffy and Angel finally consummating that relationship and then him turning so vile, it's the metaphor for 'he doesn't call the next day.' So it's the metaphor for your worst fears realized. That's also a metaphor for going a little too far, too fast, too young, biting off something bigger than you can chew."

David, who obviously has passed some of his snack-food frame of reference on to Xander, started out in the entertainment industry as Jeff Bridges's stand-in. From there, he became a screenwriter and co-authored three films: *Class, American Dreamer,* and *Secret Admirer.* The latter film was his directorial debut, and he later directed several television movies for Disney. From there, he continued to "dabble" in television.

"I really liked it," David says. "I felt there was a slightly better class of professional. As a person who has directed features, I'm not a snob against TV at all. Show me a guy who can make a great show in eight days, I'll show you a guy who could make a great show in 180 days. People work harder and longer, and, by and large, better in television than they do in movies.

"We make twenty-two hours of television a year. In terms of film on a screen, that's at least the equivalent of eleven movies. That's a lot of stuff. Plus, we do other things, plan other shows. For me, it's a throwback to the old studio system in the '30s or '40s, where someone would have belonged to a studio and would have been making five movies a year. Maybe the geniuses can, but I don't feel I could learn anything making a movie every four years. Now making three every week, I think I can learn something, so it's wonderful, it's stimulating."

David ended up writing and directing several episodes of *The Wonder Years* and *Shannon's Deal* before going to work on *The Commish* for Stephen J. Cannell. After two years on that series, he teamed up with a friend, and together they created a series called *Profit. Profit* is rare in the history of television because, though every major critic in America praised it vociferously, "nobody watched it," as David says.

Still, the series, which was unique because it had "a villain as its centerpiece," got David Greenwalt noticed in the television industry. In fact, that series helped land David a deal with Fox which would have him working on *The X-Files,* right after he helped them out with this little experiment they were doing, a new series called *Buffy the Vampire Slayer.* He never expected to fall in love.

"I remember saying to my wife, 'Anybody want to know what the best pilot of the year is? The best-written pilot is *Buffy*.' Joss had worked on *Roseanne*, he worked on *Parenthood*, his work in movies is pretty well known, but you know, he just really got this thing on its feet. He's totally devoted to it. It's always hard in a TV series, to come up with a hundred episodes. But with this show, it's worth telling a hundred stories. There is so much richness in these characters, that while it is hard, like on any show, we just feel as if we have more stories every day to do."

Needless to say, giving up *The X-Files* was quite a decision. But it's obvious David doesn't regret it at all. Still, though he's more Buffy's godfather than father, David is quite satisfied with his role on the series and his life.

"I feel incredibly satisfied," he says, and then smiles. "On the series, we say 'into every generation one is born.' That's this guy [Joss Whedon]. Mark my words, Steven Spielberg, watch out. This guy is only thirty-three years-old. By the time he's fifty, he will be as rich, and as successful, as Steven Spielberg. I have no doubt of it.

"Joss understands stories. Breaking stories with him is like playing tennis with a pro. You go play with a pro, the pro hits the ball back really hard, and really sure every time, so you're forced to be better and better in your game. I've been working long and hard to learn story and structure and emotion and humor and heart and dialogue and all these elements that we play with here. I'm playing with one of the very, very best in the business. And while he certainly runs this show, he's also very willing to let you go and do your own thing, too. He's very open to suggestion, and he's a big team player and very big on acknowledging other people's contributions to it. I can't sit here and lie and say I'm fifty percent of the show: it's just not true. But I'm the number two guy, so I'm very happy."

As for how he explains *Buffy*'s popularity, David attributes a lot of it to the show's willingness to delve deeper into the shadows than most.

"A lot of the time, television is considered a clean, safe world, as opposed to movies. There's sort of a tradition—I don't think a good tradition—of safe, easy stories, easy on the psyche," he explains. "Joss just keeps going deeper. For example, 'Lie to Me' is very disturbing. It's about the idea that there is no innocence, there is no good in the world. The bad guys and good guys aren't clearly delineated. Some of the episodes [Joss has written] I find very disturbing. You can have more depth, but you don't have to distance your audience to do it. I think that's quite an art in its own."

As for the future of the series, David says that *Buffy* is just getting warmed up.

"I actually think that this year is going to be our big year. I think we're very hot within the industry. Certainly we're ahead on the WB, which is somewhat of a fledgling network. *Buffy* is in the consciousness now. The show is mentioned on radio programs, it's mentioned on *Jeopardy!*, it's in the lexicon already. We've only been on the air a year, really. So twelve months in the national consciousness. I think season three is the year that we will come into our own. I think we'll become more mainstream. I'm sure that Sarah will get an Emmy nomination eventually, and the show will get more and more recognition. You know there are some people who are never going to come to a show called *Buffy the Vampire Slayer*. But I think there are enough people who are going to be hearing from their friends and other people that 'Oh, you should see this.'"

Of all the hats you wear on this show, which is your favorite?

DAVID: "Always the writer. Writing the story is the very hardest thing to do, but, in a sense, the most satisfying. A lot of people who want to be writers make a similar mistake: writing is not putting words on paper. Writing is understanding the way the character is, what the arc of the story is, where you want to be at the end of the story. Laying it out. That is the hard work. The writing is also challenging, but kind of fun. So that's my very favorite thing. The next thing is directing and editing."

Do you have a favorite moment from your tenure with the series?

DAVID: "Probably when I directed 'Reptile Boy,' where Buffy is dancing with the frat boy who turned out to be evil. It was a nice moment with Tom, and I had all these fancy ideas on how to shoot this thing. Sarah came in and said, 'This is really hard to choreograph, just let us dance, just shoot it, and just let us dance and move, and watch what happens.' Sure enough, it just happened, and it was great: just watching two people relate and dance, and I didn't do anything so terribly fancy, showing off with the camera. You have these moments on the set...if you're lucky maybe you get one a day, or one every few days, where you go, 'This feels true, this feels honest, this feels really funny, it just feels right.' There's that kind of quiet that comes, that sort of hush that says this is the moment, this is the little pearl for the necklace."

Were you a big fan of genre films and fiction growing up?

DAVID: "Nothing like Joss. I'm a Billy Wilder, John Ford, Preston Sturges, romantic-comedy guy. My movies were romantic comedies, and most of the TV I've done had sort of a comedic bent to it. I've learned dramatic structure form over the years, and there were horrific elements, but it's not my natural bent. Through working with Joss, I've discovered that it's really cool because...we say that people have demons, but in our world *they really have demons*. It's just making it bigger."

FRAN RUBEL KUZUI

Only Joss Whedon has a longer history with our favorite Slayer than Fran Kuzui. She was, as they say, there at the beginning and ushered the film version into being by helping rewrite and then directing the original feature film. Fran is married to producer Kaz Kuzui and together they own Kuzui Enterprises, one of the largest independent motion-picture distribution companies in Japan. How she got there, however, is classic Hollywood.

"I wanted to make films from the time I was about twelve years old," she recalls. "I was the president of my drama club in high school, and I directed all of the plays. My high school drama teacher was my mentor and really encouraged me. When I went away to college, I started taking film courses my freshman year and always knew that that's what I would do.

"In my senior year at New York University, I wrote a treatment for a TV show as part of an assignment for one of my professors. It was my final project for my last year of school. He had just been appointed head of PBS Public Affairs. He hired me on the basis of the treatment that I had written for class. I went directly from graduation to a job at the PBS station in New York, and within three weeks I was an associate producer in the public-affairs department, and I was producing documentaries."

After working in television for a time, Fran went on to produce educational films for Encyclopedia Britannica. Then came the next major turning point in her career, when she met renowned film director Milos Forman.

"I told him that I was really inspired to make movies," Fran recalls. "He had just come to live in the United States from Czechoslovakia, and his wife was a script supervisor there. He said to me, 'Why don't you become a script girl, and I'll teach you how to do it?' So I became his personal assistant, and I worked for him for two years. In the course of that time, he introduced me to his script supervisor and taught me how to be a script supervisor and helped me get into the union. I went from being an associate producer at a TV station to running errands for somebody, and I think that's sort of the dues you pay in the entertainment business."

Fran went on to write and direct the 1988 film *Tokyo Pop*, which received much acclaim at Cannes Film Festival upon its release. Her latest project as producer is *Orgazmo*, a film by *South Park* creators Trey Parker and Matt Stone.

Her involvement with *Buffy* came about almost entirely through instinct.

"After *Tokyo Pop* was shown at the Cannes Film Festival, and as soon as I came home from there, my agent sent me a script I loved, which eventually turned out to be *Cool Runnings*. I fell madly in love with this script and spent the next two-plus years trying to get the film financed as an independent film. The options on the script expired without my knowing it because I was not the person who had optioned it. I was just the director. I wasn't the producer. Without my knowing it, somebody else optioned the rights, and I lost the opportunity to direct *Cool Runnings.*

"I was really, really down in the dumps. I ran into Howard Rosenman at a birthday party, and he said, 'Oh, I have a script that you're going to fall in love with. Why don't you come to my office next week?' So the next week, I went to his office, and he threw the [movie] script down on his desk, and I opened it up, and it said *Buffy the Vampire Slayer*, and I said, 'I'll do it. Anything called *Buffy the Vampire Slayer* has to be a wonderful script. I'm in.' So I called Joss, and I got together with him, and I told him how much I loved the script.

"After we optioned it, Joss and I sat down and discussed ways that it could be re-focused. I suggested, since I was an enormous fan of John Woo, that we add martial arts. My idea, since I like to do comedy, was to make this more comedic than scary. What I do is pop art. Or what I'm interested in is pop art. So I saw the original script more from a pop sensibility or a pulp sensibility than as a genre piece. So I suggested that every time she saw a vampire she should do martial arts before she puts the stake through its heart, kind of like John Woo's *The Killer*.

"John is a friend of mine. I thought, *Well, in* The Killer *there's all this violence, but it's not very violent because it's treated as ballet.* And it's done so tongue-in-cheek, more like comic-book violence than Jean-Claude Van Damme violence. I think that's the biggest change that Joss and I made in this script.

"As we rewrote it, there were several times I said to Joss, 'Oh, that's such a silly thing for her to say, could we take that out?' And Joss said, 'But I said that myself when I was in high school,' and we started to laugh at how funny you are when you are in high school. High school is not only a scary place, but a funny place. For me, what I wanted to do in the movie was balance the scary and the funny. I think, at that point, Joss's vision was more toward the scary, but he was incredibly supportive of what I wanted to do and refocused the script more along the lines of my vision and how I wanted to make the movie.

"You know, *Buffy* has been blessed from the very, very beginning, because it took Joss several months to do the rewrite and give it to me, and I just loved it," Fran recalls.

After sending the script to Fox, Fran and Kaz took off for a vacation in Hawaii. Things in Hollywood don't usually happen very quickly. But the morning after they arrived in Hawaii, they received a call from Fox saying that Joe Roth wanted to give *Buffy* the green light and wanted them in L.A. as soon as possible. Fortunately, when Roth learned of their vacation, he gave them a week in the sun before they needed to come in for a meeting.

"The whole process from our optioning it, having it rewritten, and then green-lighted, took about six months," Fran notes. "In the movie business, that's like lightning."

As for its middling reception at the box office, Fran chalks it up to a lack of focus in the marketing of its release.

"I know the film has an enormous number of fans, but I think it was never clearly marketed to one audience. I think the film found an audience. I don't think the marketing found an audience. Gail Berman, who loved *Buffy*, came to me and said, 'Someday I'm going to turn this into a TV show.' I was still smarting from the experience of the theatrical release of the film and said, 'Well, I don't really think this is *Buffy*'s moment.' But several years later, I just had the sense that it was time for *Buffy*.

"For me, from the very beginning, *Buffy* was always about 'girl power.' I started seeing so much around me that was beginning to emerge that was similar to that. I called Gail, and said, 'Hey, remember you wanted to do this TV series? Let's go.' And the next thing we knew, everybody in town was fighting over who got to make it. It's always been pretty blessed."

When it's pointed out that her career path is a perfect example of that 'girl power' that she saw as a trend, Fran pauses a moment.

"The real challenge for me is to have made a movie that was perceived as not successful and to pick myself up and not quit," she says. "To turn the creative focus of *Buffy* [the show] over to Joss Whedon and to say, 'Well, okay, I will enable Joss to express himself through the TV show,' is where the guts come in. That's what *Buffy*'s about: dealing with the consequences of what you do, and moving on and not folding to the vampires is the really important part. Having the grace to say to Joss, 'This is yours now.' The grace to say to Joss, 'I know you had an original vision. Let's go back to that, and let's make this TV show along the lines of what you want to do.' That's the guts, and that's the girl power."

Fran also wants to make it clear that she believes "girl power" is almost more important for boys than girls.

"For me, *Buffy* was always about creating a role model for girls, but unless you show boys what that is, they're not going to step aside and let girls be that," she says proudly. "You can educate your daughters to be Slayers, but you have to educate your sons to be Xanders."

Do you have a favorite moment from your involvement with the series?

FRAN: "I'm very fond of the praying-mantis episode. Also, the entire [atmosphere] of the set. Since I'm not there all the time, there are people who don't know who I am. One day, I was on the set and asked one of the Teamsters for directions, and he said, 'Hi, what do you do?' and I said, 'Believe it or not, I'm the executive producer,' and he looked at me, and he said 'Thank you, thank you. This is one of the nicest experiences of my life. Thank you for making this.'"

GAIL BERMAN

Now that she's added running a new company to her duties as executive producer on *Buffy*, Gail Berman has had to move her office. But don't worry, she hasn't gone far. Only a few hundred feet from her old office is the new one, the home of Regency Television. When we sit down to interview her, everyone is still moving in and there's a very sort of temporary look to everything. She's a remarkable woman, sharp and in control. She had all her calls held, with the single exception of her daughter, and the warmth and pride in Gail's voice as she spoke to her were wonderful to hear.

Gail got her start shortly after graduating from the University of Maryland. She produced *Joseph and the Amazing Technicolor Dreamcoat* at the Ford Theater in Washington, D.C. "Then nine months after it closed in Washington, it opened off Broadway, and two months later it went to Broadway. So I was the youngest female Broadway producer. My first project was one of those *wunderkind* things. Then I was a Broadway producer, having never been a production assistant. I did that for ten years."

Among Gail's theater production credits were *Hurly Burly, The Nerd, Blood Knot,* as well as "all the road companies of *Joseph* at the time." She was on the Board of Trustees of the League of American Theaters and Producers, "and I was younger by thirty years than my next colleague," she says.

In 1989, Gail decided it was time for a change.

"It was a very dramatic move at that time. I had no idea what I was going to do next." She took a job at the then-fledgling Comedy Channel (now Comedy Central), her first "real" job since graduating college. "It was an extraordinary thing to have happen, because when you are starting something new, you have to learn it all. This was an operation where the day-to-day business was taking place where the production was taking place. It was really a great experience, and I learned a tremendous amount about television." During her time there, she served as the supervising producer for a new show from Minnesota called *Mystery Science Theater 3000,* among others.

After her husband's career took him to California, Gail resigned and went to work for Sandollar in L.A. "I wasn't sure what I wanted to do, but I figured it was a good way to start my career in Los Angeles. That's been my career in Los Angeles, one place. I started as the vice president and I became the CEO of the company, and then in June, I left to just do *Buffy*." In addition to her duties as one of *Buffy*'s executive producers, Gail is the president of the television studio Regency Television—a joint venture with Fox.

Gail was instrumental in getting *Buffy* to the small screen.

"When I came to Sandollar, I read a script called *Buffy the Vampire Slayer.* I thought it was a great script, I thought it was really amazing, and they were making a movie of it. Before the movie was going to be released, I went to Sandy Gallin and I said, 'I think this would make a great television series. I think we should sell it as a television series before the movie comes out.' Sandy [Gallin, president of Sandollar] said, 'Great idea, let's see if we could do that.' I called the various parties. Nobody was interested in pursuing it as a television series at that time.

"I was very disappointed and went home with my tail between my legs. I couldn't go ahead with it, so I put it on the shelf and thought, *someday.* A couple of years later, Fran Kuzui called me and said, 'You know, someone has come to see me about *Buffy*'—talking to her about it sort of theoretically, and she said that they might be interested in doing it. I said, 'Fran, nobody else is going to do this but us.' We started to work on it together. I didn't know Joss, I had only read the original script. We were contractually obligated to offer this to Joss. Everybody said he was a big movies guy now, and he'll never want to do this, including his agent, who said that to me on the phone. Then his agent called me back and said that, in fact, this was the only thing that Joss *was* interested in doing. So for me, that was fantastic. I met him, we hit it off very well, we had a very similar vision, and we went to go about selling it eventually."

Gail is quick to point out that it's Joss Whedon's show, top to bottom. "It was my idea to do this as a series, but it's his creation. Every single thing you see, every line you hear, it's him.

Obviously, there are episodes I like better than others, but I never am disappointed in the vision. The vision is unbelievable to me."

She is very grateful for the show's success, especially since it didn't seem as if it had much of a chance at first. "We were like the bottom of the barrel. We're on the WB mid-season, thirteen episodes, a show called *Buffy the Vampire Slayer,* based on a movie that was considered less than successful. You can't have any more strikes against you."

Indeed, the title was a source of contention. "The network did not want to keep this title at all. They had a lot of different ideas, none of which we were interested in. It was a very big battle to the finish. Now, of course, it seems fine, because everybody calls it that, but at the time their research told them that the title was a killer. 'Definitely don't call it *Buffy!*'"

Gail's ability to cut and run when she's had enough of something is in direct contrast to the heroine of *Buffy,* who is stuck with her destiny no matter what. When this comparison is mentioned to Gail, she says, "I just know when it's time to move on." As to Buffy Summers's inability to move on even if she is "spent," she says that is "one of the things that makes her pretty extraordinary, I think. It's something that I think Suzanne Daniels from the network pointed out in an early episode that she wasn't pleased with. She felt that it was very important that Buffy not be reluctant. She is a heroine, she accepts her responsibilities, she accepts her fate. That doesn't mean that every day she loves it, but it means she totally accepts. I think about that often when we think about the show. She is mature enough to understand her destiny."

There are a lot of strong girl-driven shows right now. Do you think this is something that is going to last, or do you think this is just a fad?

GAIL: "I'm not prescient in these matters. The only thing I can tell you is, a lot of women out there respond to this kind of material. I think women are looking for role models, or strong characters, that they can identify with in some way. I don't think that that is a trend; I think it has taken all this time to catch up with what's going on with women. Now, sooner or later, people are going to say, 'Hey, there are too many shows like this on television,' and you'll see there will be an emphasis on male shows. That will happen just simply because that's the nature of television. You sort of have to be above the curve to anticipate new trends, but I think, in the end, what we've learned here is that women are not going back to the same place they were before this all started. So this trend has moved women forward."

Who is your favorite character?

GAIL: "Willow. Young people respond so much to Willow, because so many people see themselves as her. Young girls who are scientifically oriented, or they're into math, and they're always on the sidelines. What I love so much about Willow is that she maintains that, she keeps that. It's not that all of a sudden Willow became a glamour girl for having known Buffy—she is the same Willow, but all of her strengths come out thanks to this friend of hers. Her loyalty, her brilliance, her cuteness, her everything comes out because she has been empowered by her friend. I love Willow's character, I love what's going on with her and Xander, and Oz—it feels real to me. I love the fact that she is Jewish—I can't recall ever having a Jewish character on television that isn't portrayed in some stereotypical way. For me that is very helpful to say to my daughter: Willow's Jewish."

Has there been a moment where you felt really satisfied with something, a moment where you can kind of sit back and say, "This is really cool"?

GAIL: "Well it's a much earlier moment than anybody else will remember. There was a moment at the end of the presentation [reel] where Buffy throws a stake at a poster of *Nosferatu*, and the music starts—it's not music that we ever used again, just for the presentation, and she's so satisfied with herself and she is sort of welcomed into the group. I thought to myself, *This is the best show*, and I just knew it in my heart at that moment. It was a very private moment, it's not a moment that I really shared with anybody else. It's the eeriest thing with this show, because people ask me, 'Well, when did you know?' and I can't explain it other than saying that I just have always known. It's never been something where I thought, *Well, it's not going to happen that way.* It's happening where I always knew it in my heart. It's like when people used to say to me, 'How did you know that *Joseph* was going to go to Broadway?' I just knew it. Remember the show wasn't picked up. *Buffy* was not ordered. We almost didn't make it then, and yet I thought, *We're going to get picked up.* I don't know why. Knowing Joss, believing in him, just seeing his vision, being around that kind of creativity, just watching that is an awesome thing."

SANDY GALLIN

Ask executive producer Sandy Gallin how he got where he is today, and his answer is typically direct and self-effacing: "I eat breakfast, lunch, and dinner."

A personal manager, Gallin has represented superstars as Barbra Streisand, Michael Jackson, Mariah Carey, Dolly Parton, Cher, Whoopi Goldberg, Luther Vandross, Lisa Stansfield, Renee Zellweger, and Nicole Kidman. As a film producer, he has brought to life such features as *Fly Away Home, Father of the Bride, Sabrina,* and the original film version of *Buffy the Vampire Slayer.* On the television side, Sandy has produced dozens of specials and series, including the original, long-running *Donny and Marie Show* and the Margaret Cho sitcom, *All-American Girl,* as well as the Academy Award-winning AIDS documentary, *Common Threads: Stories From the Quilt.*

Sandy's place in entertainment history is assured by his extraordinary accomplishments, but his place in the history of America itself is marked by the single most important booking he made in his early career as an agent for General Artists Group (which would later become ICM): it was Sandy Gallin who booked a little-known British band called the Beatles for their legendary appearance on *The Ed Sullivan Show,* after which he was promoted to senior vice president at the tender age of twenty-seven.

"I started in the mailroom. I became the head of the television department. I moved to California, running their music and television department, which is now ICM, and I became a personal manager. I brought the Beatles to the United States. And in 1985, I formed Sandollar Productions with a very good friend and client, Dolly Parton."

Sandollar was the main force behind getting the original *Buffy* film onto movie screens. The film, released in 1992, was written by Joss Whedon and directed by Fran Rubel Kuzui. It starred Kristy Swanson, Luke Perry, Donald Sutherland, Rutger Hauer, and Paul Reubens.

"The movie was sort of a cult success," Gallin recalls. "Not a big commercial success, but I had asked Gail Berman, who was then running Sandollar Television, to please go through all of our inventory and see what we could turn into a television series. Gail came up with *Buffy the Vampire Slayer*. We partnered with Fran Kuzui and made a deal with Joss Whedon to create, write, produce, and direct the series. In all the years I've been involved with any project, television or motion picture, this is the first time that when the creative head of the show took over as producer and director, there actually were no problems. Joss did such a brilliant job. When we made his deal, that was a difficult thing. He's a very hot screenwriter. But he was passionate and wanted to do this and is totally and completely responsible for its success in my opinion, in every way.

Though it was all very hush-hush at the time of this interview, Gallin confirms that there is a *Buffy* spinoff in the works, featuring Angel as the lead character.

When asked, as the interview draws to a close, when he knew that *Buffy* was going to be as big a hit as it has become, Gallin's answer was immediate: "When I was told that it redefined the advertising prices for the WB."

GARETH DAVIES

We met Gareth Davies in his second-floor office in the *Buffy* production wing. Most of his office wall space is taken up with production stills, air-date schedules, and the other paraphernalia of being a producer. His desk faces a rogue's gallery of guest stars, with large red dots on the ones who have been killed. He speaks with a British accent and is very gracious, very relaxed, despite the fact that it's around 9:30 P.M. There's a location shoot of the mansion going on, and the residential area in which the mansion is located has requested a "taillights at ten" curfew. This means that the shoot must be finished, wrapped, and on the way out of the area by 10 P.M. People

with radio phones periodically walk by the open door of his office to report on the shoot's progress at making the curfew. If they don't make it, there will be a hefty fine. (*Note:* They *do* make it.)

Gareth is impressed with how suddenly *Buffy* has gone from obscure WB show to hot pop-culture phenomenon. "I've done a lot of shows but never had a show that got as hot so quickly as this one. I went with Sarah to the premiere of *Scream 2*, and I was shocked at the reaction to her as opposed to the others." As a result, the production office is a trifle skittish. "You might notice," he says, "there are no names up on the outside of the studio or anything like that, and we have just left the owner's name up on the building. We don't want to draw attention to ourselves."

Gareth started out his career as an actor, but got out of it because, "I was not a very brilliant actor and didn't want to be anything less. And in England there is a huge pool of actors and, unless you're really good, you can make a sparse living, but that's about all." He went to work on the production side, first for the BBC, then for ATV. "I was sent to do a documentary all around South America, which is when I got the bug to travel. As I sat in first class going over the Andes, drinking champagne, I thought, 'Do I really want to go back to London?' I went back anyway—I was broke by the time I got to Rio—and when I arrived, a new show was being scheduled called *Broadway Goes Latin*. I asked what it was and was told, 'Oh, you don't want to do it, it's a co-production with the Americans.' Okay, but what is it? Turns out, they took the one Latin American orchestra in Europe, along with some dancers and musicians in the Caribbean and brought them to London with an American choreographer and basically orchestrated all the Broadway hits, but with Latin rhythms. I said, 'I'll do it.'

"The first show was a disaster. The American producer called me the next morning and said, 'We need to talk. Meet me tomorrow at seven.' So we went for coffee and I told him the problem was that he was an American, nobody wanted to work with him, and he stocked the deadwood for the entire network. So he said, 'Well, how do I get rid of it?' I said, 'Here, I'll give you a list of names. You go into the production office and say, "These are the guys I want."' And I gave him the names of all the young turks, and we put together a helluva show. We did nine months worth of shows. Six months later, he came back to England and said, 'You know, I want you to come to the States.' He brought me to the States with his company. His name was Milton Leer, and he had a production company called International Video Productions in Miami, and did a lot of work in Puerto Rico. With him I went to Yugoslavia, Spain, Puerto Rico, all over. A lot of work in Miami. But eventually, we were going nowhere. We did an unfortunate movie in Yugoslavia, where I realized that I had to get away. So I left him after three years and came to Los Angeles, not knowing anyone, but I thought, *I'll give this a whirl.* I got very lucky, and since then it's been one job after another, once I got the start."

His credits, once he arrived in California, included *The Best of Families*, a 1976 PBS miniseries with Sigourney Weaver, William Hurt, and Jill Eikenberry ("We nearly got Meryl Streep except her agent wouldn't let her get tied up to PBS for nine months"), which got very little notice thanks to coming out at roughly the same time as *I, Claudius; Andersonville* ("We got a lot of enemies for that"); and a number of television shows, among them *Flamingo Road, Remington Steele,* and *Shannon's Deal*.

It took Gareth some time to get into *Buffy*. "When I first saw the presentation, I thought, *Hmmm, it's okay.* It grew on me as we went along. The more I got into it, the more I saw how clever it is."

In addition to the high praise that everyone has for Joss Whedon, Gareth also singles out the set designers. "The art department is amazing."

What are the difficulties in producing a show like Buffy?

GARETH: "The amount of stunts we do, the amount of fighting, because that means stunt doubles all over the place, and it takes forever. When we first start to do the climactic scene of the show, we can board it normally, which means six or seven pages a day. Then we would find two pages we couldn't get finished in the day, because there are stunt shots all over the place. On one show, we had a situation where the director had seven vampires just beating up on everybody. So about ten pages of dialogue went to a fight there, and he went on and on about this. Eventually, I got called on the set to plead with the director, to tell him it's okay and put him out of his agony. This poor guy was sitting in the chair going, 'Oh, I'm dead.' I explained to him that it was fine. We know it's going to be tough. I would hate to be a director that had to shoot that stuff! The other problem is the prosthetic makeup. When we do it, it's a couple of hours each. When we have a fight with sometimes six vampires, we've got more makeup guys down there than almost any other department. Then the other thing from the financial point of view is that those people could be in at six o'clock in the morning and not get used until eleven o'clock. Then, at the end there's all the taking off, so their work span is terrific. That's a very expensive episode."

How did you get involved in *Buffy*?

GARETH: "I got a call from my agent, who said, 'Would you be interested in doing *Buffy the Vampire Slayer*?' I said, 'You have to be joking!' He told me to go out and see the movie. So I saw it and said basically the same thing. He said, 'Look, take a meeting.' So I did. I hadn't seen the presentation, and I didn't think we got on very well, and I walked away. Then one day I called my agent because there was something else that I wanted to do, and he said, 'Wait a minute, let's not dismiss *Buffy*.' I told him it wasn't going to work and that they didn't particularly like me anyway. So I came over and met Charlie Goldstein, the senior vice president of production. I had met him years ago and liked him a lot. Ultimately they offered me the job and I came on.

"Since then it's sort of been a love affair in that it's been great. Joss makes my job easier, because I don't always have to say no, but I can go to him and say, 'Look, Joss, this is the situation. This or that, which do you want?' Nine times out of ten he'll be very rational. Sometimes, of course, he is irrational about something he's really in love with and really wants. But he's great. And the whole group is just terrific."

DAVID SOLOMON

Co-executive producer David Solomon is in charge of postproduction, which basically includes all the things that occur to the film after it is shot: the editing of the episode, the sound effects and special effects, mixing the show's sound, and so on. He also directs all the second unit (generally, sequences where the main actors are not used) and the inserts (someone's hand opening a book, for example). In addition, to his great delight, he directed "What's My Line? Part 1."

During our visit, we watch David direct Drusilla as she slashes Kendra's throat. This is a "pickup," where bits and pieces of an episode are shot after the episode is wrapped. Although he is under pressure to get the shot finished quickly, the set is relaxed, even jovial, as Juliet Landau and Bianca Lawson go through their paces. There is a great deal of care and discussion over how much blood there should be—*Buffy* strives to be "tasteful" in that regard—and he and Todd McIntosh try various methods such as attaching a tiny tube to Bianca's throat and giving her a "blood"-soaked sponge to press against it when Juliet slashes her. It is very important that the actors maintain their "eye lines"—their line of sight—so that this shot blends seamlessly with the previously shot footage. Some directors find this difficult to achieve, but thanks to David's editing background, it's second nature to him.

Though he works at pretty much the same pace throughout the season, the beginning of a season is less hectic for him than the final weeks. However, since *Buffy* uses Avid, a very sophisticated, high-end Macintosh editing software program, he is able to move fast. In addition, Avid allows Joss to oversee every aspect of each show. "And he does," David assures us. Additionally, the more special effects in an episode, the more work there is for him in postproduction. He works closely with Digital Domain in this regard.

However, the amount of work per episode seems to "even out," he observes. "It seems that the fewer visual effects there are, the more second unit there is to be shot." He mentions "Go Fish" as an example: no visual effects, lots of second unit.

David also oversees blue-screen effects, where the actors have to act before a large blue screen, freezing and reacting to various visual elements that will be put in later. David tells us that the fifty-year-old method is very demanding for the actors.

"But we have an unbelievable group of actors," he says. "I don't know how they do it. They all work a minimum of fourteen hours every day…and there's no such thing as five minutes late."

Armed with a degree in biology from UCLA—"I use it every day," he jokes—David's first job in the entertainment industry was cutting sound effects for Hanna-Barbera cartoons. He worked in animation for a while, but like *Buffy* director of photography Michael Gershman, decided he wanted to move to live action. He was an assistant editor on a Billy Wilder feature called *Buddy Buddy*, starring Jack Lemmon and Walter Matthau.

"I had the best time in the world," he recalls fondly.

He went on to do a lot of editing on various features and TV series including *Hill Street Blues* ("those leather jackets were such a pain, drowning out the sound") and the pilot for *Miami Vice*. He went on to edit, line-produce, and direct more than thirty TV movies and pilots for Viacom. He also directed *Matlock* and the Shadoe Stevens series, *Loose Cannons,* among other TV shows.

It was in his capacity as an editor that he met Joss. An executive at Twentieth Century Fox put them together, and David edited the twenty-minute presentation that Joss and Kuzui/Sandollar showed around town in hopes that *Buffy* would be picked up.

He enjoyed editing the *Buffy* presentation and was delighted to work on the show when it was bought. By the third episode ("Witch") he says, "the show really took on a life of its own for me. Buffy is a great character, but I didn't know how great the show would be until we started rolling. The second season took off with much more complete and sophisticated shows, deeper and better ones, really, and even the humor is funnier."

We talk about "What's My Line? Part 1," the episode that he directed. He was thrilled to get the chance, as he had "drifted from directing to producing and stayed there." He was very pleased to be able to cast Kelly Connell, one of his favorite actors, as Mr. Pfister, the Tarakan assassin also known as Bug Man.

"There was a stand-in bug wrangler for the arm sequence," David recalls, but Connell assured him he wouldn't mind putting up with "a bug or two." Everyone else stayed well away of the critters. "They were disgusting."

"I was lucky," David continues. "I had a lot of interesting characters" to work with, including Spike and Drusilla.

"What's My Line? Part 1" is the episode for which Kendra's cargo bay was built. The cargo bay provided the inspiration for the sewer system beneath Sunnydale and its attendant grimy appearance for the vampires' world.

"It almost didn't get built," David recalls. "It was very expensive for use in a small scene." However, he points out that it would have cost three times as much to rent one, and it would have been even more expensive than that to go to an airport to film a real cargo bay. "So Carey has used it over and over."

Did you have any professional associations with anyone on Buffy prior to working here?

DAVID: "It's interesting that you should ask that. When I was editing *Hill Street Blues*, Gareth Davies was down the hall working on *Remington Steele*. I saw him every day for years, just to nod to in the hall."

Do you have any scars, tattoos, or distinguishing marks?

DAVID: "When I was twenty, I dumped a motorcycle on the island of Corfu. I have a big scar on my knee filled with gravel. You can see it." It is the same knee he injured as a boy growing up in Tarzana, California.

Do you have a special moment working on Buffy?

DAVID: "When I found out I would be directing an episode. I thought it wouldn't be for a while, but the scheduled director [for "What's My Line? Part 1"] dropped out. David Greenwalt called me in to the office to tell me. I'm sure I was very professional, said something like, 'Well, thank you very much for this opportunity,' but inside I was bouncing off the walls and shouting, 'Omigod! Omigod!'

"Directing is the best kind of exhaustion there is. It's a fully concentrated day."

Since your work on Buffy requires you to work with intense scrutiny on a myriad of details, does it take away the "magic" of watching the finished shows for you?

DAVID: "I watch *Buffy* at home if possible, and I watch just like everyone else. I rarely take a tape home. I watch it while it's being aired, with the commercials and everything. I really enjoy it."

MARTI NOXON

It's hard to imagine Marti Noxon as a Hollywood power broker, though that seems to be where her career is quickly taking her. She straddles an interesting line. One moment, she's all professional, intensely scrutinizing the events taking place on the set of *Buffy the Vampire Slayer,* and absorbing everything she feels she can learn from. The next, she's all social butterfly and fan girl. Everybody on the set seems happy to be here. But Marti seems as if she still can't quite believe her good fortune.

It isn't luck, however. Not at all. Marti rose to the position of story editor in *Buffy*'s second season, with a promotion to co-producer for the third. She is heavily involved in all the story conferences and has written five second-season episodes, co-writing a sixth with Howard Gordon. Among her credits are the pivotal two-part episode "What's My Line?" and the turning-point episode "Surprise."

Marti goes out of her way to be friendly to people. She is very, very "up." And she has good reason to be. She worked for seven years to break into Holllywood as a writer, and now she's not only here, she's on a series famous for its scripts.

"I was working as a secretary until last year," Marti recalls. "But I had been writing that whole time. I had had little successes here and there, and a lot of encouragement, but nothing had clicked. I finally got a better agent last year."

Amazingly enough, Marti almost passed on the chance to work on *Buffy*.

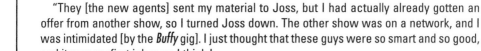
"They [the new agents] sent my material to Joss, but I had actually already gotten an offer from another show, so I turned Joss down. The other show was on a network, and I was intimidated [by the *Buffy* gig]. I just thought that these guys were so smart and so good, and it was my first job ever. I think I was afraid the bar would be too high."

In addition, it was only logical to assume that a small show on a fledgling network would be a risk.

"There were very few people saying this show was going to be a hit. There were even people at my agency who were discouraging me from taking this job. But then I called someone who knows Joss—my sister-in-law's brother went to school with him—and he said to me, 'If you don't work with Joss Whedon, you're crazy.' That's when I changed my mind, and I backed out of the other deal and came over here."

In her first year, Marti would still get the occasional odd look. "When I first started, people were like, '*Buffy*?' They would give you a kind of, 'Oh, that's nice,' and then discount you like you couldn't get a better job."

What Marti likes most about the show is the character progression, though she admits that it makes it that much harder for aspiring screenwriters. "I have a number of friends who are writing specs, and it's really tough for them, because things change so dramatically. 'Xander and Cordelia are together now? What's that all about?' That's one of the things about Joss, one of the reasons I think this show is so good, because he does things with characters. He is willing to take them places, where most average TV writers would stop. 'This is a franchise, you don't want to alienate your viewers.' And guess what? They *want* to see these radical things happen. We all crave that motion, that sense that things are happening, and they're just going to keep moving forward. It's very exciting.

"Next year's senior year, and there are all the paces we get to put them through that come with that, and all the questions about, 'Who am I going to be, and what am I going to be doing?' They all get to change; no one is going to remain static.

"When Joss pitched me the end of the second season, I went, 'What, you can't!'" Marti says. "My first reaction was, 'You can't do that to our audience.' Then I thought, 'Of *course* you can do that.' You've got to give them what you think they don't want, because if you fulfill [their expectations], it's the old *Moonlighting* thing: get those two people together and it loses its energy."

The story editor has nothing but fulsome praise for her boss.

"Thank God I get to work with a Mozart—maybe I'*ll* get a little Mozart, you know? Maybe just a touch, just a pinky of Mozart, from being around him."

She knew that this was the right place for her shortly after she turned in her first couple of scripts.

"I was riddled with anxiety, and I got a call from both David Greenwalt and Joss on my home machine. The first thing they said was, 'You know, we're really sorry to have to tell you this…'—I think this is my second script, and they called me from the set, and they were saying—'God, you really just haven't worked out at all.' Then they both started cracking up. Then they said, 'You did a really good job, and this is just great stuff, we're real excited.' I felt like, if they can tease me, then I must be okay. They must want me to stay."

We heard that you had a special guest for the *Buffy/Seventh Heaven* softball game.

MARTI: "John Ritter came out and played! He was just a guest star [on 'Ted'] that week, and he came out and played for our team. He was just the greatest. He turned out to be a great hitter, too; he was amazing. He really helped our team. Of course, *Seventh Heaven* won. God was on their side."

Could you describe your day-to-day work and responsibilities?

MARTI: "The cool thing is it changes all the time. It depends on what I'm doing. We get together and break story, no matter whose script it is—it's usually David and Joss, and then sometimes David, Joss, and me and the guys. We all sit around in a room and eat and talk about everything under the sun except for what we are supposed to be talking about. We spiral down to having really no other anecdotes, no other shockingly bad jokes to tell, right until you are really desperate enough to actually talk about the story. Then we will talk for seven or eight days. Once we have locked on the story idea, if it's my script, they send me off to take the story beats and then write out an outline. If I have ideas or pitches for jokes or things that will happen in that scene, I'll put it all in the outline, then hand it back. They'll give me notes on that, and then I go away and write a first-draft script. That usually takes between five and seven days. I usually try to write an act a day, then I try to spend a couple days and just let it sit, then I read it over. Then comes the agonizing day when you turn it in and you wait for someone to put their head in your office and say something nice to you. Those are sort of vomitory days, seasickness days."

Do you have a favorite moment, either off screen or on?

MARTI: "Recently I got asked to teach a day of school for aspiring writers, high school–age writers, through the Museum of Television and Radio. That made me almost cry, because I got to pass on my passion and my love for this thing to other people, and I have a credential now to do that, so that was kind of an amazing thing.

"The other time I remember is when we were first breaking story, everybody was working through lunch, and someone said, 'We've got to get lunch.' I stood up and started to go to the phone because I knew I had to start making calls about where we were going to have lunch. Somebody said, 'Marti, you know one of the guys who works with us, he'll get the lunch; you don't have to do that anymore.' And I was like, 'Wait a minute, I don't get the lunch?'

"It's all those little things, but in terms of the actual show, there are so many moments when I know that probably half the people watching the show just felt something, either laughed or maybe cried, if we're lucky. To me, that's the big win, if you get someone there, and that to me is so overwhelming I can't even take it in."

Are you interested in horror at all?

MARTI: "Yeah, I've written three spec features that are about ghosts. I love ghost stories. For me it's always been the metaphysical types of horror, like *The Haunting, The Exorcist*, and *The Silence of the Lambs*. It's always been about that sort of transcendence, about trying to communicate with the dead or reconcile your past—all those kinds of things. Those are the themes that I kept working on, and for some reason horror always fit. I think about reconciling your high school experience. We all had those nightmares in high school."

Do you have an affinity for any character in particular?

MARTI: "Willow is probably closest to who I really was. I was an egghead, and I didn't date until college. I was totally antisocial, and I was very, very shy. I couldn't talk to boys. So I was much more Willow, although Willow is way cooler than I was. You know, there's no one as geeky as me on this show. There's nobody as awkward and introverted, and creepy as I was. I scared my friends. I was just a big drama nerd—I was too gregarious, too silly, then I would withdraw, and then I was too quiet. A couple of other girls and I were the biggest nerds in the universe. We were pizza-faced and just completely couldn't talk. There was a hall that wasn't actually a classroom, like an in-between place, called Room 6—it didn't lead anywhere, it was just a dead end. We would stay in Room 6 because no one ever walked through there. That's where we would hide so we wouldn't have to talk to people.

"It wasn't the hardest time of my life, because I had a support system. I had what Buffy has. I had my Xander and my Willow and we had each other and we got through it. Man, thank God those weren't my glory days. I hope my glory days are still ahead."

ROB DES HOTEL AND DEAN BATALI

We met Rob Des Hotel and Dean Batali in their large, shared office. Rob's desk faces the door; Dean's is perpendicular to it. They talked about naming various characters after relatives—"Spritzer," the dog whose role was ultimately cut from "The Dark Age," is the name of one of their family pets.

From their rapport, it was clear they were a team, and comfortable working as such. Both were articulate, bright, and funny. Rob and Dean come originally from the sitcom world. They started out as writers' assistants on various shows, meeting on *Bob*. They were writers on *Hope and Gloria, Bob,* and other shows. They wrote spec scripts together—*The Simpsons* and *Duck Man,* but it was their scripts for a Nickelodeon show called *The Adventures of Pete and Pete* that attracted Joss Whedon's attention.

Rob tells us, "[Joss] was reading everything at the time. He was reading one-hour dramas, half-hour sitcoms. *Pete and Pete* was a one-camera comedy drama that actually, in retrospect, is the closest thing to this show at the time because it had some edge to it—but obviously, no vampires. *Pete and Pete* had a lot of the same character issues."

They pitch Joss a number of ideas, and Joss will pick one or more from the batch. They go off and develop those. The secret to consistent excellence comes from sitting with him and David Greenwalt "for hours and hours and try to break the story out," in other words, separating it into "beats" and acts. Then the team goes back into its office, to its white board, where the two "try to piece stuff together," then go back to Joss. This process usually lasts a week or two.

Their "beat sheet" usually consists of one line or so for each scene. After Joss approves that, they do an outline of around ten pages.

Rob adds, "For the most part, it's a lot of planning. It's one of the great things about this show is that it's planned in the story stage. We've been on plenty of shows where you're doing rewrites every day all day because you didn't have the story broken in the first place. You just

sort of had an idea, and then find, to no one's surprise, that the script doesn't work at all, so then you have to go back and do what you should have done in the beginning. So I think Joss is really really good at planning ahead, knowing where he wants to go."

As an example of their creative process, Rob and Dean discuss their favorite episodes. Rob's was "Phases," and Dean's was "The Puppet Show." Rob tells us, "Werewolf was what Joss gave us for the story. He said, 'Okay, Oz is a werewolf.' It was his basic idea, and then we went to him and said, 'Here are some ideas....How about if there's a bounty hunt going on here?'"

Dean says, "Last season's episodes—especially the early ones—were really big on teen situations. 'The Invisible Girl' was about people who had a lack of popularity, for

example. And even 'Puppet Show' was at one time more about being the geek of the school and being around all the other geeks at the school. We felt that in 'Puppet Show,' the angle that everybody freaks out worked. But once we got deeper and deeper into the script, that just kind of stood out. In rewrite, the basis became a subtle kinship between Buffy and the puppet."

Rob gives us another example of the way in which stories are devised: "Joss said, 'Giles did something bad in his past, so pitch ideas about that.' It felt like we pitched at least a hundred ideas. About things that he could have done or things that could have happened, and we had all sorts of 'could be this, could be that,' different things, different ways things are happening."

Once the idea is approved, the team does a first draft. They get notes back. Then they rework the material into a second draft, and then "usually the third and sometimes the fourth. From first to fourth, that can change a lot."

As with "Killed by Death," the "hospital episode," as they shorthand it: "The first draft actually took place at a day-care center, so that tells you the transition that can happen. Story ideas will change, things can move around, the monster can be different. The only person who really changes [things] is Joss, mostly, although David does a little bit here and there. We've done a rewrite of a script or two for other people, but normally it just goes from the writer to Joss. And even if we do a rewrite, Joss still takes it after that."

So moving from pitch to completed final draft of the team's script is probably an eight-week process.

"Getting the story down is, of course, always harder than the actual writing of the script."

They also point out that they can—and have—sped the process up. They've had to turn scripts around in five or six days. They wrote the second draft of "The Puppet Show" in thirty-six hours straight.

Pitching stories to Joss can sometimes amount to a discovery process of Joss's long-term vision of the show: "He has story arcs and stories that he wants to tell through this season and next season and next season. Occasionally, you do come up with a happy accident. Jenny Calendar [being a Gypsy and then getting killed]—that just sort of fell in place perfectly at the perfect time in the perfect way. And really, you know, sometimes you have an element in your story, and you're not sure what it is that's not making it work and it presents itself.

"So, like we were saying, [when we] pitch to him, probably thirty to forty percent of them, something's already being done like that in a future episode, or he's got an arc plan that negates it. So sometimes we do find ourselves pitching stand-alone type things—one episode, a contained episode, like "Puppet Show" or the hospital show that we just did. Often he'll give us stories where he says, 'Okay, here's a story where by now this is happening, and I want this kind of development happening.'"

But they add, "It's really rare that any one episode can just be plunked down anywhere in the season and still work. Even 'Killed by Death' had part of the Angel–Buffy story. You can't throw it anywhere."

"Killed by Death" was originally scheduled to be one of the first thirteen episodes, but there were production problems in that they would have to shoot on a hospital location for at least half the time, so they postponed it. By then, so many developments had occurred in the show that the script had to be reworked. In its original incarnation, Buffy and Angel were fighting side by side, and Angel was the one who brought Buffy to the hospital.

In fact, it was almost the "great lost *Buffy* episode." Rob and Dean explain that it had some conceptual problems in the beginning as they tried to get a bead on what the *Buffy* story of it was. "And the monster was just way too difficult to comprehend.

"In the second or third draft, there was an old lady sharing Buffy's room, and instead of the cousin who had died, it was Buffy's grandmother who had died. So that changed things."

How do you break down the work when you work together?

DEAN: "I do most of it." (They laugh.)

ROB: "We are a weird drama team. We write like comedy. We do everything face-to-face, word for word. We do it all together."

DEAN: "One of us sits at the computer. Occasionally, once we have an entire script, we'll take it away and work on our own, and then come in with pitches written on the script and say, "We could do this here, or this here" and go back and forth and decide what we like the best. It's usually Rob's stuff we like the best. That's weird because then we look back over the script, and in all honesty, it's hard to tell who came up with what. We might remember a line or something."

ROB: "And hope we have something that flows."

Would you say it is the strengths you brought into your work as sitcom writers that have given you your longevity on *Buffy*?

ROB: "Yeah. The staff from last year, of which I guess we remain, was a real combination. There were two or three teams and a single person. We were a comedy team, and the single person was a comedy team. The other two...were hourlong teams, so it was a real mixture. Then Dana Reston came on. She did the witch episode. And then Kiene and Reinkemeyer were hourlong writers. They'd come from *Space* and *Law and Order*. And then Gable and Swyden, who were hourlong writers. They were brand-new, but they got this off their hourlong scripts."

From studying the shooting scripts, we have seen that actors almost always deliver their lines exactly as written. Do the actors request many dialogue changes prior to this final draft?

DEAN: "Well, Joss is the final arbiter on that, ninety-nine percent of the time. Nicholas wanted to say 'red rum' in the 'Puppet' episode. Sarah had a good note for us a few months ago, in "Phases." She thought there was a word in there that Buffy wouldn't know, and that she was being too pushy in her advice to Willow. [We] thought she had a good point, so we toned down the advice and rephrased it. But usually that's a thing that Joss deals with."

When you come up with your pitches, do you keep budgetary considerations in mind?

ROB: "Well, our best example of that was right in the beginning where we knew what the budget was, but we had no clue as to what that would buy or what we could do. In our first episode, 'Never Kill a Boy on the First Date,' there was going to be a [vampire] uprising. Giles had this prophecy that he was reading to Buffy, and it was something like, 'Seven will die, and five will rise.'

"As production went on, Joss would poke his head in about once a week and say, 'Okay, five are going to die, and how many are going to rise?' By the time production came around, it was 'Five will die, and one will rise.'

"We had this fight choreographed with Buffy, Xander, Willow, Giles, and Owen—her date—and five vampires. It included urns crashing down, flipping over caskets, falling into caskets, and none of us had any idea if this was possible or not, and that was actually why we had to do a third and fourth draft of that particular script, because we had done two drafts, and we were done. But Joss came in a few weeks later and said, 'We can't do this anymore, we're going over budget, and we really have to tone down a lot.'

"So we rewrote a big thing like a duel from the movie, *Duel,* with the two vampires who take the van off the road. And then it became the airport minivan with both vampires standing in the middle of the road. We still had them crash into the light post. It was cool."

Do these budget considerations frustrate you?

ROB: "It's almost not fair in horror to have a huge budget because it's so easy then to manipulate the audience the way you want to. With our little budget, we have to rely more on classic, old-fashioned scares. More eeriness and suspense rather than huge special effects.

"We catch ourselves occasionally going, 'That'll be too expensive.' We try not to, but then [the producers] will go, 'No, we can't do that, it's too expensive. That sounds like a lot of outside stuff' [location shooting]."

So, any tidbits for next season?

DEAN: "Nothing you'll hear from us. We don't even tell our wives. We don't tell our friends. Oh, there is a chance that Xander is an alien....'"

MICHAEL GERSHMAN

In the egalitarian dress of production professionals, Michael Gershman wears the standard jeans and casual shirt. A quiet, affable man, he is perhaps the antithesis of the stereotypical director of photography, very soft-spoken, although extremely enthusiastic about his work.

Michael began his career as an animation cameraman in the late '60s, shooting *Peanuts, George of the Jungle, Tom Slick,* and Captain Crunch cereal and other animated commercials. But as he sat all day in a semidarkened room, his colleagues were on the streets of Hollywood shooting movies, and he decided live action was where the real action was.

While continuing to shoot animation, he began working for Pylar Camera Systems, which specializes in aerial cinematography. They trained him on the job and then began throwing jobs his way, until he dropped the animation work and concentrated on the aerial jobs. He worked in aerial cinematography for about five years, but became increasingly nervous about flying so much. As he had before, he started transitioning into another line of work: episodic television and movies of the week. One of his first projects was *Columbo.*

He worked on *Days of Heaven,* a feature that was shot in Canada and went on to win an Academy Award. He worked with famed cinematographers, such as Haskell Wexler and Vilmos Zsigmod, on such films as *The Deerhunter, The Rose,* and *Heaven's Gate,* moving from assistant cameraman to camera operator .

Then, in the mid 1980s, Michael's life took a big turn: he became a single parent as a result of a divorce. He eliminated travel and concentrated on working in Los Angeles, which led him back into television. He worked on the pilot of a show called *Shannon's Deal* as camera operator and moved up to director of photography when the show was picked up. Through that project, he became DP on *Middle Ages,* and that was where he met Gareth Davies, *Buffy's* producer. They worked together on a number of other shows before Gareth persuaded him to come to *Buffy.*

Recalling his initial reluctance, he tells us, "I thought, *Buffy the Vampire Slayer,* 16 mm. [the format the first two seasons have been shot in]...no.' Gareth called me a number of times and said, 'You just have to meet with them.' I just kept saying, 'Well, I don't really want to get involved with that.'

"Finally, I said, 'Okay. Within ten minutes of meeting Joss, I wanted to work with him. So here I am."

So this actually...is a sort of shift content-wise. A little different from the other stuff you have done.

MICHAEL: "It is different because of the subject matter. I have tried to bring a look to most of the shows I have done. I have always tried to make them interesting. This [show] gives me the ability to be much more interesting than anything else around. There are no rules. In a normal situation, you would not put a light on someone from below and bring it up. But I can light from below; I can light from above; I can use camera moves, and I pretty much have carte blanche.

"Joss told me what he likes and what he doesn't like...and I think that the material that we are dealing with is so good and so well-written, I feel an obligation to keep the show looking on par with the information we are delivering. I am just trying to make it interesting all the time."

What about the challenge of shooting in 16 mm? Does this affect the look of *Buffy*?

MICHAEL: "To me, it is much harder to make it look interesting. It tends to flatten everything out....The *Buffy* look is just to stimulate the audience's interest and to keep it original. To light it with depth in the frame and put texture in the frame. I use colors and I use pools of light to set up contrast, so that I will have light, dark, light, dark, light, dark. To set up areas of contrast for perspective. Then I will use various colors, warm colors, or cool colors, to help shape and mold the actors a little bit."

What about the Bronze set?

MICHAEL: "It is really one of the easiest sets to shoot. Because I have so much lighting in place, I can leave it very dark. I try to keep the show dark. . . . I let things go into darkness, where another show may not.

"I like to keep it simple. I like to work with as few units as I can. . . . I like camera movement. We use Steadicam. We use all the tools. At night we use helium weather balloons, white balloons that I fly and bounce light off of to light the sets. I just use any tool that I think will do the job. There is not a set pattern. If I need something, they [the producers of *Buffy*] have been very good. I explain to them what I think I will need to do in the scene and why, and they say okay when at all possible."

When we were watching you work today, we thought it looked very much like a tag-team kind of operation between director and DP. Is it difficult for you with the TV system of rotating directors, given that you are the constant and they are the variable?

MICHAEL: "It is difficult, inasmuch as it is physically demanding. It is difficult in the area...that some of our directors who come in don't communicate as well as others. When I work with Joss, he can start a sentence and I can finish it or vice versa, because our minds go the same way about where to put the camera and what we are trying to get. And, of all the directors, he is my favorite director. So we have fun.

"It is very much a collaborative effort when it comes to the camera. [Joss] knows what he wants, and he says, 'What if we put the camera over here; yeah, move it over here instead, that is exactly what I want.' It's great when you can work with somebody like that."

"Passion" was your directorial debut. How was that experience?

MICHAEL: "I had a great script [by Ty King], and I was able to do things. I know the sets, I know the actors. The actors were incredibly helpful to me. All of our producers were helpful to me. They left me alone and just let me do my thing. I think we got a great show out of it."

Do you light actors in different ways?

MICHAEL: "All of our actors on the show photograph so well. They are young. They have character. The camera loves them. If I were working with actors who were twenty years older than this, it would be more difficult, but you can't light these people badly. Sarah takes any kind of light you can throw at her. She takes it and she looks beautiful. The same with Aly and Charisma. And the guys. You can do anything you want and they look good.

"Again, it is really about keeping it interesting and keeping up with the material, the written word. That is where it all comes from, it comes from Joss. These are Joss's visions that I am trying to interpret. The show is about him. That is where it stems from. Sarah brings it all to life, Sarah and the other actors. These kids have such great personalities. They are kids. They are fresh. Sarah, at twenty, being the youngest member of the cast, has as much or more experience than any of the rest. Other than possibly Tony.... But she nails it time and time again. She is right on. She finds the light, she finds the camera angle, she clears herself if another actor blocks her. She is special.

"I love the show. Everybody on the show works so hard to make it into the show that it is. It's not like any other series that I have ever worked on....

"Everybody loves it, even when we complain, even when we get tired ... and we're saying, 'We have been here too many hours, let us go home, and we are hungry'...the bottom line is that we all still love it."

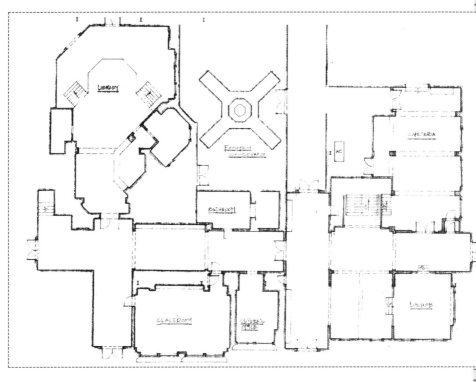

CAREY MEYER

Carey Meyer became the production designer for *Buffy* at the beginning of the second season after working as the first-season art director. That means he heads the art department, designing all the sets and overseeing their construction and decoration. The title came into being because the art director of *Gone with the Wind* had such a huge impact on the set work, and became such an involved person in the production as well, that the producers felt they needed to give the person a more meaningful credit.

When he begins designing for a new episode, Carey gets the script from Joss and the writers, taking careful note of the list of new sets and locations that he and his team "have to sort of make real."

A soft-spoken man, he sits behind his desk in an office filled with sketches, blueprints, a drafting table, color wheels, and assorted design paraphernalia. A number of sketches dot the wall behind him, including one of the new mansion set.

Armed with a degree in architecture, he studied production design at the American Film Institute in Los Angeles. Then he realized that "nobody wants to hire production designers just because they have a degree," and set out to get some practical experience. He worked as a swing man (a grip) on a few productions, then became a production assistant. Around that time, he had a chance to design a "really, really low-budget" independent film. He got together with a friend who was fresh out of architectural school and they created a team for the film—"very unorthodox, but we put a lot of fun into it."

After that, he started getting more design work, in commercials, music videos and a few more small independent films. He was also art-directing for other designers on various low-budget shows. One of those designers hired him to art-direct a show called *VR Five*—a show on which Tony Head was a regular cast member. All this took approximately six years to achieve after graduating from the AFI.

He worked on TV series, including **Nash Bridges**, and then Steve Hardy, the first-season production designer for *Buffy*, asked him to be the first-season art director. Carey was delighted. "Steve was somebody I had been wanting to work with for a really, really long time. We sort of crossed paths several times, but just hadn't had the opportunity to hook up."

So Carey came to *Buffy*. He "just got really into the show, had a great time, and really, really loved working for Steve." They worked together on a feature titled *Denial* with Adam Rifkin during the first-season hiatus.

Hardy decided to concentrate on feature work, so *Buffy* producer Gareth Davies called Carey and asked him to move up to production designer. It was a big opportunity for Carey, and he decided to cement his position by pitching the idea for the Factory, Spike and Dru's lair, which Buffy burns to the ground during the second season.

Carey reminisces that he wanted to prove to Joss that he could design the show, so the Factory set was very important to him. Though he looked at many pictures of factories from different time periods, what eventually inspired him most was an English library from the Craftsman period. Since much of the vampire look of the show is industrial, he enjoyed creating a set that retained that flavor, yet was layered with something more.

"There's this bizarre kind of amalgamation of different styles and things. As long as it has a feel that is cool.…You know, things happen by chance," he says. "It's not like something that you set out with the rule books saying that 'this is going to be this.' It just evolves."

As an example, Carey tells us the genesis of the underground motif for the vampires:

It began with the lair of the Master, the underground church where he was imprisoned. To get to the lair from aboveground, Steve Hardy introduced sewer pipes. Over time, it became established that there was an extensive sewer system beneath the town. As a result, the underground world of the vampires became "industrial, low-ground, cement, dirt, rust, and grime and that kind of stuff."

Carey recalls that when Kendra was scripted to emerge from the cargo bay of a 747, "We had a bunch of curved walls and things from the set, and I said, 'We could make a really great sewer tunnel out of this stuff, and so all of a sudden, we started shooting all this sewer, this great sewer.…"

The sewers got used in more and more creative ways. Floors broke away beneath characters to drop them into the sewers; characters chased vampires down into the sewers; or someone popped up from beneath a manhole or a grate. The underground grotto in "Go Fish" is another extension of the underground sewer theme. As is the cavern of the Zeta Delta Kappas in "Reptile Boy."

Over time, the *Buffy* team also realized that the sewer system worked almost like a "transporter" à la *Star Trek*, allowing them to move from one place to another in a confined area.

"It allows us to get somebody in and out of the set in an interesting fashion and having [a connection] from one set to another . . . getting somebody to go somewhere [while trying] to keep the time line going in real time."

FUMIGATION PARTY
Find a cockroach, get a free drink

It was also very important to the *Buffy* production company because it cut back on the need to go on location and do big night exteriors. It's more technically difficult and expensive to go on location, especially night location. Carey tells us that a typical day shooting on location lasts for fourteen or fifteen hours, while shooting the equivalent amount of footage on a stage takes twelve or thirteen.

"When we're here on the lot," he continues, "we don't have to do a whole night out. We can have a slightly later call and do the work inside on the stage, and move out to our little graveyard and do half a night, then do the same thing the next night. So it's enabled us to keep all the night work in the show, but also not have to go out for a whole night. If you go out, you're going to go out at six o'clock sundown and be out until morning.

"Gareth [the producer] really got excited about building sets this year and bringing the show to the stage as much as possible.... We've been able to just go hog-wild and build tons of stuff."

How much stuff?

CAREY: "On every other show I've done, we've built one or two permanent sets and then built like one and a half, maybe two, sets per episode. With twenty-two episodes, you figure you can have maybe twenty-five or thirty sets. But this show, I've easily done three sets an episode, so on top of eight permanent sets that we have on stage, we've built between sixty and eighty sets this year, easily. And Caroline Quinn (the set designer) has drawn every one of them."

Where do you build all these sets?

CAREY: "Everything is built essentially in the El Niño building or on the stage, The El Niño building is a temporary structure that we built outside to cover up material and have a dry workspace during the rain, because we didn't have enough space inside to build, and sometimes there will be shooting on both stages. We're constantly creating scenery, and we do everything right here. We don't build anything away from here and then bring it here."

How big are the stages?

CAREY: "Stage I is 26,000 feet. Stage II is 19,000 feet. And the third stage [will be] 14,000 square feet, wedged between the two."

Did you have any professional connections with anyone prior to working on *Buffy*?

CAREY: "I knew some of the costume people from working on *VR5*. Cynthia Bergstrom, the costume designer. And I worked for my decorator, David Konoff, as a swing man on my second job in Los Angeles. It was on *Eve of Destruction*. David and I have worked together ever since I moved to Los Angeles; we've known each other for eleven years."

Tell us about the new mansion set.

CAREY: "When we first started conceiving of the mansion and the secret garden, Joss was driving out of the lot one day and stopped his car, and said, 'By the way, we're working on burning the Factory down.'

"It was a really fun set and I really loved it, and I hated to see it go, but you know Joss. I think Joss likes chaos. Which is good. I like it that way. I don't get very precious about [the sets]...you build them for the camera, you film them, and you rip them down.

"And now we were looking at trying to create a new permanent site. I had to think of a way to utilize the same structural stuff and the same space to create the mansion. So I conceived a floor plan that would mesh with the space of the Factory before I even thought about what the mansion would be like. The geography of the set.

"From there, I found a very Gothic mansion, arches and fireplaces and things like that. But what really attracted me was the coloring of the photograph. It was a photo shoot, so there was a very pretty lady in a large dress, standing in the middle of this decrepit place, which had been in an earthquake or something. The vampires have a sort of different look than Sunnydale, which is very pastel and bright in daytime, aboveground. Our underground spaces for the vampires are industrial and dirty. So I really liked the photograph.

"Joss hated it because it was very Gothic. He wanted to stay away from Gothic because that's very Anne Rice. He said, 'Maybe it could be [Art] Deco or something.' I can do Deco, but I wanted to keep it very cement. If you notice, the set looks like cement."

Do you have a special moment where it all just clicked for you?

CAREY: "I feel like that seventy-five percent of the time. I really love putting these sets together, bringing everything to a point of completion. We are able to generate sixty or eighty different spaces, making everything look different...without cramming everything into every nook and cranny. It's something you can be proud of."

MARCIA SHULMAN

A native New Yorker, Marcia loves all things Italiano: the food, the culture, and the language, which she now speaks because she goes every year to Tuscany, where she hopes to eventually retire.

When asked about her professional life and how she came to *Buffy*, she chuckles at the memory. "I was so naive," she says, that when she graduated from college, she went to an employment agency and informed them that she would take their typing tests and all the rest, "but that I really wanted to work in show business."

The agency placed her in a secretarial position at Children's Television Workshop. She was promoted very quickly to the title of talent coordinator, "which had nothing to do with talent. It was more like a production manager kind of function."

A freelance producer had an office next door, and he noticed that not only did Marcia have a photographic memory, but she was obsessed with keeping track of actors and roles: "I always had to know, as long as I can remember, [maybe I was] three years old.... I used to watch credits, look at *TV Guide*, and match the names to the actors. I call myself the Rain Man of casting." The producer informed her that she was a casting director.

As a result of working for CTW, she knew every child actor in New York, and in her capacity there had negotiated contracts. The producer suggested she open her own casting agency, which she did. Her first project was *A Christmas Story*. From then on she did many after-school specials, and then went out to the West Coast to do television. She was on her way back to New York in January 1996 when Gail Berman, her best friend, asked her to talk to Joss about *Buffy*.

She remembers the meeting with fondness: "I think part of it was because I wanted to go home, [so I] threw caution to the wind [with her casting suggestions]. If he didn't like them, I could go home.

"So I said to Joss, 'I read your script and I know casting directors come in with lists and ideas, but I have a problem: Everyone I thought of while I read your script is dead.' And I started naming these really obscure character actors from movies of the '30s and '40s.

I mentioned the name Franklin Pangborn to him. [Pangborn] used to play the butler in Fred Astaire movies."

Marcia chuckles. "Joss said, 'I can't believe it. You're the only person who has ever mentioned that to me. In the *Buffy* movie I made a reference to Franklin Pangborn and they cut it.' It was just such a funny meeting. We have always had that connection. . . . It is really easy to cast for Joss because there is so much trust there. He knows what he wants."

When we asked her about the process of casting for *Buffy*, Marcia explained that she has three different ways of casting: Sometimes when she reads a script, she immediately thinks, "I know who this is." She gets a tape of that actor to show Joss, who knows everybody himself, and he has never disagreed with her suggestion. Sometimes she will jot down a short list of four or five names and ask them to come in and read for the part.

The third process is perhaps what most people think of when they think of casting. Marcia uses it primarily for smaller speaking roles: She breaks down the part, then looks through the voluminous numbers of submissions (she points to an enormous file cabinet brimming with agent submissions), and then she sits down on the floor and looks through all of them. Then she does a pre-read of those actors who make that cut, and then she presents Joss, David Greenwalt, or Gail Berman with a handful of possibilities.

In some ways, she tells us, it is more difficult to cast the smaller roles. Generally, the actors have less experience, and are hungry for a chance to show their stuff. So they "try to do more, but they only have one line to do and then it becomes over the top. It is really hard for somebody to come in and throw it away."

She gives the example of the shoot today, when they were filming the "Buffy gets arrested" scene. When she was casting for the cops' roles, "there were people who came in and they were like, 'FREEZE!' It was like the *Airplane* version. We said, 'This is a cop, he does this every day, these are kids.' Less is more."

She adds, "The thing about *Buffy* is that it is very real. The acting is very real. You can't comment on the show [in your acting]. When I first started casting for the pilot, people would come in and do *Dracula* kind of readings. But now that it has been on the air, people see it, and they get it."

Casting about seven parts per episode, she says that the process takes "as long as you have. It's like water seeking its own level. It's like production: if you have five days to shoot something, it will take five days. If you have eight days, it will take eight....There have been many times in my career where a director I am working for will say, 'It's fine. I got it', and I will just continue to cast, secretly. I have to keep looking. Thank God I have this job."

She adds, "The other very interesting thing about this project as opposed to a lot of stuff is that there are really fun, great, fantastic characters to create. We sort of live in a world of typecasting, and on this show, which is what I love about the show so much, actors get a chance to act and create. These are characters. It is like why you want to be an actor. It is playing. You really don't get a chance to do that on other television shows."

What about the famous "David Boreanaz was walking his dog" story?

MARCIA: "[Angel] was supposed to be in just the first episode. Sort of like a vision. . . . The character was supposed to start working the next day. I said to Joss, 'Just give me one more day. I don't feel like he is there yet.'

"[The person who became David's manager] was looking out the window as David was walking his dog. He's a friend of mine, and he called me and he said, 'I am telling you, I just saw Angel. I can send him.' David walked in and I ran down the hall [to Joss."]

She flips through her casting book. "9-9-96. I wrote, 'He is the guy.'"

How did you know Sarah Michelle Gellar was Buffy?

MARCIA: "We didn't know she was Buffy. I knew Sarah from New York, when she was a kid, as I knew Seth Green from when they were eight years old. At the time we were all trying to find our way to make the show something, its own thing apart from the film. Sometimes it's sort of hard to get a new vision going. So we didn't think of Sarah as Buffy because we thought she [Sarah] was too smart and too grounded and not enough of a misfit in a sense, because Buffy was this outsider. How could Sarah be an outsider? She's so lovely.

"So we brought her in as Cordelia, and she was fantastic as Cordelia. We still kept looking for Buffy. Then when we went to the network, they [knew] that Sarah was a star [from her previous work], and that she could be a Buffy, and that we could do that Buffy. It was a different Buffy. It was a great Buffy."

Then how did you cast a new Cordelia?

MARCIA: "I had met Charisma before, and I brought her in and she just nailed it. She was hysterically funny. . . . She was just great and beautiful and she brought so much to it."

What about Willow?

MARCIA: "Willow was really hard. Because when you think about it, the kind of character Willow is—a sort of shy, insecure person—is the exact opposite of what somebody has to be as an actress. So it was like working against who came in and had the nerve to audition.

"When Alyson came in, we all got her immediately. I had pre-read her first and then brought her to everyone else and we felt good. She just brings so much vulnerability. She makes me cry all the time and she is also funny. She is an 'everygirl.' I think Willow is the kind of character that there is someone like her in high school...or most of the girls in high school are like her."

What about casting Nicholas Brendon as Xander?

MARCIA: "Nicky also came in [via the pre-reading process]. I read him and then I brought him to the guys and every time he came for callback, he brought more and more to it. When we went to the network for everybody to see him, he improvised a line, which was, 'Let's go get some schwarma.' And now we have used it in the show. I think that gave him the part. We all just died and so the part was his."

Tell us about Tony Head as Giles.

MARCIA: "I had brought him in the first day and we all just completely fell in love with him. I was so happy because when you start working for somebody new, you always want the first day of casting to be good. Because you want [your boss] to say, 'Good,' so you can stay for the second day. When everybody responded to Tony the first day, I said to Gail, 'I'm so happy Joss is happy today.' Tony was a no-brainer. Like David [as Angel]."

And the newest regular, Seth Green.

MARCIA: [smiling] "Seth and I...we get each other. When I knew Sarah Michelle Gellar and Seth [in New York], you brought them in on everything. They were really star kids. And now they are star adults, and no surprise."

What about some guest stars?

MARCIA: "James Marsters came in on the pre-read process. But I am always partial to theatrical training on a résumé [which James had]. In New York, it's not even a question. Out here it is very different. With Juliet Landau, I knew her. I got a tape of her and I went in to Joss. Same with Armin Shimerman. Merrick is Richard Riehle, a really wonderful actor I know from New York."

Did you have professional associations with anyone prior to the show?

MARCIA: "When I met Joss, I didn't think it was appropriate to say anything, but when he hired me, I said, 'I have a question for you: is your father Tom Whedon?' When I was just out of college, and working on *Sesame Street*, Tom was a writer on *The Electric Company*. And Gail and I have been best friends for seventeen years, and we get to work together. That is so great for me. That never happens. You know, you get to work with one of your best girlfriends every day, and we have this sharing and this mutual respect. It is an incredible thing."

Do you have any tattoos, scars, or other distinguishing marks?

MARCIA: "Since I started working on this show, I have broken both my ankles. . . . I kept saying, they're going to talk about me like, you know, 'that casting director, the one with the limp.'"

Do you have a special moment?

MARCIA: "Well the David moment, because it was so hard to find [Angel] and he walked in the day before we were shooting, but there are so many moments. This is a really special group.

"Joss has such a complete vision and you sort of come not to expect in your career that [working on a show] is going to be such a cohesive thing. It is crazy to produce this number of shows on this schedule. That goes with the territory. I am always amazed that a group of people can carry out a vision that it is somehow communicated through the writing, and through who Joss is as a person. It is a very unique situation. It is why I want to do *Buffy*."

CYNTHIA BERGSTROM

From the chaos of the set, we enter the relative calm of the costume-design department. At first glance, it seems like either a particularly odd flea market or the private closet of a particularly eclectic dresser. Either way, it's fascinating. Off to the left is the office of the series' costume designer, Cynthia Bergstrom. A former model, Cynthia is tall and beautiful...and an impeccable dresser.

The office is unlike any other we see on our visit. Candles burn brightly within. When she wants a glass of water, Cynthia pours from a crystal decanter. Her dog, Sammy, who has an injured paw, makes himself at home. It's a very soothing retreat for a woman whose job is often the opposite. But you don't hear Cynthia complaining. She loves it. Clothing and fashion have always been her passion.

"I've been doing costumes for about ten years, but I've always been involved in fashion;

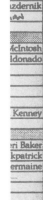

when I was a little girl, I was a runway model and I did some print work. I used to sit with the encyclopedias as a kid and look at the history of clothing. Look at period clothing and historical pieces and patterns to see how the clothes were constructed. I'd watch old movies.

"One of things that really sort of, I think, tied Joss and me together was the fact that we both grew up watching *Creature Feature*. I watched all those bad horror movies, and I loved them. I especially loved the Dracula movies—the vampire movies—because I just was so mystified by everything. I loved the fantasy of it. So that kind of solidified our relationship right there. We had bonded through Bela Lugosi and Christopher Lee."

Cynthia attended Brooks College in Long Beach, California, where she majored in fashion design and merchandising. She entered the working world as a wholesale rep for ESPRIT.

"I handled thirteen western states, and then I went to another company, and I was really longing for something else. I just felt there was something else. Then I remembered watching movies and watching television as a little girl and wondering who put the clothes on these people. I just woke up one day and I said, 'I want to be a costume designer.' It must have been one of those things that was meant to be because a friend called me a week later and said he was doing a film and he needed my help. One thing led to another, and ever since then, I have been designing."

That initial film was a low-budget horror piece called *Zombie High,* with Virginia Madsen. Though it was never what she set out to do, it seems Cynthia's early love of horror films set a course for her. From that first picture, she worked on several other horror films, all the way up to the smash hit *Scream,* which is what drew the attention of *Buffy*'s producers.

"As I recall, Joss really liked the way the kids looked, because they were so believable; they were so real," she says. "So they tracked me down. I'm not one hundred percent sure on that story, but that is what I've gathered from Joss and the producers."

Interestingly, though she worked on so many horror films, Cynthia confesses to a distaste for most of the current crop.

"I like the older ones," she says. "I don't like the new horror films. I don't like slash gore. I like stories. Like in this show [*Buffy*]. There is nothing like it out there. It is fantasy, yet it is real at the same time. A lot of the story lines are so metaphoric for what really goes on in life."

Cynthia buys much of the show's "contemporary" wardrobe (as opposed to historical costumes) in stores in Los Angeles. Some designers send her things directly, such as Cynthia Rowlie and Vivian Tam. In L.A., she often shops Fred Siegel, Barney's, American Rag, Contempo Casuals, Rampage, Macy's, Neiman Marcus, Traffic (in the Beverly Center), Bloomingdale's, and the Tommy Hilfiger store on Rodeo Drive.

"I really go just about everywhere," she says.

On historical or "period" costumes, there is a great deal of research involved. Cynthia enjoys the challenge.

"I look at costume books," she explains. "I'll pick a painter that I particularly like that was of that time and look at his treatments of color. I have some books here and I have tons of books at home. Sometimes I'll call the research houses and I'll have them pull things for me, but I am typically a pretty hands-on designer, so I like to do my own research. I always figure there is something that I'm going to see that nobody else is going to see. I go to museums and I study paintings; knowing your periods is part of being a costume designer. Knowing the construction of a garment; being able to look at something and being able to say, 'This is the sixteenth century; this is the seventeenth century.' It is important to know those things. I do continually study, and also movies are a great way to study periods, you know. You can always turn on AMC and catch those period films."

It isn't just the look of the clothes that's important, however. A Hollywood costume designer has to worry about other things, including how the clothes *sound*. It sounds like a joke, perhaps, but it isn't. Cynthia puts rubber soles on the bottoms of all the actors' shoes so they don't make noise that could be distracting if picked up by the sound equipment during shooting.

"I've taken fabrics and washed them in softener," she adds. "Especially rayon, because it can get kind of noisy. Heat will soften the fabric as well."

The clothing also has to be treated to fireproof it.

"Everything has to be of natural fibers: wool, cotton…rayon is actually a natural fiber. But I can't use any synthetics because they'll burn. We have a certified fire-proofer that does it. It's dipped and sprayed. A lot of things are taken into consideration when the clothes go on these people. Buffy has multiple costumes. She is either getting dunked in water or she is fighting, whatever might be happening, she needs a change."

Cynthia needs to have a philosophy about each character she dresses. To understand exactly how that is developed, it would help to know how she analyzes them. Jenny Calendar for instance.

"Though she was a computer instructor, she was a very beautiful woman," Cynthia explains of Jenny. "She was a combination of old-world guile and the kids she was teaching. A combination of her past as well as today's technology. I knew that she was a Gypsy and that she was sent to watch over Angel and that her family had cast a spell on him. With all that in mind, I gave her colors and silhouettes and textures and patterns that were somewhat of that Romanian Gypsy influence. If you notice, her colors have sort of a vibrant, earthy tone, and I used really tiny little paisley, and everything was new yet old. Her jewelry was always some sort of reproduction of a vintage piece. She was the easiest one to find things for, because I was so specific about what I wanted for her. It was really hard to stop looking for clothes for her when I was out in the stores. Cindy [Rosenthal, one of Cynthia's costumers] and I would go around shopping, and she'd say 'You know, Jenny isn't on the show anymore.'

"Then there's Angel," she continues. "Angel's shirts have to be spectacularly different and European. But lot of times you don't get all of the detail on TV that is really there in his wardrobe. I've taken that into consideration and—especially now that he is bad—I've really toned down a lot of detailing on his shirts. The clothes on him should be sexy, whether he is good or bad. I experimented with lighter colors in the beginning, when he was still good; it just didn't work, it wasn't really his thing so I stuck with the darker colors."

Drusilla has also changed, Cynthia notes. As Angel went from good to bad, Dru went from weak to strong.

"We first saw her in her ivory gown that to me was a timeless image of a woman," she recalls. "She was killed in 1860, and this dress is about the late 1800s, from the romantic period. She started out as a very sort of insane, willowy, soft, sickly, consumptive woman. I was really taking off from the women that you sometimes saw in the Dracula movies from the '60s. I sort of saw her like that, but not quite so, you know, girly. I toned down the dress, and I just gave her an empire waist. Then, as she grew weaker, I put her in bad clothing, and I had that nightgown she walked out of the Factory in [in the second part of "What's My Line?"]. Then when she does her ritual, she's in a black dress. I wanted something that looked very medieval, but yet still had a sense of the future. It needed to look powerful yet soft at the same time, that is why I chose velvet."

Then there's Drusilla's paramour:

"Spike is just a bad-ass character," Cynthia says. "He's just great. He's really funny, and he's quirky, and he's got this white-blond hair and this English accent. He just needs to be a bat; to just sweep in like a bat. His coat cost $1,600, and we literally beat the heck out of it. We took down the shine and sandpapered and really distressed it. And his clothes are also just a bit distressed."

Cynthia loves the writing on the show, particularly when it offers her a challenge.

"When I am able to do something different, when I see an opportunity to build something, that's exciting," she says. "In 'Inca Mummy Girl,' there was a dance where we had people coming dressed as their nationality, and that was so fun. Then, of course, the 'Halloween' episode; it wasn't just dressing people in Halloween costumes, it was doing Buffy in her dress and Cordelia in her cat suit, and I just went to Joss and asked, 'Can I do something a little fun?' It is such a wonderful opportunity, because I know they trust me. I am given a lot of creative freedom. It's a great feeling."

It's impossible not to ask if Cynthia envies the wardrobe she buys for the characters. What does she like?

"I like all of it. Fridays I'm in jeans and T-shirts. But I have a tendency to dress a little conservatively. Some of the miniskirts that I put the girls in, I'll try them on. It is so fun. Little black miniskirts and knee-high boots, which I did end up buying a pair of for myself. It is so much fun to dress like that. I couldn't wear that to work, of course. In my personal life, I'll go a little bit more out on the edge, but at work I have to keep things rather serious."

JEFF PRUITT

It's impossible to look at Jeff Pruitt and believe a word of his résumé. He seems far too young to have risen so high in his chosen field. Now stunt coordinator for *Buffy*, Jeff has held that position on more than fifteen feature films and five television series, including *Mighty Morphin Power Rangers* and *The New Adventures of Robin Hood*. Previously, he had performed stunts in dozens of films and TV series.

Jeff is the only American stunt coordinator to have belonged to an Asian stunt team. He has specialized in Hong Kong–style stunts for more than ten years. He has more than twenty years experience in martial-arts combat, and, surprisingly, Jeff himself directed and edited more than half of each episode for the second season of *Power Rangers*.

During our visit to the set, Jeff was omnipresent. Setting up stunts, or "gags," he was informative and inclusive at all times. We interviewed him at a picnic table on the grass by the cemetery set on the lot. He was friendly and forthcoming and broke the news that he was engaged to Sophia Crawford, the stunt double for Sarah Michelle Gellar. Sophia is also one of only four women in America who do both stunts and martial-arts fight sequences. The two seem quite evenly matched. When they see each other on the lot, their faces light up.

He's at the top of his game. But one must wonder, what leads a person to get into this very dangerous game to begin with?

"In the '60s I watched *The Green Hornet, Our Man Flint*; *Wild Wild West* was a big show. All of these shows and the 007 films—they all got me interested in stunts. I knew that's what I wanted to do, and that is where I headed—especially with the martial-arts action. *The Green Hornet* was the first time I had ever seen someone leaping and kicking and I knew this is what I wanted to do.

"From the time I was a kid, I trained in martial arts and I did motocross racing and I raced cars and things like that. As things progressed, I started working on films and also worked as a production assistant and as a cameraman and things like that, until I was able to break through. This is a tough business. Finally, when I made it to Hollywood in the late '80s, it took me a couple of years to get in the door here, even though I had some credits. I started coordinating some shows here in about '89, and that's all I've been doing."

Though his time is at a premium, Jeff knows the value of his fans. He spends time on the official *Buffy* Web site talking to them. "I have a whole closet full of sweatshirts and T-shirts made by the fans," he says happily. "They know all about me and Sophia and our show."

"I normally block everything out with my story boards and choreograph the fight with Sophia. Then Sarah and I will watch it. We shoot closeups of her doing the stunts, and then we edit it together."

Now that Jeff's brought her up, of course, we want to know everything about his love, Sophia Crawford.

"Sophia trained in Hong Kong," Jeff says. "She came here and starred in a film series. When I did *Power Rangers,* I hired her to be the Pink Ranger, so she did all the stunts for the Pink Ranger. We worked together for four years before *Buffy* ever started."

They didn't come as a package deal, however. Sophia was on the series from the beginning. After the first season, a new stunt coordinator was hired, but he didn't work out after the first episode. "I wanted to come in and meet Joss, but he was nervous because of us being a couple. He'd seen my work, and he liked my work but he thought *Well, we've had problems with people who are couples and then have a fight and then they don't want to work together.* For the girl who does all the fighting for Buffy and the guy who designs all the fights…for them not to be able to get along would be terrible. But, he gave me a chance, and I started working, then he saw that we worked together well."

In the early days, though, Jeff and Sophia spent a lot of time just checking each other out.

"For two years, she would wear the Pink Ranger helmet and she would be looking at me. But I couldn't see that she was looking at me and I would try to work on my story boards, but I was really looking at her. We kept doing this for so long. Finally, during the Power Ranger movie, we started dating and we never stopped. And we are going to get married now."

Jeff reveals their impending nuptials casually. You'd never know there was a moment of anxiety that spurred on his proposal. It was after a stunt that, Jeff says, "scared me so much that I decided that I had better marry her now.

"It was during the episode 'Phases.' Sophia had to walk onto a net, and the effects guys had rigged the net with 300 pounds of counterweight. I told them that I weigh 150 pounds and normally when we do stunts like this, I just jump down and jerk her straight up. They felt that they needed extra weight. They said they had tested it with some dummy weights before and it was okay. So we did it and she shot up….We had the camera up at about thirty feet in the air. She went past the camera and came out at the top of the net. Then as she

was falling, she grabbed hold of the outside of the net and snapped to a halt before she hit the ground, and it snapped her neck back. She was okay. She got up and she did it again. We took all the weight out and we did it the right way. After that, that same night, I asked her to marry me.

"We do so many hard stunts, and we're not blasé. Sometimes Sophia and I will fight each other, I have her really kick me, really hit me, because we come from that background of more Hong Kong–style fighting. They're not really used to seeing that, so it freaks them out a little bit, but it's our job; it seems like normal, everyday stuff to us. It was just that one time it did bother me, because I wasn't in control of it. As long as we're in control, it's okay. Equipment failure I don't like."

BUFFY THE VAMPIRE SLAYER

Stunt Coordinator: Jeff Pruitt

PAGE 13.

BUFFY & KENDRA EXCHANGE HAND TECHNIQUES AND BLOCKS BUFFY'S PUNCH...

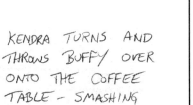

KENDRA TURNS AND THROWS BUFFY OVER ONTO THE COFFEE TABLE - SMASHING IT TO PIECES.

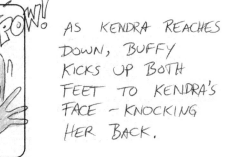

AS KENDRA REACHES DOWN, BUFFY KICKS UP BOTH FEET TO KENDRA'S FACE - KNOCKING HER BACK.

Even though he's the coordinator, Jeff doesn't miss out on the action. Anytime he gets the itch, he jumps right in.

"Sometimes I put myself in just for the heck of it. I still like getting out there. As a matter of fact, in the episode "Lie to Me," you see Buffy whaling on this guy with a trash-can lid. That's me. That was one of those days when I told her to just go ahead and hit me as hard as you can. So every shot she was hitting me and the crew was just freaking out. Certain stunt guys I know will do that. "

Though at times, fights are described in the series' scripts, and Jeff doesn't necessarily follow those directions.

"I find out what the feeling is before, during, and after the fight. Unless there is something specific, some specific prop or someplace a character has to be...then I know that's where they have to end up. But what happens during the whole thing is pretty much up to me. I guess Joss has come to trust me pretty much on that.

"This final fight that we are going to do [for season two] involves some very specific attitude between Buffy and Angel and how they feel about each other. So that was not as fancy as some of our other fights but more emotional. Each fight has a different flavor to it."

In the case of Buffy, because Sophia has exactly the same body type as Sarah and the ability to do fights and stunts, she does all the doubling for Buffy. For other characters, however, Jeff chooses from a range of stunt people whose services he calls upon depending on what the particular fight calls for.

Of his favorite moments on the set, Jeff says there is one that doesn't have anything to do with stunts or fighting. That would be working with John Ritter.

"'Ted' is not a great fighting episode," he says. "But I enjoyed John Ritter. Now there was a nice guy to work with. He was so sick that day, and he brought me my pads back all separated neatly and put in little plastic bags and gave them back to me. No one had ever done that before. They usually just rip them off and fling them. I have never met a guy like him before, he is so great. He's super."

Despite the fact that there isn't much fighting in "Ted," Jeff remembers that episode for another reason. After shooting a fight from several angles, one particular shot was included that was from the wrong angle.

"There is a miss," Jeff says incredulously. "There is an actual miss. There is a high angle of John Ritter's stunt double just before he goes upstairs, and it is a big miss. I made a big deal about that, because it makes me look bad. But those things happen."

One of the things that Jeff enjoys most about working on *Buffy* is that it is a story-driven show.

"I've walked into a room full of executives as they are rewriting a script," he recalls. "These are guys whose experience in movies is watching movies when they were in law school. That was their experience in making films. But there they are, saying, 'And then the old master trains them....' and I'm saying, 'We've seen all of that before a million times.' So many shows have been like that. But now, with *Buffy*, the writers are actually in charge of the show. God, it's great. It is original, it is witty, it is different, and it is cool."

TODD MCINTOSH AND JERI BAKER

Todd McIntosh is more than merely the makeup supervisor for *Buffy the Vampire Slayer*. He is friend, father-confessor, and sometimes even chef to many of the people who work on the series with him. Chef? Well, don't tell Hanna Mourad, who is the on-set chef for the series, but Todd has been known to whip up a meal now and again. One particular night, he cooked for David Boreanaz, Nicholas Brendon, and James Marsters, who all then went online on the official *Buffy* web site's posting board. Marsters called the meal "amazing," and everyone enjoyed chatting on the posting board. That's something else Todd does a lot of—taking care of the fans. Everyone talks about the series' star, Sarah Michelle Gellar, as being nurturing. It's a sure bet that Todd gives her a run for her money.

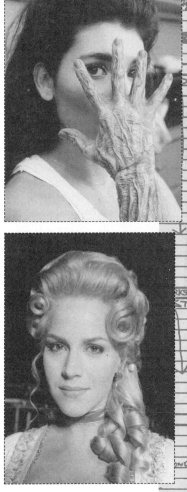

He's also one of the best makeup men in the business.

After the morning's makeup session is through, Todd and hair department head Jeri Baker invite us into the trailer where the makeup and hair crew work. The room is festooned with photographs of actors and stuntmen in very nasty-looking monster makeup and, of course, in the glamour makeup that the cast wears while filming.

As makeup supervisor, Todd is also the department head, and liaison to Optic Nerve, the special makeup effects house that creates the prosthetics for the show.

"The design phase of everything that we do goes on between Joss and whoever upstairs needs to do the budget and John Vulich at Optic Nerve," Todd explains. "They design, then they send me the drawings. I look at the drawings, give my input, then when it comes to actually doing the makeup, they drop the appliances on my doorstep. I pick them up and take them to work. I put the makeup on that day, and the coloring and finishing of the makeup is my end of the deal. So it's a complete symbiotic group among Jeri Baker, John Vulich, the actor, myself, and, of course, Joss, who comes in to see what I've done with the coloring and okay it."

The department includes Todd, his second-in-command, John Maldonado, Jeri Baker, Dugg Kirkpatrick and Francine Shermaine. When necessary (for instance, when there is a larger-than-usual number of vampires in an episode), Todd and Jeri both use union makeup and hair artists for additional coverage.

As for how long the actors have to sit in the makeup chair, the answer differs, of course, depending on exactly what needs to be done that day.

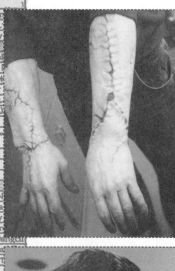

"Beauty makeup on our show takes no more than half an hour," Todd says. "The monsters, if you're doing regular vampires, take about one to two hours. If I do it, I can get it down to forty-five minutes, but if new people who have never done the show do it, they all get two hours to put one on. The removal time is about half an hour to forty-five minutes, whether it has been put on to last all day or put on for five minutes."

He notes that when an actor, in this instance, David Boreanaz, has to morph into vamp face only briefly, they are able to put the vampire prosthetic on with a water-soluble glue.

"It's not very stable and won't stay on for long, but we can peel it off without damaging the skin too much," Todd explains.

The conversation turns to the subject of stunt doubles, and the difficulty involved in making them look like the stars they're doubling for on film.

"Unlike feature films again, where you can take the time to make a prosthetic so that the stunt double looks like the actor, we don't have that luxury," Todd explains. "Buffy's stunt double is Sophia Crawford. Sophia is a magnificent martial-arts person. There are times when we will be watching the show and it's her, but it's so perfect, and Sarah and Sophia have found a way to look like each other. Sarah watches Sophia, and Sophia watches Sarah, and the two of them have merged into twins, in their expressions, turns and movements. You really have a magnificent combination of actors and stunt people, hair and makeup people."

Obviously, McIntosh and Baker are true professionals, individuals working a fine craft that is often overlooked. But how does one prepare for a career doing makeup or hair in film and television? Good question, but one without a simple answer. Or, perhaps, many different answers. For instance, one would be hard put to find two individuals who came at the industry from more divergent origins.

Todd McIntosh knew what he wanted to do from childhood.

"I was about seven years old, watching *Dark Shadows* on TV, and I was so totally fascinated with what I was seeing," he recalls. "*Star Trek* was on at the same time. I started to do what makeup I could, to make myself into a vampire or whatever, with my mother's eyeliner pencil that was lying around. I used to Scotch tape my ears into a point like Mr. Spock, and that moved me into theater makeup.

"I was in the theater by the time I was twelve, doing makeup. I was at a TV studio at seventeen, being paid to do makeup, and in my early twenties I was chairman of the local union in Vancouver, doing makeup full-time. I moved here when I was in my thirties. So I'm over twenty years in the business now. But it all started with *Dark Shadows*, and that, to me, was a perfect makeup show. Again, you had beauty makeup—you had Angelique, you had all the pretty young girls—your regular characters and your monsters. It was the closest possible thing that I could ever hope for as a model for this show.

"For me, *Buffy* is like coming full circle. I'm doing a vampire show, which I've always been fascinated by, doing beauty and horror, and it's a chance to really shine in all of those fields. There have to be at least 800 makeup artists in the Hollywood local. Out of that 800, there are really not very many who do beauty makeup and special makeup in equal quantities, with equal dedication. For those of us who do that, and like to shine that way, this is the place. This is the best gig in town."

Jeri Baker's background couldn't be more different from Todd's. She didn't start out with any intention of working in Hollywood. In fact, she was in medicine.

"I was a surgical nurse for thirteen years," she explains. "I developed an allergy to one of the chemicals we used. Allergies are all the same. If you don't find out what the allergy is, you keep on getting exposed to it until your body builds up so much resistance to it that it is dangerous. By the time they figured out what was wrong with me, I was too toxic, and they told me I wasn't going to survive. For two years, the therapist was trying to keep me alive and when they finally did, they decided I had to have a new career, so they came in and retrained me.

"Hairdressing was the only thing that they felt was cheap enough to put me through. So I went through hairdressing school, but I had problems with some of the chemicals. Then a makeup artist in Burbank named Laurie Stein helped me do a project, and he liked my work, and we started talking and he asked me what my background was, and when I told him he was quite interested. He felt my nursing background and art talent would be great assets. So I did all the training films for the medical corps for the Navy and makeup simulation and then one thing led to another....When you're breaking into the industry you have to do both hair and makeup and climb the ladder. So that's what I did.

"I was on a television series that turned union, and I had to make a decision," she recalls.

The union required that members be one thing or the other. Jeri was leaning toward makeup, but was already working with one of the best-known makeup artists in the business. In order to stay with the show, and make a decent salary, she chose to do the hair on the series. She hasn't regretted it for a moment.

"In nursing, you're problem-solving, and in this you're doing the same sort of thing. You have to figure things out, some things I didn't know, or weren't possible, but I made do and it worked. For instance, one of my first experiences was with a wig that the director hated. He didn't know what he was going to do since the whole story hinged on the actor—who had very short hair—having long hair. I took the wig and took the actor with me and opened up the wig and started to find all these little bands inside. I cut them out and placed each one of them at the hairline, all the way around, so it looked more like hair. It became what today would be called hair extensions, but in 1990 hair

extensions for Caucasians weren't that big. It wasn't something you were taught in school, just something you had to figure out.

"That's the fun part about the job. A lot of our work is pulled out of our imagination and has to be done quickly. Sometimes it's the best work we do, because it's done with a whole lot of energy. Without a doubt, it's a craft; it's a skill, but then after you learn a skill, you have to be able to take it further than that."

Jeri has her own take on vampires as well, one that ties in rather nicely with the blood-suckers on *Buffy*.

"Vampires are the ultimate seduction. This a creature that can seduce on any level. It can seduce a dog, a child, an adult, an elderly person, on their level. There has to be a certain amount of physical attraction for anyone to start a seduction. If you make everything ugly, there is no seduction. You have to make it so that you're pulled into it. Like, I want to be there but 'ooh that's bad.' That gives the woman the feeling of 'Wow, the big bad boy.' That's what Angel came out of. It had to be beautiful. There had to be something about them that you would rather be with them than be safe."

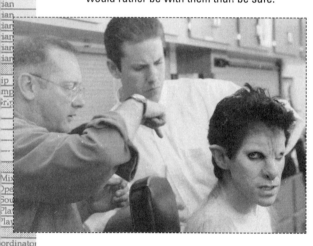

One aspect of doing makeup for television and motion pictures that people rarely consider is the lighting. How a set is lit is something that makeup artists must consider very carefully.

"The makeup that you use for film and television is already color-balanced for the lighting and for the circumstance. So I don't need to change the makeup for each scene when they change the lighting. But, if I walk through a scene and everything is amber and I didn't expect it to be, then all my colors have to be changed. I may have to take makeup out there [onto the set] and do the final touches in that lighting.

"The first season, we had a character called the Master who required a lot of subtle highlight, shadow, and coloring because he was so white. Every time I did it, he went out onto the set and the thing was lit for candlelight [amber] and everything was gone, and he just looked like a big, blobby head. So I finally had them light this end station [in the makeup trailer] with gels that matched the set. I would come in here, turn out all the lights, close the doors and paint the appliances under that light so it would look normal. I finally got this system down, painted the appliances, put them on him, took them up to the set and they hit him with a white spotlight! I don't know, you do the best you can. That's all you can do.

"The lighting alters all the colors. Sometimes you've got a problem area on a prosthetic; if the light is coming from one direction, the edge is huge. If it's coming from another direction, it's gone. So we often coordinate with Michael Gershman, the director of photography. I tell him what my problems are, and he does what he needs to do to adjust it. If he sees something that he thinks I can help him with, I go in and do that. We work very hand-in-hand, and Michael is really good that way. He's one of the few I have found who is very open to communication both ways. A lot of DPs are just, 'That makeup doesn't look any good. Change it,' when really the problem is the light. There's no back-and-forth communication. But we work very well on this show."

Despite that teamwork, however, Todd and Jeri agree that some mistakes just can't be helped.

"Sometimes you can't do anything about it. We knew it was a mistake, we knew going in it was a problem, but couldn't get it changed," Todd says.

"People are walking in and out of lights," Jeri notes. "At one point, they may look absolutely fabulous, and the next thing they walk into the light and it's turning them a whole other hair color, and you just look at it and people are saying, 'Look how it keeps changing back and forth!' The light sources make the effect."

Because synthetic hair will change color differently, and because it almost never looks quite right, Jeri tries to use real hair whenever possible. Even better when a desired 'look' can be achieved with an actor's own hair.

"Ninety percent of the time, we try to work with what we have, because of the lighting problems," she notes. "Nothing looks more wonderful than someone's natural hair. If I have to do a piece, I like to try to match the person's hair or try to use the hair piece in the back of the head, with the front of their own, and try to make a great color blend. Wigs are wigs. You can spend $5,000 on a wig, but it doesn't necessarily mean the audience is going to buy it. That's when you really have to talk to everyone involved and try to come up with a solution that works best. The worst thing that can happen to a hairdresser is that you get this gorgeous hairstyle going and then somebody comes along and dumps a hat on it, or they put the actor up against a dark background when they're brunette and the hair just kind of fades off into the background. We spend so much time trying to make something happen, and then all of a sudden it's gone in the light."

Talk in the trailer turns to the looks of individual characters, and then Jeri drops a bombshell. She whips out a head shot of James Marsters before he was cast as Spike. The dashingly handsome brunette actor looks more like a soap opera star than a punk bloodsucker.

"He was so flamboyant that he needed to be either one way or the other, either have black hair or white hair," Jeri says. "But since Drusilla has dark hair, I thought he should go to white hair. It needed to be a statement one way or the other. So they were afraid, and asked that I just make him blond, so I sent him out to a friend of mine, asking that he be made white. I took a chance. His hair was very curly and very close to his head, but when he came back after having his hair bleached, the texture of the hair had changed. So when I cut it, I came up with this beautiful wave pattern because the bleach allowed the hair to mellow out. He walked into wardrobe, put his outfit back on and walked in front of Gail and Joss, and they all just went crazy. 'That's what we wanted all the time!' When everybody's ideas come together, it's the best.

"That's what I really love about Joss and Gail and David, is that they have allowed us and trusted me with changing some things that they were kind of not sure would be the way to go, but they trusted me. They've let me do some really cool things. I don't think Spike would be Spike without it. We had a character called the Master, and his original design came up with hair. Todd showed me the pictures of it, and I said no, I didn't want that. So he said, you go fight for it.

"I went to the producers and told them that he had to be bald. So they said, 'You're a hairdresser, why are you going to take someone's hair off?' 'Well, this is a character that's been dead for a long time and has no human characteristics and no heart for anyone. Hair is a very human characteristic. If you take hair away from them, all of a sudden they lose their human connection. Just like that. That's the way I think we should go with it.' They agreed to give it a shot and the Master was amazingly cold and cruel and heartless, and you felt nothing for him in any sense as a human being. As a hairdresser, it's hard to give up the idea of hair, but Todd is a magnificent artist, and we talked about it, and he agreed with me that it was a good fight, and he fought for it."

Back to Todd and monsters. It's interesting to note that the maestro waxes poetic about beauty makeup and about monster makeup. One wonders if he has a preference.

"*Buffy* is the perfect show for me, because I like both in equal amounts," he explains. "I started out wanting to do special makeup, but I was raised in Vancouver, and at that time there was nothing up there. Now they have *Outer Limits*, but at that time I couldn't get a job. There was nothing. So I taught beauty makeup and ended up doing beauty makeup in film and television more than effects. While it wasn't my first love, I grew to enjoy it very much, and this is an example of the kind of show that is a perfect meld between the two. I enjoy that more than anything else about it. There's not one makeup I like more or one person I like working on more. People keep asking me what's the most difficult makeup, what's the most elaborate—it's the whole show. It's being able to have two stations set up at a time and jump from a beauty makeup to a prosthetic makeover, all within the same morning. That's what makes this exciting, for me anyway."

Todd is also quick to note that one isn't necessarily more elegant than the other. Though it might be hard to imagine for those who have seen too many low-budget horror films.

"The trouble is that people seem to think that if you throw a lot of blood on something, everybody goes, 'Ooh, isn't that wonderful?'" he notes. "But if you take the blood away and take a good photograph of the work, it's often really crude, you can see the edges sticking out, where they've used a false strip and it's not even glued down properly."

"I'm never going to do shows with a lot of gore. I have done them. I did *Hideaway*, for example, but most of the gore effects were cut out at the end to get the ratings down. But that's not where true artistry lies. [Watch] a movie that Dick Smith has done, such as *Marathon Man*. When the old man gets his throat cut in the street? I have gone over that frame by frame on laser disk, and it is so beautifully done, so artistically done, I can't even see the edges. There are very few zombie-type films that would stand up to that kind of scrutiny. So that level of artistry is what I'm striving for. I want each thing, whether it's a vampire that we paint or Sarah's beauty makeup, to be as good as it can be, as polished as it can be, within the realm of TV."

Soon, the talk begins to turn toward fans and how the television audience perceives what it has seen on the small screen.

"A lot of people want to know 'How do I get my hair to look like so-and-so's?'" Jeri observes. "They go to their hairdresser with a picture and say, 'I want to look like that.' Now, first of all, styling hair in the television industry does not necessarily have anything to do with a haircut. It's styling, and the audience has to realize that this is a style that is maintained all day long. They don't walk out of the trailer and never get touched again, like normal people in the regular world. They have somebody chasing behind them, making sure that every hair is in place. So to take a photograph of an actor and expect to look like that, they can cut your hair the same way, but if you don't do the styling, all you're stuck with is a haircut you don't know what to do with.

"I think the most important thing is that everybody needs to seek their own look, what makes them beautiful. It has nothing to do with what the actress looks like and nothing to do with wanting to be like them. You have to be yourself. I'm hoping that's what has evolved on *Buffy*. She kinda looks like herself. She doesn't try to create a hairstyle that takes hours to do. Fifteen minutes. Sometimes you have to work with the hair that you have. She is sixteen years old. I don't want her hair to look like she came out of a salon. I'm hoping that we're creating things that people can do, they're not difficult to do. It's a matter of really liking your face and being able to stand in front of the mirror and move [your hair] around until you balance your face."

Todd is very pleased that Jeri brought up the fact that hair and makeup are constantly touched-up during a day's shooting.

"People who don't really know our business seem to think that we come in in the morning, put the makeup on, and we go home. It is the weirdest thing. What do they think we do all day?" he asks, mystified. "We are there every minute of the day during filming, making sure that everything is still on. Lipstick has to look fresh for fifteen hours, and that's our job, to wipe their noses and make sure there are no problems. Every five minutes, you are going in and primping."

On a side note, our experiences on the set bear this out. Todd and Jeri seem to be there before almost anyone else arrives, and they're on set until "cut" is called for the last time that night.

The conversation continues on the subject of the Hollywood image versus reality, and it's clear that both parties wish people knew a bit more about Hollywood. Perhaps people wouldn't be quite so uptight about their appearance.

"They went through a period in movies where they would take the classic Greek face, with a set of actual measurements that the Greeks used in their sculptures. They measured the distance between the eyes, lined up the nostrils with a certain part of the features, and came up with a mathematical formula. That's what it was all about, looking at an actress's face and seeing how far off it is from 'perfection,' and then adjusting the face through the illusion of makeup to make it perfect. That's insane in the same way that all of the current controversy about what a woman's perfect figure is and weight is. It's insane to try to fit everybody into a common mold. What we do in the movies is all illusion. It's all about creating something that isn't real.

"When you've got Marlene Dietrich up on that screen, that's not what she looked like when she went shopping at Ralph's. She had this mask that was built for her, the makeup illusion, which included lighting and film stock, and everybody worked together. In the old days, for example, when an actress stepped out of makeup, she went straight onto the set and got her closeups. Then they would pull back and do the master. Because it was fresh and she looked perfect."

In case anyone was wondering, by the way, the men wear makeup, too.

"Xander [for instance] doesn't wear a ton of makeup. He wears a foundation. We do have a problem when his beard shows. It's a little heavy, so to make him look younger we do a beard correction. It's not a huge amount of makeup."

And on the subject of the actors in the makeup trailer, Jeri really enjoys watching them. Sarah, for instance, "comes into character" in the chair.

"I start putting in her hair pieces, and before I know it, she's moving like this, like that. It's really fun," she says.

Working on *Buffy* is a delight for both of them, and Todd is always amused to hear from other makeup artists.

"I got a little bit of a last laugh," he says. "On the first season, before we hit the air, I could not get a makeup artist to come and help me on the show. '*Buffy the Vampire Slayer*, I don't think so.' This season, they're calling us, two or so a week."

JOHN VULICH

As the driving force behind Optic Nerve Studios, the company that supplies *Buffy the Vampire Slayer*'s demons and other nasties, John Vulich is living his childhood dream.

"I'm the classic kid who had the *Famous Monsters* magazines kind of stuck behind my text-book in class. I've always had an interest in filmmaking. I was always making 8 mm horror films, and, inevitably, I ended up doing my own effects for them. I was just a kid in Fresno, and I learned how to do effects as a by-product of being interested in being a filmmaker."

Vulich's interest in filmmaking consumed him. So much, in fact, that he dropped out of high school his senior year to work on an installment of the *Friday the 13th* movie series.

"At a certain point, I realized that I needed to go and get a job, and really all I knew how to do was make monsters and make films. It seemed more practical to try doing something like makeup effects rather than trying to jump into directing right off the bat. It seemed more accessible to me, I think."

Because of his interest in horror and monsters, John made contacts with makeup wizards like Tom Savini. Savini promised that the next time he worked in L.A., he would hire Vulich, and he "stuck to his word."

Vulich and his team at Optic Nerve came to *Buffy* via an existing relationship with the series' makeup maestro, Todd McIntosh.

"We had originally worked with Todd on a series called *Great Scott*, which was really kind of a neat Walter Mitty kind of show," Vulich notes. "That was a clever show, but it never really found an audience. There was another [similar] show called *Pete and Pete*, which is on Nickelodeon and is one of my secret favorite shows."

Unbeknownst to Vulich, two of *Buffy*'s staff writers, Dean Vitale and Rob Des Hotel, actually wrote for *Pete and Pete*. Another bit of kismet among a cast and crew who seem to have been literally made for one another.

But, back to *Great Scott*, where Vulich hooked up with Todd McIntosh. That relationship led to Optic Nerve working on a pair of Mel Brooks films, including *Robin Hood: Men in Tights*. Optic Nerve went on to become the special makeup and prosthetics provider for *Babylon 5*. When McIntosh began to work on the "presentation reel" for *Buffy*—essentially a *Reader's Digest* version of the pilot to show to network execs—another special makeup and prosthetics firm was being used by the producers. Fortunately for Optic Nerve, the other firm turned out to be too expensive; McIntosh recommended them, and Optic Nerve was in!

"It was a very good opportunity," Vulich notes. "At that point, we had done three or four years of *Babylon 5*, and I feel I learned a lot of the ins and outs of getting it done on that kind of [severely deadline-oriented] schedule."

Indeed, *Babylon 5* required Optic Nerve to create special makeup effects in extraordinary volume and with incredible speed. In comparing their job on *B5* to any of the *Star Trek* spinoffs, Vulich believes that the amount of work his team does for *B5* is "certainly comparable, if not more work—or more elaborate work—than on *Star Trek*.

"So much of what we do, other than trying to learn, is trying to work faster and [find] ways to cut corners without really affecting the quality," he notes, before confirming that Optic Nerve will also be working on the "sequel series" to *Babylon 5*, currently titled *The Crusade*.

For all three shows, the amount of work Optic Nerve has done continues to pay off in other, very cost-conscious ways.

"We have a decent backlog of a lot of, like, backs of the heads, ears, necks—all kinds of different things—that we tend to recycle from project to project. We kind of pull a 'Mr. Potato Head.' We'll have four or five sets of demon horns, two or three sets of demon ears. Out of respect to the original people that we had built it for, we won't necessarily reuse the same face twice. But we might use the back of the head, something that's not as recognizable."

Buffy has been a challenge for a number of reasons; among them, of course, are the eight-day shooting schedule (each episode is shot in eight days) and the tight budget. But what's the biggest challenge the Optic Nerve team has had to face on the show?

"I would say maybe the Hellmouth, in the first season's finale," Vulich replies. "We only had a week and a half to do this really large, elaborate creature. If we were to have done it for a feature, it could easily have cost half [*Buffy*'s per-] episode budget."

Obviously, Vulich had to come up with some other options for the enormous, tentacled demon that seemed to be the embodiment of the Hellmouth itself—or perhaps just the first of the Old Ones to cross over. And he had to come up with it quickly—the producers needed a resolution in about four days. Vulich's first instinct was to go with CGI, a prospect he quickly abandoned."

"Our next idea was that maybe we could do it in miniature. But the creature had to interact so much with people, and a miniature copy of the set seemed prohibitive. We can't spend $500,000 to do this, and we only had a week and a half to do it."

Vulich's answer was the last thing anyone might have expected in an era so filled with technology.

"The Hellmouth beast is really three guys inside these tentacles, who are holding these mechanical poles, and the [tentacles] are actually almost like suits. We used a different technique to make the [tentacles]. The standard technique is to sculpt something in clay, mold it, and then pour rubber into the molds that you make, and that's how you end up with the piece. That is a simplified version."

The technique Optic Nerve went with required them to use sheets of a certain type of foam, cut and glued to form the desired shapes.

"It's a type of technique they use a lot for walk-around suits that you see at amusement parks," Vulich explains. "It cuts out the sculpting and the molding process, so that saved us about a week, a week and a half right there. It's not quite as refined a look, but you try to make up for it in a paint job. We knew it was going to be gooped up and all that, and that would help. Some elements were sculpted, like the teeth and the mouth and the eyes. We did sculpt those.

"I also made some suggestions to the producers as to how to shoot it. They were very gracious about listening to my ideas—which oftentimes doesn't happen—but they actually took me seriously. I suggested [they use] a couple of cameras and shoot some very tight closeups, so you almost don't know what you're looking at. You're just looking at masses of flesh, and one of my big beliefs with creatures is that oftentimes context is almost everything. If you were to see the alien in the movie *Alien,* in full-frame, walking through a shopping mall, it would [look] kind of stupid."

Vulich was happy, however, with the end result of this challenge when it finally aired in "Prophecy Girl."

"I thought it all came together very nicely. It was a lot better than I thought it would be," Vulich admits. "We were basically using the same stuff they would have used in *Lost in Space* back in the '60s, so we had to try to pull every trick we could to make it look that much better."

Vulich is also proud of the "suit" for the demon Machida, from "Reptile Boy." Once again, the look was achieved with a mixture of techniques. The upper body was sculpted, and the lower, tail portion, made use of the same foam construction used for the Hellmouth tentacles.

"We were very pleased with that," Vulich notes. "We hid the actor's body in there, in a kind of slip he fit into, which bound his legs together. It was made of different plastic sections that were glued together with foam wrapped around it, kind of interlocking. It was almost a forced perspective, in a way. The tail is actually a lot smaller toward the back than it is in the front, something we did hoping to make it look longer than it really was. Again, it's using whatever illusions or tricks you can, you know, to make these things look more dynamic."

In both cases, Vulich observes that the final product works on film in large part because of the environment. In the case of "Reptile Boy," he notes that Machida lived in a "really neat basement, and was kind of coming out of this pit."

An observation that leads to a discussion of the show in general, and his feeling—as a long time horror enthusiast—about why the show works as well as it does. For instance, he says of "Reptile Boy" that "there is certainly some kind of Freudian symbolism going on, the idea of a snake coming out of a hole in the frat." He also notes the date-rape subtext of Cordelia and Buffy's abduction by frat brothers.

"It's kind of indicative of the show in general, to basically take teenage angst and turn it into some kind of metaphor through a monster. I think that is really the brilliance in the show. For any kind of fantasy, horror, or sci-fi to really touch anybody, it has to be a metaphor for some real, true emotion; otherwise, why would anybody care about it if it is pure fantasy? You have to somehow relate to it in a way that actually touches you. A lot of the episodes are about taking real teenage angst and then doing the nightmare version of that."

From there, the conversation quickly turns to the creative process and the balancing of the intent to entertain with the urge to share one's philosophy through that entertainment. And it is a balance Vulich believes all artists reach for on some level, conscious or otherwise.

"Intuitively or through trial and error, creativity is just editing. You generate a lot of ideas, and you pick the good ones or the ones you like. You can't even necessarily explain why it feels right. If you try to rationalize it intelligently, at a certain point you just like it. I'm sure there is a reason, but it's probably so deeply buried, and there are so many layers of your consciousness, there's no point in even trying to go after it, and probably not even healthy to try to do that," he reasons.

Back to the series in question, however. We've heard from Vulich about the things he's proud of having pulled off. It's tempting, then, to wonder what he was unhappy with. The answer: the werewolf.

"[The producers] weren't pleased with the way it turned out, but I maintain that a lot of it is the context. It was shot in people's living rooms and stuff, and I think it makes it that much tougher to make the monster—it's a lot easier if you're in the basement, because the basement is half the mood, you know?

"We looked at a lot of videos, and there wasn't anything we really liked, except for *The Howling*. I think a lot of what made the werewolves in that film work was the way it was shot and the context it was all within—they are all silhouetted and backlit. Actually, oddly enough, sometimes a lot of tighter shots are better. If they are quick, close shots, they are disorienting enough. To me, that always seems to be the answer when you're shooting something that you're not quite sure about."

Of later episodes, the entire team at Optic Nerve was quite happy about the fish-boys from "Go Fish." That "team" will, at any given time include about fifteen people. Among them, Vulich's right-hand man, studio supervisor Mark Garbarino; John Wheaton, who does a lot of the designs with Vulich; and a number of others, including Andrew Sands, a novelist and screenwriter who is part of the studio's office staff. One key player Vulich wants to be sure to mention is Mike Pack, who makes all the fangs for the series' vampire characters.

The basic vampire prosthetic was something that Optic Nerve and Joss Whedon differed on originally. While Whedon wanted something distinct and dramatic, Vulich and his staff were thinking of something more subtle. Subtlety had worked well for them in the past, on the remake of *Night of the Living Dead*.

"If it's bloodier or more rotted or more angry or has an evil-looking forehead, to me, that's not necessarily what makes it scary. To me, what makes things scary is if they're believable. The fact that it's a wrinkled, shriveled puppet doesn't necessarily make it believable. That's why we tried [in that film] to think of them as characters instead of monsters. That was our whole aesthetic on that, and I think that to a certain degree, we were successful. We try to look for little holes, things that other people would miss, and that's why we did oversize ears [on the zombies]. We also took contact lenses and made people's eyes look bigger, because in real life certain parts of your features don't shrink.

"Cartilage doesn't shrink, so when you see emaciated people, their ears look huge because the rest of them is shrinking but ear cartilage doesn't. There are all these little things we tried to do to make them look more natural. When we started doing that with *Buffy*, we were trying to go in that direction, and it just wasn't really the tone that they were looking for. They encouraged us to be a little bit more heavy-handed in it."

Obviously, the process of putting an episode of the series together is complex and rigorous for all involved. It requires, more than anything, vast amounts of cooperation. As soon as Optic Nerve receives a script for an episode of the series, Vulich and his staff do a breakdown of the scenes and what they need to supply for that episode. Then they begin to create designs for a meeting with the series' producers. Usually, they bring no more than three designs for any one creature, to limit the choices to the best they have to offer. Once again, aesthetics come into play.

"Our primary concern is to figure out what serves the story. We try to be really aware of the fact that we're providing elements that are part of the story-telling process. We are not just making the cool monster, but we're making a story-telling device. What does this design need to be? Is it scary? Is it something that you start thinking of as scary but later on is benevolent? The design needs to reflect that. Not that we want it to be obvious, but we want a kind of resonance to it. With 'Reptile Boy,' there is a certain kind of phallic aspect to the story. That should be reflected in the design, so instead of making him green, we went for lighter flesh tones.

"Secondly, we try to find what's been done before," Vulich says. "We'll scour magazines, books, and videos. We usually have a day or two to do this. We'll try to find out what everyone else has done before, bring in photos, and figure out if there's anything anyone else has missed. Or how we can avoid some clichés."

Once Vulich's designs are approved, it becomes a question of budget.

"I will try to make whatever suggestions I can to try to make it as cost-effective as possible," he admits. "The show is very limited financially, and that's a really major concern. Part of what makes me valuable in what I do is actually saving people money. In the case of the fish-guys [for "Go Fish,"], we had to build three of them. We used some existing body casts that we had, and pretty much told them what size person to get to fit into it."

Once again, cooperation appears to be the key. And that doesn't seem to have been any problem. Vulich and Whedon share a love of horror, and of films in general, that makes their communication very simple and direct. Any reference Vulich can think of, Whedon is likely to be familiar with. That communication has served both John Vulich and the producers of *Buffy*.

"I think we're very much simpatico with Joss's vision," Vulich notes. "Once we initially got the tone down, from the first few episodes, I think we really got a good feel for what he was looking for."

DIGITAL MAGIC

"It's really cool when you can say part of your job is blowing up vampires."
—Stephen Brand, 3D and visual effects supervisor, Digital Magic

And how do they blow up those vampires?

Loni Peristere of Digital Magic, the computer-graphics company that creates *Buffy*'s "CG" effects, told us that it was an exciting challenge to create the show's signature effect...and to do all the other things they've been asked to do. But Digital Magic was up to it: founded in 1990, it has worked on shows such as *Star Trek Voyager, Teen Angel, Early Edition, You Wish, Dawson's Creek, Rodgers and Hammerstein's Cinderella,* and *Dr. Quinn, Medicine Woman,* as well as the feature films *Mortal Kombat: Annihilation* and *Species II*. A dedicated team working in a 30,000-foot facility in Santa Monica, they searched for the perfect image to represent what happens to a vampire when Buffy stakes it: all the moisture is sucked out of its body, which then turns to dust and explodes.

To their delight, the teeth fall out last.

Loni explained that to create this effect, a "dust man" double of the live character is created, then positioned frame by frame to match the live action actor. As Loni continued:

"Stephen [Brand's] integrated dust elements are designed around the scene. They possess as many realistic qualities as the scene provides, as well as the dramatic impact suggested by the actors. They can be languid and touching, as Angel's turn in Buffy's nightmare sequence in "Surprise," or pointed and quick, as Xander's killer lunge in "Bewitched, Bothered, and Bewildered." Each shot is layered with detail. The skin turns, the teeth fall, and the body crumbles."

In addition to the vampire "dustings"—each episode averages a minimum of two—Digital Magic provides two to four more effects per show. They provided the sequence where Drusilla's and Angel's blood mingles in "What's My Line? Part 2." They've risen demons and mummies from their sleep, and opened the mouth of Hell in the second-season finale, "Becoming, Part 2."

They also transformed a certain Dingoes Ate My Baby guitarist from his creature self back to Oz. Again, as Loni vividly describes it:

"Lying on the floor of a very realistic wood setting is an actor dressed in an impressively frightening six-foot werewolf costume (created by makeup and prosthetics specialists Optic Nerve). Later on, he will be replaced by two increasingly less-hairy actors, before the real actor takes his place on the set." (Indeed, Todd McIntosh told us how they painstakingly inserted the hairs onto Seth Green's body one by one.)

"It will then be up to our special-effects team to blend these four different stages into a seamless transformation from werewolf back to man."

Working on a relatively tight budget, and required to produce completed effects on a schedule unheard-of in the world of feature film, Digital Magic usually receives the scripts for *Buffy* two weeks before they must provide two to eight graphic sequences for the episode in question. Co-producer David Solomon adds that since *Buffy* isn't a show heavy on special effects, the few they do use in an episode need to look "fantastic."

Back to that dusting thing. It seems that in an effort to find just the right look, Digital Magic filmed exploding bags of flour and smashed plaster models. They researched their vampire lore, watching cinematic vamp death scenes from the old masters, including Bela Lugosi. They decided they wanted to find an "organic" look, rather than go for the super-slick hi-tech superclarity that often betrays a shot composed of computer graphics. They refer to this organic look as "CGI gore."

Live actors are combined into the computer-graphic elements much more often than one might expect. Loni told us that when shooting the demon-possessing-Angel sequence in "The Dark Age," David Boreanaz had to repeat his "wild involuntary convulsions" in three different makeups. Alyson Hannigan had to let the floor fall out from under her for the vortex scene in "I Only Have Eyes for You," and in that same episode, Charisma Carpenter "marched through stage after stage of extra makeup and applications" for the snakebite infection sequence.

And he excitedly remembers the first successful test shot for that all-important dusting: "...and the 4 A.M. realization that what we had on screen was right, that yes, indeed, a vampire turns to dust just like that, and Joss, Sarah, David, Alyson, Nick, Tony, Charisma, and all the show's creators believed it just as we did. This first experience set the precedent for the year, and we've all continued to work together as such."

The Digital Magic Visual Effects Team includes:

JEFF BEAULIEU, executive producer

STEPHEN BRAND: 3D and visual effects supervisor

LONI PERISTERE: visual effects producer-supervisor

BILL LAE: Henry compositor (an editing and special effects "suite in a box")

KIKI CHANSAMONE: flame compositor

DAN SANTONI: CGI animator

CASEY DAME: CGI animator

MICHAEL SCHNEIDER: Telecine colorist (converts film to digital video format)

Carey Meyer
ne Quinn
d Koneff
ustafson
Brennan
on Webb
Starlight
ve West
ecauwer
on Hight
ngblood
Wilson
Grastait
he Barry
rgstrom
osenthal
Shapiro
n Dunn
zdernik
McIntosh
ldonado
Kenney
ri Baker
kpatrick
ermaine
Vankum
C. King
Kimble
Kim Ray
Domald
oodman
Saldutti
ryl Cain
an Casas
hip Hall
L. Perez
Mendez
li Flores
bert Ellis
ath Culp
McEntyre
McEntyre
McGivern
arry Fee

FUMIGATION PARTY

Find a cockroach, get a free drink

MUSIC

Buffy the vampire slayer

Buffy: "It's not noise. It's music."

Giles: "I know music. Music has notes. This is noise."

Buffy: "I'm aerobicizing. I must have the beat."

Giles: "Wonderful. You work on muscle tone while my brain dribbles out my ears."   **—"THE DARK AGE"**

The post-production department has a policy of listening to every demo sent to them. They are particularly delighted when they find songs from up-and-coming groups to help them get exposure.

The band that really plays for Dingoes Ate My Baby is called Four Star Mary. If you listen closely, you can hear Giles humming very softly in the segue from the scene with Buffy in front of the burning Factory to their standing beside Jenny's grave. (And did you spot the uncredited appearance of Sean Lennon in one of the Bronze's headliners?)

Here are the songs and the bands who played in the first two seasons of *Buffy:*

SEASON ONE song list

Artist	Song Title	Episode #
Sprung Monkey Surfdog—1995's "Swirl"	*Saturated, Believe, Swirl, Things Are Changing, Right My Wrong*	4V01
Mindtribe Independently recorded; not yet available	*Losing Ground*	4V01
Dashboard Prophets No Name Recordings— 1996's "Burning Out the Inside"	*Wearing Me Down, Ballad for Dead Friends*	4V02
Superfine (a.k.a.: Abbey Normal) Fish of Death Records; available on label's website	*Already Met You, Stoner Love*	4V04
Three Day Wheely Capitol—1996's "Rubber Halo"	*Rotten Apples*	4V05
Velvet Chain Overall—1997's "Warm"	*Strong, Treaon*	4V05
Rubber Independently recorded; not yet available	*Junkie Girl*	4V05
Kim Richey Mercury Nashville—1995's "Kim Richey"	*Let the Sun Fall Down*	4V05
Sprung Monkey Surfdog—1995's "Swirl"	*Reluctant Man*	4V06

| Dashboard Prophets | All You Want | 4V06 |
| No Name Recordings—1996's "Burning Out the Inside" | | |

| Far | Job's Eyes | 4V06 |
| Epic/ Immortal—1996's "Tin Cans with Strings to You" | | |

| Sophie Zelmani | I'll Remember You | 4V07 |
| Epic/ Immortal—1996's "Sophie Zelmani" | | |

| Patsy Cline | I Fall to Pieces | 4V12 |
| MCA—1961's "Patsy Cline Showcase" | | |

| Jonatha Brooke | Inconsolable | 4V12 |
| Blue Thumb and Refuge/MCA | | |

SEASON TWO song list

Artist	Song Title	Episode #
Cibo Matto	Sugar Water, Spoon	5V01
Warner Brothers—1997's "Super Relax"		
Alison Krauss and Union Station	It Doesn't Matter	5V01
Rounder—1997's "So Long, So Wrong"		
Nickel	Stupid Things, 1000 Nights	5V03
Independently recorded; available on band's website		
Four Star Mary	Fate, Shadows	5V04
Independently recorded; available on band's website and at Aaron Records in Hollywood, CA		
Act of Faith	Bring Me On	5V05
Expansion—1997's "Release Yourself"		
Louie Says	She	5V05
RCA—1997's "Cold to the Touch"		
Epperley	Shy	5V06
Triple x—1996's "Epperley"		
Treble Charger	How She Died	5V06
RCA—1997's "Maybe It's Me"		
Willoughby	Lois on the Brink	5V07
Fuzz Harris Records—1996's "Be Better Soon"		

| Creaming Jesus | *Reptile* | 5V07 |

Import—"Dead Time"

| Shawn Clement and | *Blood of a Stranger* | 5V07 |

Sean Murray
Independently recorded; e-mail requests to smurray@cinenet.net or clemistry@aol.com

| Rasputina | *Transylvanian Concubine* | 5V13 |

Sony—1996's "Thanks for the Ether"

| Shawn Clement and | *Anything* | 5V13 |

Sean Murray with vocals by Care Howe
Independently recorded; e-mail requests to smurray@cinenet.net or clemistry@aol.com

| Lotion | *Blind for Now* | 5V15 |

Warner Brothers—1996's "Nobody's Fool"

| Four Star Mary | *Pain* | 5V16 |

Independently recorded; available on band's website and at Aaron Records in Hollywood, CA

| Naked | *Drift Away* | 5V16 |

Red Ant—1997's "Naked"

| Average White Band | *Got the Love* | 5V16 |

Atlantic—1974's "AWB"

| Morcheeba | *Never an Easy Way* | 5V17 |

WEA/Sire/Discovery2—1996's "Who Can You Trust?"

| Puccini | *La Bohème: Acte 10* | 5V17 |
| | *Soave Fanciulla* | |

| The Flamingos | *I Only Have Eyes for You* | 5V19 |

Collectables—1959's "Flamingo Serenade"

| Splendid | *Charge* | 5V19 |

Independently recorded; CD in spring 1999

| Naked | *Mann's Chinese* | 5V20 |

Red Ant—1997's "Naked"

| Nero's Rome | *If You'd Listen* | 5V20 |

Lazy Bones—1995's "Togetherly"

| Sarah McLachlan | *Full of Grace* | 5V22 |

Arista—1997's "Surfacing"